A NIGHT TO TREASURE

Gabrielle slipped the bolt on the cabin door and walked slowly toward Alex. When he held out his arms to her, she had no power to resist.

"You know I can make you no promises," he told her as she embraced him with trembling arms.

"I know," she whispered. His lips met hers, and she accepted them hungrily.

"I cannot stay here."

"And I cannot go with you," she replied, her eyes filled with tears of love and longing.

Alex eased her gently to the floor as she clung to him, forcing his mouth down to hers. "Are you sure you want to do this?" he asked huskily.

"I'm sure. I need you; I want you, if only for tonight." Her fingers teased the dark red curls at the nape of his neck, and she marveled at their softness. She gazed up at him, needing to see his reaction to her words. Would he think her wanton? The ache for him inside her was so great she wondered if she would care. . . .

Snowfire

COLLEEN FAULKNER

ZEBRA BOOKS
KENSINGTON PUBLISHING CORP.

ZEBRA BOOKS

are published by

Kensington Publishing Corp.
475 Park Avenue South
New York, NY 10016

First printing: July, 1988

Printed in the United States of America

For Joyce Flaherty,
who believed in me. . . .

Prologue

Trembling, Gabrielle LeBeau pressed her body against the rough shingled wall of a warehouse and forced back the tears that welled up in her brown eyes. She was certain Taylor had seen her cross the street, and she knew he wasn't far behind. Slipping her gloved hand into the velvet drawstring purse, her fingers touched the hard, cold steel of a Colt 45.

Drawing in a deep breath of the tangy, salt air, the slim young woman stepped from the late afternoon shadows of the building and started down Water Street. *Just four more blocks,* she told herself, keeping her hand inside the purse. *Four blocks to the dock and you're free.* Ignoring the mud that splashed the hem of her elegant, black brocade gown and rose over her high-buttoned boots, she hurried, keeping to the middle of the street.

Glancing over her shoulder, she spotted Taylor

again, his hat pushed forward to shadow his leering face. As long as there were people on the street, men moving crates and hauling materials in wagons, she was certain she'd be safe. But if he caught her alone . . . Gabrielle bit down on her lower lip until she tasted her own blood. She'd not let him get the best of her! Just a little farther now. . . . She could hear the sound of steam being exhausted into the summer air as a ship prepared to get under way. She'd come this far; she couldn't lose her nerve now.

Crossing the next street, Gabrielle broke into a run. She hadn't counted on the warehouses being locked tight, the rutted street winding between the dirty buildings being empty. Yanking up the burdensome skirts to her knees, she raced down the middle of the paved street. Behind her, she could hear the sound of the murderer's feet hitting the brick. She was still ahead of him when she turned the corner, veering left, desperately searching for other people. She had to get back out in a crowd; he wouldn't dare harm her in front of witnesses.

Suddenly, she spotted a well-dressed, redheaded gentleman on the far side of the street. She hesitated for only a heartbeat before rushing up and throwing her arms around the stranger. "John," she cried impulsively. "I didn't think you'd make it before the steamer sailed." She stared into the honest face, her dark brown eyes pleading. "Just play along," she whispered beneath her breath, pressing a kiss to his lips. "You must believe me! My life's in danger. Please, help me. I need you to escort me to the *Lady Yukon,* pier three."

Jefferson Alexander the fourth stared at the young woman who'd thrown herself so enthusiastically into his arms, then glanced up to spot a man in a dark coat coming around the corner. The fear in the girl's haunting, raspy voice made him turn and start down the street, his arm wrapped possessively around her shoulders.

"Thank you," Gabrielle murmured. "I don't think the bastard'll lay a finger on me in front of anyone."

Alex blinked, looking down at her lovely face. Vulgarity was not something he expected from this bundle of femininity; she was obviously a lady. Dressed in the height of fashion in a heavy brocade, bustle and all, she wore a black straw, capote bonnet tied with a flourish of silk and velvet. Only the somber black of the gown seemed out of place on the young woman.

"Why is the gentleman following you?" Alex linked her gloved hand through his arm. Was he aiding and abetting a thief, a swindler? There were certainly enough of those in this town.

"I haven't done a thing." Gabrielle took a quick look over her shoulder. Taylor was still following her but had put some distance between them. "He's the guilty party." She raised her chin a notch, her brown eyes cold and aloof. "Just to the *Lady Yukon,* and then I can care for myself."

Alex raised a dark eyebrow, keeping up his pace. The wharfs were only another block down.

"What? Don't think I can? I could have out-run the weasel if I wasn't dressed in all of this fluff." She tugged at the brocade skirt of her gown, after seeing the look that crossed Alex's face.

Alex didn't know what to make of her. She certainly was like no *Southern* young lady he'd ever met. One of his sisters would never have spoken to a stranger in this

9

manner. Of course, none of his sisters would have ever gotten themselves into a situation where they needed assistance from some man off the street. Alex was strangely intrigued. "Heading north are you?"

Gabrielle looked over her shoulder again, her arm still linked in Alex's. "Where else might the *Lady Yukon* be going, the tropics?" Her reply was curt, but no malice seemed to be intended. "Here we are. Out-fooled the fool, haven't I?" She released Alex's arm, hurrying up the ramp that led to the steamer. "Thank you!" she called, waving over her shoulder. "I won't forget it."

"Last aboard!" shouted a hand on the deck.

"Wait," Alex shouted, his voice drowning in a sea of sounds. "What's your name? Where are you going?"

Gabrielle stepped onto the deck, refusing the uniformed hand's assistance. "What difference does it make?" she shouted back over the railing. "You'll not see me again." She was smiling now, a smile that brightened her delicate oval face.

Alex pulled his round hat off his head, running down the dock as the steamer began to move. "Humor me!" he called, leaping over massive mooring lines.

Gabrielle just tipped back her head, laughing as she slipped the black gloves from her hands. Tossing them over the rail, she turned and disappeared.

Alex watched the black gloves float through the air, one landing in the water, the other on the edge of the filthy dock. Leaning over, he picked up the bit of material and stood watching the *Lady Yukon* disappear into the channel. Then, raising the glove to his lips, he started back up the street.

Below decks on the *Lady Yukon,* Gabrielle yanked

10

the black capote bonnet from her head and tossed it onto the narrow ship's bed. Twisting to unhook the long row of black buttons down her back, she let the heavy brocade dress slip to the floor. "Didn't think I'd manage it, did you, Papa?" Her voice echoed in the small ship's cabin, shattering the lonely silence. Running her hand through her short, cropped chestnut hair, she shook her head letting out a deep breath. "It's okay, Papa," she whispered. "You never answered me when you were alive, either."

No, not far enough away from me. I could have touched the ... as I leaned away. ... to drown the ... one of them from about here, I said. "I ... question is did you, Poe?" Her voice seemed to be ... coming closer, interacting. Her voice ... Raising her head toward me, and I stopped over the ... on to tilt her head letting our system to me. She ... again, she whispered. There never was a word she didn't like saying, never.

Chapter One

Somewhere on the Tanana River
Alaska Territory, October, 1885

Indian Jack settled himself on the step outside the cabin and relit a half-smoked cigar. Inhaling deeply, he leaned his back against the door and pursed his lips to try a smoke ring one last time. When he spotted two men with a sled and a handful of dogs coming over a hill to the south, he shook his head, a twitch of a smile crossing his windburned face. *Too late to be headin' north,* he thought to himself. *Too late by a couple of days.*

When the strangers reached the cabin, they had to speak twice to Indian Jack before he finally pushed his hat up off his forehead and gazed at them through pitch-black eyes. "What'cha want?" He didn't like strangers, especially foolish ones.

The man with greying temples spoke up. "We want to buy provisions. We were told we could buy food here." Simone Parsons slipped the pack off his back, letting it hit the snow-covered ground with a thump.

"That right?" Indian Jack gave a nod, glancing at the man's redheaded partner. "Who told you that?"

"Listen here, Indian." Parsons raised his voice impatiently. "Can we, or can't we buy food here?" He glanced up at the small, crude cabin doubtfully.

Without bothering to reply, Indian Jack slowly got to his feet and disappeared into the cabin, closing the door soundly behind him. "Gabe, got visitors." He gave a little chuckle. "Looking for provisions."

Gabrielle turned from the crate she was pushing across the floor and let out a sigh, shaking her head. "How much do they need? I hadn't figured on anyone else coming through for a while." She slapped the crate with a hand. "It's doubtful I'll be able to find anything in this mess. I think Papa was right; I'm going to have to build on next spring." She surveyed the crates and boxes piled ceiling high in the small log cabin.

Indian Jack just gave a shrug, chewing on the end of the cigar butt still in his mouth.

"Well—" Gabrielle wiped her hands on her heavy cotton breeches and reached for a wool sweater hanging on a wooden peg—"guess I'll go see what they want. The sooner they can load up, the sooner they can be on their way." She pulled a brimmed wool hat over her short, dark hair. "Awful late to just be getting supplies isn't it?"

Suddenly, the sound of snarling dogs filled Gabrielle's ears, and she flung the massive hand-hewn door open, stepping out into the bright sunshine. "What's going on out here?" she demanded with authority. Her glance shifted from the dog fight just outside the door to the two strangers standing a few feet away.

14

"Get him off my dog!" Parsons shouted, taking a step back. "He'll kill him."

Anger rose in her cheeks as Gabrielle tried to get her sled dog's attention. "Tristan! Back! No!" she shouted, coming down the step.

"Well, aren't you going to do something?" The younger stranger shouted to the boy that had just stepped from the cabin.

"Do something? What do you suggest?" Gabrielle snapped. Fur flew in great puffs through the air, and the sound of the growling, barking dogs sent a primeval chill down her spine.

When sled dogs got into a fight like this, they fought to the death like their ancestral wolves. The strange dog had invaded Tristan's territory, and he would die for it. Anyone who dared get between them, risked being maimed or killed by the huge canines.

Running to the side of the cabin, Gabrielle snatched a long piece of firewood from a pile and started to beat the dogs in the head, taking care to keep out of the way of their powerful snapping jaws. "Get back, Tristan!" she ordered, wincing as her lead dog sank his teeth into the other's hip. "No! Bad dog! Back!" she shouted vainly.

But it was of no use, by the time she got Tristan off the stranger's dog, the husky was lying on its side howling with pain.

The younger man moved forward, reaching his hand out to his dog.

"Get back!" Gabrielle shouted as the dog snapped at the man. "He'll take your arm off." Dragging Tristan around the cabin to a make-shift dog pen, she returned to confront the strangers. "Have you lost your minds?"

15

she demanded through clenched teeth. "Look what you did to him." She gestured with one hand to the dog rolling and whimpering in the snow. "Why did you unhook him from his traces?"

"What we did to him!" The younger of the two men stepped forward, confronting Gabrielle angrily. "Listen, boy! It was your damned dog that attacked mine!"

Gabrielle's eyes narrowed dangerously. "You should have had him under control." She gave him a shove on the chest with the palm of her hand. "This is my dog's territory; he was protecting it, protecting me!"

The man twisted around at the sound of the husky howling in pain. His belly was slit, and his entrails rolled in the snow. "Can't you do anything for him?"

"Yea, I can do something for him," she answered bitterly. Stepping in the cabin, she returned in a second, a rifle in her hand.

The young man, Alex, stood frozen in horror as Gabrielle slid back the bolt on the rifle and pulled the trigger. His eyes drifted shut at the sound of the shot, and he struggled to control the bile rising in his throat. "You killed my dog," he accused through tight lips.

"No," Gabrielle spat. "*You* killed him." Turning on her heels, she took four long strides to the cabin steps and disappeared inside, slamming the door behind her.

Uninvited tears rolled down Gabrielle's cheeks as she hung the rifle on its peg and yanked her hat off her head. Damn him! Damn the tenderfoot and his stupidity! Why did these men keep coming? They came, they killed and they died hunting for gold that didn't exist.

Brushing the tears from her face with the back of her

hand, she went back to the crate she'd been moving from one side of the cabin to the other. She wanted to get her supplies in order before winter really settled in. Between the trading she did with the Tanana Indians and scattered gold seekers, and the money from the sale of the sled dogs she raised, she could keep herself well fed and add to her growing savings. If all continued to go well, another two years and she'd have enough cash to hire loggers to clear land and build her road. It had been her father's dream, and now it was hers.

When Indian Jack came through the door, she kept her head lowered over the crate of packaged flour, continuing to count. She wouldn't want her friend to know she was crying over one stupid dead dog. She didn't want him to think she was just another weak white woman. She had earned Indian Jack's respect, and she wanted to keep it.

Jack cleared his throat. "Sorry 'bout the dog, Gabe." It wasn't like him to express his feelings, but he felt bad for his friend. He knew what her dogs meant to her and what a waste of life he'd just seen.

"What do they want?" She didn't look up.

"What do they always want? Flour, sugar, coffee." He laughed, scratching his stubbly chin. "Sulfur matches."

Gabrielle looked at him. "Matches? They didn't bring matches?" She got to her feet. "How far did they think they were going to get without matches?"

Jack shrugged his stocky shoulders. "Guess they didn't know it was cold here."

She shook her head sadly. "Never make it, will they?"

He started to pick through the wooden crates,

counting bags of flour and packets of salt. "Too late to be moving north, I say. My grandfather saw a fox chasing his tail just two days ago. He says that means the snow will fly heavy within the week."

"Did they say where they were headed?" She ran a hand through her short curly hair. "Guess it doesn't matter, does it? Someone will find them frozen on a path, or their bones'll wash up on a river bank in the spring." Taking the flour from Jack, she slid it into a clean feed sack. "Life must not mean much to them, to risk it on a few specks of shiny rock. If you ask me, they'll not find it. No one will."

He tossed a bundle of jerky into the feed sack. "Oh, it's there. Don't know that they'll find it, but it's there. My people talk of the river running gold someday. It is a legend we tell our children."

"You'll never see me digging in the dirt; I promise you that!" Tying the feed sack shut with a bit of string, she grabbed her hat off a crate. "Let's get this over with. I want them out of here."

Out in the sunshine, Gabrielle dropped the bag of provisions in the snow. When the younger man turned around, she was startled to see that without his hat on she recognized him. It was the redhead, the man who had escorted her to the *Lady Yukon!*

"Everything in there we asked for?" Alex's face was hard, his cloudy, blue eyes steely. He appeared to be in his mid-thirties, a ruggedly handsome man with brawny shoulders and a head of dark auburn hair.

"Yes." She tore her eyes from his. "And the price is not negotiable. Take it or leave it." She hooked a thumb in the pocket of her wool pants.

"Hard as nails, are you, kid?" Alex searched the

18

young boy's floured face for some sign of remorse.

It was obvious to Gabrielle that her rescuer didn't realize who she was beneath the man's bulky clothing and big hat, and that suited her just fine. Originally, she had begun dressing in men's clothing because it was warmer and more comfortable. Then, when she began to grow into a young woman, she and her father had agreed that with all of these lonely men passing through, she'd be better off if they didn't know she was a woman. There was no telling what some of these drifters might do. The icy solitude played with their minds turning honest men into thieves, rapists, even murderers sometimes.

Through the years she had grown used to the charade. She was Gabe, Rouge LeBeau's son. She saw so few people that she was able to get away with it; only a few friends here on the Tanana knew her true identity. Gabrielle turned her back on Alex. "Pay Jack and be on your way," she called over her shoulder. "And good luck, fellows, you're going to need it."

Late in the evening, Gabrielle sat in front of the fireplace, a cup of steaming coffee cradled in her hands. Breathing deeply of the heady scent that rose from the china cup, she stared at the flames that licked at and consumed a log she'd just tossed in.

Indian Jack had gone home to his wife and daughter across the river, leaving her alone until the next time he came by. Jack came and went as he pleased, running on what Rouge called "Indian Time." He never made plans or said when he would be back; she would just look up, and he'd be gone again. To Jack, time meant nothing. He ate when he was hungry, slept when he was tired. Theirs was a special relationship; they grew up together under his parents' care, and though he now had a family of his own, he still came by when it pleased him to help her with the dogs and the trading business.

Gabrielle sighed, taking a sip of the aromatic coffee. "Can you believe it, Papa?" she called aloud to the empty room. "You saw it, didn't you? I had to shoot. I had to put that beautiful animal out of its misery." She ran her finger around the rim of the hot cup. "Why do they do it, Papa? I know they must have paid good money for that husky; he couldn't have been more than three years old. How could they have been so foolish to let one of their dogs get with mine?" She paused for a moment. "Are you listening to me, Papa?"

She shook her head. Probably not. Chances were, he was somewhere up there playing cards or cornering some tart. A smile crossed her face as an image of Rouge LeBeau flashed through her mind. He had never been much of a father to her, but he'd done the best he could. He had hired Indian Jack's mother and father to care for her when she was still a babe; then, after they had drowned crossing the river, Rouge had sent his daughter to school in Seattle. It wasn't his fault that he didn't realize she would never fit in with the other young girls. It wasn't his fault that she had hated every day of the three years she'd spent in Sister Kathryn's School for Girls, either.

Gabrielle picked at a thread that hung from her bright red union suit. It was time she settled down to sleep. What good was it to sit here and dwell on the past? Nothing she could do could make those years in Seattle go away, and nothing she could do was going to bring her father back from the dead.

Slowly getting to her feet, Gabrielle threw another

log into the fire. When winter settled in, she'd have to light the aged woodstove too, but for now, the stone fireplace kept her comfortably warm. Draining her china cup, she slid it onto the mantel her father had cut with an axe and retired to her bed on the side wall.

That night, to Gabrielle's delight, a thick blanket of snow fell, giving her the first chance of the season to take her young dogs on a trial sled run. If she hoped to sell all seven in the spring, she'd have plenty to keep her busy through the long winter months. In the morning she loaded her small sled and hitched two young males and her lead dog in their harnesses. *Always leave like you're never coming back,* Indian Jack had warned. *No telling what could be ahead of or behind you on the trail.*

"Mush!" Gabrielle commanded, her clear voice ringing in the trees. When Tristan moved forward, the other dogs followed, and Gabrielle found herself running easily beside the sled.

She breathed deeply as she ran, letting the cold, sharp air revitalize her weary soul. It was going to be a hard winter, this first one without her father, but she would be all right. She had to be. This was where her life was: the snow, the dogs, the breathtaking silence. How could anyone prefer the filthy streets of Seattle to this frigid paradise? No, she was sad that her father was gone, but as he said, "The Tanana River keeps freezing . . . life goes on."

Since she was a small child, she had known Rouge wouldn't always be there for her. Hell, even when he'd been alive, he'd never been dependable. Sometimes he'd go on a binge and stay soused for a week; other times he'd pack a bag and just walk away. She didn't know where he went, sometimes to one of the nearby Indian camps, or to one of the squatter's cabins. He'd play cards, drink, and then he'd wander home when the mood struck him. He hadn't been much of a father; but he was all she'd ever had, and he didn't deserve to die like that.

Gabrielle swallowed hard. She had promised she wouldn't do this to herself. Slowing the dogs to a walk, she forced all thoughts of her father from her mind. She had so much to be thankful for, why dwell on it? Patting one of the young dogs on the head, she shaded her eyes with a mittened hand. The trees glittered, reflecting the bright sun off sugar-dipped branches. The ground was covered in a blanket of crystal white, minifying the earth's imperfections.

Kicking at a drift, Gabrielle laughed aloud, listening with amusement to the sound of her voice echoing in the trees. It was so good to be home! Commanding her lead dog to quicken the pace, she broke into a run again, heading north.

Coming around a bend in the river shortly before noon, Gabrielle stopped short. "Slow, boy," she ordered, falling into a walk. Up ahead lay a motionless body, face down in the snow. Immediately, she slipped a hunting knife from the belt she wore around her waist. It could be a trap; she had heard tell of men pretending to be injured, then ambushing their would-be saviors, taking their belongings and leaving them to die along the river.

Leaving the dogs on the path, she moved cautiously toward the body, keeping an eye on it as she checked out the tracks in the snow. Two men . . . no, three, she surmised. There had been a tussle, sometime early that

22

morning from the looks of the depth of the tracks. Two men had gone off to the west . . . together, and they'd taken the dead man's coat. They had wanted to be sure he'd not live to tell any tales. There must have been a camp nearby because there were no sled tracks, and the men couldn't have been carrying anything on their backs. "Tracks could tell it all in the snow," Indian Jack always said.

For a moment Gabrielle just stood there. It was so early in the season to already be finding dead men in the snow. They always found a few every winter, but they increased with every year as more men set out to find their fortunes. She shook her head. Good sense would have told her to just leave him. He couldn't be buried anyway; the ground was already frozen. But she couldn't leave him; no man deserved to die without even a prayer spoken in his name.

Pulling her red, brimmed hat down on her head, Gabrielle approached the dead man. With one booted foot, she pushed his leg. It moved easily; he hadn't been dead long. . . . Tucking her knife back into her belt, she turned around to tuck the man's socked feet in her arms. The bastards had even taken his boots! Giving a hard tug, she started to drag him slowly in the direction of her sled. Tristan gave a howl, moving nervously in his traces.

"Stay, Tristan. Good dog, good flop-eared mutt." Slowly she dragged the lifeless man down the path, leaving the imprint of his body in the snow. She'd take him home and bury him beneath rocks in a small quarry near her cabin. It wouldn't be the first nameless gold seeker buried in the territory, but it would be the first she buried on her own.

Finally reaching the sled, Gabrielle dropped the man's feet, gasping for air. Even as strong as she was, it was still difficult to drag dead weight through the snow. Wiping her mouth with the back of her hand, she leaned to grab the feet again . . . and then he moved.

Startled, she dropped the foot. Had she imagined it? The metallic taste of fright filled her mouth. The man couldn't be alive, not as long as he'd been out here. He should have died of exposure hours ago. Still . . . she waited for a moment, and when he didn't move, she gave him a nudge with her boot.

The man groaned, and Gabrielle was on the ground in an instant, rolling the body over.

Chapter Two

"Oh, my God," Gabrielle whispered, dropping to her knees to brush the snow from the man's placid face. It was the stranger . . . the red-haired man that had helped her in Seattle . . . the man whose dog she'd shot and killed.

Pulling her mittens off, Gabrielle slapped his face sharply with her bare hands. "Wake up, wake up," she insisted. "You're still alive, wake up." But the stranger only moaned, mumbling a few words of gibberish.

Slipping his head into her lap, she pulled off his black wool cap to reveal a thick head of shining auburn hair. "Are you hurt?" She began to shake him by the shoulders. "Can you hear me?"

When he didn't answer, Gabrielle eased his head back into the snow and crawled to his feet, yanking off a sock. His toes were a deathly white, but when she rubbed the skin briskly, streaks of red appeared, telling her that some of the flesh might still be alive. Running back to the sled, she grabbed her fur-lined parka to throw over the unconscious man.

Standing for a moment in the ankle-deep snow, Gabrielle planted her hands on her hips, trying to decide what she should do first. She had to get him to shelter. She could see that his forearm was broken, but the most important thing to do was to get his feet back to their normal temperature. Even if he survived the hypothermia, he might still loose his toes, and then he'd never walk again.

Shading her eyes from the sun, she tried to guess at the time. It was awfully dark; had she lost track of how long she'd been gone? She didn't think so. It was around noon. She'd only been traveling a few hours. Even though the sun shone less and less each day with the coming of winter, it should have been brighter than this. Turning to the southwest, she swore under her breath. How foolish could she be? She'd been so caught up in daydreaming that she hadn't kept a close watch on the weather. A big storm was brewing, and it was moving fast. They'd never make it back to the cabin in time.

Gabrielle swallowed hard, trying to push back the terror rising within her. "Fear is what kills people out here. Nothing else." She'd heard her father say those words a hundred times. Indian Jack had his own way of putting it, but it meant the same thing. "Keep calm," she said hoarsely to herself. Her voice seemed to echo through the ice-glazed trees. "Panic is another word for corpse."

Slipping her waterskin from beneath her sweater and leather jerkin, Gabrielle forced herself to slowly take a long pull and then knelt beside the still body of the man. She held the waterskin to his lips. Most of the liquid dribbled out of the side of his mouth, but she

26

managed to get a little down him.

Pacing back and forth in the snow, Gabrielle began to think logically. It was simple; she had food, a gun and ammunition. She never left the cabin without it. All she had to do was figure out somewhere to hole up until the storm passed.

"You're right, Rouge." She laughed wryly. "All I have to do is get past the fear."

With a twinkle in her eye, she dropped down to grab the man's feet and started dragging him toward the whining dogs. Successfully rolling the stranger onto the sled, she collapsed into the snow to rest, thankful that he was still unconscious. If he hadn't been, the rough treatment his arm was getting would have been excruciating. Getting back on her feet and brushing the snow from her wool pants, Gabrielle stuffed the man's feet into one of her provision bags and threw her parka over him. She could do without the coat; as long as she kept running, she'd be warm enough.

"Mush!" she commanded, giving the sled a push. Caesar and Anthony were young dogs; they hadn't learned to pull a full load yet. She hated to put so much weight on them; it could ruin them at this point in their training. But she had no chioce. She could never move the stranger any distance on her own. "Come on," she cried out. "You can do it."

Letting the dogs go at an easy pace, Gabrielle kept her eye on the dark sky, estimating the storm's distance as they followed the river. Reaching Crooked Neck Bend, she turned west through the straggly forest.

Not more than a mile and a half away on a small tributary of the Tanana River was a squatter's cabin. She hadn't been there for years, so she wasn't even sure

27

it was still there; but she had to take that chance. From the look of the sky, the way the dark angry clouds moved, they were in for a snowstorm of blizzard proportions. Jack had warned they were due for one.

As Gabrielle continued to move, pushing the pace, the storm began to descend on them. One moment there were dark skies and howling wind, and the next moment the world became a flurry of blinding white. Running beside the sled, Gabrielle followed a small tributary branching to the left of the Tanana until it narrowed into a small stream.

"If my guess is right, this has got to be it," she yelled above the wind to the panting dogs. Checking to be sure the stranger was still situated on the bent-wood sled, she turned to the left and moved through the wall of white, calling out soothing words to her overworked dogs. Brushing her arms briskly, she ran beside the sled. She couldn't see more than a few feet in front of her. The cold snow stung her face and eyes, but she kept running, knowing the shack had to be near. Her memory was good; her father had always given her credit for that. Once she had been somewhere, she didn't forget it.

Falling into a walk, she passed what she thought was the old hangman's tree and signaled the dogs to move right. Knowing that if the forest got any denser, she would have to leave the sled behind, she strained her eyes, searching in the nothingness for some sign of the cabin.

"Just a little farther," she coaxed the dogs. "Mush."

Finally, just in the distance, she spotted the dark shadow of a structure. Jubilant, she raced past the dogs, calling to them as she reached the squatter's cabin. Groping with her cold-stiffened hands, she yanked the door open and went back to the sled to unload the still-unconscious stranger.

By the time Gabrielle had dragged the man into the cabin and settled the dogs just outside the door, she was nearly frozen. Lighting a few pages of an old *Harper's Bazar* magazine she carried in her pack, she started a fire in an old stove in the corner of the room. Fueling the flames with bits of wood and broken chairs she found in the cabin, she soon had a decent fire going.

Lighting one of the candles she carried in her bag, Gabrielle surveyed the cabin. Not more than ten by twelve feet, it was in relatively good condition, though the dust was an inch thick on the rickety table and snow was blowing in around the door. The floor was littered with broken chairs and assorted junk, timber that Gabrielle knew would make good firewood in the dilapidated stove in the corner. Taking a pan from her bag, she retrieved clean snow from outside the door and got down on her knees to observe the stranger.

She would have to warm his feet slowly by immersing them first in cold water, then slowly adding warmer water until they reached room temperature. The odds weren't good that she could save his toes, but she knew she had to try.

It was late in the afternoon by the time Gabrielle had cared for her patient and cleaned up the cabin as best she could. She had brought his feet back to normal body temperature and now could do nothing but wait. The purpling bruise on his temple told her that it was probably a blow to his head that kept him unconscious. After a beating like this, it was hard to tell how things would turn out. He might wake up tomorrow as if nothing had happened, he might wake up with no more control of his body than a newborn babe . . . or he might not ever wake up.

Listening to the howl of the wind as the storm raged around them, Gabrielle huddled near the stove, cradling a cup of hot water with a few bits of tea leaf floating in it. She had stoked the fire and watered the dogs and now had nothing to do but try and stay warm and keep vigil over her stranger.

Time dragged on as the snow began to pile inside the door where it flew through the cracks. Gabrielle sang to herself as she flipped through the pages of her magazine, knowing the pictures by heart and mentally subtracting the pages she'd burned.

At last she grew so sleepy she could barely keep her eyes open, and then she laid down to sleep. Making a pillow from an evergreen bough and the feed sack she carried her belongings in, she laid her head beside the stranger's, pressing her body against his. It felt odd to hear his breathing, light and even in her ear, and her body tensed when it touched his. She had never slept this close to a man before, except for Indian Jack and her father, and they didn't count. But even with the fire in the small stove, it was frigid in the cabin, and Gabrielle knew she couldn't afford to be squeamish over laying so near someone else. She had to conserve their body heat; besides, what harm could he possibly do her? He was an unconscious man with a broken arm and frostbitten feet. Relaxing on the floor, Gabrielle pulled her overcoat over them both and drifted into a dreamless sleep.

*   *   *

Slowly Alex climbed from the depths of unconsciousness, the waves of nausea pushing him under as he struggled to surface. A howling sound filled his ears, drowning out his thoughts. His body felt as if it had been crushed into a million shards of frozen glass. His legs ached, and his body trembled with cold; but somewhere in the corner of his mind he could feel a warmth radiating from something . . . someone . . . someone soft and sweet smelling. Alex wondered if it was death he walked toward. But he wasn't ready to die. There was his daughter, Alexis, waiting for him in Richmond. There was the family home crumbling in ruin, destroyed by Northern soldiers. His family was depending on him. He had promised. . . .

The howling became louder but less overwhelming, and hot, searing pain ripped through his limbs as Alex forced his eyes open. He was alive, and there was someone warm snuggled beside him. Moving his head slowly, he waited for his eyes to adjust to the darkness. His body jerked involuntarily. The boy who had shot his dog had his arm flung over his chest!

The moment Alex moved, Gabrielle was awake, her heart pounding. She sat up to meet startled blue eyes.

Alex was confused. The proprietor of the trading post had appeared to be a youth, but this body beside him was no boy's. Even through the sweaters, he'd felt her breasts pressed against his side; he'd smelled the tantalizing scent of a woman's flesh.

"You're not a boy," he accused through cracked, parched lips.

"You're alive," she whispered. "I was afraid I was going to wake up to find you dead." Her large brown eyes met his, eyes so soft and liquid a man could drown in them.

"You haven't answered me." Alex's throat was dry, and his voice cracked with each word. Was he dreaming?

Gabrielle shook her head slowly. "No, I'm not a boy," she murmured. She could feel the heat of his arm against hers; it felt strange, but a good kind of strange. It had been so long since she'd felt another's touch. Since she had returned from Seattle, she had seen only a few travelers and Indian Jack—and he kept to himself. Far back in the recesses of her mind, Gabrielle recalled the feel of the stranger's arm around her shoulders on the Seattle dock. She licked her lips nervously, remembering when she had touched her mouth to his. Her breath came raggedly, the sound of her pounding heart filling her ears.

"I thought I *was* dead," Alex muttered. "Can I have some water?" His eyes drifted shut as he combated the pain.

Gabrielle was immediately up on her knees, thankful to have something to do. "I thought you were dead, too. Some partner you had there, huh?" She offered her tin cup to his lips.

Alex strained to lift his head high enough to take a sip and then let it drop. "Yeah. Some partner."

Gabrielle held the cup between her palms. "Let me guess, your partner's *real* partner ambushed your camp, took all you had, and then tried to kill you."

He swallowed hard, no longer trying to keep his eyes open. His head hurt too much. "How did you know?"

Gabrielle crawled to the stove to throw in some more wet wood. "Seen it before, too many times. You're lucky, most don't live to tell their story." Suddenly her voice was laced with sarcasm. Any man who was fool enough to be swindled like that deserved to freeze to death!

"How'd you find me?" Alex's voice was becoming distant as his mind drifted to escape the pain. His feet felt as if they had been set on fire, the flames shooting up his legs.

"I was running my dogs along the river. Thought I'd found another body to bury." She didn't know why she was being so cruel. She just didn't like him. She didn't like fools and liked gold miners even less.

"Thank you . . ." he murmured drifting off to sleep again.

Gabrielle woke in the morning to the sound of the wind still lamenting, howling and whining as it whipped at the eaves of the old cabin, threatening to rip it to shreds. Snow still blew in through the cracks in the door she'd wedged shut, forming drifts on the worn wood floor.

Snuggling deeper beneath the parka she shared with the stranger, Gabrielle turned hesitantly to study his face. She had never seen anyone with such beautiful hair; it was clean and shiny, a deep startling red that appeared brown in the darkness. Hanging at the same length as her own, it framed his angular face reminding her of a painting she'd once seen on the wall of a church. His lips were parted slightly, his eyelids heavy with sleep. A day's growth of red beard shadowed his face, but it didn't matter. Gabrielle was used to men with beards and saw them as being natural. No, the only thing that marred his serene face was the ugly purple bruise on his temple that spread across one cheek.

Suddenly the lips moved. "Good morning."

Gabrielle scrambled to get out from under the parka, startled by his voice. He knew she had been looking at him. "Good morning," she answered briskly, opening the stove's door with an old rag. She felt so foolish. What had possessed her to lay there beside the stranger and stare at him like some brazen hussy? Alice LeBeau she was not!

Alex opened his eyes, moving slowly to pull Gabrielle's parka up to his chin. His entire body ached as it never had before. Not even when he had fallen forty feet from the mast of the whaling ship and broken six ribs had he hurt this badly. "It's cold in here. Where are we?"

"Yes, it's cold in here," she snapped before she could catch herself. "This is just a squatter's cabin. I'm sorry if you don't like the accommodations. A storm came up fast. I had to get you in out of the weather." She busied herself stoking the fire and adding wood to the fresh blaze.

Alex followed Gabrielle's movements through half-closed eyelids; there was something about her that was familiar. She moved like a dancer, smooth with no wasted or jerky movements, yet she was dressed in dark, baggy wool pants and a bulky sweater. There was no evidence of femininity in the clunky leather boots or unfashionably short-cropped hair, yet something about her lit a spark deep within him. "Do I know you?" He raised one dark eyebrow.

"I think not." Gabrielle scooped up a pot of snow from the drift near the door. No sense in telling him if he doesn't remember, she thought. No need in it.

"I do. I know you." Alex wouldn't give up so easily.

"I'm Jefferson Alexander . . . Alex. Have you ever been to Richmond or maybe New Bedford?" Slowly he eased himself into a sitting position, putting all of his weight on his good arm.

"Nope. Born and raised on the muddy banks of the Tanana." She placed the pot of snow on the stove and waited for it to melt, deliberately keeping her back to him.

"Have I done something to offend you?" Alex asked hoarsely. He was tiring quickly as the pain washed over him in great waves. "I'm certain I'd remember if I'd wronged you." His head hurt; his brain seemed foggy. She was little more than a child. How could he have done anything to her? How could anyone? "I know I've caused you a lot of trouble, but . . ." His voice sounded like it was coming from a long way off. "I'll pay you whatever you ask."

She glanced at him, hearing the strain in his voice. "You'd better lie back down before you pass out and hurt yourself."

Alex slid his body down until he rested flat on the floor again. "How bad are my feet?"

"Bad."

"Am I going to lose my toes?" He closed his eyes, running a palm over his shaggy face. He was badly in need of a shave.

"Might."

Alex's eyes flew open. "Look, have we got a problem here?" He inhaled sharply when a fierce stab of pain ripped through his chest.

"You've got broken ribs, too, so I wouldn't go shouting for a couple of days." Gabrielle's voice was as chilling as the wind that blew through the cracks in the walls.

Alex took a deep breath. This was all he needed. First he'd been robbed and beaten with the butt of a rifle, then his coat and boots were taken and he'd been left in the snow to freeze to death, and now he had this little snit of a woman to contend with. "I apologize for the inconvenience this has caused you, ma'am. I'll pay you for your trouble." His voice had a touch of a southern drawl. "I assure you I'm no more pleased with this than you are."

"Keep your money and your highfalutin words, okay?" She pulled a cloth sack of beaten biscuits from her feed sack and slammed them onto the dirty table. She didn't know why she was so angry with this man, but she was. He had invaded her privacy; he had forced her to care for him. She went on. "We're stuck with each other for the time being, so we'd just better accept it and go on from here." She pulled a biscuit from the bag and threw it at him.

Alex's arm shot up to catch the biscuit, and he took a bite, a smile tugging at the corner of his lips.

Gabrielle continued to speak as if nothing had happened, but secretly, she was pleased. Maybe he did have some survival instinct. She took a deep, calming breath. "From the color of your toes, I think I found you in time. You're not going to lose them, but the recovery is slow. You have to give the flesh time to heal and replace the dead meat. It will probably be weeks before you can walk."

He gnawed at the dry biscuit; it was too salty, but he was starving. Weeks? He couldn't believe his bad luck. "I couldn't have been out there too long; it was past morning light when he attacked me."

36

"It doesn't take long out here, Mr. Alexander. Don't you know anything about cold weather?" Gabrielle dropped a few leaves of tea into her hot cup of water. He would have to wait for something to drink; she had to have her tea in the morning.

"I know a little. I was on a whaling ship for a couple of years off of New England. It gets cold at sea, damned cold." He tried to swallow, but the dry biscuit caught in his throat until he thought he would choke.

"Well, you should have stayed on your ship and chased your whales, Mr. Alexander." *Probably all a pack of lies,* she thought. Men, they were all liars. He sure didn't seem like any deep-water sailor she'd ever known. He was too tall, too clean.

"Considering the circumstances, don't you think Mr. Alexander is a little formal? I never cared much for Jefferson. My friends call me Alex." He forced another bite of biscuit down and waved the remainder at her. "This is the worst damned biscuit I've ever eaten in my life. Who made these awful things?"

Gabrielle's dark eyes grew cloudy with checked anger. "I made them, and if you don't like it, give it back. I'll eat it. I don't usually carry fancy food with me when I'm out dragging jackasses out of the snow." She took a swallow of her tea, burning the roof of her mouth.

Alex tucked his good arm beneath his head. This girl was vicious, quite a sparring partner. "What's your name?" he asked with an equally gruff tone.

Instinctively, Gabrielle hesitated, reluctant to give any information about herself to this stranger. "What difference does it make?" She laughed nervously, taking another sip of the hot tea.

37

Alex's grey-blue eyes grew wide as he struggled to sit up again. "What did you say?" He stared at Gabrielle in disbelief.

She laughed again. "I said what difference does it make."

"It's you," he whispered huskily.

She turned to tie her biscuit bag, knowing she'd been found out. "Who? What are you talking about?" She was stalling for time. She didn't want him asking questions. It was none of his business, any of it. He'd done her a favor, and now she was returning it. It was as simple as that.

"Seattle. You're the girl on the wharf." He pointed a long, tapered finger at her. "You sailed on the *Lady Yukon.*" His voice was laced with an emotion Gabrielle didn't recognize. "You're the woman I keep dreaming about."

Chapter Three

Gabrielle's cheeks grew flushed; her pulse quickened. "I am not." Her voice wavered. "I don't know you."

"I know you remember," he whispered. "Someone was after you. You said you feared for your life. You had me put you aboard the *Lady Yukon.*" He shook his head. "No one could forget that."

Gabrielle turned slowly to face the man who lay on the floor of the old cabin. She could feel her hands trembling at her sides. She'd left Seattle to escape the prying questions. She'd wanted no part of the investigation into her father's death; she had just wanted to be left alone.

Alex studied the slender girl's face, reading the fear in her heavenly dark eyes. Something was very wrong, but he couldn't fathom what. "Tell me your name," he implored.

"Gabrielle," she answered without hesitation. "Gabrielle LeBeau."

He smiled. "Gabrielle, what a beautiful name.

You're French. Do you speak it?" He spoke softly, intrigued by her haunting voice. It was a husky, utterly feminine voice that hinted at untapped sensuality. Even through the pain of his injuries, he felt a shudder of pleasure race down his spine.

"My father was French-Canadian, but I don't speak the language. He never bothered to teach me." She averted her eyes, trying to release the tension strung between them. There was something about this man that made her tremble. No one had ever made her feel this way before, and it frightened her.

A lump caught in Alex's throat. Never in his life had he felt so strongly for a complete stranger. She appeared to be a tower of strength, yet beneath that façade he sensed a frightened child. He suddenly wanted to take her in his arms and kiss the hardened lines of her angelic face. He wanted to smother her biting words with his mouth, to taste her lips again. His eyes drifted shut, and he laughed beneath his breath. Was he mad? A woman was the last thing he needed in his life!

Gabrielle watched Alex through lowered lashes, sipping her hot tea-laced water. He appeared to be sleeping now, and she was glad of it. She needed time to think. Reaching for her parka, she slipped into it and started for the door to check the dogs. She had to get rid of this Alex somehow, and the sooner the better. Something deep inside her told her he was dangerous—dangerous to her orderly plans for the future, dangerous to her way of life.

Hours later Gabrielle sat in front of the old woodstove, its door swung open, watching the flames lick at the leg of a broken chair. She could feel Alex's eyes boring holes in her back, but she refused to turn and face him. The snow storm still raged around them, howling and tearing at the cabin walls, but she knew they were safe within. There was another day's worth of firewood lying about on the floor, and she had food and her gun. Her dogs were safe just outside the door, sleeping comfortably beneath a snowbank. Her only problem was the stranger.

"Why do you dress like a boy?" Alex's voice startled her.

Gabrielle picked up a stick to poke at the fire. "Been doing it for years. My father made me dress in breeches to keep strangers from knowing I was a girl. There's not a white woman for hundreds of miles, and these gold seekers sometimes get funny ideas."

He strained to sit up, leaning against the cold wall of the cabin. "The gown I saw in Seattle was far more becoming."

She gave a snort. "But not very practical. Of course you wouldn't know anything about practicality, would you, Mr. Alexander?"

"I said call me Alex."

She spun around on the floor to face him. "You *said* your friends call you Alex. I'm not one of your friends, and I have no intention of becoming one."

"How can you dislike me? You don't even know me." He ran a hand over the red stubble of his beard.

"I dislike stupidity." She drew up her knees, hugging them against her chest. "And I've seen enough men like you to know you."

"Oh, so you're an expert on men are you?"

She grinned, giving a shrug. "Stupid ones at least."

Alex tipped back his head to laugh in disbelief, and

41

Gabrielle squirmed in discomfort. No one had ever laughed at her before. No one had ever not taken her seriously.

Alex shook his head. "If only we'd met at a different time . . . a different place."

"I don't know what you mean."

"I think you do, Gabrielle." Alex's eyes rested on hers for the briefest moment, and then she turned away.

"Tell me what brings you to the Tanana."

"I thought you weren't interested in sad tales. . . ."

"I'm not actually." Gabrielle had gained her composure now. "But I thought it would make for entertaining conversation. Not much else to do, is there?"

Alex studied her face in silence for a moment, watching the way the firelight cast shadows over her features. The bright light filtered through her short, curly hair like a halo, tinting the ends with gold and red. He sighed, letting his eyes drift shut to ward off the pain that still streaked through his legs. "It's a simple tale."

"I'm sure it is—" Alex's eyes flew open, and Gabrielle hid a smile behind her hand. "All right." She put up her hands in surrender. "I'll keep quiet."

He gave a nod. "Do that, or I'll not provide the entertainment." His eyes drifted shut again, and he began to speak in a low, masculine voice. "I'm from Richmond, Virginia. Ever been there?"

"Never been out of the territories."

"It's the same old story. My family owned land and prospered before the war. My father and brothers were killed at Sharpsburg. The Northerners called it the

42

battle of Antietam. We sold much of the land after the war for taxes." He laughed wryly, his voice echoing in the tiny cabin.

"You didn't fight?" Gabrielle asked quietly.

He shook his head. "I wanted to. They'd have taken me. Hell, they were taking them younger than sixteen. But I promised my papa I'd look after my mama and sisters."

"No need in all of you dyin'."

Alex opened his eyes, tucking his hands behind his head. "After the war, I tried a couple of things, but nothing worked out. I wrote for a newspaper, I shoveled grain in a mill, but I just couldn't make enough money to support my family. We were planters, but with the slaves gone, we couldn't plant more than a few acres. Then I met Amber; we married, and a friend hired me on as a deck hand on his whaling ship out of New Bedford." His voice took on a new pitch. "The pay was good, it was terrific, but it bothered me slaughtering those beautiful creatures." He looked up at her. "Have you ever seen a whale, Gabrielle?"

She shook her head, intrigued by the emotion reflected in the stranger's eyes. "Never." She drew closer, listening intently. Storytelling was as natural as breathing to the people who lived this lonely life in the territories. They thrived on it.

"Ah, they're one of God's most beautiful creatures, huge and glistening. They're the size of the sailing ships we track them on." His blue eyes sparkled as he raised a hand to arc in the air. "Time seems to lose all meaning as they surface and dive again crying out in this strange, haunting voice. I hear their songs in my dreams. . . ."

43

He paused staring into nothingness for a moment. "But anyway. I left New Bedford and returned to Richmond to find my wife buried in the family graveyard and my sister caring for my newborn daughter."

"So you came north?" Gabrielle was so close to the stranger now that she could see the dark streaks that ran through his intense blue eyes. He had a light sprinkling of freckles across his nose and high, handsome cheekbones.

"Tried some other things that didn't work out. So, I came north. I read about the tales of gold in a Richmond newspaper and packed my bag. My daughter Alexis is with my sister Clarice and her Yankee husband."

"How old is she?"

"Alexis? She'll be five in the spring." He struggled to sit up, and Gabrielle took his good arm to help him. The broken one she had set with wooden slats from a crate and strips of flannel from her favorite shirt.

"What does she look like?"

"An angel." He laughed. "Red-gold curls and an impish smile."

"You must love her very much," Gabrielle dared hesitantly.

"I do." He looked up at her. "So, that's my sad tale. How about yours?"

Gabrielle stiffened. "Mine?"

"Sure."

"Oh, no." She got to her feet to throw more wood on the fire. "You'll not find me spouting my life story to a complete stranger." She kept her back to him. "Besides, there's nothing to tell."

"Liar."

44

Gabrielle spun around. "Pardon?"

"I said you're a liar, Gabrielle LeBeau." He slid his body down until he rested on the floor again and closed his eyes.

For a moment she just stared at him in disbelief, then grabbed her parka and stepped outside, slamming the door. Behind her, she could hear his laughter filtering through the cracks in the cabin's outer walls. She covered her ears with her hands, lifting her chin to let the snow sting her face. She breathed deeply, letting the frigid air fill her lungs, and gasped in response. Conceited jackass, she thought, stuffing her hands in her pockets. Who was he to laugh at *her?* She stood in knee-deep snow, staring out at the forest blanketed in white.

One of the younger sled dogs crawled from his haven in a snowbank to nuzzle her leg, and Gabrielle patted his head, smoothing the thick coat that protected the husky from the elements. "What's the matter, Anthony, boy?" she crooned. "I've no meat to give you." She scratched the underside of his chin. "The snow's just about stopped, though. We'll go home tomorrow." The dog whined in response, and Gabrielle laughed.

She preferred the company of her dogs to human companionship. The dogs were loyal and affectionate, and they didn't call people liars. She shook her head wondering how she got herself into messes like this. She didn't want to take Alex back to her cabin. She didn't want to be responsible for him. All she wanted was to be left alone.

When night fell, Gabrielle stoked the fire in the old stove and laid down on the floor beside Alex. Begrudgingly, she spread her parka over them both, turning her back to him.

"I don't bite." Alex's voice came out of the darkness.

"You sure?" she asked, the sarcasm plain in her voice.

"You'd be warmer if you moved closer." He propped himself up on his elbow, staring at her through the darkness. With the door to the woodstove closed, there was barely enough light to see the outline of her slim body stretched out beside his. "You're shivering."

"And you're going to take care of that for me, are you?" She wrapped her arms around her waist, hugging herself for warmth.

"You're awfully suspicious."

"Not suspicious, just realistic."

"Look Gabrielle, the farthest thing from my mind right now is taking advantage of your feminine wiles. And I use that term lightly. You've nothing to fear from me. Dressed like that, it's hard for me to believe you'd have to worry about anyone." He rolled onto his back. "Now come on. Roll over. You'll be warmer next to me."

Reluctantly, she inched her way closer to him. He was right. Sharing body heat was important out there. Still, she wished it wasn't him. She was warmer next to him, but still, her body trembled as an unfamiliar shiver raced through her veins. Her arm brushed against his, and she recoiled. Her ears rang with Alex's laughter.

"Come here; you're shaking like a rabbit." Before Gabrielle knew what was happening, he had wrapped her in his good arm and drawn her against his hard body.

"Take your hand off me!" she insisted between

clenched teeth. She strained against him, surprised by his strength in his invalid state.

"Hush and go to sleep. I told you I won't hurt you. I'm cold, too."

Gabrielle opened her mouth to speak again, but then clamped it shut. She shouldn't be doing this. She knew she shouldn't be letting this man touch her like this, but the truth was she *was* much warmer.

When she finally relaxed, Alex spoke again. "That's better. Now go to sleep. You said the snow was almost stopped. Tomorrow we'll go back to your cabin."

She sniffed. "You mean tomorrow I'll load you in my sled and take you back. You won't be doing any walking for some time."

Alex scowled in the darkness but said nothing. She certainly was a woman who liked to rub in a man's mistakes. Not much of a woman at all as he saw it. Her breath was even now. He could feel her chest rising and falling beneath his hand. Even through her bulky sweater he could feel the curve of her breast. He groaned inwardly pushing all thoughts of Gabrielle from his mind. He had to be crazy to find her attractive, her and her waspish tongue.

Gabrielle breathed slowly, trying to calm the flutter in her stomach. She could feel his hand pressed against her side, his warmth radiating through her. She wanted to roll away; she wanted to sleep on the other side of the room, outside with the dogs even! She didn't want to be laying next to Alex like this. She didn't want to feel his warm breath on her cheek. But she stayed, drifting off to sleep.

With the coming of light in the morning came the sound of rapping on the door. "Gabrielle? It's Jack.

47

You all right?" He rattled at the door she had tied shut from the inside.

Jack? Gabrielle's eyes flew open. Recoiling from Alex's touch, she leaped up to run to the door. Was she mad to have her arm flung over Alex like that? "Jack," she called. "I'm coming." Thank God it was Jack. He would know what to do with Alex; he would know how to get rid of him.

Gabrielle untied the knot of string that held the door shut and flung it open. "Jack!" She grinned, half-tempted to throw her arms around her friend.

The native bore a broken-toothed smile. "You all right, Gabe?" He stared through the door at the waking Alex. "No harm come to you?"

"No, no. I'm fine." She motioned to Alex, feeling her cheeks redden. "Mr. Alexander was beaten by his partner and left to die on the river path. I found him when I was out running the dogs." Why did she feel like she had to explain? She had never had to explain anything to Jack before.

Jack nodded his head, his inky-black, shoulder-length hair sweeping the collar of his seal-skin coat. "He bad off?" He stepped inside the door, and Gabrielle closed it.

"Toes were bad, but I think he's going to make it. I found him in time." She stood between Alex and Jack, looking from one to the other.

"Morning." Alex gave Jack a nod. "We're glad to see you."

Jack lifted a black eyebrow studying Alex but said nothing. Gabrielle moved to the stove to get her pan and start hot water. "He's right. I could use some help getting home. He can't walk, and he's a load for my

48

dogs. They're young to be hauling in snow this deep. They're barely broke." She dipped snow from outside the door and put the pan on the stove to melt. "How'd you find me, Jack?"

He stood in the middle of the room staring blatantly at Alex. Gabrielle couldn't help smiling as she watched Alex squirm. Jack did what he pleased, having none of the social mores of the white man. If he wanted to stare, he stared.

"I came to the post yesterday," Jack said evenly. "You were gone. I started walking."

"You were out there all night?" Alex asked in awe, struggling to sit up. His chest ached with every movement.

Jack shrugged, turning from Alex. "Didn't leave the post 'til after dark."

"You didn't sleep?" Alex winced as he moved one leg and then the other.

"I didn't sleep." Jack dropped his pack to the floor, dismissing Alex without a glance. "I brought meat for the dogs," he told Gabrielle.

"Oh, good. They haven't eaten since the night before I left." She grabbed a piece of wood from the floor and threw it into the old stove. "You came just in time. I've burned all of the fuel in here. I was going to have to go looking for dry wood this morning."

"I will feed the dogs. You have your tea. Then we go." Jack picked up his pack off the floor and stepped outside, closing the door behind him.

Alex inhaled sharply. "Quite a character," he remarked.

Gabrielle whipped around. "He's my friend."

"A little blunt isn't he? Probably not much of a

conversationalist at a party."

She noted the hint of a teasing tone in his voice. "Jack is what he is. A good friend. He'd do anything for me."

"So how did he find us?"

Gabrielle shrugged. "I don't ask. He probably wouldn't say anyway. He knows about this squatter's cabin, too. Good guesser, I suppose." She poured her heated water into her tin cup and threw a few tea leaves into it.

"You don't really believe that do you?" Alex watched Gabrielle as she moved about the room gathering her things. Beneath the baggy woolen pants and heavy sweater, he could make out the slim form of a shapely woman.

"I told you. I don't ask. He just knows things sometimes. He knows when I'm in trouble. His mother and father were the same way." Gabrielle could feel a tightening in her chest as images of her foster parents flashed through her mind. A sad smile played on her lips. Even after all of these years, she still missed them. They had been so good to her. They had given her such a wonderful childhood.

"Sounds pretty odd to me." Alex stroked his growing red beard.

"Well, Mr. Alexander, what might be odd to an outsider is perfectly normal here. We live among the natives of the Tanana, and we accept without question." She refilled her cup with hot water and handed it to him. His hand brushed hers as the cup passed between them, and a pleasant shiver ran down her arm. She turned her back to him. "We'll take you back to my cabin on the sled, and then we'll decide what to do with you."

Alex sipped the hot water with a trace of mint in it. "I haven't thanked you properly."

"It isn't necessary," she answered gruffly.

"It is, and I'll repay you somehow. I know you don't want to be burdened by me, and I'm sorry."

Something in Alex's voice made her turn to him. She studied his azure-blue eyes for a moment, caught in their depths. "I said it's all right. You helped me, remember?" She smiled the way she had smiled that day on the steamer, and Alex grinned. She was beautiful when she smiled.

Chapter Four

". . . cabin's a bit small, isn't it?" Alex leaned against the door frame, catching his breath. Pain shot up his legs nearly rendering him senseless. Only Jack's arm wrapped securely around his waist kept him upright.

"This isn't the Full Moon Hotel, Mr. Alexander," Gabrielle replied irritably. She glanced at Jack. "I suppose you'll have to put him in my bed for now."

Jack chuckled deep in his throat, half carrying Alex to the frame bed that ran along the east wall. Gabrielle and the red-haired stranger had been scrapping like sled dogs since early morning. In all the years he'd known Gabe, she'd never behaved like this, and it amused him. If he didn't know better, he'd think she was stuck on the man. Jack dumped Alex unceremoniously onto Gabrielle's bed and went outside to care for the dogs.

For a few minutes Alex just lay there, waiting for the pain to subside. His face was ashen white, his lips tightly compressed.

"It's good that it hurts," Gabrielle offered from

across the room. She pulled a precious sulfur match from a tin box over the fireplace and struck it, lighting the wood shavings that littered the inside hearth.

"That right?" Alex groaned.

"Yup. When there's no pain, that's when you begin to worry. Only live flesh can hurt. I don't think you'll even lose any toes."

"That's a relief," he responded dryly. His eyes were open now as he studied her back.

Gabrielle spun around. "Look Mr. Alexander—"

"Alex," he interrupted.

"Alex," she conceded with a nod of her head. "I'm not any happier about this than you are. What? You don't think I've got anything better to do than drag fools around on my sled?"

"At least you're not one to dwell on things." Alex was resting on his side now, his head on a duck-down pillow.

Gabrielle ignored his comment. "Now, if you could just keep your mouth shut long enough for me to do a little thinking, maybe I'd be able to come up with a way to get you out of here."

Alex watched her as she turned her back to him and knelt to feed the newborn flames that licked at the woodshavings. Slowly she added small bits of kindling, then branches as thick as her wrist. She worked in silence, each movement fluid and unwasted. Alex could tell that she had followed this ritual many times. Finally she lifted a log and dropped it onto her masterpiece, then she turned back to him.

"Have you got any money?" She was stripping off her parka now and hanging it on a wooden peg near the door.

"Not any more I don't. You think they took my coat and boots, but left me the money?" He laughed ruefully.

Gabrielle made a face. "I wouldn't be laughing if I were you. You haven't got any money to pay anyone to haul you out of here, and by the time you can walk, the passes will all be closed for the winter."

"What about your friend Jack? Wouldn't he get me out? I could send money later."

"Not for all the gold he could carry on his back. Jack doesn't do that sort of thing. He cares for himself, his family and for me. You're lucky he carried you in the door here. I thought he was going to leave you on the sled for the winter."

Alex raised himself up on one elbow. "God damn, woman, you've got a sharp tongue!"

Gabrielle grinned. "So I'm told." She lifted her chin. "And I'm proud of it. I don't take anything from anyone, men especially."

"A man hater are you?"

She shook her head. "I don't think so. I'm just not going to be pushed around." She tugged her red, wool hat off her head and ran her fingers through her short, curly hair.

"For a woman who hates men, you're doing an awfully good job of disguising yourself as one."

"I told you, I don't hate men. And I dress like this because it's comfortable and it's safe." She tossed her hat onto a peg and crossed the room to him.

"That how you live? Safe?"

"I try." She reached for the sleeve of the seal-skin jacket Alex wore and gave a tug, removing it for him. Jack had loaned it to him for the sled ride back to the cabin.

"Not much happiness in playing it safe," Alex murmured. "You're not happy, are you?" He caught her hand, but she pulled away.

"Perfectly happy. Let me get a look at your feet."

"Habitual liar too?"

Gabrielle turned to meet his gaze. A sarcastic remark lurked on the end of her tongue, but she bit it back. What was it about this man that grated on her so? He just stared at her. He should be grateful, she thought, tearing her gaze from his. He should be apologetic. She tugged at the wool socks she'd put on his feet this morning.

"Ouch!" Alex cried out. "You're ripping the flesh off my bones."

"Oh hush. Don't be a baby. You don't know what pain is. I once saw my papa saw off a man's leg, right there on that table." She indicated a rectangular wooden table burdened with crates near the fireplace. "And he lived to tell about it."

Alex squeezed his eyes shut. She pulled off the other sock, but this time he didn't flinch. Who did she think she was this little up-start? He was nearly old enough to be her father.

"I've a salve to put on that will take away some of the surface pain. It's one of Jack's wife's recipes."

"He has a wife?" Jack swallowed hard, battling the pain.

"He does. And a daughter. They live across the river in a village." Gabrielle went to fetch a tin from her medicine chest and returned to kneel next to the bed.

"So why does he come here?" The cold salve she

spread smoothed away the pain, and his breath came easier.

"We were brought up together. His parents cared for me when my father was gone."

"Off on hunting trips?"

"Off getting himself soused. My father was a drinker, Mr. Alexander." Gabrielle didn't know why she'd told him that. It wasn't his business; it wasn't anyone's. Her throat tightened. She wished her father was here right now. He'd know what to do with Alex; he'd know how to get rid of him. Who was she kidding? Her father had never made a decision in his life. It was Gabrielle who ran the trading post. *She* was the one who bought the supplies. *She* was the one who solved their day to day problems.

"I'm sorry." Alex brushed her arm with the tips of his fingers.

Gabrielle doctored his other foot in silence and returned the tin to its proper place. Without another word, she ducked out of the cabin.

Indian Jack stood leaning against the cabin's exterior wall, a cigar dangling from his mouth. Gabrielle leaned against the wall beside him, stuffing her hands in the pockets of her wool breeches. It was barely supper time and already the sun was setting. For a long time the two stood in silence, listening to the call of a ptarmigan and watching the flight of a covey of grouse when one of the dogs spooked them from the brush. Finally, Gabrielle spoke.

"What am I going to do with him, Jack?" She dug in the snow with the heel of her boot.

"Not much you can do with him, is there?"

She exhaled slowly. "He's the one, you know. The man who saved me on that street in Seattle. Taylor would have had me if it hadn't been for Alex."

"You feel like you owe him, huh?" The Indian blew smoke into the frigid air, watching the patterns it created before disappearing with the wind.

Gabrielle wrapped her arms around her waist. It was getting too cold these days to be out without a coat. Even her wool sweater couldn't keep out the biting west wind. "I don't know what I feel. He scares me."

"I could stay awhile," Jack commented matter-of-factly.

Gabrielle laughed. "No, that's not what I mean. I'm safe enough. Good Lord, in his condition he can barely take himself to the outhouse. He wouldn't have the strength to wrestle a hare." She shook her head. "I can't explain it. He makes me feel funny. Know what I mean?"

Jack grinned. "Yea, I think I do. But you just watch yourself. Don't get tangled with that stranger. He doesn't belong here. He's not one of us."

Gabrielle lifted her hands. "Oh no, you don't have to worry about that with me. You'll not find Gabrielle LeBeau with any man strapped to her side. Not ever."

He chuckled beneath his breath. "So he's stayin', is he?"

"Not for long he's not. Only until I can figure out how to get rid of him. Maybe Beans Magee will know someone who'd be willing to haul him out. Hell, I'd pay 'em myself just to get rid of him. What do you think? You think I can get anyone to take him out on his sled?"

"Maybe."

She slumped against the rough hand-hewn slabs of

the cabin. "But probably not, though, huh?"

"Probably not," Jack responded.

Dejected, Gabrielle watched the setting sun. It was glorious there on the horizon with its brilliant yellows and golds against the stark white of the snow-filled trees. Finally, she pushed off the wall. "Guess I'd better dig up something to eat."

Jack gave a nod but said nothing. He just went on puffing on the cigar and scratching a young pup's head.

As darkness settled on the tiny cabin nestled on the bank of the Tanana River, Gabrielle moved about the cabin fixing the evening meal. She worked silently, beating the batter for flapjacks, ignoring the man who lay restless on her bed.

Alex tossed and turned in the narrow bed along the wall, trying to find a comfortable position. The salve Gabrielle had spread on his feet eased the pain of the frostbite, but his broken arm ached beneath the homemade splint. Alex watched Gabrielle with an odd curiosity, finally breaking the quiet spell. "Where's your friend?"

"Jack?" Gabrielle did not turn around. "Don't know. Gone."

"Gone? Gone where?"

"I dunno." She shrugged, ladling batter onto the cast-iron griddle that rested on the wood stove. "Probably home." The batter hit the hot griddle, and the room was filled with the sound of spattering grease.

Alex considered Gabrielle's words and then spoke again. "I thought you two were friends."

She flipped the first flapjack over. "We are."

"Then why don't you know where he's gone, or even if he is gone?"

Gabrielle turned to the stranger in her bed, licking the batter from one of her fingers. "I'm no one's keeper."

"I didn't say you were. I just thought . . ." Alex ran his hand through his thick, red hair. "I thought he must have said good-bye or something."

"Nope." She flipped another flapjack, sending this one airborne before it hit the griddle again. "Jack just comes and goes. Doesn't bother with hellos and good-byes."

He watched her drop two burnt flapjacks onto a cracked china platter. "And you don't think that's odd?"

"Why should I? He's done it all his life."

Alex gave up the subject with a heavy sigh and tried another. "How long have you lived here?"

"My whole life." Gabrielle slid the platter onto one of the wooden chairs that furnished the stark cabin. She would have put it on the table, but it was piled high with wooden crates and empty cloth sacks. She dropped some more batter onto the griddle. "Born and raised on the banks of the Tanana, Mr. Alexander. Except, of course, for a brief, unsuccessful stay at boarding school in Seattle a few years back."

"You left school?" Alex propped himself on her pillow.

"Kicked out. The sisters said my soul was beyond hope." She laughed. "Actually, I just think I was too smart for them. You could have put the three of them together, Sister Agatha, Sister Mary, and Sister Ruth, and combined they didn't have the sense of a moose."

"Why here? Why the Tanana?" Alex inquired softly.

"Because this is where I belong." She turned to him,

60

the flapjack turner in her hand. "How about you? Where do you belong, Mr. Alexander?" Their eyes locked for a brief moment, and then she turned back to the stove.

"Touché, Mademoiselle LeBeau." Alex slid back in the bed.

Gabrielle lifted the griddle from the stove and set it on the floor. Then with her platter of flapjacks in hand, she grabbed a jug of maple syrup, a tin plate and a fork off the fireplace mantel and sat down on one of the chairs. Dropping two flapjacks on her plate, she rested the platter on the floor and poured a healthy portion of syrup over the fried cakes. Cutting a piece off, she stuffed it in her mouth, licking the syrup from her fork.

"You going to bring me some?" Alex asked, lifting an eyebrow.

"Nope." Gabrielle stuffed another piece into her mouth.

"You rescued me on that path to bring me back to your cabin so I could starve to death?" His voice was indignant.

"There's plenty here." She indicated the platter resting on the floor. "Help yourself."

Alex scowled. "You know I can't walk."

"You can't walk *far*." She finished the flapjacks on her plate and reached for more. "It's what, five or six feet from this platter to that bed?" She poured more syrup onto her plate. "I'm no one's servant. You'll come that far if you're hungry enough."

Alex swore beneath his breath. The first thing he was going to do when his broken arm healed was give that woman a good throttling! What was wrong with her that she couldn't bring him one lousy plate of food? He

61

wasn't asking to bed her! All he wanted was something to eat!

After a few minutes passed and Gabrielle went on eating zealously, Alex realized that if he wanted something to eat, he'd better get moving before she ate every scrap. Slowly, painfully, he got to his feet and forced himself to cover the distance between the bed and the chair next to Gabrielle. It was the longest journey he'd ever made. Perspiration broke out in beads across his forehead, and his heart pounded painfully in his chest. But somehow he managed to reach his destination. Panting, he pointed to the mantel above the fireplace. "Might I have the plate and fork, dragon-lady?"

A smile twitched at the corners of Gabrielle's mouth. "Might you say please?"

"Please." Alex watched her get to her feet and retrieve the other plate and fork. "If I'd said please a few minutes ago, would you have brought me the flapjacks?"

"No." She dropped the plate onto his lap. "It's going to be weeks before you heal. You can't lay around forever. Your muscles'll grow so weak your legs will never carry you again." She picked up two flapjacks with the end of her fork and dropped them onto his plate. Then she gave herself two more.

Alex watched with amazement as she poured more syrup onto her plate, drowning the fresh flapjacks. He took the jug of syrup and began to pour. "Do you always use that much syrup?"

"Yup." She stuffed in another large piece, and a long string of syrup ran down the corner of her mouth. Her tongue darted out to catch the thick, sweet liquid.

Shaking his head, Alex put the jug on the floor at his feet and cut off a piece of flapjack. Pushing it into his mouth, he grimaced. "God-sakes, woman! This has got to be the worst pancake I ever put in my mouth!"

Gabrielle devoured another mouthful. "Now you know why I use so much syrup." Her laughter filled the cabin as Alex reached for the jug at his feet.

Later, after the meal was finished and Alex had made his way back to the bed, Gabrielle stepped outside and filled two huge kettles with snow, placing them on the stove. She dug some rope from beneath the bed and strung it from one wall peg to another. Taking an old quilt, she draped it over the rope, screening off the corner the stove occupied. Emptying an old tub of flour sacks and assorted junk, she dragged it behind the blanket. With interest, Alex watched her carry three buckets of snow in from outside. Then she disappeared behind the blanket.

Alex began to chuckle as Gabrielle's clothes appeared. First her wool pants were thrown over the rope, then socks, cotton underdrawers and her shirt. He could hear her pouring the hot water from the stove. Closing his eyes, he imagined the snow in the tub melting as the hot water hit it. When he heard her slide into the tub, his mind filled with images of her slender body. He imagined her full breasts, her small waist, her rounded hips. Groaning, Alex pulled the pillow over his face.

"You all right?" Gabrielle called from behind the curtain.

"Quite," Alex responded cooly. After a moment of silence, he spoke again. Anything to keep his mind off her. . . . "You said this was your father's cabin. Is he

63

coming back?" He glanced at the man's red-plaid shirt hanging on a peg and the razor strap on a nail near the mantel.

"I doubt it." Water splashed, and Alex heard the distinct plop of a bar of soap. "He's been dead a couple of months."

Alex's brow furrowed. "I'm sorry," he murmured.

"So am I" came the feminine voice from behind the curtain. After another moment of silence, Gabrielle spoke again. "I don't mean to be flippant. I loved my father very much, drinker or not."

"How did he die?"

"I don't want to talk about it."

Respecting Gabrielle's privacy, Alex didn't press the issue. "Don't you have anyone else?"

"What, a guardian? A protector? A knight in shining armor?" She laughed. "I'm afraid, Mr. Alexander, that we've long passed the age of chivalry." The air was beginning to smell of some wild flower unknown to Alex's sensitive nose. "I'm of legal age," Gabrielle continued. "I have no one but myself . . . and my dogs and Jack. A few other friends I see on and off."

"Aren't you lonely, Gabrielle?" Her name rolled off his tongue, easily, sweetly. Alex's eyes drifted shut as he listened to her move in the tub of bath water.

"I miss my papa. But lonely? No. I have the birds, the animals, the trees, the ice and snow. They'll speak to you if you've got the time to listen."

"And what do they say, Gabrielle?" Her voice was an anesthetic, drawing the pain from his aching arm and legs.

"They tell me about beauty, about honesty, about hard work."

"Would they tell me the same?"

"They might. If you listened."

Alex heard Gabrielle move in the tub, and the sound of splashing water filled his ears. He imagined her running the bar of sweet-smelling soap over her long limbs. He could almost see her cupping the water with her hands to rinse her legs, her back, her breasts. He glanced up at the blanket that separated them. His fingers ached to give the old quilt a tug, to remove the barrier that hung between them. Slowly, he reached with his good hand until it brushed the soft fabric of the curtain.

"I wouldn't do that if I were you," Gabrielle's voice warned as she went on, splashing, rinsing.

"And if I do?"

Alex heard her move, and then the old quilt lifted and the barrel of a rifle appeared. His laughter echoed in the small cabin as he released the blanket and watched it fall.

Chapter Five

The following morning Gabrielle was awake before dawn making coffee. She hadn't slept well on the quilt on the floor in front of the fireplace, and she was feeling irritable. It wasn't that she wasn't comfortable enough; Rouge had always said she could sleep anywhere . . . standing on her head if she had to. No, it was the stranger. It was thoughts of Alex that had kept her awake most of the night. No matter how tightly she squeezed her eyes shut, no matter what she tried to think about, sleep eluded her. All she could think of was Alex, his laughter, his questions, his clear blue eyes. And this morning she was mad as hell with him.

"Morning," Alex called from her bed. He smiled at the sight of her in her red union suit. Though she was covered from head to toe, he had no need to use his imagination this morning. The heavy cotton, one-piece suit revealed every curve of her lithe body.

"Morning," Gabrielle grunted in return. She had her back to him, pouring herself a cup of coffee. The blanket screen had been pulled down, but she had left the rope. Alex presumed she intended to use it again. "Want coffee?" she asked gruffly.

"Please." Alex sat up, running his hand through his hair. He felt filthy this morning. What he needed was a bath and a shave. When Gabrielle brought him a steaming cup of coffee, he nodded in the direction of the tub she'd used the night before. "I think I could use that this morning."

She gave a nod, sipping her coffee. "I think you're right."

Alex shook his head, inhaling the heavenly scent of the rich, hot brew. "What's that supposed to mean?"

"How long's it been since you had a bath, Mr. Alexander?" A bare glimpse of a smile was visible over the rim of her cup.

Alex reddened. "Too long."

She turned away chuckling, relieved to know that if she was going to be stuck with this man all winter, at least he wouldn't stink like a bear. Though it was common for most folk this far north to dispense with bathing through the winter, Gabrielle's father had insisted on personal cleanliness. It was he who had brought the old copper wash tub from Seattle on one of his supply trips more than ten years ago. "I'll fill the tub for you, but from there you're on your own," she said. "I'm going to take my dogs down the river, so I'll be gone most of the day. Think you can manage it?"

Alex eyed the tub, seriously doubtful. He looked back at Gabrielle pulling her wool breeches over her union suit. "If I can't, you'll help, right?"

"Like hell!" She whipped around to face him, a faded green flannel shirt in her hand. "But I'm warning you." She shook a finger at him. "You start stinking up this place, and you're out with the dogs."

Her voice was light, but Alex knew she meant every word. "You don't see me getting out of here any time soon, do you?" He watched distractedly as she pulled the bulky pants over her shapely buttocks.

"Not unless you intend to sprout wings." She gave a smirk, putting an abrupt end to the conversation. "I'll get your water, and then I'm off." Pulling on a heavy sweater and her wide-brimmed hat, she grabbed her parka and disappeared out the door.

Gabrielle returned late in the afternoon to find Alex sitting where she'd left him, propped on pillows in her bed. His hair had been washed and combed into soft waves, and he was sporting a clean shirt and pants.

"I hope you don't mind my borrowing your father's clothes." Alex ran a hand over the soft flannel of the worn, red plaid shirt. "Mine were filthy—what was left of them."

Gabrielle stood in the doorway of the cabin for a moment staring at Alex. That familiar tightening in her throat made her turn away. *Oh, Papa,* her heart cried silently. *I miss you, Papa. I miss you so bad.* "No, not at all," she managed, pulling off her parka to hang it on a peg. "If Papa had been here, he'd have given 'em to you."

The strain in Gabrielle's voice tugged at Alex's heart. Where was his sense, to put on the girl's dead father's clothing? He should have put his own things back on, stinking or not. It was just that he wanted to be presentable. Something about this sultry young harridan made him want to look his best.

Gabrielle moved to the table and sat down to remove her heavy leather boots, glancing up at Alex. "I left the

69

razor out for you. Couldn't you find it?" She suddenly felt tired, worse than tired. She felt weary. She was just beginning to realize how hard it was going to be to fill the void her father's death had left in her life. She took off her hat and ran her fingers slowly through her hair.

Entranced by the sight of her slim fingers tousling the bright chestnut hair, Alex didn't answer at once. Was her hair as soft as it appeared? Would those curls feel like silk against his cheek? "No, well . . . yes, I found it, but . . ." His fair skin colored as he tapped his splinted arm. "My right arm, it's my shaving arm. I was afraid I'd slit my throat."

Gabrielle dared a slight smile. He was actually quite handsome, this stranger of hers. He was an honest man; she could see that in his smokey blue eyes. And he was a caring man; she could see that, too. "I could do it for you," she heard herself say.

"Could you?" Alex straightened. "I'd appreciate it, Gabrielle." He liked the sound of her name ringing in his ears.

Peeling off her wool sweater, Gabrielle stoked the fire, then moved to the mantel to find her father's razor and strap. The metal felt good in her hands, cold and hard, but familiar. How many times had her father sent her to fetch his razor? How many summer mornings had she sat on the step of their cabin . . . watching him shave in front of the mirror that hung on a tree branch just outside the door? Memories . . . sweet memories.

Fetching a basin of hot water from the stove, a bar of soap and an old cotton towel, she sat down on the side of the bed. "I have to warn you, Mr. Alexander, I'm not very good at this."

"I thought you were going to call me Alex, us being cabin mates and all." He knew he was pressing his luck. He knew she wasn't any more pleased about this situation than he was, but he wanted to see her smile. He wanted to hear his name on her lips. His eyes rested on them. They were full and pink, her upper lip slightly heavier than the lower. His pulse quickened as he watched the tip of her tongue unconsciously trace the shapely line. He had a sudden impulse to kiss those lips.

Gabrielle caught Alex's odd stare, and she squirmed uncomfortably. Other men had stared at her—on the streets of Seattle, on the steamers—but no man had ever looked at her like this before. She'd never seen such a strange light in anyone's eyes. She lifted her gaze until it met his. It was Alex that broke the spell this time.

"I'm ready. Do what you will to me."

"Huh?" Her cheeks colored. "Oh, all right." Gabrielle dipped the corner of the towel in the hot water and applied it to one cheek.

"Ouch! Damn! That's hot, Gabrielle!"

Startled, she pulled back the towel. Her wide eyes met his, and they both laughed breaking the tension. "I'm sorry," she murmured.

"Remind me not to ask you to ever do this again," he chided good-heartedly.

Gabrielle gave a nod, pressing the air-cooled cloth against his cheek again. She looked away, waiting for the damp heat to soften his red whiskers. It felt good to laugh. It was nice to have someone to talk to. This was how she and her father had been—at least when he wasn't drinking. They laughed and teased. They played practical jokes on each other and told long

71

bald-faced lies.

Alex caught Gabrielle's wrist, and she flinched. Slowly he moved her hand to the other cheek. He was watching her now, studying her dark brown eyes.

"You're very pretty you know."

Despite herself, Gabrielle blushed again. "Am I? No one's ever told me that before." She took the bar of rose-colored soap and began to lather his cheek.

"I can hardly believe that."

She shrugged. "Who would there be? My hounds are not much for compliments."

"You're serious." Alex's jaw dropped. His brows knitted as he caught her hand and took the soap. "Hey, what is this? I'm going to smell like a bouquet of flowers!"

Gabrielle was lathering both cheeks now, her hands running the length of his fine jaw, caressing his high cheek bones. "Sorry, but it's all I've got. Jack's wife makes it for me. Smells good, doesn't it?"

"On you maybe, but certainly not on me!" Alex relaxed against the pillow, enjoying the feel of her hands on his whiskered face.

Gabrielle laughed, running the razor over the sharpening strap. This was oddly comforting somehow—sitting on the edge of the bed, shaving Alex. It made her wonder if this was what it would be like to be married. The laughter . . . the closeness? She had once asked her father about married life and what it was like. "Pure hell," he'd replied. "Pure hell, daughter. An entanglement I never intend to get myself into again, and I recommend the same to you."

Gabrielle pushed her father's words from her mind, leaning to run the razor over Alex's left cheek. She comforted herself with the fact that her father's advice was rarely worthy and more often than not, completely erroneous.

"Boy, does that feel good," Alex remarked, letting his eyes drift until they were almost shut. "If you ever get tired of living alone here, you could always open your own little shop in Seattle."

Gabrielle made a face, and he laughed again. She dipped the razor into the pan of water and moved to his other cheek. Alex raised his good hand to touch a lock of her chestnut hair.

"Why do you wear it so short?" He fingered a silken curl. It was softer than he'd imagined. He yearned to press it to his lips.

Gabrielle pushed his hand away with her elbow. "I dunno. Just always have."

"Even when you were a little girl?"

"Well no. I used to wear it in long braids. Jack's mother could weave my hair so tight it made my head hurt." She smiled at the memory.

"So why did you cut it?"

Gabrielle dipped the razor in the water again. "Lift your chin," she ordered. The steel razor glided expertly down his neck. "Actually it was a prank. One of the sisters at school accused me of being more like a boy than a girl, so I cut it all off. I was nearly bald."

"And you didn't mind?"

"Oh, I minded. I cried for days afterward. But I'd never have let that old witch know!" She was making the finishing touches now, lingering when it really wasn't necessary. For some strange reason, she didn't want to pull away. Gabrielle ran her hand over Alex's smooth cheek, blotting at a patch of soap with the towel. "How's that?"

Alex brushed the back of his good hand against his cheek. "Better than I could have done myself." His hand touched hers for a moment, and then she pulled away. Gathering her implements, she got to her feet and began to put everything away. "Now it's time to find something to eat around here."

"What are you making?"

"I shot a rabbit. It's hanging outside. How about fried rabbit and biscuits?"

Alex raised his arms in mock horror. "No! No! Please, ma'am, not the biscuits!"

Gabrielle spun around. "How dare you insult my cooking. I don't see you getting yourself up to make anything!" She knew he was barely fit to cross the room, nevertheless cook a meal, but it made her mad. What right did he have to say anything? He didn't have a cent in his pocket nor a place to go. He ought to be damned grateful!

Alex smiled, but his voice became more serious. "You're right. I know I've invaded your privacy, and I'm sorry. I'll make it up to you." He didn't know how or when, but he'd repay her for her kindness. "Now how about letting me try a hand at biscuit making."

"You?" Gabrielle raised an eyebrow skeptically. "Where'd you learn to make biscuits?"

"For your information, ma'am, I am multi-talented. I can speak French, bale cotton, write newspaper reports, shovel horse manure, harpoon a whale and make the best damned beaten biscuits this side of Richmond, Virginia!" He sat up and swung his feet over the bed. His face grew instantly pale, and he paused to let the waves of pain subside. His chest ached from the broken ribs with each breath, but the dizziness passed.

Gabrielle eyed him suspiciously. "Let me guess, you went to the finest schools to learn how to hold that shovel just right." To her own surprise, she was at his side now, helping him across the room. His good arm was around her neck, her arm around his waist. She shivered involuntarily, and her stomach gave a flip-flop. His arm felt good around her, sure and strong.

Alex could feel a tightening in his groin as Gabrielle slipped her arm around his waist. He turned his head ever so slightly until his chin brushed the soft cap of curls that covered her head. It was difficult for him to understand how this short-haired girl in men's breeches could attract him so. Gabrielle was nothing like his wife. Whisper-thin Amber had been tall with long locks of silver-blond hair to her waist. Amber had been soft-spoken, a sweet blushing bride as delicate as the china tea cups she sipped from. But Gabrielle—she was a wharf rat, part boy, part wild creature, part woman.

Gabrielle eased Alex into the chair at the wooden table, wishing it had been farther away. Confused by her feelings, she turned her back to him and lifted a wooden crate to the floor.

Alex couldn't help chuckling as he watched her move the other crate filled with flour. His Amber had barely had the strength to lift her own tea pot, but this girl—he had a notion she'd be stiff competition in an arm wrestling match!

"What are you laughing about now?" Gabrielle demanded, dropping her hands to her hips.

Alex just shook his head. "Nothing, just ignore me. I'm prone to these fits. Now, if you'd be so kind as to fetch me the necessary ingredients, I'll do my best to make you some *real* biscuits."

"What do you need?" She was already digging out a tin mixing bowl and a wooden spoon.

"Flour, sugar, leavening, a little salt, lard and milk."

"Milk?" Gabrielle spun around to stare incredulously.

Alex's face was blank for a moment, and then the realization of his foolish words washed over him. "No, I don't guess you would have milk."

"Not one cow more here than you had on that whaling ship of yours." Gabrielle shook her head, turning back to look for the salt. "Not very prepared for this territory, were you, Alex?"

"I thought I knew what it would be like. I thought I could make it."

"Then you'd be one tenderfoot in a hundred that did."

Alex stared at her back, her words biting into his flesh. Anger rippled down his spine as he looked away. Damn her! She made him out to be such a buffoon. Who was she to judge him, to sum up his entire life on the basis of one mistake?

One mistake? He shook his head. This one stupid mistake might cost him his little girl. The gold he'd been certain he'd find this winter was going to be the means to support Alexis. If he didn't find a way to make a great deal of money in the next two or three years, it would be a lost cause. By then, his daughter would have lived too long with her aunt to separate them.

Gabrielle turned from the stove to see Alex's eyes growing misty. His gaze dropped to the floor as she neared. She was intrigued. What was this man thinking of that would bring tears to his eyes? Until this moment it had never occurred to her that a man could cry. "Here you go." Her voice was as smooth as honey again. "I'll fetch the rabbit and be back in a minute."

Alex gave a nod of dismissal, leaning over the table to dump flour in the bowl with his good hand. Gabrielle paused, wanting to say something else. But she didn't know what to say. Should she tell him it's all right to stay? Should she tell him that suddenly she was glad he'd be here all winter? Could she admit that she was just a tiny bit afraid to stay there alone through the heavy snows? She caught her parka off the peg on the wall and slipped out the door before her foolish words got the best of her.

Outside, darkness had settled upon the tiny cabin nestled on the bank of the great Tanana River. Gabrielle took a deep breath, welcoming the sharp sting of icy air as it filled her lungs. The snow crunched beneath her feet as she walked to a leaning pine to cut down the rabbit she'd left strung in the trees. One of her young dogs gave a long eery howl, and she turned to stare into the darkness.

The other dogs were up on their haunches now, peering upstream. Gabrielle swore beneath her breath as she moved toward the cabin straining to see into the icy blackness. Where was her sense, coming outside without her rifle this time of year? There was too much movement, too many men trying to settle before the first heavy snows. There were too many vagabonds who would think nothing of killing to have a warm cabin and plenty of food.

Her dog Tristan growled deep in his throat and

moved to stand beside Gabrielle as she eased the cabin door open and felt for her rifle against the wall.

"What's wrong, Gabrielle?" came Alex's voice from within, but she ignored him. Relief flooded her as her fingertips met with the ash stock of her father's rifle. Keeping her attention focused on the darkness upstream, she cradled the Winchester. It was loaded, she was sure of that. She'd been loading it for her father since she was five, firing it since she was seven.

A great horned owl wailed mournfully in the distance as Gabrielle raised the rifle to her shoulder. "Show yourself," she ordered, her voice echoing in the tree tops.

No answer came from the darkness, but Gabrielle knew there was someone there. She could feel his presence in the emptiness of the new-fallen snow. Just behind her, she heard the cabin door swing open.

"Gabrielle," Alex called quietly.

She waved to him to be silent, nodding into the distance. The light from the cabin had spilled into the snow, creating an aura of golden light. The trees hung low, laden with sparkling frost, casting long-fingered shadows against the rough-hewn log walls.

Alex swallowed hard, leaning against the inside of the door. In his hand he held Gabrielle's Colt 45, his finger poised on the trigger. Streaks of sharp, stabbing pain shot up his legs, and he swallowed hard to force down the nausea. He hated himself for getting into a position like this. Because of his own stupidity, he had almost lost his own life, and now he was too weak to protect the woman who'd saved him.

Gabrielle heard movement to the left, just outside the circle of light, and she swung around, aiming the rifle carefully. "Hold it right there, mister," she called in her gruffest voice. Alex was beside her now. Somehow he'd managed to get down the step.

A lone figure took one step into the light, his hands raised high in the air.

"You son-of-a-bitch!" Gabrielle shouted, lowering her rifle. "What's wrong with you, Peg? You almost lost your other leg!"

"You know this character?" Alex's voice was weaker than it had been a moment ago.

Gabrielle broke into a grin, dropping the butt of the rifle to the ground to hold it by the barrel. "Know him? Why that man there is Peg-Leg Laurence. He's the one I was telling you about. My father sawed his leg off when he got frostbite and it turned green on him." She leaped off the step and ran toward Peg.

He put out his arms to greet Gabrielle, wrapping her in the folds of a bear-skin cloak. "Gabe, you sweet thing! How about a kiss for your ole Uncle Peg?"

Gabrielle kissed the old man's grey-whiskered cheek. "What's wrong with you, sneaking up on me like that? Have you lost what little sense you had left in that head of yours?" They walked toward the cabin, linked arm in arm. Peg limped, dragging one foot behind him, but kept up with Gabrielle's long-legged gait.

Spotting Alex on the steps, she held out a hand with a flourish. "Peg, I want you to meet Mr. Jefferson Alexander the fourth of Richmond. Alex, this is Peg."

Alex took one dizzy step forward, meaning to offer his hand, but was overcome by a heady blackness. He saw a whirl of snow and heard Gabrielle call his name . . . and then there was nothing.

Chapter Six

"Alex?" Gabrielle called softly. "Can you hear me, Alex?"

Alex sighed. Yes, he could hear her, but he couldn't answer. Her voice came to him as if he were under water, muffled and from a distance. He could feel himself rising slowly to the surface, but as he rose, the pain of his injured limbs began to seep into his being. For a moment he was caught between wanting to climb toward Gabrielle's hushed voice and wanting to stay below where he was warm and void of pain.

"Alex, answer me!" Gabrielle's voice came sharper this time. She eased a cold, wet cloth over his forehead, jolting him back to reality. "Can you hear me?"

"I can hear you," Alex mumbled, catching her hand. "I'm all right."

"Don't look much all right to me," she chided. "If you hadn't fallen into us, you'd have been headfirst in that snowdrift." She thought she should brush his hand aside, but she didn't. As she spoke she could feel the heat of his hand radiating through her arm. A delicious

81

tingle ran down her spine.

Alex heard a male chuckle and lifted his heavy eyelids to see Gabrielle and the old man watching him intently. Alex let his eyes drift shut again. He couldn't believe he had fainted! To his knowledge, in the history of the Alexander family, no male had ever fainted.

"What were you doing out of the chair?" Gabrielle removed the cloth from his head, and Alex let his hand fall. She dipped it into the icy basin and eased it onto his head again. "You could have hurt yourself."

"I was trying to help," Alex answered beneath his breath.

"What?" She smoothed his pillow, tugging a woolen blanket over his chest.

Alex cleared his throat. "Do I have to spell it out for you in front of him?" He lowered his voice. "I was coming to your rescue."

Gabrielle covered her mouth with her palm to stifle a giggle. "I really didn't need any help." She thought it funny, but at the same time she felt a strange tightening in her chest. Was he so concerned for her welfare that he would risk injury to come to her side?

Alex frowned. "That's pretty obvious isn't it?" Damn it! he thought to himself. How was it that this girl could continually make him out to look like such a jackass?

"Well, I thank you just the same," she told him quietly, smoothing the blanket she'd covered him with. It was a subtle gesture that did not go unnoticed by either man in the room.

Another chuckle came from Peg near the fireplace. "I didn't mean to bust in on you two. I hope I'm not interrupting anything."

Gabrielle lifted her hand aimlessly to smooth her

chesntut hair, laughing nervously. "Just like you to come around at supper time, Peg." She got up from the edge of the bed and crossed the room to the stove.

The bearded man shrugged off a fur-lined coat and sat down to pull off his boots. "Come to think of it, I am famished."

Gabrielle rolled her eyes for Alex's benefit. "Peg can't talk like the rest of us. He's got to be fancy about it." She dropped the coffee pot on the stove with a bang. "He was a professor at Princeton before he came north during the war."

"Were you?" Alex rolled onto his side. "I had a friend who attended Princeton. Fine school. Why did you leave it for this?"

Peg gave a snort. He had removed both boots and was now pulling on a pair of red, knitted socks he'd fished out of his coat pocket. "Just t'weren't the life for me. Couldn't stand to see my country pulled apart like that. The way I looked at it, no matter who won, North or South, we were all going to lose."

Alex gave a nod of understanding. "I've never heard it put so well, sir. And from a Northerner, no less. Glad to meet you."

Gabrielle turned from the stove to stare at the two men. They were actually going to get along! Why that mattered to her, she really didn't know. "So," she asked, "how about fried rabbit and some of Mr. Alexander's beaten biscuits?"

"Good God, Gabe, for a moment there I thought you were going to offer me some of your own!" Peg laughed, banging his pipe on the table.

Alex's laughter mingled with Peg's, and Gabrielle ducked outside to retrieve the rabbit, giving the door a good slam behind her.

An hour later the threesome had settled at the wooden table for the meal. Alex sat on one chair with his feet propped on pillows on another. Gabrielle sat across from him and Peg on the end. They laughed as they ate, swapping stories and complaining about the age of the rabbit Gabrielle had brought home for dinner.

"Toughest damned hare I ever had, but these biscuits, they melt in my mouth!" Peg dropped a bone on his plate and reached for another round biscuit.

Gabrielle made a face but reached for another as well. "So who invited you anyway?" she asked, smothering the bread with salmonberry preserves. "I'll remember this next time you come begging."

Alex leaned back in the wooden chair, licking his fingers. "Come on now, admit it, Gabrielle. Are these the best beaten biscuits you've ever had or what?" He settled his gaze upon her. "Milk or no?"

"I don't know that I can say. Never had beaten biscuits before." Her mouth turned up in a grin. She was so pleased to have some company to keep her mind off her father . . . to keep her mind off the man who had murdered him. . . . Somehow this stranger Alex took some of the ache from her heart.

"Well, all and all, it was a superb meal, Gabe." Peg was up now, carrying away plates. "I don't know about you two, but I'm ready to turn in."

Alex got slowly to his feet, surprised to find Gabrielle at his side. She looped her arm easily around his waist and started for the bed. "I could get used to this," Alex dared.

Gabrielle looked up at him, her dark eyes searching his. "Hush," she murmured. "Or it's out in the snow with you."

Long after Peg and Gabrielle were asleep on the floor of the cabin, Alex lay awake. His mind churned over the events of the past few days. His life was going so poorly, and yet here in the middle of the mess he'd created, appeared Gabrielle. His logic told him to leave her alone, to get through the winter as best he could and get on with his life. But when he closed his eyes, he could see her oval face smiling down on him. He could smell the fresh, clean scent that clung to her hair.

Gabrielle LeBeau was a paradox of femininity. One moment she was tromping about the wilderness dressed in men's breeches and toting a loaded gun, the next she was here in her own cabin, moving like a dancer, her hips swaying sensually beneath the heavy wool pants to some imaginary tune.

Alex needed no woman in his life right now, yet he needed Gabrielle more than he had ever needed anyone. There was something about her that made him see hope when there was no hope. She made him laugh like no one ever had before.

Alex groaned, rolling onto his side in Gabrielle's bed. Opening his eyes, he saw her slim form in the darkness. She was asleep in front of the fireplace, and though he could not see her face, he could imagine how beautiful she must be with her head resting on a rolled-up sweater, her lips parted slightly as she breathed. He smiled in the darkness. He had never seen anyone look so peaceful. Once she was asleep, she never moved until morning, unlike himself who tossed and turned his night away. Rolling back over, Alex closed his eyes, letting thoughts of a dark-haired beauty lull him to sleep.

Alex woke in the morning to silence. Bright light filled the small cabin, and he blinked, adjusting to the golden rays. Gabrielle and Peg were gone, where he didn't know. Moving slowly, he got to his feet and stumbled across the room to where the wash basin and razor strap hung on the wall. While they were out, he thought he would clean himself up and try shaving on his own.

It was only when he began his morning ritual that he realized what a help Gabrielle was. Just getting out the door to get a basin of snow and take it to the stove took all of the strength he could muster. As he sat on the side of the bed trying to catch his breath, he shook his head beginning to fully realize the extent of his injuries. Even if he had been able to find shelter, if it had not been for Gabrielle, he would never have lived. It was her doctoring and the crushed herb poultices that had saved his legs from gangrene. Though she said he would be many months healing, she assured him he was out of danger. He had only to give his legs time and he would be as good as new.

As the morning passed and the shadows in the cabin lengthened into afternoon, Alex began to get nervous. Where had Gabrielle gone? He hobbled to the cabin door several times to look out on the snow-covered forest but saw no sign of them save for the footprints that disappeared to the north. He went over the conversations from the night before, trying to remember if she had said anything about leaving this morning.

She must be all right, he told himself as he ate two

cold biscuits near dark. She left with Peg; she must still be with him. But by the time he had to light the lamp over the fireplace, he was almost frantic. Why did this girl mean so much to him? She had taken care of herself this long. She had escaped Seattle and the clutches of the man who was pursuing her. Why didn't he think she could look out for herself now?

Alex thought of the man who had chased her into his arms in Seattle. Who was he and why was Gabrielle so adamant about not speaking of him? When she returned safely, Alex vowed to question her again.

When the sound of barking sled dogs filled the clearing, Alex was on his feet, hurrying across the room. He swung open the door, letting light fall into the darkness. "Where have you been?" he shouted over the howling dogs.

Gabrielle got down on her hands and knees in the snow and began to release the dogs from their harnesses. "What do you mean? I went up river with Peg to lay a trap line."

"I was worried about you," Alex said before he could catch himself. It was snowing now, and the flakes caught in Gabrielle's hair creating a halo of bright white.

"Worried about me?" She gave a laugh. "Why would you be worried about me?" She had freed all eight huskies and was patting them on their backs, calling their names.

Alex shook his head. "God only knows why," he murmured to himself. He stood there in the doorway, watching her feed the dogs from the fresh fish she carried on the sled. Finally, she came into the cabin, brushing past Alex.

"Look, if we're going to live together all winter, we're going to have to get a few things straight." She put her parka on the peg on the wall and began to pull her wool sweater over her head. "You're not my father."

"I didn't say I was."

"So why are you worrying where I am? I've been coming and going through these woods since I was a babe." She planted her hands on her hips, waiting for an answer.

Alex shrugged. "I don't know . . . all right? I don't know why I care."

Gabrielle gave a nod, her dark eyes meeting his for just an instant. "All right. I'm sorry. I guess I should have told you I'd be gone all day. I just didn't think about it. I'm not used to checking in and out with anyone. My father never paid much attention to where I was going."

"What about your mother? Didn't she care where her five-year-old was?"

Gabrielle turned her back to him. "Not hardly. I haven't seen my mother more than twenty or thirty times in my life."

Alex was silent for a moment. "I'm sorry. I didn't mean to pry."

"You weren't." Her back was still to him as she busied herself with the fresh fish she'd carried in. "It's no secret around here. My mother left my father and I before I was a year old. She lives in Seattle. Works at the Red Sash. You know what that is?" She turned to Alex slowly.

"You don't have to tell me this, Gabrielle. It doesn't matter to me." He could see the pain in her eyes; he could see how tightly she held the tin cup in her hand.

"It should matter to you if you come from the kind of family you say you do." Her eyes dropped to the floor for a moment, and then she looked at him again. "My mother is a whore, Alex. Always has been. Always will be." She spun back around and began to chop the fish vigorously with a knife.

Alex leaned on the wooden table, resting his chin in his palm. His chest ached with her pain. All he could think of was wrapping her in his arms and holding her against him. "I'm sorry, Gabrielle," he told her.

"So am I," she answered softly. She wiped her hands on a towel and poured two cups of black coffee from the pot on the back of the stove. Silently she brought Alex one, but then instead of returning to the stove, she just stood there.

He pushed himself to his feet. She was just standing there, staring as he reached out slowly with his good arm. Gabrielle's head spun as she leaned toward him, allowing him to pull her against his broad chest.

The world suddenly came to a standstill as she rested her head on his shoulder. Her eyes drifted shut, and she raised her arms to loop them over his shoulders. She breathed deeply, mesmerized by his heady male scent. No one had ever touched her like this before. No one had ever made her feel so good, so safe.

Alex moved slowly, afraid he would frighten her. He brushed her curly hair with his fingertips, daring to touch her smooth, pale cheek. "I'm going to kiss you, Gabrielle."

"No," she breathed. But she lifted her head from his shoulder to study his smoky blue eyes.

"Why not?" His face was so close to hers that she could feel his breath on her cheek.

"No one's ever kissed me before," she answered shakily.

"No one?"

She shook her head as he caught her chin to raise it. He lowered his mouth to brush his lips gently against hers. Gabrielle sighed, her eyes drifting shut as she felt his flesh make contact with hers. Did all men have such soft, inviting lips? He withdrew slightly, and she raised her eyelids to study his face.

"I liked that," Gabrielle murmured, wide eyed.

Alex laughed softly, brushing his lips against the springy curls on her forehead. "I'm glad. I liked it, too."

"Could you do it again?" she asked hesitantly.

Alex marveled at her honesty as he leaned to kiss her again, this time lingering for a moment over her trembling lips. He wanted to deepen the kiss, to taste the sweetness of her mouth, but he didn't want to push her too far.

Gabrielle clung to Alex, letting the heat of his flesh seep through her flannel shirt. Her breasts tingled as she moved to rest her head on his shoulder. For a few moments Alex held her, listening to the sound of her soft breathing, enchanted by the feel of her heart pounding against his chest.

Finally, he pulled back. "Enough kissing," he told her, brushing his lips against her forehead. "How about something to eat, and then we'll talk."

Gabrielle brushed her fingertips against her lips. What was wrong with her? She had let this man, this stranger, kiss her! Yet she had never felt anything so glorious! Nothing had ever made her heart beat like this. Nothing had ever made her feel so deliciously warm inside. "All right," she murmured, turning away from him. "Something to eat." She couldn't help smiling as she dug for her frying pan in the side cupboard.

Long after Alex had fallen asleep, Gabrielle lay on the quilt on the floor staring at the dying embers in the stone fireplace. She brushed her fingers over her lips again and again, trying to recall every ripple of pleasure that had surged through her body as Alex had kissed her. She was in awe. How could a man make her feel that good? The act was so simple, so meaningless. She smiled in the darkness. Her first kiss.

But where was this going to lead? Would he expect another kiss tomorrow? Would he expect more? She groaned inwardly, rolling onto her back. She shouldn't have allowed it to happen. It was her own fault. She knew what one kiss would lead to. Hadn't her mother started with a single kiss? And now look at her . . . Alice LeBeau, the best whore on News Street.

Gabrielle's face hardened with determination. She would not be her mother's daughter. She'd be no whore! Her feelings for Alex would pass if she'd just let them. *The best way to handle this,* she told herself, *is just to pretend it never happened.* It was a mistake—a sin of the flesh—and it would not happen again.

Chapter Seven

"Damn it, Gabrielle! Don't do this to me!" Alex clenched his fists in frustration. He'd kissed her over a week ago, and since then, she had been treating him as if he carried the black plague. She had stopped assisting him in and out of bed; she was going out of her way to keep from coming in any physical contact with him. She barely spoke.

Gabrielle looked up from the ground where she was kneeling on a quilt in the snow. Across her lap was the new set of dog traces she'd been hand stitching. They had been outside more than an hour, soaking up the fall sunshine. She hummed while she worked, trying to ignore Alex who sat in a chair, his feet wrapped in a blanket. "I don't know what you're talking about," she replied as nonchalantly as possible.

"The hell you don't! I've had enough; now tell me what's wrong."

"Nothing's wrong. Why would you think anything

was wrong?" She had left her hat inside, exposing her dark tresses to the noonday sun. Outside, her curls lit up with bright golds and reds, mirroring the sun's rays. It was all Alex could do to keep his eyes off her.

"Gabrielle, all I did was kiss you." He extended an arm. "Have I upset you that much? Did I misunderstand?"

She leaned over the leather harness, forcing a needle through the soft leather. "It was a mistake," she murmured. She didn't have the courage to lift her head.

"What do you mean it was a mistake?" He ran a hand through his dark red hair. "You liked it so much you asked me to do it again!"

Gabrielle's cheek colored against her will. "I said I made a mistake. I'm sorry."

"That's not good enough, Gabrielle."

"I don't know what the problem is, Alex." She forced the needle through the leather, jabbing the tip of her index finger. "Ouch!" She pushed the injured finger into her mouth, nursing it.

"We can't live like this all winter." He shoved up the sleeves of the wool sweater he wore, suddenly feeling overly warm. It had been Rouge LeBeau's sweater.

She raised her head, lifting a dark eyebrow. "Have you got a better offer?"

Alex regarded her in silence for a moment. "As cold and uncaring as the ice on that river, are you?" His jaw jutted out, the line of his lips taut with anger. "I don't need this, Gabrielle. I'm too old to play games with virgins. We both feel something for each other, but let me tell you something. I'll not chase after you. You're going to have to meet me halfway."

"Me, feel something for you?" Her voice was uncommonly high-pitched as she pointedly ignored his statement about virgins. "What makes you think I want some man chasing after me, tugging at my drawers?"

"Do I look stupid, Gabrielle? I see you watching me in the darkness after you've blown out the lamp. Come on now, admit it. You're not as innocent as you seem. You feel it too." He lowered his voice. "Don't worry, it scares me too."

"I'm not afraid of anything and certainly not you," she spat, getting to her feet. "And I think this is all damned well presumptuous of you."

"Where are you going? Why do you keep running from me?" He watched her shake the snow from the quilt and gather her things.

"Look, this is my cabin, my property. I did you a favor by letting you stay here. I'm not doing you any other favors. You got that?"

Alex listened to her stomp off, dragging the new harness behind her. He looked skyward, beckoning with a hand. "Why me?" he asked aloud. "How do I get into these things?" But no answer came. The snowy forest was silent except for the occasional call of a distant ptarmigan.

Moments later Gabrielle came out of the cabin, a pack on her back. She brushed past Alex without a word, heading south down the path that led out of the clearing.

"Where are you going?" he taunted. "You going to spend the rest of your life running . . . from the fellow on the dock . . . from me?"

Gabrielle spun around, startling Alex. He hadn't expected her to reply. He hadn't anticipated the full-fledged wrath plain on her windburned face. "You don't know anything about him! I had to run! He wants to kill me!"

"You're right. I *don't* know anything about him. So tell me. You've got to tell someone." Alex pushed himself to his feet. The pain was not as great as it had been, but it still knocked the wind out of him.

She yanked her red wool hat over her head. "I don't have to tell you anything. I don't have to tell anyone! I can take care of myself!"

"If you could take care of yourself, he wouldn't have been chasing you."

"You son-of-a-bitch!" Her gaze locked on his. She was so mad she wanted to hit him, to beat him with her fists.

"You know, I thought that somewhere beneath that façade there was real woman, a woman who could laugh, could cry. A woman who could love." He sat down. "Guess I was wrong. . . ."

Gabrielle's hand went to cover her trembling lips. *Please don't let me cry,* she begged silently. Exhaling, she turned slowly around. If she spoke again, he would hear the pain in her voice. He would know how much his words hurt her. Without another word, she disappeared into the forest.

For a long time Alex sat in silence, listening to the snow fall from branches that grew weak and splintered.

It was an intriguing sound—first just a creak, then a snap and the snow would come whooshing down to form a heap beneath the weary pine. He sighed, rubbing his hands to warm them. Finally he got up, leaving the wooden chair where it was to go inside. All he wanted right now was to get out of there. He wanted to be rid of that hellion, because he knew that if he'd let her, she'd break his heart.

Not more than an hour later the cabin door swung open. To Alex's surprise, Indian Jack came walking in.

"Gabrielle's not here," Alex said.

Jack gave a nod. "I know. I passed her on McNally's path. I came to see you."

"Me?" Alex's eyes narrowed. "Why?"

"I want to tell you about her." Jack shrugged off his seal-skin jacket and began to dig through his pack. To Alex's surprise, he was sporting a new pair of Levi's beneath his leather jerkin. "My Mya sent you a tea to make you strong. I will make it."

Alex studied the native Indian as he retrieved a pan of snow and put it on the stove to heat. His movements were much like Gabrielle's, smooth and unwasted. He was comfortable in the cabin, seeming to know where everything was kept. How long had Gabrielle said she'd known Jack? Since childhood?

Jack sat on the chair opposite Alex and withdrew a cigar from beneath his jerkin. "I want you to know. Gabe is different from the others."

"Different from who? Different how?" Alex leaned forward to study the Indian's weathered face. His cheeks were broad, his nose long. His skin was the color of fresh-turned soil left to bake in the sun.

Jack took a long time to answer. "She's not like other white women. I won't have her hurt."

"I have no intention of hurting her."

Jack studied Alex for a long moment. "Her feelings run deeper than most. She has suffered much for her years."

"You're talking in circles." Alex leaned back in the chair, crossing his arms over his chest. "Tell me what she's been through. The only thing that she's told me is that her mother's a whore and that your parents raised her, here in her father's cabin. What happened to her father?"

"Gabe wouldn't want me tellin' her business." Jack poured hot water into a cup he'd sprinkled powder into and brought it to Alex. "But I tell you this. The man who killed Gabe's father seeks her as well. He was the man chasing her in Seattle. Gabe is safe here, but if she ever leaves the Tanana, her life will be in danger."

"Who's after her? Why? You're still not making any sense." Alex took a sip of the hot brew. The taste was odd but not unpleasant.

Jack sat down across the table from Alex. "She could never leave with you. When the river breaks up, you must go and Gabe must stay."

"Why would Gabe go anywhere with me?"

Jack smiled. "Are you such a foolish man that you don't recognize that light in her eyes?" He chuckled. "She loves you, white man." He shook his head. "But she'll get over it if you let her be. You understand what I'm saying?"

"Gabrielle is of legal age, isn't she? Any woman who

can take care of herself out here"—he gestured with open arms—"can certainly make her own decisions, don't you think?"

Jack toyed with his unlit cigar. "She's never known a man."

"And you'd prefer it stayed that way?" Agitation was evident in Alex's voice. He understood that Jack was just looking out for Gabrielle, but he didn't like being put on the spot like this. What did Jack think he was going to do to her? If there was any woman that could look out for herself, it was Gabrielle.

"No. I didn't say that. I hope Gabe will find someone to share her life with. But this is her life here. She will find someone here. You're not one of us."

Alex set the tea cup on the table and leaned forward. "What if I told you I was falling in love with her?"

Jack studied the red-haired man. "I would tell you don't, but if you do, never tell her."

"Don't tell her! That's ludicrous! Don't you believe that if two people love each other, they should be together?" Alex slammed his fist on the table.

"Because two people love"—Jack extracted a tin of sulfur matches from beneath his jerkin—"that does not mean they can live in happiness."

"So what you're telling me is to stay away from her?"

Jack got slowly to his feet, lighting his cigar. "What I tell you is that if you hurt her, I will hurt you."

Alex stood up. "You threatening me?"

The cabin filled with a deep, resounding laughter as Jack picked up his pack to go. "I'm making you a promise."

Alex stood in silence watching Jack go. These were

the strangest damned people he'd ever met! To look at Jack with his rounded stomach and small stature, he'd have never thought he had a violent bone in his body. He smiled to himself. Gabrielle was lucky to have him. Few men, let alone women, could claim to have such a loyal friend. He knew he didn't.

Gabrielle returned late in the afternoon to find Alex sitting just where she'd left him. Her anger had subsided, and she felt in control again. She liked Alex and wanted him for a friend. If she would just watch herself, she knew she could control that friendship, making sure it didn't become anything more.

"Evening." Alex spoke first, giving a nod as he pulled the quilt tighter around his legs. The sun was setting now, and it was growing colder by the minute.

Gabrielle planted her hands on her hips. "You still here? If I'd been gone three days, would I have come back to find you still in that chair?"

Alex grinned. "Yea. But I'd be frozen solid."

She couldn't resist a smile. "Look, Alex . . ." Her gaze fell to the snow-covered ground.

"It's all right, Gabrielle."

"No, it isn't. I shouldn't have let you kiss me. It's not what I want."

He stood up slowly, picking up the quilt. "It was what you wanted at the time."

"I know, but . . . I mean . . ." Gabrielle looked off into the distance. "I want to be your friend, Alex, but nothing more."

He threw the quilt over his shoulder. "Not you, too?"

"Me, too, what?"

"Your friend Jack was here not too long ago, giving

100

me the same story."

Gabrielle's cheeks colored. "What did he say?"

"Don't worry about it. I'll keep my distance, I promise." He hobbled toward the door.

A strange disappointment came over her as she stood there watching him disappear into the cabin. *What's wrong with me?* she asked herself. *He's promised to leave me alone.* But she knew what was wrong. As much as she hated herself for it, she was dying to kiss Alex again.

The following afternoon Alex decided to try his hand at fishing on the Tanana. With a wooden pole and a bit of biscuit dough, he hobbled down the path toward the bank, promising to return with fish for supper. His feet were healing with each passing day, and he was regaining his strength. Every day he tried to get outside and go for a short walk somewhere, just to keep his muscles from atrophying.

Waving to him, Gabrielle went back into the cabin to get a bucket. Deciding this would be a good chance to take a bath, she began to heat water to fill the ancient tub. Sliding into the heavenly water, she relaxed, closing her eyes. *This is going to be nice,* she thought. With this new agreement between her and Alex, he would be such good company to her. With winter settling in, she was glad to know she wouldn't be alone. Everything had all happened so fast; she needed time to adjust. By next winter, she knew she would be all right. By the time spring came and Alex left, she'd be over her father's death. And by then, Lucas Taylor would have completely forgotten about Rouge LeBeau and the map . . . she hoped.

Sinking deeper into the tub, Gabrielle began to lather herself with sweet-smelling soap. Leaning back, she dipped her head into the water and scrubbed her scalp until it tingled. Finally, when the water had grown luke-warm and she began to shiver, she stepped out of the tub.

At that moment the cabin door swung open and Alex came up the steps. Gabrielle stood frozen as his heavenly blue eyes moved over her slim, dripping form.

Alex swallowed, murmuring beneath his breath. He knew he should turn away, but he couldn't. His gaze went from her bare feet, up her long, graceful legs to her rounded hips. He had never seen such a tightly clipped waist, such beautiful taut breasts. The bath water shimmered in the firelight playing off her silken, quiescent flesh, and Alex took a step forward.

Gabrielle's eyes met Alex's, and she trembled, unable to tear her gaze from his. A warmth spread from the core of her womanhood, bathing her in a throbbing, incandescent heat. Her cotton towel hung from her fingers, but she was unable to raise her hand to cover her nakedness. Her tongue darted out to moisten her lips as she stared at him, wanting him to come nearer, yet frightened he would. She knew she should send him away, but when she tried to speak, her throat constricted until nothing but a squeak escaped.

Alex could hear his own ragged breath. God, she was beautiful . . . those dark, oppressive eyes, those trembling lips that taunted him even when he slept. Images flashed through his mind, images of his limbs twisted with hers. He could feel his heart pounding beneath his breast, and the strain of his loins. He

102

wanted Gabrielle like he had never wanted a woman before. Swallowing hard, he turned, stumbling down the steps, and slammed the cabin door. "Not now, not this way . . ." he murmured.

After Alex was gone, Gabrielle stood in frozen silence. Finally, her limbs obeyed her will, and she raised the towel to dry off. She was still shaking as she pulled on her breeches and flannel shirt over her damp body. *My God! I stood there and let him see me, let him stare at me!* The word "whore" pounded her brain rhythmically as she fumbled with the buttons of her shirt. Tears stung her eyes as she fought them.

"What's wrong with me?" she murmured. Had she been born a brazen hussy? Was it inherited? She cursed her mother beneath her breath as she searched through a crate for a pair of matching socks. Tears blinded her vision until finally she slumped to the floor. "I don't want to love him," she repeated over and over again. "Help me, Papa, don't let me love him. I'll hurt him; I'll hurt him just like Mama hurt you." Once the tears had started, Gabrielle couldn't hold them back. She cried for herself, for the loss of her father. She cried for what her mother was and what she could never prevent her from being.

When Alex finally came back in the door, Gabrielle was sitting on the floor against the bed. She had long since stopped crying but still sat there, her head cradled in her arms.

"Gabrielle," Alex called softly.

She lifted her head, frantic words bursting from her mouth. "How dare you! You had no right!"

"I'm sorry. But how long did you expect me to stay

out there?" He stared at her, huddled there on the floor, her eyes red and strained from crying. His ardor cooled as he watched her brush frantically at her eyes. All he wanted to do was hold her, to soothe the pain of her clouded past.

"It hasn't been more than an hour," she spat.

"An hour! It's been at least an hour and a half, maybe two. In case you didn't realize it, it gets damned cold out there after dark." He shrugged off the caribou-hide parka he'd inherited from Rouge.

"You should have left. A gentleman would have knocked first." She stood up, her hands trembling. The sight of him made her heart flutter. The depth of his eyes as he stared at her body would be forever branded in her mind.

Alex could feel his anger rising as he took a step closer. "A lady wouldn't have stood there bare-assed looking at me!"

Instinctively, Gabrielle raised her hand to strike him. The only thing that prevented her palm from making contact with his cheekbone was his iron-clad grip that caught her wrist in midair.

"Don't you ever, ever hit me," Alex ordered through clenched teeth. "Because I'll hit you back, and I can promise you I'll hit harder."

Gabrielle stared with numb incredulity. No one had ever spoken to her like that; no one would have dared. Her lower lip trembled as she forced contact with Alex's stormy blue eyes. They were grey now, with streaks of anger. "I'm sorry," she whispered.

"I'm sorry," he returned, slowly releasing her wrist. With a rough impulsiveness, he pulled her into his arms, crushing his mouth against hers.

Gabrielle clung to him, her blunt nails digging into his back as she strained against his hard male chest. When he pressed to deepen the kiss, she succumbed to the power of his embrace, forfeiting the control she usually held over herself and others. She was frightened by a physical contact she'd never had, but at the same time, she yearned to know.

"Ah, Gabrielle, what am I going to do with you?" Alex breathed, his tongue darting out to taste the honey of her lips.

"I don't know." She shook her head, lifting her chin to let him nibble at the soft flesh of her throat. "I don't know." Her dark eyes drifted shut, heady from the shivers of pulsing pleasure that raced through her veins. Boldly, she ran her hands over his broad back, exploring the field of taut muscles. She had never felt a man's back like this, and it was glorious!

Alex brushed his knuckles against the outline of Gabrielle's breast, and she moaned deep in her throat. Hesitantly she accepted the thrust of his tongue in her mouth. It was a strange sensation, this mixing of breath, but it made her heart pound and all conscious thought fly from her mind. All she knew at this moment was Alex, his mouth on hers, his stroking hand, his whispered words.

"Please," Gabrielle groaned as Alex lowered his mouth to her breast. She could feel his hot, wet breath through her flannel shirt, and she strained, arching her back, unable to resist the excruciating delight that filled her being.

"Please what?" Alex laughed, his eyes shining as he

raised his head to brush his lips against hers.

Gabrielle lifted her heavy lashes, joining in his laughter. "I don't know. . . ."

He smiled at her, and she returned the smile, lowering her head to the crook of his neck. Never in her life had she ever felt as secure as she did right now.

"Come here," Alex murmured against her hair.

"What?" She looked up at him.

"I have to sit down." He caught her by the shoulder when she tried to back up. "I'm not through with you," he teased. "But my foot is killing me. If I don't sit down, I'm going to fall down." He lowered himself onto the wooden chair at the table and pulled her into his lap.

Gabrielle lowered her head to Alex's shoulder again, inhaling his heavenly male scent. She toyed with the dark red curls at the nape of his neck.

"What are we going to do about this, Gabrielle? I know I said I wouldn't touch you, but . . ." his voice trailed off.

"It's my fault."

"It's not anyone's fault, but the fact remains that you and I have got a long winter ahead of us." He sighed, pressing a kiss to a short tendril of chestnut hair. "I can make no promises, Gabrielle. Even if I could, I don't know what you want."

She laughed, lifting her head from his shoulder to study his eyes. They were calm again, the streaks of anger gone as if they'd never existed. All she saw now was a sea of heavenly blue and a twinkle in their depths. "It's all right, because I don't know what I want either." She sighed, looking away. "There's so much I want to tell you. Yet I want to tell you nothing."

Alex stroked her flushed cheek. "I know. Let's just

take it easy. We'll take our time. We both have a lot to consider."

Gabrielle gave a nod, slipping from his lap. She was surprised to find that her legs were still shaky as she crossed the room to the stove. "So where's the fish? You did bring home dinner, didn't you?"

Chapter Eight

"Come on!" Gabrielle shouted over her shoulder breathlessly. "You're holding the dogs back."

Alex stopped in the sled tracks in the snow, breathing laboriously. "Go on without me. I told you I couldn't go far," he shouted to her on the crest of the hill. "Go up and around and then come back. I'll wait!" His breath clouded in the frigid air and rose above his head.

Gabrielle clapped her mittened hands together to warm them, her dark eyes sparkling mischievously. The past three weeks had been a delightful dream. Alex had demanded nothing of her, and Gabrielle had never been so content. When she refused to speak of her past, he filled their evenings with tales of whaling ships and southern battlefields. They just took each day as it came, embracing it and reveling in each other's laughter. Neither spoke of the tie that bound them closer each day, or what would happen in the spring when Alex would leave.

"Weakling!" Gabrielle accused. "Come on, just a

little farther." She patted her lead dog's head, giving him a scratch behind the ears. The eight-dog team shifted in its harness, anxious to move on.

Alex pulled his wool cap off his head, running his fingers through his bright head of hair. "Watch your mouth! You wouldn't dare say that if I were a little closer." His deep tenor voice echoed in the tree tops, and snow fell to the ground under the strain.

"All right, I'll just go up a ways and come down along the river. It's about half a mile east of here. Think you can find it?"

He picked up the stick he'd been using as a cane. Gabrielle had reset the splint on his broken forearm so that he could use it sparingly. "That where we're going to camp?"

She gave a nod, preoccupied by the sight of his handsome clean-shaven face and brilliant cap of thick auburn hair. She smiled to herself. It was difficult to believe that she, Gabrielle LeBeau, had herself a man. True, they'd done nothing more than kiss a few times, but he was hers for the time being, just the same.

Breaking herself from her thoughts, she waved and started over the crest. "Mush!" she commanded. The dogs leaped forward pulling the bent-wood sled behind them, and Gabrielle ran to leap on the back of the metal runners.

Alex stood listening to the sounds of the jingling leather and metal harnesses and the howl of the dogs until they disappeared into the distance. Leaning on his make-shift cane, he turned east and started out through the fresh snow.

He and Gabrielle had decided this morning to take advantage of the mild November day and hike up river with the dogs. They were going to camp on the bank of the Tanana and return to the cabin the following day. Though his legs still pained him, Alex had been anxious to escape the confines of the cabin. Outside, in the frigid air, his thoughts came easier. Out there in the bright sunshine and sparkling blanket of crystalline white, his life seemed to come into perspective.

Thoughts of gold and his failure to reach his mining destination before winter plagued his mind. He knew there was gold somewhere north of here on the river, and he still intended to find it. His few attempts to discuss the possibility of gold on the Tanana with Gabrielle had been disastrous. She cursed the gold miners, accusing them of destroying the precious balance of nature on the river. She said they left their tin cans along the paths and slaughtered caribou and moose for a single night's meal, leaving the carcasses behind to rot. The gold miners supplied whiskey to the Indians and took advantage of them, robbing them of their dignity and making them dependent on the white man's society. Alex sighed, ducking beneath a low-lying branch. Gabrielle also said that there was no gold on the Tanana.

Stopping to catch his breath, Alex loosened the neck of his parka. He could hear the river now, still rushing, but it was not as loud as it had been a few weeks ago. Parts of it had begun to freeze. Great chunks of blue-green ice flowed past the cabin each day. Many of the tributaries were a solid sheet of ice already.

Reaching the Tanana's banks, Alex perched himself on a fallen log to wait for Gabrielle. Not more than an hour later, he heard the sound of barking dogs and her voice clear and sharp in the crisp air.

"Beat me here did you?" she called as she leaped off the back of the runners. "Whoa! Whoa!" She slowed the dogs to a walk as she came into the clearing. "I would have been here sooner, but Caesar and Anthony got themselves tangled in the harness, and I had to stop and straighten them out." She got down on her knees and began to release the sled dogs one at a time.

Alex kneeled beside her in the snow. "Show me how to do it."

Gabrielle turned to him, lifting an eyebrow.

"I want you to teach it all to me. If you've got another sled, I'd like to take it out. People learn best by doing, don't you think?"

She smiled. "All right, your lessons start today. By spring you'll be the best musher on the river . . . next to me of course!"

An hour later the dogs had been fed a mixture of ground fish and caribou and had curled into balls to sleep in the snow. Alex had built a fire and started roasting chunks of caribou he'd pierced with a long pointed stick.

"Smells good," Gabrielle commented, rubbing her hands together for warmth. "It's the last of the caribou. I'll have to go hunting when we get back."

"You always carry all of this stuff on your sled?" Alex indicated the tin container of frozen meat for the dogs.

"Sure do. Enough at least for a day or two. I'd forgotten dog food the day I was sledding and found you. That's proof that an afternoon's outing can drag into days. My dogs mean a lot to me. I don't want them going hungry."

"They look a little bigger than the ones I bought." He

grimaced at the thought of all of that money gone to waste. Pulling a chunk of meat off the stick, he blew on it and popped it into his mouth.

"They're mostly husky, but I like a little hound in them. They're larger, leaner, definitely faster. I'm becoming known for my dogs." She smiled with pride. "People on the river come to me when they're ready to buy."

Alex nodded, offering the stick of roasted meat. "Have some, it's pretty good."

Gabrielle accepted, taking a seat on a hide mat by the fire. She patted the place beside her. "Sit down. I know your feet must hurt."

"They do, but it feels good to be out." He pulled up his collar to ward off the wind. The sun was setting already, disappearing below the line of trees in the distance.

Gabrielle suddenly turned to look at the huddle of sleeping dogs. "Leopold . . . have you seen him?"

"Who?"

She scrambled to her feet. "Leopold. He's Tristan's brother. He's gone." She made a head count again just to be sure. "Only seven dogs. Leo's missing."

Suddenly they heard a yelp and a crashing in the trees. Out of the woods came a husky, howling in pain. His back was covered in blood, his hide and one back haunch slit open. The dog raced toward his master, barking warning to the other dogs.

A thundering sound filled the clearing, and Alex spun around to see a monstrous moose come crashing out of the forest.

Gabrielle screamed at the dogs, and they leaped in the air, barking and howling. The camp broke into

113

pandemonium as the moose charged forward, headed straight for Gabrielle and the injured dog.

"The rifle!" Gabrielle shouted as she dodged right, dragging Leo by the collar to avoid the creature's deadly antlers. "It'll kill us!"

Alex turned to go to the sled for the rifle, and Gabrielle screamed again. "Look out! Here he comes!"

Alex threw his body through the air landing in a snowdrift with a bump. The moment his chest hit the hard-packed snow, he groaned in pain, praying he hadn't rebroken his ribs. Brushing the snow from his face, he turned to see the moose tip over the sled and send their belongings flying in every direction.

Gabrielle whistled to the dogs, coaxing them toward the river. It was frozen on the edges now and seemed the safest place for her team. In the woods, she would lose them in the confusion, but here she could keep them together. "Get out of his way, Alex! Try to get the gun, but stay out of his way!" She slid down the bank, dragging a dog under each arm.

Alex stumbled to his feet to stare at the frenzied animal. He stood as tall as a man, with a shaggy rack of antlers nearly five feet across. The moose lowered his head, and Alex grew still. He could see the gun lying in the snow, but to get to it, he would have to cross the moose's path.

"Get the rifle and kill him!" Gabrielle shouted, reaching for another dog. One by one she was hauling them over the steep bank and out of the rampaging bull's line of vision.

Alex moved slowly behind the moose, putting the turned-over sled between them. The creature lowered his head to charge again and bellowed mournfully.

114

Just a few more feet, Alex told himself. He prayed the rifle was loaded. Just as he raised the Winchester to his shoulder, the moose charged toward the remaining dogs on the bank. Alex took aim and pulled the trigger. He squeezed it again and again, watching the crazed creature fall to its knees. The shots rang sharp in the early evening air, and the ground shook as the beast went down.

As Alex lowered the rifle, he heard a creak and a splash and then Gabrielle's shrill voice. "Alex! Help me!"

Throwing down the rifle, he ran through the snow to the bank of the river. The dogs huddled on the ice-shelf, whining to reach their master who clung to an ice flow.

"Gabrielle!" Alex shouted, standing on the snow-covered bank. He spotted her on the edge of the ice-shelf struggling to keep her head above water. The heavy parka and leather boots she wore were water logged and threatened to pull her under. "Hang on!" he commanded sharply.

The water was so cold that Gabrielle was finding it difficult to breathe. Clinging to the chunk of ice that held her afloat, she cursed herself for being so foolish. Though the edges of the river were frozen, she should have known better than to take those extra steps to catch Anthony's collar. She'd have been better to have lost a dog than to have risked her own life.

"Hurry, Alex! Please!" she cried. She could feel herself slipping, and she kicked her leaden feet, clawing desperately at the ice floe.

"I'm coming, Gabrielle! Hang on!" Alex slid down the bank on the seat of his pants with a rope in one hand and a tree branch in the other.

"I can't hang on!" she moaned as her fingers slipped and she went under.

"Gabrielle!" he screamed.

Kicking with her feet, Gabrielle willed herself upward until her head surfaced. She gasped for breath, forcing her arm out of the water to grab the branch Alex held out to her.

"Take it, Gabrielle. Take it!" Alex insisted. "I can't come to you, love. The ice won't hold me so near to the edge."

Her mittened hand touched the tip of the branch, and she grasped it, struggling to get the other arm out of the water. When she finally held the branch with both hands, she gave a nod, too numb with cold to speak.

"Just hold on." Alex tugged at the branch, praying it would hold. *Another moment and she'll go under for good,* he thought. He knew from experience how long a man could live in water of this temperature . . . not more than a few minutes.

Ignoring the pain in his legs, arm and chest, Alex heaved with all of his might. The dogs yiped and leaped back onto the bank as he pushed them aside, making room to pull Gabrielle onto the solid ice. Slowly, her body rose out of the water as he slid her to safety.

Dropping the branch, Alex got down on his knees. "Gabrielle!" He ran his hand over her blue-tinged cheek. "Can you hear me? Open your eyes. Let me see those beautiful brown eyes."

"So cold," she chattered, forcing her weary lids open.

Stripping her of her coat and parka right there on the ice, he swung her into his arms.

"Put me down; I can walk," she objected weakly.

"Your arm."

"My arms are just dandy, now hush. We've got to get you warm." He climbed the bank with ease. Reaching the campfire, he slid her to her feet, holding her up as he began to strip off her clothes.

Gabrielle was dimly aware that Alex was undressing her. She wanted to protest, but she was so sleepy that she just didn't have the energy to speak.

"Gabrielle, open your eyes. You can't go to sleep; you know that. Not until we bring your body temperature up." He shook her. "Gabrielle!"

"What?" she asked curtly, opening her eyes.

"That's better." He stripped off her sweater, her wool breeches and flannel shirt. Then came the union suit.

"Alex!"

"I promise I won't look." He eased her onto the hide blanket near the fire and ran to the turned-over sled to get the wool blanket. He ignored the body of the monstrous moose that lay still in the snow. Finding the blanket in the snow, he shook it, then wrapped it tightly around Gabrielle's shivering body.

Uprighting the pan for hot water that had been turned over in the commotion, Alex filled it with snow and put it over some coals to heat. Going back to the sled, he found Gabrielle's canvas knapsack and rifled through it, looking for her tin of tea leaves. In an instant he was back at the fire, leaning over her. "Sit up. Get closer to the fire." He took her wrist, pulling her up.

"My dogs," she murmured. "Check my dogs."

"Gabrielle!"

"Please." She took a deep breath. "I'll be all right. I'll sit here. Check my dogs. Leo's hurt."

With a sigh of surrender, Alex went back to the bank to call the three dogs still on the ice. "One, two, three," he counted aloud, watching them scurry up the slight hill. Two more near the sled, two sniffing the dead moose—where was Leo? "Leo!" he called. "Leopold, here boy."

A low whine came from just beyond the trees. Passing Gabrielle, he gave her a pat on the back. "I'll be right back. Stay awake." In the woods, he found the injured husky and brought him back to the campfire. Washing the blood away with handfuls of snow, he examined the wounds. "Got a needle and thread, Gabrielle?"

"I think so," she managed, her teeth chattering so hard that he could hear them.

Dumping some tea leaves into the tin cup left near the fire, Alex added water and pushed it into Gabrielle's hands. "Drink. Old Leo needs a few stitches."

"I can do it," she told him. Her voice was barely audible.

"Not hardly. I'l be fine. Aboard ship we had no doctor. I've sewn up more than my share of busted heads and sliced hands."

Gabrielle shivered uncontrollably as she watched Alex care for her sled dog. Wrapping him in a piece of cured hide from the floor of the sled, he covered the dog's head to keep him from biting. Then quickly, but meticulously, Alex sewed up Leo's two gashes with the sewing needle and thread and released the dog to join the others.

"There, you happy now?" He dropped the needle and thread back into the knapsack and sat down beside her.

"I'm so cold, Alex."

He immediately began to shrug off his parka. "I'm sorry, here. Why didn't I think of it?"

"No," she shook her head. "You keep it. It won't be enough. I haven't any body heat to hold in." She was huddled beneath the wool blanket, a corner pulled up over her head to cover her wet hair.

"I'll stake up your clothes to dry."

"I can't wait. I'm so cold." She lay down on the mat again, and he rolled it up over her.

"I'll be right back." A few minutes later Alex was laying her clothes near the fire on brush he'd brought from the woods. He retrieved her parka and boots and laid them out as well. It was pitch dark now, with only the firelight to see by.

Getting down on his hands and knees, he brushed his hand across Gabrielle's pale face. "What are we going to do, sweet?"

She forced her teeth together to speak. "You're going to have to get under here with me."

Alex slipped beneath the wool and hide blankets, taking Gabrielle in his arms. She's so cold, he thought as he brought her against his chest. Even with the fire roaring, out here in the open, he just couldn't produce enough heat to warm her. "I could build a bigger fire," he murmured against her dark, wet hair.

"No. Body heat is the fastest way. You're going to have to take off your clothes, Alex," she heard herself say.

Holding her in his good arm, he lifted his hand to brush the clump of wet hair off her forehead. Her face was ashen white; her dark eyes had lost their sparkle. "You sure?"

119

She managed a smile. "I figured this would be the chance you were waiting for."

He laughed, kissing her lightly on the lips before he slipped out from beneath the blanket.

Gabrielle watched by the light of the fire as Alex dropped his parka to the ground and began to unbutton his old flannel shirt. She couldn't tear her gaze from his as he shrugged it off and reached for the buttons of his wool pants. Her pulse quickened. . . .

Alex's hands hesitated at the band of blue wool. He'd never stripped off his clothes for a woman, and it excited him. With his wife Amber, their lovemaking had been discreet . . . lamps out, fully dressed in layers of bedclothes. "I don't want to shock you, Gabrielle." He could hear his own breath coming faster against his will.

"I've seen men before . . ." her voice trembled, but not from the cold. "But it's different with you. . . ."

Never lifting his gaze from her pallid face, Alex slipped off the coarse pants. The firelight played off the rippling muscles of his chest and arms, bathing him in a glorious glow of yellows and golds. "But maybe not in this state," he whispered gently.

Gabrielle laughed, feeling a flush of warmth across her cheeks. He was right. She'd never seen a man aroused, but it didn't shock her; it made her feel warm and tingly, as she welcomed that warmth. "Alex, I think you're blushing. . . ." She smiled, lifting the blanket for him.

Alex crawled in beside her, pulling the wool and his hide blankets over them. "You certainly are chatty for a woman near frozen to death." He pulled her into his arms, flinching as skin met skin. "Damn! You

120

are cold!"

Gabrielle snuggled against his chest, resting her head on his shoulder. Hesitantly, she ran her hand over the mat of fine curly hair. "How are your ribs?"

"Sore, but I don't think I rebroke anything." He smiled in the darkness. No woman had ever dared to explore his body like this. Gabrielle's fingers were light and thorough as they caressed the flat, hard muscles of his chest, not leaving an inch of flesh untouched. She was finally beginning to warm up. When her fingertips brushed over the taut muscles of his stomach, he inhaled sharply.

"Does that hurt?" Her hand was instantly still.

Alex laughed. "Not hardly." He laid his hand on hers. "It feels wonderful. You feel warmer already." He was touching her too, now, running a hand over the curve of her hip.

"I was already getting warmer before you got back under the blanket." She lifted her chin to study the blue eyes she knew were gazing upon her.

"Ah, Gabrielle." His eyes drifted shut as she brushed her lips against his. "I'm falling in love with you."

"Shhh," she hushed. "Don't say that. You can't." Her slim body was molded against his muscular one, absorbing the heat of his rising ardor.

"What do you mean I can't?" Alex's breath was ragged. She was kissing his eyelids, his cheeks, the ridge of his nose. Her kisses were soft and fleeting, innocent, yet all-knowing.

"I mean you can't. I don't want you to. I don't want anyone to."

"That's silly, Gabrielle." He rolled over, pressing her onto the animal-hide blanket that protected them from

121

the snowy ground. "Everyone needs to be loved."

She shook her head, slipping her hands up over his shoulders. "It's too complicated, Alex. You wouldn't understand." The firelight was filtering through his dark auburn hair setting it aflame with bright red and gold flecks of magic. Never in her life had she thought any man was beautiful . . . not until this man.

"I would understand, if you'd let me, Gabrielle," he implored.

"In love there's a future, Alex. There's no future here, not with you and me. There's just now." Her voice was a raspy whisper, soft and haunting.

Alex sighed heavily. "I wish you'd tell me what happened to your father. I want to know why you're afraid."

"It's not just that." She stroked his bare back beneath the blanket, exploring the hardened muscles of his sculptured form.

"What? Your mother? It doesn't matter. She's not the first woman to be forced into that kind of position."

"No, you don't understand, Alex. There was no forcing to it. She likes what she does." Gabrielle's body stiffened. "She likes being a whore. She's made a career of it."

"It doesn't matter."

"It does."

"Gabrielle—"

"Alex," she interrupted. "I don't want to talk about it."

Alex could feel her withdrawing as she spoke. Her hands had fallen to her sides; her voice seemed to come from a distance. He exhaled slowly. "All right. You win for now. But this isn't the end of this conversation." He pulled her tightly against him, and slowly she raised her arms to his shoulders again. After a long silence, he spoke again. "I want to make love to you."

"I know." She could feel his manhood pressed against her thighs, hot and swollen with desire.

"Do you want to make love with me?"

She moistened her dry lips with the tip of her tongue. "I don't know."

"Then it's not right. We won't."

There was another stretch of silence as Gabrielle held tightly to Alex. She liked the feel of his hard body against her soft curves, and she yearned to calm the heat of her churning insides; but she was frightened. If she gave herself to him—if she made love with him—would she ever be able to recover and go on with her life? Would the pain of his leaving ever subside?

For a long time Gabrielle lay in Alex's arms listening to the pop and crackle of the fire, to the sound of the rushing river, to the sound of his steady, even breathing. Finally she lifted her head. "Are you angry with me?"

He opened his eyes, and by the light of the fire, she could see the depths of his soul. "I'm not angry."

Her lips trembled. "I want you, you know."

"I know," he breathed.

"It's just that—"

Alex pressed his fingers to her lips, silencing her. "Go to sleep, Gabrielle. I'm going to be here all winter. I'd never force you to do anything you didn't want to."

She sighed, snuggling down beside him. "Goodnight, Alex."

"Goodnight, love."

Chapter Nine

Alex gave the cabin door a vicious kick, and it swung open, slamming into the wall. "God damn it, where are you, Gabrielle?"

Gabrielle leaped off the floor, dropping the brush she'd been currying one of her dogs with. The look on Alex's face made her tremble. She knew he would be angry when he woke up in the morning to find her gone, but she hadn't suspected this fury.

"What the hell is wrong with you packing up and taking off like that?" His windburned face was taut, his lips tightly compressed.

She clasped her hands. "I was going to come back for you. . . ." she offered quietly.

"That's not the issue and you know it!" It took only four long strides for him to reach her. "I'm not your boy that I need to have you leading me around by my nose. I can fend for myself."

Gabrielle dropped her hands to her hips. "Then what are you so mad about? You found your way back."

He took her by the shoulders, forcing her to look at

him. "Last night you were lying in my arms. I told you I loved you. The next thing I know you're bounding off like a rabbit."

Gabrielle winced as his fingers sank into her soft flesh. "You're hurting me."

"I'm going to hurt you if you don't start giving me some answers!"

Gabrielle bit down hard on her lower lip, averting her eyes as tears threatened to spill over. "Alex, I don't know what you want from me."

"I want you to start acting like a mature woman instead of a foolish child. I don't have the time or the energy for these games."

"Who's playing games?" *Please don't let me cry,* she begged silently.

"You are. Last night—"

"Last night was a mistake," she interrupted.

"Oh, no. I'm not going to listen to that again." He clasped her chin with his good hand, forcing her to look at him. The tears in her dark eyes made his throat tighten.

Gabrielle's entire body was trembling now. "Alex . . . I'm afraid." One tear trickled down her cheek.

He gave a sigh of surrender, pulling her hard against him. "Oh, God, Gabrielle." He brushed his lips against the cap of soft, chestnut curls that covered her head. "What are you afraid of?"

Tears ran unchecked down her cheeks. "You name it. Of you . . . of you and me. Of being alone, of not being alone." A sob managed to escape her lips. "And then there's Taylor. . . ."

Alex held her against his chest, stroking her back. He

didn't know what to say. Everything was so complicated. He had his daughter at home, Gabrielle had her life here . . . and then there was the man. He wished to hell she'd tell him the entire story. He couldn't imagine anything she could have done that would make someone want to kill her!

"Gabrielle," Alex murmured. "Let me take off my coat. You're getting soaked."

She looked up through tear-reddened eyes. The snow on his parka had melted and was puddling on the wooden floor. Her flannel shirt was damp and cold. She backed off, murmuring an apology.

"Let the dogs out and throw another log on the fire," Alex told her gently. "There's a storm moving this way."

She sniffed, wiping her eyes with the back of her hand. "What about the rest of the moose?" She'd cut up a good-sized section of the moose Alex had killed and brought it home on her sled this morning, but the remainder of the great beast was still lying on the river bank. That much meat would keep her dogs in food for months.

"I strung the carcass in a tree with rope. It was already freezing." He shrugged off his parka and hung it on a peg. "It'll be safe from the wolves until we can go back for it. I left the blankets, too."

Gabrielle opened the cabin door and ushered out the two dogs she'd been grooming. "I'm sorry I left you. It was a stupid thing to do. You're right, I was running from you."

Alex sat down on the bed and removed his boots, fingering the worn leather. They had been Rouge's. "Apology accepted." Going to the fireplace, he spread

127

out the bearskin rug Gabrielle slept on and knelt. "Now come here, Gabrielle."

She slipped the bolt on the cabin door and walked slowly toward him. When he put out his arms for her, she had no power to resist. "You know I can make you no promises," he told her.

"I know," she whispered. His lips met hers, and she accepted them hungrily.

"I cannot stay."

"And I cannot go," she replied, fumbling with the buttons of his shirt.

Alex eased her gently to the floor as she clung to him, forcing his mouth down on hers. "Are you sure you want to do this?" he asked huskily.

"I'm sure. I need you; I want you, if only for tonight." Her fingers caught at the nape of his neck, and she smoothed the dark red curls, marveling at their softness. She gazed up at him, needing to see his reaction to her words. Would he think her a whore? The ache for him inside her was so great that she wondered if she would care.

"That's fair . . . for us both." He kissed the tip of her nose and then rolled onto his side, cradling her with his injured arm. He tried to unbutton her damp flannel shirt with his left hand, but after several unsuccessful tries, she brushed his fingers away.

"Let me." She laughed nervously. "I'll have pneumonia by the time you manage." Sitting up, she tackled the buttons one by one, never taking her eyes from his.

As Gabrielle revealed her pale flesh beneath the old green shirt, Alex's eyes moved to her hands. "You're so beautiful," he breathed. With one hand he reached out to brush his knuckles against the stiff peak of one breast.

Gabrielle's breath caught in her throat, and she looked down as his thumb made contact with the tip of her hardened nipple. She looked back up at him with surprise. "It feels so good," she murmured.

Alex tipped back his head and laughed, removing her shirt. "Promise me you'll always be so honest." He eased her onto her back, smiling down on her.

"What? I'm not supposed to say that?" Her face was instantly a mask of concern. "I've never done this before . . . I don't know."

Alex leaned to kiss the hollow of her throat, touched by her words. "There are no rules, love." He traced an invisible line with his lips, leading to the valley between her breasts.

Gabrielle held his head between her hands, innocently guiding his mouth to the ripening bud of her breast. When Alex's tongue brushed against her nipple, she arched her back, crying out with surprise. She could feel her pulse quickening as he suckled her gently, sending a rush of tingling pleasure through her body.

Alex explored the arched fullness of her breasts with his mouth and hand in awe of her reactions. She sighed and moaned, laughing when his day's growth of beard tickled her tender flesh.

"I'd have tried this sooner if I'd only known," she teased. Alex chuckled, lifting his head to nip at her lower lip as she tugged at his shirt. "Take it off," she ordered.

When he slipped out of the shirt, Gabrielle rolled Alex onto his back. "What are we doing?" he asked, brushing his fingers against her flat stomach.

A smile tugged at the corners of her mouth as she lowered her head to his chest. "Is it the same for a man?" she whispered huskily.

"I don't know, I never—" Alex's voice caught in his throat as her lips touched his hard male nipple. He inhaled sharply, and she lifted her head.

"Is it all right? Am I doing it all right?" She blinked, studying his handsome face.

Alex laced his fingers through her rich brown hair. "Please, continue," he managed with a throaty laugh.

Gabrielle spanned his broad chest with a hand, lowering her mouth to imitate Alex's actions. She wanted to make him feel just like he had made her feel. She brushed the tip of her tongue against his nipple and then took it gently into her mouth. He moaned, running his hands over her bare back as she taunted him with her innocent exploration.

"God, Gabrielle," he groaned, lifting her head. "You'll be the death of me." Pulling her down on top of him, he crushed her mouth to his, deepening the kiss as he thrust his tongue between her lips.

Gabrielle kissed Alex hungrily, touching his tongue with the tip of hers, daring to survey the hot, wet cavern of his mouth. Her hand brushed against the wool of his pants, and boldly she let it rest on his thigh.

Delivering soft fleeting kisses over her face, Alex unbuttoned Gabrielle's wool pants, and she lifted her buttocks to let him slip them off. He couldn't help smiling at the sight of the soft, lacy, cotton underdrawers she wore.

She laughed at his surprise, slipping her hand to toy with the waistband of his pants. "I have to wear something, don't I?" Her voice purred with warmth as her fingers brushed against his stomach. "Now you have to take off yours."

Tugging off his own wool pants, Alex laid down on his side, running a hand over the soft cotton of her drawers. "They're very pretty."

Gabrielle's eyes drifted shut as his fingertips sent waves of delicious desire coursing through her veins. She felt as if her body was not her own, as if it was on fire, a flame fanned by her lover's hand.

Cradling her head in his arms, Alex drew off the lacy garment, shuddering at the pleasure of finally seeing her unclothed again. "Are you sure?" he asked, brushing at the dark triangle of curls. "I'll stop. You have only to say the word."

"No." She arched her back, urging him on. "I'm sure, Alex. Love me, please . . ."

Alex rested his head on her breast, tracing intricate patterns across her bare stomach and thighs. As he stroked the folds of her womanhood, he listened to her sighs of pleasure. They were the most beautiful sounds he had ever heard. Amber had never enjoyed his lovemaking, or if she did, he never knew it. This was a whole new world for him . . . a woman who enjoyed his touch, a woman who wanted to give pleasure in return.

"Alex," Gabrielle murmured, rolling her head from side to side. "I need . . . I need—" She laughed at herself, forcing her eyelids open. "I don't know what I need. I hurt." She ran her hand over her stomach. "But I feel so wonderful."

Alex moved over her, lowering his body down until his damp flesh met hers. They fit together as one, a solid bit of clay split and then reunited. "I know what you need," he whispered, brushing back a tendril of

131

hair off her forehead.

Gabrielle stroked the lean, hard muscles of his buttocks, lifting her hips with unknown instinct. Alex kissed her cheeks, flushed with desire, moving against her until her thighs were parted. He prayed he could hold back. He didn't want to frighten her; but already his heart was pounding in his chest, and his manhood was throbbing with desire for release.

"It might hurt a bit," he offered quietly in her ear as he slipped into her, giving aid with his hand.

She cried out with bittersweet anguish, rising to meet his first thrust.

"You all right, love?" He supported himself with his good hand, brushing her cheek with the other.

He kissed her dewy eyelids, and they flickered open. A smile played on her love-bruised lips. "I'm fine," she whispered as she rose up again, welcoming him. Her eyes remained open, staring up at his heavenly blue ones as she matched his rhythm.

Alex groaned, trying to move slowly, his stroke long and deep. His heart was bursting with joy as Gabrielle murmured endearments in his ear, encouraging him, lifting her hips in reception of each thrust. Then suddenly she was moving faster, her breath coming quicker.

"Alex," she cried, clutching his shoulders.

"It's all right," he murmured against her cheek.

Higher and higher Gabrielle soared until all conscious thought was gone from her mind. Then there was just she and Alex and this glorious, throbbing, incandescent heat. Her muscles tightened as she made the last leg of the journey, and then she was falling, wrapped in a blanket of shooting stars.

"Gabrielle," Alex called hoarsely. "Gabrielle." One thrust and then another and he too was falling. Catching hands, they drifted slowly back to reality, bathing in the joy of their first union.

Gabrielle's eyes flew open. She couldn't help laughing; she was so happy. "That was wonderful," she whispered, reaching up to run her fingers through Alex's auburn hair.

He pressed his lips to hers and slid off her onto his side, cradling her in his arms. "You're terrific for a man's ego," he teased, wiping his damp brow.

"I'm not supposed to say that, either?"

"I told you, you can say anything you want; it's just that . . ." He paused searching for the right words.

She propped herself up on an elbow. "What? It's just that what, Alex?"

"It's just that most women . . . the women I've been with . . . my wife." He exhaled softly. "They don't usually let themselves enjoy making love."

"Then, why do they do it?"

"Good question." His voice was laced with mild amusement. "For a wife, I suppose it's sense of duty, as for the others . . . I don't know. They want to be loved, to be held, some want to be kissed. I guess they figure the rest must go with it."

"Have there been a lot of others? For you I mean." Gabrielle brushed her fingers over his bare chest, toying with the mat of curly hair.

"Gabrielle! That's what you're *not* supposed to ask." He nipped at her bottom playfully. "But to answer your question. Yes, besides my wife Amber, there have been a few."

"Before or after her?"

He lifted a dark eyebrow. "You're embarrassing me."

"Why should it embarrass you? I don't care. I'm just asking."

"You don't care?"

"Well, maybe just a little." She pinched two fingers together.

"Well, Miss Nosy-Box, I refuse to give you particular numbers, but I *can* tell you," he lowered his voice until it was barely audible, "that you were perfect. We're perfect together. No woman, not even my wife whom I loved dearly, ever made me feel like you did . . . like you do."

Gabrielle gazed into his blue-grey eyes, studying his face. "You're not giving me a story, are you, Mr. Jefferson Alexander the fourth? Because if you are, I'll string you up like that moose." Her words were teasing, but beneath the surface, he could detect the concern in her voice.

"No, I can promise you that I speak from my heart." He gathered her in his arms, and she rested her head in the hollow of his shoulder. "You're the most beautiful woman I've ever met. I dreamed about you, you know?"

"You did? When?"

He ran his hands over her back and buttocks, caressing the pale skin beneath his fingertips. "After I saw you on the dock. I couldn't get you out of my head. You were there, and then you were gone. It was as if you'd never existed, yet I knew you had."

"If you hadn't been there," she said quietly, "he might have killed me."

"Who, Gabrielle?" he tread lightly.

134

"Lucas Taylor." Her voice trembled. "The man who murdered my father in the Full Moon Saloon."

"Will you tell me about it?"

There was a long silence before Gabrielle spoke. "Yes. But not tonight." She lifted her head to look down on him. "I'm so happy tonight. Can't we just be happy?"

Alex brushed her cheek with his palm, wishing he could smooth away the pain so stark in her face. "Yes. You're right. For tonight, let's just be happy."

Gabrielle lowered her head to his chest again and began to run her hand over his muscular thighs. The cabin was growing dark now, as the sun set in the west. The flames from the crackling fire sent long fingers of bright light dancing across their naked flesh. She smiled to herself as she heard Alex groan, running his fingers through her dark hair. Proof of his growing arousal was already evident as she lifted her head to speak softly. "Do you think we could do it again, Alex?"

Chapter Ten

"Alex," Gabrielle called. "Alex, wake up." She tickled him beneath the chin with the corner of the bearskin rug they'd slept on.

For two days the snowstorm had raged around them, and they had remained there in front of the stone fireplace, snuggled naked beneath the blankets, basking in the closeness they both needed so desperately. Other than to feed and water the dogs and bring in firewood from the shed, they had done nothing but eat, make love, sleep and make love again.

For two days they had laughed and talked. They spoke of everything, yet of nothing. Alex had not questioned her about Lucas Taylor again, and she had not offered any information. She knew she had to tell him, but she didn't want to encourage his thoughts of gold mining upriver. He had already told her he thought there was gold near Jeremia's Bend, three days by dogsled from there. If she told him about the map her father had claimed to own, it would only fuel his fever for the gold. She didn't want Alex mining; she didn't want him to become one of them, and she didn't want him to die trying.

"Alex . . ." she called softly again. She ran her hand beneath the cotton blanket, stroking his bare chest. "The snow's let up. Time to get up, sleepy-head."

Alex blinked, opening his eyes, then squinting as he adjusted to the bright sunlight that poured in through the cabin windows. "Morning."

"Morning." She propped herself up on his chest, staring down at him, a smile on her face. She would never grow tired of looking at his astounding blue eyes. "You going to lay here and sleep all day, or are you coming with me?"

"The snow's stopped?" He lifted his head to brush his lips against hers.

"Umhmm. We've got to fetch that moose. I need dog food." She ran a finger over his lower lip. "You certainly slept well."

"Because you wore me out!" He tucked an arm beneath his head.

"Aw, poor thing!" She pressed her mouth to his and then leaped up, dragging the blanket with her.

"Gabrielle!" Alex shivered as the frigid morning air met his bare flesh, and he yanked the corner of the bearskin rug over him. "It's freezing in here!"

"That's because someone was too lazy to go out last night and get more wood." She slipped into her underdrawers and reached for her grey wool pants that lay on the floor.

"Me? What about you?" Alex grumbled good-naturedly.

She turned up her nose impishly. "That's who I meant!"

138

"Oh." He nodded absentmindedly, watching her slip on her clothes. He was still in awe of her lack of embarrassment when it came to his body and her own. Growing up here in the territory, far from the "civilized" states, she possessed none of the mores of society. She used her own head to decide what was right and wrong, not some silly social rules that his own sisters were guided by back home in Richmond. He couldn't help chuckling to himself as it occurred to him that never in his married life had he seen Amber totally unclothed. And here, Gabrielle was standing before him without a shirt, teasing him with a sway of her full-rounded breasts.

"What are you laughing about? Me?" Gabrielle pulled a soft sweater of lamb's wool over her head.

Alex shook his head. "Never you. I was laughing at myself." He smiled, his face glowing with a new-found happiness. He hadn't known what was missing in his life until now. To his delight, in the past two days, he'd found that not only was he falling in love with Gabrielle, but he liked her as well. She was bright, humorous and filled with an enthusiasm for life. Her mind was filled with a vast knowledge of the wilderness around her, and she was genuinely happy to share it. She had already promised that when the snow stopped, she would let him harness her smaller sled and they would take two sleds out to bring home the moose. "What better way to learn to mush than to get on the back of a sled?" she'd said.

Gabrielle's eyes narrowed suspiciously as she opened the wood-stove door to start a fire. "Well, are you getting up or not? I'm leaving in half an hour's time."

"Naw . . . I thought I'd just lay here and look

at you."

"That right?" Gabrielle's eyes sparkled mischievously. "Well, I can think of a good way to get you up." She grinned as she swung open the cabin door and stuck out her head. "Tristan, Anthony, Leo! Come on!"

A great whoosh of frigid air swept through the room as Alex threw up his hands. "No!" he shouted as the snow-covered huskies came bounding in. "Call them off!"

The dogs poured in through the door, barking and nipping at each other's heels as they raced through the cabin. Tristan bounded across the room pouncing on Alex and licking his face.

Alex batted at the great ball of wet fur, laughing as he tried to push the affectionate canine off his blanket. "Gabrielle, do something about these mutts!" he ordered good-naturedly. He pushed and shoved the lead dog but to no avail.

Gabrielle only laughed, counting as the dogs still came pouring through the door. "One little, two little, three little sled pups, four little, five little, six little sled pups . . ." As the seventeenth and final dog made his way through the cabin door, she closed it, shutting out the snow that blew into the single room.

Pandemonium reigned as the dogs barked and howled, chasing each other around the table and climbing over the bed. Anthony had found the cupboard where she kept leftovers, had pulled out a brown sack of muffins and was chewing through the paper. Lawrence was beneath the bed, gnawing on a half-cured deer hide, and two yearling pups were playing tug-of-war with Gabrielle's red felt hat.

140

Alex struggled to sit up as Tristan settled his large brown and white frame on his human companion's lap. "Good God! How many dogs have you got?" He scratched beneath Tristan's long snout, and the dog whined contentedly.

"Seventeen." She crouched down to study Leopold's injuries, pleased that no infection had settled in. "You did a good job on them. He's going to be fine."

"Good." Alex pushed the dead weight of the dog off his lap and got to his feet, reaching for his pants which hung on the chair.

Gabrielle couldn't help smiling as she watched him draw the red tweed over his hard-muscled thighs. "You've got nice legs, you know." She bit back a smile as Alex's head bobbed up.

He lifted an eyebrow, easing the rough material over his lean hips. "Have I?" The air was filled with sensual tension. "What else have I got, missy . . ." his voice was low and teasing, "that's nice?"

Gabrielle walked the few feet between them, ignoring the sled dogs that barked and raced around them. Reaching out with nimble fingers, she did up the buttons of his pants, letting her fingers brush purposely against his tightening groin. "Getting confident, aren't you?" She leaned against him, pressing her palms on his bare chest. She had grown used to this chest in the past few days and had grown to love the feel of the short, curly red hair beneath her fingers.

Alex groaned audibly, taking her mouth with ardent fervor. "God, Gabrielle, I can't get enough of you." His tongue delved in the moist cavern of her mouth, savoring her nectar.

Gabrielle's tongue met with his in a sweet dance of

love as she molded her body to his, threading her fingers through his thick hair. She wouldn't let herself think about the future, about him leaving her; all she would think about was now, here. It was all that mattered. Just a few brief months of bliss, she had decided, and then she could live out the rest of her life on memories. "Tell me you love me, Alex," she whispered in his ear.

"I love you, Gabrielle." He ran his fingers through her chestnut curls, pressing a kiss to her forehead. "Now tell me honestly," he said, his blue eyes somber. "I've not heard the same words from you. It doesn't matter if you don't; it couldn't stop my feeling for you if you didn't, but . . ." His voice was soft and lilting, with an edge of trepidation.

Gabrielle smiled, brushing her fingers over his full lips. "I've not said it because I was afraid . . . because I don't want to. But yes, Jefferson Alexander the fourth, I love you, like I never thought I'd love anyone." She brushed her palm against his cheek, embedding the image of his handsome face in her mind forever. "Little good it will do me . . ."

Alex studied her dark eyes, his hands resting comfortably on her waist. "Don't be so pessimistic. Life's full of surprises."

"Don't try to fool yourself," she told him in a hushed voice. "In the spring you have to leave. There's all that gold just waiting upriver for you." She couldn't keep the sarcasm out of her voice.

"I've got my daughter, my family, and you've got your dogs and that silly road to build through this wilderness," he countered. Sometime in the past two days when they had laid in each other's arms, she had told him about the road she would someday build with her profits from the trading post. It would be a road that would join her and her friends and make passage possible even in mid-winter.

"We could never stay together," she forced. There was a tightness in her throat. Her head knew the words rang true, but her heart cried out with pain.

His voice was equally careworn. "It was never meant to be." As he spoke he tried to convince himself of the truth of what he said, but deep inside he ached for what would never be.

A tense silence strung between them, and then Gabrielle lowered her head to his shoulder, tightening her arms around his neck. "But let's not think about it now, Alex. Let's just be happy with what we have, all right?"

He stroked her back through the soft lamb's wool, enjoying the feel of her fingers at the nape of his neck. "All right, Gabrielle, it's a deal. We live for today, for the winter, and then like you said, I'll go."

She blinked back the moisture behind her eyelids, releasing him. "It's a deal." She kissed him lightly to seal the pact and walked away, afraid he would see the tears in her eyes. She didn't want him to think she expected him to stay. Of course she didn't, but deep within herself, she wished just for a moment that it was possible.

"Now let's get these dogs out of here and have some breakfast." He changed the subject with ease, refusing to let her know how difficult it had been for him to agree there could be nothing between them. There's no possible way it could ever work, he told himself as he swung open the cabin door and began to usher out the dogs one at a time. "Come on, here dogs . . . come on, out."

"Get Tristan out and the rest will follow," Gabrielle offered, putting water on for coffee.

"Tristan, come on boy, out." Alex clapped his hands, and the lead dog came bounding across the room and ducked out the door. Just as Gabrielle had said, the others followed one by one.

"You feed them, Alex, and I'll make breakfast."

"I don't know if I can stand your flapjacks again." He reached for his parka. "What do I feed them?"

"Take that tin of dried fish; each dog gets a scoop. Then use another scoop of frozen moose bits from the large can outside. There'll be no time for a hot meal for them today if we're going to get that moose home before nightfall."

Alex buttoned up his parka and went out the door with a wave, Leopold following behind him.

"Looks like you made a friend," she called after him.

"Looks like I have!" He gave the spotted husky a pat on the head, closing the door behind him.

Gabrielle sighed, watching the door swing shut. *If only I could freeze time until it stood as still as the river,* she thought . . . *let the winter never end.* She reached for her skillet and slid it onto the stove. *I'd be happy to live right here with him forever, no gold, no Richmond or family back home, no Lucas Taylor and no stinking map.* But such thoughts were only childishness. She couldn't freeze time, and the sooner she realized that, the better. Alex was leaving in the spring; she was staying, and that was the way things were. It was just like Rouge had always said: "Life's not supposed to

144

be fair."

After breakfast Gabrielle and Alex hitched the dogs to two sleds and mushed up river to where they had camped a few nights before. They cut down the moose from the tree and dressed it as best they could in its frozen state and hauled it home.

Once Alex received instruction from Gabrielle on dogsledding, he caught on easily, taking pride in what she taught him. He found he liked the sound of the dogs barking and the whoosh of the snow beneath the steel runners. He liked the feel of the biting wind in his face and the sled handles in his hands. A born musher, Gabrielle called him. He had laughed at the time but couldn't help wondering if this was where he belonged.

The two arrived home before dark and had the dogs cared for and meat put away by night fall. "Let's make an early night of it, shall we?" Alex asked. "We haven't tried out that bed yet."

Gabrielle laughed, helping him pull his parka over his splinted arm. She was pleased to see that the bone was healing nicely and that there'd be no permanent disability. "A little early to go to sleep isn't it?"

"Who said anything about sleep?" He lifted a dark eyebrow suggestively.

Gabrielle swung his parka at him, hitting him across the middle with it. "Don't you think of anything else?" She sat down on the chair to pull off her boots.

"Do you?" He dropped both of their parkas on pegs on the wall and picked up the half-thawed moose steak he'd brought in with him.

"Just make the supper, mister, and keep your comments to yourself."

145

Alex crossed the room to the stove and threw on another log. "How about a bath while we wait?" he suggested.

"We?" Her dark brows crinkled in confusion.

"Sure, why not? You know . . . you scrub my back and I'll scrub yours. . . ."

"Do people do that?"

"You're such an innocent, Gabrielle. Of course people do. Want to try it?" He dropped the meat on the frying pan to thaw on the stove. "I could pull the tub over in front of the fireplace."

Gabrielle wrapped her arms around her waist. "I don't know . . ."

"Oh, come on! Where's you sense of adventure? If you can wander all over this territory with those dogs and that Colt strapped to your thigh like some gunslinger, you can certainly take a bath with your lover."

"My lover?" She smiled. "Is that what you are? I like the sound of that word on my tongue."

Alex took her in his arms. "And I like the taste of *you* on my tongue." He brushed his lips against hers, his tongue darting out to tease her lower lip. "Now start bringing in the snow. I'll get the water boiling on the stove. We're going to have a bath."

In half an hour's time, Alex had the fire in the fireplace blazing and the tub filled with steaming water. He shucked off his clothes and got in first, allowing the relaxing water to seep over him. "Come on, Gabrielle." He put out his arms for her. "Come sit here in my lap."

Her cheeks blushed rosy as she clutched a couple of cotton towels. "It seems so personal, bathing with someone, Alex." She watched him drip water from a

146

sponge over his well-rounded shoulders.

"And you think what we do on that bearskin isn't personal?" His laughter echoed in the shadowy cabin. "Oh, come on, sweet!"

Hesitantly, Gabrielle stripped off her clothes, leaving them in a pile beside Alex's. Taking a deep breath, she stepped into the tub, sinking in between his legs.

"Mmmmm, now doesn't that feel nice?" Water overflowed from the tub as he wrapped his arms around her bare breasts, holding her against him.

Gabrielle's eyes drifted shut as she relaxed against him in the hot bath. The heat of the water seeped into her bones until she felt like she was drifting in some tropical ocean. "You're right, it's wonderful."

Alex nibbled at her neck, sending tremors of delicious sensation through her body, and she dropped her hand to his outer thighs, massaging the taut muscles. His thumb brushed against one pink nipple, teasing it to a ripe peak, and Gabrielle moaned softly, guiding his hand with her own to the other breast.

The two were so caught up with each other that they didn't hear the click of the latch. As the door swung open, they both turned to see Jack coming in the door.

"Oh my God," Gabrielle moaned. Mortified, she slipped beneath the surface of the water, hoping she'd have the nerve to drown herself.

Alex burst into laughter, looking from Jack to the bubbles surfacing in the tub. "Looks like you've caught us in an awkward moment," he managed, pulling Gabrielle up by the shoulders.

Gabrielle sputtered and coughed, covering her bare breast with her crossed arms. "What are you doing here, Jack?"

"Come to visit you folks." The dark-skinned native bit back a grin, but his amusement was plain in his voice.

Alex came out of the tub, wrapping a towel around his middle and then held out one for Gabrielle. He was still laughing as he covered her dripping form with the towel and lifted her out of the tub. "Have a seat, Jack. We'll be with you in a moment."

Jack sat down at the table and extracted a half-smoked cigar from his pocket. "That moose I smell cooking?"

Gabrielle let out an exasperated sigh. "For God sakes, Jack. The least you could do was look away!"

Her old friend lifted a sooty eyebrow. "Does this mean I'm going to have to take to knocking before I come in?"

Alex tugged his tweed pants over his wet skin. "It means we're going to start sliding that bolt. I never even heard the dogs bark."

Jack shook his head. "They don't bark, know me too well. They lift an ear, hear it's my footsteps and burrow deeper in their snowbank."

Gabrielle stood listening to the men's relaxed conversation, her anger at both of them rising with each moment. There wasn't even a place she could dress in privacy in the cabin, and she certainly couldn't step outside!

Sensing her dilemma, Alex handed her her clothes and held up the towel to shield her. "Get dressed, and then we'll have something to eat."

Gabrielle forced her damp limbs into the clothes, still too embarrassed to speak. Finally dressed, she yanked

148

the towel from Alex's hand. "You needn't look so smug!" she snapped. Strutting across the room, she tossed the towel on a chair and got down on her hands and knees. Climbing halfway under the bed, she came out with a full quart of good Irish whiskey. "I don't know about you two, but I need a drink!"

Chapter Eleven

Alex threw back his head in laughter, his deep tenor voice echoing his masculinity in the small, cramped cabin.

Gabrielle looked up at him sharply. "I guess that means you'll not be having any." She got up off the floor, brandishing the sealed bottle of whiskey.

Alex stuffed his fists in the sleeves of a dark, grey corduroy shirt, covering his bare torso. He tried to wipe the grin from his face as Gabrielle glared at him, unamused. "I'm sorry, Gabrielle. But you have to admit, all of it is rather funny."

"I'm not laughing," she told him dryly, rummaging through a wooden crate she kept her dishes in. Extracting three dusty glasses wrapped in faded newspaper, she looked over at Jack. "You staying for supper?"

A smile twitched on Jack's face. "Guess I am, Gabe."

She unwrapped the glasses one at a time and dropped them carefully into a dishpan of water that sat on the sideboard near the stove. "I suppose you'll be wanting some of Papa's whiskey, too."

"Suppose I will."

Alex chuckled, his back to Gabrielle as he stabbed at the piece of moose meat frying in the pan with a long fork. "Didn't I see some potatoes in one of those boxes over there?" He motioned in the direction of the supply crates piled ceiling-high on the far side of the room.

"You did," Gabrielle answered.

Alex spun around, resting his hands on her hips. She tried to push him away, but he was insistent. "Then why not dig a few out, sweet, and I'll fry them up, too?" His blue eyes sparkled with amusement.

"Alex," she whispered between clenched teeth. "Let go of me."

"Why?" he asked. "Jack's already seen the worst of us . . . or maybe it was the best of us." He broke into a wide grin.

Gabrielle groaned, trying to pull away. "Can't you see he's watching? I could just kill you!"

"What do you care if he's watching? I'm the one who's in trouble. I'm the one he threatened." He gently brushed a lock of curly hair off her forehead. Her hair had grown since he first saw her in Seattle; it nearly brushed her shoulders now.

"Did he?" She couldn't resist a smile. "I didn't know Jack had a violent bone in his body."

"Well, when it comes to you, he does." Alex kept his voice down, his words meant only for Gabrielle. "Look, I'm sorry he walked in, and I know you're embarrassed; but there's nothing to be done about it now but laugh." He lifted her chin to kiss her tightly compressed lips. "But next time, the door will be bolted."

"There won't be a next time."

"Oh, yes, there will," he breathed in her ear.

An hour later, Gabrielle, Alex and Jack sat around the table, devouring the fried moose steak and potatoes and sampling the fine whiskey. Once Gabrielle's ruffled feathers had been smoothed, the meal had been an enjoyable one. The three got along well, laughing and telling stories, each revealing small glimpses of himself.

"Who taught you how to cook moose?" Jack asked Alex as he pushed his cleaned plate back.

"Never cooked it before, but as far as I could see, it wasn't much different than beef." Alex grabbed his own dirty plate and slid his hand across the table to take Jack's.

Gabrielle handed Alex her plate, allowing her hand to brush against his. The whiskey had lulled her into a pleasant mood, making her feel warm and safe here in her cabin with her two best friends in the world. Best friend and her lover, she silently corrected herself. She couldn't help smiling as she watched Alex move across the room to clear the table. He barely limped now, his stride long and masculine. She watched as the firelight played off his well-sculpted face, emphasizing his high cheek bones and well-shaped chin. His dark auburn hair was tousled giving him the appearance of being far younger than his thirty-five years.

Alex returned to the table, dragging his chair around to sit beside Gabrielle. He patted her leg, reaching for his glass. "How about another round?"

Jack pushed his glass forward. "Another." He pulled a cigar from his leather jerkin and went to light it from the coals in the blazing fire.

"You, Gabrielle?" Alex's voice was soft and teasing.

She dropped her hand to his thigh. "I shouldn't." His gaze held hers, making her feel hot and tingly.

"But you will . . ."

She nodded her head, her eyes fastened intently on his. "But I will . . ."

Alex poured a generous portion of the amber liquid into her glass and then leaned to refill Jack's. Putting down the bottle, he laid his hand gently over hers, giving her a wink out of the corner of his eye.

Jack dropped back into his chair and pushed it back, resting one foot on the table. Smoke from his cigar circled his head, rising to form a cloud in the ceiling's rafters. "Gabe here tells me you're a gold seeker." His eyes narrowed. "Don't look much like one."

Alex laughed, squeezing Gabrielle's hand when he felt it tense beneath his own. "What does a gold miner look like?"

"Not a gentleman." Jack studied his leather boot propped on the edge of the table, flexing his foot. "Gabe's father was a miner." He glanced over at Gabrielle as if for approval to go on.

Alex saw the slightest nod of her chin and spoke cautiously. "Was he? She never told me that."

"Probably hasn't told you a lot of stuff. . . ."

Alex sighed, seeing it was obvious it was going to be as difficult to get any information out of Jack as it was Gabrielle. "Where did he mine?"

Jack removed his cigar, waggling it at Alex. "Ah hah! More than one man has asked that same question."

"You never really believed those stories of Papa's,

did you, Jack? You know as well as I do that he was the best liar on this side of the Tanana." Gabrielle took a sip of the whiskey from her glass, savoring its taste as it slid down her throat, burning a path to her stomach.

"I'll tell you, Gabe, they were no stories. I saw the money he played faro with. Even saw a chunk or two of gold."

"God sakes, Jack! The money you saw was what he'd won from someone else, or cheated them out of!" Gabrielle knew the liquor was loosening her tongue, but she didn't care. Maybe this was the best way to tell Alex. The whiskey would serve as a buffer against the pain of the loss of her father over that damnable map.

"I don't understand; Rouge said he struck gold?" Alex held Gabrielle's hand tight in his. He wasn't going to let her slip away from him this time. No, tonight he'd hear the story of Rouge LeBeau and the murderer, Lucas Taylor.

"Lied and said he struck gold." Gabrielle took a deep breath as Jack settled back in chair, letting her go on with the story on her own. "It was while I was in Seattle at that boarding school. My father said he won a map in a poker game, a map that led to gold somewhere north of here. He *told* me he went there, mined and struck gold."

Alex studied her dark eyes, lifting his glass to his lips. "So why didn't you ever see any gold, or money at least?"

"Because there never was any gold." She got up from the chair and went to stare at the fire blazing in the fireplace. In one hand she cradled her nearly empty glass. "His story was that he lost all of the gold gambling. 'Course Papa told me a lot of things, and

155

most of them were lies."

Alex watched her intently. "You said there was a map. Where is it now?"

"*He* said there was a map." She laughed bitterly. "I never saw it, never believed it for a minute. But he always promised me that one day we were going to go back and mine the gold, and then we were going to build that road we always talked about."

"He never once showed it to you, never took you back to the place?"

"When I first came back from Seattle, I almost believed there was a map, but as time passed, I realized it was just another one of his stories. That was when we really started trading to make money. I knew by the time I was fifteen that the only way that road of his was going to get built was if I earned the money to hire those loggers myself."

Alex got to his feet and went to stand opposite Gabrielle. He placed one hand on the mantel of the fireplace, leaning toward her. "Where does Lucas Taylor come into all of this?"

"Lucas Taylor?" She gave a snort of disgust and drained her glass. "We met Lucas Taylor in a saloon on the docks in Seattle. He started following us around, being all friendly-like with my father. Papa was so gullible, he thought the man liked him. I never liked him . . . never trusted him." She paused.

"And . . ." Alex urged softly.

"Taylor tried to get my father to tell him where the map was, or least what was on it. He had to have heard about it from someone else. But Papa was tight-lipped. He kept telling Taylor the map was mine, that the money belonged to me." Tears welled in her eyes.

156

"Papa and I, we had a big argument. I was getting scared. I told him either to tell the man he lied or give him the damned map." A sob escaped her lips, and she turned away.

"Gabrielle . . ." Alex rested a hand on her shoulder. "Tell me what happened. I can't help you if you don't tell me."

"They were playing cards one night, just like any other night in the Full Moon Saloon. I was there, but Papa didn't know it. He didn't like me in the saloons, but if I didn't go, there was no one to drag him home when he passed out from drinking." She set her glass gently on the mantel. "I was sitting behind a curtain in another private playing room. I was watching the game. My father was a cheater at cards, but for some reason that night he was rolling high all on his own." Tears rolled freely down her cheeks. "Taylor accused him of cheating, but he wasn't—" Another sob racked her body. "He wasn't. He had three kings, an ace high. He won fair and square. But the next thing I knew, Taylor was shouting and pulling out his gun." Her voice became barely audible. "It was a setup. Taylor searched his body for the map after he went down. Rouge LeBeau never had a chance."

Alex turned Gabrielle around, drawing her trembling body into his arms. He didn't care if Jack saw him; he really didn't care what the man thought. All he wanted was to comfort Gabrielle, to wipe the tears from her cheeks and make her laugh again. "Oh, Gabrielle. Why was that so hard for you to tell me? That's why he's after you, isn't it? He thinks you have the map."

Gabrielle clung to Alex, molding her body against

157

his. "Hold me," she whispered. "Please, Alex, hold me. . . ."

"Shhh," he hushed, smoothing her dark curls with the palm of his hand. Behind him he could hear Jack moving, putting on his parka and then leaving quietly.

Gabrielle lifted her arms, encircling them around Alex's neck. "I'm so afraid," she murmured against his hair. "So afraid."

"The authorities . . . didn't they—"

"Oh, they investigated, but Taylor said it was self-defense. No one would listen to me. I think he'd paid them off . . . the sheriff, the judge, all of them. I was told it would be best if I just left, and soon." She was calmer now. It was Alex that gave her the strength to go on. "I had to get him buried, then there were the supplies to be shipped, and my mother . . . God, my mother, she came around wanting to know if there was an inheritance coming to her. Seems she'd heard about the map, too."

"Go on, what about Taylor?" Alex kissed her cheeks, her eyelids, the end of her nose.

"He started following me." She raised her head, wanting to feel his lips on hers. "He said he wanted to talk, but I knew better. It was his talk that killed my father."

He brushed his lips against hers again and again, savoring the smell of wild flowers that clung to her hair. "That man who was chasing you when you ran into me?"

"When he found out I was leaving soon, he cornered me in a hotel. He had his hands all over me. He said he'd kill me if I didn't give him the map. I was scheduled to leave later in the week, but I had all of my supplies

158

transferred to the *Lady Yukon* because she was sailing two days sooner. I almost got away, but someone informed him of my change of plans. If it hadn't been for you . . ." She lifted her dark lashes, and her eyes met his.

"Don't think about it. I *was* there. It was meant to be." Lifting her gently into his arms, he carried her across the cabin to her bed along the wall.

As they made the short distance, Gabrielle leaned her head against his hard, muscular chest, listening to the comforting pound of his heart. *I love you,* her inner self cried out. *Don't leave me . . . please don't ever leave me.* But she refused to let the thoughts surface. Those were words that could never be spoken. He would leave. He had to go home to his daughter, and she had to stay here where she was safe from Taylor. He could never find her here, not this far north. Jack said so himself.

"Oh, Gabrielle," Alex sighed. He held her in his arms, stroking her trembling body. "You've been through too much for a girl your age, more than some people go through in a lifetime. You deserve better."

"It's all right." She sniffed, suddenly feeling a little silly. "It's just the whiskey talking. I've been through the worst. Things can only get better, right?" She managed a weak smile. "I have you, don't I?"

"Yes, you have me, here in your heart forever." He tapped her left breast lightly.

"Jack left?"

"And without killing me." Alex slipped his hand beneath her sweater, cupping the fullness of one breast, and she leaned in toward him in encouragement.

"Actually, I think he likes you a little." She rolled

159

closer, wanting to feel his hard, lean body pressed against hers. "It was all a setup you know."

"Was it?" he teased softly. He rained silken kisses over her face, inhaling the sweet smell of femininity that clung to her dewy skin.

"Uh huh." Her nimble fingers made quick work of the buttons on his corduroy shirt. "You plied me with hard whiskey and then made me sing." She laughed, her voice raspy with rising desire.

Alex groaned as her hands caressed the hardened muscles of his chest, her fingers lingering over his budding nipples. She liked the feel of his short, crisp hair beneath her hand and the smell of his bare skin. Leaning into him, she lifted her head to kiss him full on the lips, her tongue darting out to tease. "You taste like whiskey."

"So do you." He raised his hands, tucking them beneath his head. "Do what you will with me, sweet. I'm all yours."

Gabrielle giggled, climbing astride him. First she removed his shirt, then slowly pulled her own sweater over her head. She took her time, watching him watch her.

"You're so beautiful," he said hoarsely. Unable to resist, he sat up to take one bud of her breast in his mouth, stroking it with the tip of his tongue.

She arched her back, moaning softly as she threaded her fingers through his thick auburn locks. "Are you the devil to make me feel this way, Alex? Is this the way it's supposed to be?"

"It's the way it's supposed to be," he returned, burying his face in the sweeping valley between her breasts, ". . . when two people were meant for each other." He was pressing hot, wet kisses to her face and breasts now, caressing the long fluid line of her back with his fingers.

"But how can that be, Alex? Our lives are too different." She took his head in her hands, forcing him to look at her. His blue-grey eyes were stormy with passion.

"I don't know, love. I just don't know." With a sudden movement, he rolled her over on her back, tugging at her pants. "Take these off before I rip them off." He slid them easily down her silken thighs, kissing the bare skin he uncovered.

Gabrielle laced her fingers through his hair, innocently guiding his head to the soft skin between her inner thighs. "Oh, Alex," she cried out, lifting her hips rhythmically. Waves of molten pleasure washed over her as a heavy-limbed aching filled her being. Finally, consumed by fire, she beckoned him. "Please, I need you," she cried out.

Sitting up, Alex pulled off his pants and laid down beside her, enfolding her in his arms. Her breath was hard and unsteady, her pale skin covered with a sheen of moisture. She quivered in his arms, accepting his mouth hungrily. "You're teasing me," she moaned. "I need you; I need to feel you in me."

"All right, love," he whispered in her ear. Pressing another kiss to her lips, he straddled her, taking her with one long, hard thrust. She cried out in ecstasy, lifting her hips and rejoicing in response. As he moved, he filled her with pulsating shimmers of light, drawing her closer to the bright sun of fulfillment.

Caressing the hard, lean muscles of his buttocks, she cried out, writhing against him. He called her name, his voice strained and throaty as both of them peaked, clutching each other as they glided home.

Gabrielle's laughter filled the cabin, her voice soft and lilting, and Alex raised his head to take in her dark, laughing eyes. "What's so funny?" He couldn't resist a smile.

"Nothing." She brushed at a tendril of his hair. "I'm just happy."

He slid off her, coming to rest beside her. "I'm glad you're happy. I'm glad I can make you happy. I haven't been able to do that for many in my lifetime."

Gabrielle ran her fingers over his lips, and he pursed them, kissing her fingertips. "I love you," she whispered in his ear, snuggling close to him.

"I love you," he answered, his voice hushed. Sitting up, he reached for a blanket to pull over them and drew her into his arms, tucking them both in. "Good night."

"Good night" came her sleepy voice as she curled up, her head resting on his chest.

Long after Gabrielle was sleeping soundly, Alex lay awake mulling over the past day's events. It was difficult for him to believe a man would kill for something so elusive as a map, but he knew Gabrielle was telling the truth. She was the most honest person he'd ever known. He exhaled sharply, glaring up at the rafters above his head. His chest ached for the pain of Gabrielle's loss and for the terror Taylor had put her through. Alex's fists instinctively tightened at his sides at the thought of someone threatening his Gabrielle.

He laughed aloud in the darkness of the cabin. His Gabrielle? What right did he have to call her his own? What right did he have to love her or expect to be loved in return? She was right and he knew it. There could be no future in this love. His eyes grew damp at the thought of leaving her, but then images of his daughter flashed through his mind. "Alexis . . . what are you doing right now?" he whispered. "Papa misses you, misses you so much. . . ."

Alex swallowed the lump in his throat, wrapping his arms tightly around Gabrielle's sleeping form. His heart ached with the pain of the choices he knew he had to make. He had to make that trek north for gold in the spring, he had to return to Richmond, and he had to leave his Gabrielle behind. Letting his eyes drift shut, Alex forced those thoughts from his head. He would live for today, just as Gabrielle did. It was the only way to accept the heartaches in life. Rolling onto his side, he held her tightly, drifting off to sleep.

Chapter Twelve

"Alex, if you say one more word about that blasted map, I'm going to put a hole in your head!" Gabrielle shook the disassembled rifle she held in her hands at him. They had picked this morning to clean her firearms because it was snowing too hard outside to do much else. Alex had her Colt 45 pistol in pieces on a blanket on the floor, while she reassembled her Winchester. Two more rifles stood propped against the wall awaiting their attention.

"I'm sorry, but I can't get it out of my mind, Gabrielle. The map has got to be here somewhere. It could make you rich." He laid a hand on Leopold, who slept contented at his feet. Since Alex had doctored the dog on the trail, they had become constant companions. When Alex took Gabrielle's small sled out, it was Leopold who acted as his lead dog.

Gabrielle wrapped a wad of clean cotton on the end of a metal rod and plunged it into the barrel of the rifle. "I've been telling you for weeks now, there is no map, and even if there was, I don't want to be rich."

"What about that road you want to build? If we found the gold this spring, you could have the loggers in by June."

"I'm telling you, there is no map, but even if there was, you'd not find me digging in the dirt." She shook her head. "I'm not a miner. I haven't got the fever."

Alex let out an exasperated sigh. "What would you do with the map if you did find it?" He took aim and pulled the trigger on the pistol, checking to be sure the hammer glided smoothly.

"I'd give it to you." She got up to toss another log on the fire. It was Christmas Eve, and the snow had been flying on and off for a week, keeping them in the cabin most of the time.

Alex looked up at her. "Would you?"

"It's yours." She put up her hands in absolution. "You find the map, and you can have it."

"I thought you said there was no map." He laid the Colt on the blanket on the floor and got to his feet.

"I don't think there is, but if it exists, I don't want it. It killed my father." She caught his hand with hers, entwining his fingers. "Besides, if there was a map, don't you think I would have found it by now, after all of these years?"

Alex brushed a lock of chestnut hair off her cheek. "I don't know. I guess so."

"It's becoming an obsession with you. Just forget the map, all right?" Gabrielle beckoned softly.

Alex gave a nod. "All right. I won't ask you any more about it." He wrapped her in his arms, kissing her soundly on the lips.

Gabrielle leaned into him, lifting her chin to accept his warm mouth. That familiar shiver of desire ran

166

through her, and she sighed, resting her cheek on the broad expanse of his chest. "Wanna make love?" she asked, her voice throaty.

Just then Leopold leaped to his feet and stuck his long muzzle between them, whining.

Gabrielle and Alex burst into laughter. "You see that," she chided. "I told you, you were spoiling that dog. He doesn't belong in the cabin, Alex. You'll make him soft."

Alex let go of Gabrielle with one hand to scratch behind the husky's ragged ear. Somehow, when the moose attacked him, a piece of his ear had been torn off. But his body had healed, and except for a few neat pink scars, he was as healthy and strong as he'd ever been.

"I know, you told me I shouldn't bring him in, but when he looks at me with those sad blue eyes, I can't tell him no. Isn't that right, boy?" Alex crooned.

Gabrielle shook her head, breaking away. "You're getting to be a real dog man, Alex. First you beat me in that sled race the other day, and now you're talking to that mutt like he's a person!" She clucked between her teeth.

"I think Leo makes nearly as good a lead dog as Tristan." Alex caught the dog by his collar and started pulling him toward the door. "Don't you?"

"There's no dog this side of Tanana as good as Tristan." She walked across the room, pulling her sweater over her head.

Alex watched the material slip over her creamy skin, and his pulse quickened at the sight of the arched fullness of her breasts. "Sorry boy," he murmured as he urged the dog out the door. "But this is where you and I part." He slid the bolt of the cabin door home and turned to watch Gabrielle slip out of her wool pants and lay down on her bed.

"You coming?" she asked, putting out a hand for him.

"I am," he breathed, unable to take his eyes off her as he made his way to the bed. Her hair had grown long enough now to frame her delicate oval face in a halo of chestnut ringlets. She was more feminine than he ever could have imagined she could be. "When did you say everyone would be arriving for the Christmas party?" he asked huskily.

She took his hand, pressing her lips to his palm. "Tomorrow." Her dark eyes met his sea of blue. "Sometime in the afternoon."

Her sultry voice lured his mouth to hers, and Alex's eyes drifted shut as he tasted the honey of her lips. "That should be enough time."

"And if it's not," she whispered, "then they'll just have to wait, won't they?"

Gabrielle's cabin rang with laughter as Alex threw open the door to greet her final guests. They were all here now: Peg, his woman Lily, Beans Magee, and now Jack and his wife and daughter.

"Afternoon to you, Jack," Alex called, holding open the door to let his wife pass.

Jack gave a nod. "This is Mya." He rested his hand on the shoulder of the short, plump Indian. "And this—" he caught the small girl around the waist and swung her into the air—"is my little dove, Mary."

The child dissolved into laughter, speaking to her

168

father in their own tongue. Jack gave her a pat on the backside and shoved her in the door. Mya grinned, entering the cabin with a parcel tucked beneath each arm.

"Mya!" Gabrielle shouted across the cabin. "I'm so glad you came!"

Mya pushed back the hood of her parka, blushing profusely. "It is good you ask us. We bring food, dry fish, berries, also presents." Her pitch black eyes sparkled enthusiastically.

"You know you didn't have to do that, Mya." Gabrielle took the hide-wrapped bundles from her. "I told Jack to tell you no presents."

The native woman caught her daughter by the arm and tugged off the child's seal-skin parka, then her own. "It's Christmas! I would not come if I could not bring presents to you."

Gabrielle turned to Alex as he came in the door carrying another bundle off Jack's sled. "This is Alex, Mya." She felt her own cheeks flush with color.

Alex gave a nod, his smile genuine. "It's nice to meet you finally, Mya. Gabrielle talks often of you and your family."

Mya grinned, baring two broken front teeth. "Gabrielle is our family." She winked in Gabrielle's direction. "She is a sister to my Jack and me. Always will be."

"Come and sit down, Mya." Gabrielle gestured with a hand. "You know Peg and his Lily." She pointed to the two of them seated at the table. Lily was a native too, small and round, just like Mya. "And of course this here is Beans Magee himself." She wrapped her arm around the tall, blond-haired man with the ragged

169

beard, giving him a hug.

Alex took all of this in as he carried Jack's bundles and deposited them against the far wall. He suddenly felt like an intruder. These people had been friends for years. They knew the land; they knew each other. He wondered what had ever made him think Gabrielle needed him. These friends had been here before he came to the territory. They would be here long after he left.

Taking an empty chair near the fireplace, Alex lifted his glass of Christmas punch to his lips. It was a crude mixture of homemade spirits, canned fruit and chunks of ice from the frozen river. Gabrielle had called it her papa's special recipe, Alex recalled, and then she and Peg had burst into uncontrolled laughter over some private joke.

Sitting back in his chair, Alex watched everyone through half-closed eyes, wishing he were home in Richmond with Alexis. He couldn't bear the thought of leaving Gabrielle, but he longed to see his daughter. He sighed, studying little Mary playing on the hearth with stick-figure animals carved from wood. Why did life have to be so difficult? Why did so much depend on money? If only he could find that map—

"Hey, you . . ." Gabrielle broke Alex from his reverie. "Didn't you hear me? We're going to open the presents now." She took the glass from his hand, studying his grey-blue eyes. She couldn't help but see the mixture of emotions that troubled him. "You all right?"

"Yea." He gave a nod, shifting his gaze to the floor.

Gabrielle straddled his knees to sit on his lap. She didn't care what the others thought. She only cared that Alex was hurting. "You miss Alexis?" She brushed back the hair off his forehead with her fingers.

"Yea."

"Wish you were there?"

"Yes. But I wish you were there with me." His eyes met hers.

"You know that's not possible," she whispered.

"Why not?"

She chewed at her bottom lip apprehensively. "You know why."

"Taylor could never find you in Richmond, Gabrielle." The voices in the cabin faded into the background as he studied her dark, frightened eyes.

"It's silly even to talk about it. You have your gold to find, remember?"

"If we found the map, we could find the gold together."

Gabrielle slid off his lap. "I thought you weren't going to mention the map again."

"You're right. I'm sorry." He got to his feet, taking her hand. "Now come on, let's see these presents."

The guests, Gabrielle and Alex all sat on the floor in a circle in the center of the room and with a flurry of conversation, began to pass their gifts around. Some were wrapped in hides or old newspaper; some did not come wrapped at all. There were hard candy and trinkets for little Mary, a new pipe each for Beans and Peg, mittens for Alex and yard goods for Mya and Lily. Gabrielle received new leather straps to repair her harnesses, canned fruitcake and a new pair of snowshoes. To Alex, she gave a tunic of soft wool with moose and wild birds embroidered across the front.

"You weren't supposed to give me anything, Ga-

171

brielle," he told her, kissing her softly on the lips. "I've nothing for you."

Her eyes shined with the gaiety of the Christmas spirit. "That's all right. I'll collect mine later," she whispered.

Finally, when all of the gifts had been passed out and thank-yous had been said, Mya spoke up. "There's one more thing," she said shyly as she pulled a small bundle from behind her. "It's for you, Gabrielle. Something I found in Jack's stuff." Hesitantly she offered the bundle wrapped in blue ticking.

Gabrielle lifted an eyebrow questioningly, but accepted the present. Sitting cross-legged between Alex and Jack, she unfolded the layers of new cotton. "Oh . . ." She looked from Mya to Jack, tears brimming in her eyes. *"Laura!* Where did you find her?" It was the rag doll her father had made for her the winter she was born.

"I found it in a bag of old clothes your father gave me. I don't know how long I've had it." Jack pulled a cigar from his pocket and stuck it between his teeth. He wasn't much for emotions. Mya had said she would want the old doll, though he couldn't figure out why.

Gabrielle held the faded cloth doll to her chest. "Thank you, Mya . . . Jack. I thought she was long gone. She just disappeared one day. Papa said he didn't touch her, but I always thought he'd thrown her out thinking she was junk." She studied the doll's black-button eyes, fingering her yarn hair.

"Now how about some more of that punch?" Alex asked everyone. He gave Gabrielle a squeeze as he collected empty glasses and tin cups.

Later, after a meal of Mya's moose stew, corn bread

172

and baked apples, the friends all settled down on the floor and in the chairs. Gabrielle gave Alex a nudge as she settled on the floor at his feet. She held a cup of steaming black coffee cradled in her hands. "Now comes the real entertainment," she told him, grinning. "Listen up, because you're about to hear some of the tallest tales heard in this territory."

"Tales?" Beans Magee plopped himself on Gabrielle's bed. "What are you talking about, woman? It's the honest truth I tell, as God is my witness!" He lifted a glass of straight whiskey in salute.

"Truth!" Peg chimed in. "You wouldn't know the truth if it bit you in the ass!" Lily gave him a sharp elbow in the side, and he grunted, giving her a kiss on the cheek to appease her. "'Scuse my language, ladies. But you know it's the truth. Beans is the best liar on the Tanana." He looked over at Gabrielle. "'Course he couldn't hold a candle to Rouge LeBeau, could he?"

Gabrielle smiled. Instead of being sad at the mention of her father, it made her feel good inside. He would have been glad to know his friends thought so much of him. "All right, all right you two. Who's going to be first?"

Jack cleared his throat and spoke, going into a long meandering account of how an owl once guided him in a snowstorm, leading him to his mother's home. Next, Beans Magee recited his favorite story, swearing it was God's own truth as he elaborated on the tale he'd told the Christmas before. Peg followed in turn explaining how he went hunting earlier in the week and managed to kill a moose, a deer, two rabbits and a handful of grouse, all with one single shot.

Gabrielle broke into laughter, giving Alex a nudge.

"Come on, who could believe him? Peg, you're the worst liar in this snowbank. You're going to be barred from this house if you can't come up with anything better than that." She smiled teasingly, a sparkle in her dark eyes. "You honestly expect me to believe that you shot that moose, he ran and fell on the deer, who fell on the rabbits, who fell on the grouse, and you carried them all home on your sled?"

Peg grinned, stroking his bleached beard. "Nope, nope, don't expect you to believe it. Had to make a second trip back in my sled to fetch the moose!"

Everyone groaned, bursting into conversation as they reached to refill their glass with punch. "How about you, Gabe?" Beans Magee called from the bed. "We haven't heard from you tonight."

"That's right. What's Christmas without a story from a LeBeau?" Peg questioned.

Gabrielle put up her hands in defense. "Not me tonight, gentlemen. I haven't the belly for it." She turned to look up at Alex, a mischievous grin on her face. "But Alex, here, he's been telling me what a good storyteller he is. Seems he's had all kinds of adventures in newspaper printing places and cow stalls." She giggled, prodding his knee.

"A story!" Jack called out, raising his glass of punch. "It's the price a man pays for my Mya's meal." He lifted a sooty eyebrow, challenging Alex.

"Thanks, Gabrielle," Alex muttered beneath his breath. But he took a sip and set down his glass, crossing his arms over his chest. "I have a tale to tell you, but it's for your ears only, a tale so unbelievable, yet true, that I wouldn't dare tell any others but you . . ." His voice took on a soft, mellowing tone as he

174

lured his listeners into his confidence.

Gabrielle sighed, drawing up her knees as she listened to the yarn Alex spun. As his clear tenor voice filled the small cabin, pride swelled in her heart until she thought she would burst. He was a born storyteller. She had suspected he might have the gift when he first began to tell her stories of the great war between the states. Late at night they would lay in front of the fire, and he would repeat tales he had heard from his uncles, friends and grandfather. Even though he had never been on a battlefield, he could make her hear the roar of the cannon and smell the sweat of human blood. But here, in front of an audience, his storytelling ability was intensified. He added gestures, gentle intonations in his voice, even an occasional hushed whisper.

Alex held his listeners spellbound as he told the tale of a great whale that swam in the cold waters of the Atlantic. The sperm whale was said to lift drowning sailors from the depths of the sea and toss them onto the decks of whaling ships, thus risking its own life to save the men that threatened his extinction. It was a bold, daring tale with enough credibility to send a cold tingle down Gabrielle's spine.

As Alex's story came to an end and he leaned back in the chair, everyone in the room gave a sigh. Gabrielle hugged her knees, smiling up at him. *Papa would have been proud,* she thought.

Beans Magee stood up. "A finer tale I've not heard. The boy has my vote." He lifted his glass of whiskey.

"Aye, he has mine as well." Peg got slowly to his feet in honor of the winner.

"And mine . . ." Jack pushed himself out of his chair and plucked the unlit cigar from his mouth. "To Alex."

175

He raised his glass, as did the others, and they drank to the newcomer's acceptance.

Alex nodded, his face sober. This was a rite of passage for him, for he knew with the raising of each glass, Gabrielle's friends gave their approval of him. And for some reason, at that moment, their approval was more precious to him than the gold he had come north seeking. Catching Gabrielle's hand, he pulled her to her feet and kissed her gently, his blue eyes sparkling with accomplishment.

A few days later a warm spell hit the Tanana, and Alex and Gabrielle took advantage of it by spending the afternoon outside making up dog food in a large caldron over an open fire. They mixed moose meat, fish and wheatflour, and heated, then poured it into tin molds to let it freeze into chunks. The single servings could be carried on a sled and would stay frozen until spring.

"Now, when you're running your dogs hard, they need nearly four pounds of food a day," Gabrielle instructed as she stirred the contents of the huge pot. "And remember, they need hot food just like you do. When I'm on the trail, they get frozen chunks of fish during the day and a hot meal at night."

Alex nodded, continuing to fillet the fish they'd caught this morning. "What happens when you run out of food?"

She dropped the stirring stick into the snow and arranged the molds in front of her. "You don't, but if you do, they can go days without it. Probably longer than you can."

"I suppose as long as you hunt you can keep yourself and your animals alive." Alex tossed a piece of fresh fish into the air, and the dogs leaped for it, snapping and growling playfully.

"Yea, but there are times when the snow gets too deep and the wind blows too hard to hunt, Alex. You've got to know when those times are coming and be prepared." She shucked off her parka, overheated by the exertion of stirring the thick mass and the heat from the fire.

Alex tossed another piece of fish into the air. "Have you seen Leo?"

"No." Gabrielle eyed him sternly. "I told you about leaving him in the cabin. He'll be into my supplies, and I'll run short."

He dropped his knife on the flat surface of the log. "Sorry. I'll get him. I'm sure he's just sleeping in front of the fire." He sank his hands into the snow to clean them and started for the cabin.

Gabrielle followed him. "You're going to spoil him, Alex. He'll be useless on the trail."

He stopped and waited for her. "Alright, nag, I hear you." He hugged her playfully with one arm.

Swinging open the cabin door, Gabrielle stepped inside. Her hand flew to her mouth. "Leopold!" she shouted. "Put that down! Bad boy." She ran across the room, yanking her rag doll out of the husky's mouth. "For shame," she chastised, hugging the torn toy to her chest.

"Oh, Gabrielle. I'm sorry." Alex grabbed the dog by the collar and pushed him out the door. "Bad Leo, bad boy."

Feeling silly, Gabrielle turned around. "It's all right,

it's just an old doll." She picked up a severed arm that lay on the floor, the stuffing spilling from it.

"It doesn't matter," Alex answered. "It was yours. It had good memories."

Gabrielle held up the doll to see if she could reattach the arm. "She's not too bad, I can fix—" Her voice caught in her throat. "Alex," she breathed.

"What?" He looked up from where he'd been stooped, picking up stray stuffing.

"Alex . . . there's something in here."

"In where?" His eyebrows furrowed.

She shook the ragged toy. "My doll." Gently with one finger, she poked at the arm hole. Holding her breath, she slowly withdrew a rolled sheet of paper and tucked her doll beneath her arm.

Unrolling the brown, tattered paper, she looked up at Alex. Her face was ashen. "My God, Alex," she whispered. "It's the map. . . ."

Chapter Thirteen

"Gabrielle, come with me, please..." Alex entreated.

She tossed her fishing line through the round hole she'd cut in the ice. "I can't. You know I can't."

"You can't spend the rest of your life being afraid of Taylor. Who knows, maybe he's given up on you. Maybe he's found some other poor soul to pray on."

"It's not just Taylor, and you know it." She lifted her chin in defiance. "It's the gold. I won't have anything to do with it."

Alex tightened the hood on his parka to keep the driving wind off his face. "Why do you have to be so obstinate? The gold didn't kill your father, and you know it. Taylor did."

"It's the same thing. If there hadn't been any gold, if there hadn't been a map, my father wouldn't have been murdered in that saloon."

Alex felt a nibble at his bait and tugged gently at the line to entice the fish. "You understand why I have to go."

"I understand," she answered coldly.

"Jesus, Gabrielle. Why are you acting like this? You don't understand, and you're not trying." He rubbed his hands together for warmth, thankful for the wool mittens Mya had made him for Christmas. "I have responsibilities, my daughter, my family. Why can't you see that?"

"There's got to be another way." She shifted on the log, stomping her feet to keep them warm. It wasn't much past noon, and already the temperature was dropping. A light snow was beginning to fall, and the wind was picking up, driving harder out of the north.

"There isn't. I told you I can't make the money I need working for someone else. I've tried."

"I don't understand why you need all that money anyway. How much do you need to put food on the table for a kid? The war between the states has been over twenty years. If your mother needed money to pay the taxes, she'd have lost the damned place a long time ago!" Gabrielle's sharp stinging words echoed in the trees, and snow fell under the strain of her voice.

"I told you," Alex answered testily. "The house my great-grandfather built is nearly in ruins. I need to make repairs and to get the land back in shape for planting. My mother's been renting it out, but she's getting on in years. She deserves to see Alexander's Folly restored to its beauty before she dies."

"Folly is right," she scoffed. "The way I see it, this Alexander doesn't owe them anything."

Alex jerked his fishing line out of the water and stood up. "You're right, I don't owe them anything." His steely blue-grey eyes met hers in rising fury. "It's honor, Gabrielle. Pure and simple . . . honor and

180

loyalty. But then I don't guess you'd understand that, would you?"

Before she could speak, he jerked his knapsack off the frozen ice and started for the bank, his stride long and determined.

Gabrielle sighed, turning back to her fishing. She could feel her hands trembling as she pulled up her line to check the bait. *Honor? Where did he think I was supposed to learn anything about this gallant honor of his? Responsibility? Who have I ever been responsible for except myself and my dogs, and maybe Papa when he was too drunk to come in out of the snow?*

She sighed, staring off at the far bank of the Tanana. *I've been kidding myself thinking we could ever have a life together.* She hadn't said anything to Alex, but she'd been wondering what his Richmond was like. She'd even toyed with the thought that maybe the two of them could go back to Virginia together. "Damned foolishness," she muttered. Those dreams had ended when the map appeared. Alex was hell-bent on finding the gold. She'd given him the map, that was true; but she wanted no part of any gold miner, and he knew it. He had made his choice. . . .

Gabrielle sat out on the ice until she was stiff with cold before she finally brought in her fishing line and gave up. It hadn't been a good day for fishing on the Tanana; the dogs would have to eat dried meal and frozen fish from last week. Darkness was settling in on the riverbank as she walked wearily home. When she arrived at the cabin, Alex was already packing the smaller of her two sleds.

He barely looked up as he spoke. "I'm going to take the smaller sled, Leo and the four dogs I've been

181

mushing with. I can't pay you for them now, but I promise I will later."

"Take the dogs." Her voice rang with an emptiness that reflected the leaden weight in her heart. She couldn't help feeling betrayed. She knew he had never made any promises. Alex had always said he would leave and go north to search for gold, but she had hoped somewhere deep in the recesses of her mind that when the time came for him to go, he wouldn't be able to do it. She had fantasized that Alex would come to love her so much that he couldn't bear leaving her.

Alex strapped a pack onto the sled, securing it with rope. "Gabrielle, it doesn't have to be this way. You could go with me."

She spun around heading for the cabin door. "You've made your choice," she threw back bitterly.

"Is that what you think?" he shouted across the snow-covered yard. He came after her, catching her inside the door. He grasped her arm, twisting her around and forcing her to face him. "That's what it is, isn't it? You think it was a matter of choosing between you and the gold, between you and my family?"

Gabrielle squirmed under his scrutiny. He had always seemed so easy-going to her, so gentle. She didn't recognize this fierceness in him, and it frightened her. "I don't need you, Alex," she spat through clenched teeth.

"No, you don't need me; you don't need anyone do you? Well, I've got news for you; I need someone, someone that needs me." He eased the grip he held on her arm but refused to let her go.

"You're hurting me," she whispered.

"I don't care," he told her viciously. "You think this

has all been a game, don't you? A way to amuse yourself on cold nights?" He glowered at her. "You never cared about me. You've never cared about anyone but yourself."

"It's not true!" She dropped her knapsack on the floor and brushed at her eyes with the back of her hand. She wouldn't let him see her cry.

"I loved you, Gabrielle. I expected better of you than this. I trusted you. I trusted you to understand why I couldn't have what I wanted more in life than anything." Slowly he released her arm. "I wanted you, but if you can't come with me, I can't have you. My life is in Richmond once I find that gold. My life is with my daughter and my responsibilities."

She yanked back her arm as if she'd been burned. "Get out of here! Get out of my house! I hate you! I hated you the first day I saw you." She jerked her knapsack off the floor and threw it onto the bed. "You came here, and you took advantage of me. I was lonely, and you knew it!" she accused.

He laughed, his voice frighteningly steady. "Took advantage of you? You came willingly." He shook his head in disbelief. "You asked me to make love to you. You told me you loved me."

"And what am I supposed to know about love?"

"Oh, come on, Gabrielle. I don't want to hear your sad story about how your mother was a whore and your father was a drunk. We've all had our problems in life, haven't we? It's no excuse for hurting someone." He lowered his voice an octave. "It's no excuse for hurting me."

At a loss for what to say, she spun around, presenting her back to him. She couldn't stand the pain so clear in his voice. She couldn't stand the ache in her own chest. Tears slipped down her windburned cheeks as she stood in silence. The truth was, she still loved him. She loved him more than she'd ever loved anyone, and now he was leaving.

"Does it have to be like this, Gabrielle? Do I have to leave with you hating me?" Alex sighed heavily. "You knew I was leaving. I told you I couldn't stay. You gave me the map. Why would you give it to me if you didn't want me to use it?"

"You're a grown man." Her voice cracked, and she was silent for a moment. "You made your own choice."

He came up behind her, grasping her shoulders. "Don't you see? I have no choice. My daughter has to be more important than my personal life. Whether I'm happy or not makes no difference. Alexis is what matters."

Gabrielle held her body stiff, refusing to turn around and face him. Finally he let her go and walked out the door, closing it quietly behind him.

It was well after sunset when Alex stepped inside the cabin to find it dark, cold and quiet. He lifted his lantern to cast shadows on the walls. "Gabrielle," he called softly. He heard movement on the bed and turned to shed light on it.

There was Gabrielle, asleep, still clothed and wrapped in a wool blanket. He sighed, walking to the fireplace to set the lantern on the mantel. She'd nearly let the fire go out, and it was freezing inside. Methodically he gathered kindling from the wood box and soon had a roaring blaze in the stone fireplace.

Silently he came across the room to sit on the corner of the bed beside her sleeping form. "Oh, Gabrielle," he whispered, brushing a lock of hair off her cheek. "Maybe you're right. Maybe I should never have come here. Or at least I should have had the willpower to resist you." He listened for a moment to her light, easy breathing. She looked so peaceful, asleep like this, with all of the heartaches wiped from her face.

"But how could I resist? You came to me with open arms, with an open heart. You gave me your love and your honesty without any demands." He studied her delicate oval face, trying to recall the first moment he realized he loved her.

Gabrielle sighed in her sleep and turned on her side, oblivious to Alex's presence.

Alex smiled sadly in the semi-darkness. "I've half a mind to tie you to that sled and take you with me," he told her. "Because without you, I'll never be the man I could have been. I'll never be the man I was." He leaned over cautiously to brush his lips against hers, just once more. "I love you," he whispered. "I hope someday you'll realize just how much."

When Gabrielle woke in the morning, the room was empty. The fire was blazing in the fireplace, the cookstove was lit, a pot of coffee simmering on it, but Alex was gone.

"Alex!" she shouted leaping from the bed. "Alex?" She raced to the door, stepping out into the snow in her stocking feet. "Alex?"

Her dogs came running at the sound of her voice and pushed their muzzles against her, begging to be petted. It was a clear day, so cold that she could feel her own breath freezing as she released it. The cleared yard stood empty, except for the dogs and the sled tracks that ran north.

"Alex," she whispered once more. The cold brought her out of her stupor and forced her back inside the cabin. "You son-of-a-bitch," she murmured. "You didn't even say good-bye!"

Pouring herself a cup of strong coffee, she pulled a chair up to the fireplace and peeled off her wet socks. "You could have said good-bye!" She sat down and propped her feet on a wooden crate to warm them. She couldn't believe he was gone. He'd left her life as suddenly as he'd entered it.

She buried her face in her hands as the tears slipped down her cheeks. "Oh, Alex. Why did it have to be like this. I love you," she sobbed. "I still love you."

Long after her tears were spent, Gabrielle sat there, staring at the flames of the fire, wishing for what might have been. Finally, she roused herself. *I can't stay here all day,* she thought. *I'll go crazy!*

"I'll go see Jack and Mya, that's what I'll do," she said aloud. "You think that's good idea, Papa?"

God, she thought. *That's the first time I've talked to you like that since . . . since Alex came.* She groaned, getting up to pack her bag. She decided she'd walk instead of taking the sled. With her new snowshoes, she could make it in a few hours.

"I'm so glad to see you, Jack!" Gabrielle threw her arms around her old friend, startling him.

"Is something wrong, Gabe?" He stepped back to let her enter their tiny home. Built more like a hut than a cabin, with a dome roof and tree boughs, the place was only half the size of Gabrielle's. But the ancient woodstove was burning, and a warmth and friendliness reached out to envelope her.

"Wrong? No, nothing's wrong." She left her snow-shoes near the door and moved to the stove with her hands outstretched. "Where's Mya?"

"Her mother's." Jack eyed Gabrielle suspiciously. "You sure nothing's wrong?"

"We found the map," she said starkly.

Jack said nothing.

"Doesn't that surprise you?" She turned to face him, beginning to unbutton her parka.

"It does not." The Indian's face was void of emotion. "I told you the river would run with gold one day. You deserve it."

Gabrielle shook her head. "But you don't under-stand. I didn't want the map. I—" Her voice caught in her throat. "I gave the map to Alex and now—" She couldn't go on.

Jack helped her out of her camp parka. "And now?"

"Alex is gone," she blurted. "He's gone to find the gold. He left me."

Jack reached in the pocket of his shirt and pulled out a cigar. "I didn't know he was going to stay."

"Whose side are you on?" she shouted fiercely.

He gave no reaction except to lift a sooty eyebrow.

She ran a hand through her curly hair. "Oh, Jack. I'm sorry. I didn't mean to yell at you. It's just that . . ." She cast down her eyes, ashamed of her behavior.

"That you love the white man?"

She looked up at him. "Yes," she answered tiredly. "I love him."

"Then why didn't you go?" Jack pulled a small, crude bench closer to the stove and sat down, patting the spot beside him.

187

Gabrielle sat. "What do you mean? You know why. I hate the gold! I hate it!"

"You hate the gold more than you love the man?"

"It's not that simple, Jack. It's the principle of the thing."

He shrugged, opening the door of the stove to light his cigar. "I don't understand this principle, Gabe. I only understand that if you love him, you do what you have to. If you don't . . ." He shrugged again.

She twisted her mouth. "Now you sound like Alex. You know I can't go with him. If he finds the gold, he's going back to his Virginia."

"You are still afraid of Taylor?"

"Yes, I'm afraid of him!" She watched the flames of the fire through the door in the stove he'd left open.

"Want me to kill him?"

Gabrielle sighed, turning to look at Jack. "You really would, wouldn't you?" She studied his dark eyes.

He nodded, inhaling on the cigar that dangled from his mouth. "If it will make you happy."

"A part of me wants him dead, but a part of me . . ." She shook her head. "I just keep thinking he'll get his own one day." She folded her hands in her lap. "I just don't know what to do, Jack. About Alex, I mean. I'm afraid I'm never going to love anyone as much as I love him."

"Then go after him."

She looked at him wide-eyed. "I can't!"

"You can do what you want, Gabe."

She gave a laugh. "And what if we find the gold? Wouldn't I look silly at one of those fancy balls, dressed like a tart? I'd look so much like Alice LeBeau that you wouldn't be able to tell us apart!"

Jack grinned. "I knew your mother. You are nothing like her."

Gabrielle stared in indecision. "You'd want me to go, to leave you and Mary and Mya? Since when did you start liking Alex. I thought you hated him."

"I did not hate him. I was afraid for you. But now . . ." He pulled the cigar from his mouth. "After seeing you two together, I know your life can never be the same."

"You'd risk your life to be with him if you were me?"

Jack rolled his cigar in his thick fingers. "Life is a risk. Would you risk being unhappy forever to be safe and warm in your cabin?"

"What if Taylor comes after me?"

"Then you will kill him. But maybe he will not come after you. Maybe he is dead; maybe he has found better fishing ground. Maybe, maybe, maybe. . . . I don't know. I don't have the sight."

"You're not much help," Gabrielle muttered.

"All I can tell you is to follow your heart. It is what Rouge would have said."

She swallowed against the rising lump in her throat. Jack was right and she knew it. It was what Papa would have said. Even though he was against marriage, he would have wanted her to be happy. And he would have liked Alex. *Marriage?* she thought, laughing to herself. *Who'd ever said anything about marriage? Alex had made no proposal of marriage. But it doesn't matter,* she told herself with sudden resolution. *Jack is right. Life is full of risks.*

Gabrielle pushed herself up off the bench. "I'm going. I've got to talk to him."

Jack nodded, returning the cigar to his mouth. "You

know where he's headed? You want me to go?"

She reached for her parka, smiling. "I know where he is. If I leave in the morning and mush hard, I'll catch him by nightfall."

"You want me to take you back on my sled?" Jack stood up.

"Nah, you stay here where it's warm. With these new showshoes, I'll fly over the hard-pack." Stuffing her fists into her parka, her fingers flew over the buttons. "Thank you, Jack," she told him, picking up her snowshoes. On impulse she leaned forward and brushed her lips against his cheek. "You're a good friend."

Jack lifted his hand to touch the place on his cheek where she'd kissed him. He smiled, raising a hand to say good-bye, and closed the door behind her.

Gabrielle set out for home, moving at a grueling pace. It didn't matter that the sun was already setting; she knew her way between Jack's village and her own place like she knew her way around her cabin in the dark. The forest that surrounded the Tanana was familiar to her and its winter sounds comforting. She wasn't afraid of the crash of falling limbs or the haunting call of the great horned owl. All she could think of as she crossed the forest was Alex and being in his arms again.

When Gabrielle entered the clearing near her cabin, it was well after dark. She called to her dogs, and they came racing from behind the trees, their paws crunching in the snow. It was a black, moonless night, and she could barely make out their forms as they came bounding toward her.

"Hey! What's the matter with you?" She reached out

to them, scratching ears and patting backs. The dogs howled, pacing nervously in front of her, blocking her path.

Gabrielle pushed her way through the pack, laughing as they tripped her and nipped at her heels. "I don't know what's gotten into you," she told them as she reached the door. "You must need to get out!" She pushed Anthony aside, and he growled, deep in his throat.

Puzzled, Gabrielle pushed open the cabin door. As she stepped through, a hand shot out of the darkness, descending upon her. She screamed, trying to wrench free, and a hand clasped over her mouth. She kicked and flailed her arms as the door slammed shut behind her, locking out her growling, barking dogs.

Suddenly the room filled with light. The man who held her was Simone Parsons, the man who had almost killed Alex. "You son-of-a—"

Parsons slapped Gabrielle hard across the face, silencing her words. "Shut up, you little bitch," he whined. "Before I shut you up." He pinned her arms behind her.

"So, at last we meet again," a harsh voice rasped.

Parsons twisted her hands viciously, forcing her to turn around. "Taylor . . ." Gabrielle breathed.

Chapter Fourteen

"Surprised to see me, Miss LeBeau?" Lucas Taylor rested his arm on the mantel. "I told you back in that hotel in Seattle that you'd not heard the last of me. You know Parsons, of course, and this is Lawrence and Gaddy . . . friends of mine."

She eyed the rough-looking henchmen, calculating her chances of getting out of the cabin alive. "What are you doing in here?" she demanded through clenched teeth. She strained against her captor, trying to jerk her hands free.

"What do you think?" Taylor smirked. "Let her go, Parsons. That is if she promises to be a good girl. . . ." He looked up at her, waiting for a response.

Gabrielle nodded her head in agreement, but the instant Parsons released her, she spun around bringing her knee up sharply to his groin. He groaned, doubling over, and she clasped her hands together, hitting him over the head. She had almost made her way over his prone body when one of Taylor's other companions caught her by the arm and swung her around.

"Oh, no you don't, you little whore." The blond, pig-tailed man, Lawrence, jerked her hard against him, pulling her back over Simone's body and away from the cabin door.

"Call me a whore, you son-of-a-bitch!" Gabrielle swung her right fist, catching the man square in the jaw.

Lawrence laughed, rubbing his jaw, then swung easily, catching Gabrielle in the side of the face. She went down under his blow, crying out against her will. Lawrence yanked her back on her feet by the collar of her parka and drew back his hand to hit her again as Taylor spoke up.

"That's enough, Lawrence," he said dryly. He hadn't moved from the spot near the fireplace; his arm still rested on the mantel. "Maybe you can have her later."

Lawrence lowered his fist slowly, reluctantly. He grinned, his dark eyes glittering with sadistic pleasure. "Just tryin' to teach her a lesson, boss. Put 'er in 'er place."

Gabrielle panted, trying to catch her breath. The wind had been knocked out of her when Lawrence hit her, and her head was reeling. "What do you want with me?" She raised her hand to touch her injured cheek. The bruised flesh was already tender.

"Come, come, you know what I want." Taylor stroked his clean-shaven chin. Some might have thought he was handsome with his pitch-black eyes and well-defined jaw, but all Gabrielle could see was the aquiline nose and the twist of his mouth as he spoke. He was the man of her ghoulish nightmares.

She lifted an eyebrow in defiance. "I assure you, I don't. I have nothing you could possibly want."

He lunged forward. "You have the map!"

Gabrielle refused to flinch, though his face was suddenly only inches from hers. "I told you. There is no map; there never was."

"Your father—"

"My father," she interrupted, "was a drunk and a liar, and you, sir, are a fool to have believed him!"

Taylor lifted a thick forefinger, pressing it into her parka. "You had better learn some respect, Miss LeBeau, for myself as well as for your deceased father."

His eyes were suddenly devoid of any humanity, and an uneasiness swelled in Gabrielle's chest. The stark realization came to her that she would likely die at this man's hands, and the thought turned her fear to anger. What right did one man have to ruin so many lives? Though there had been a time in her life, right after her father was killed, that she wished she was dead, her desire to live was overwhelming. She wanted Alex and a life with him, and she'd not give it up so easily.

Gabrielle lowered her gaze to the floor, deciding to be more cautious. "So what are we going to do about this, Taylor? You say there's a map. I say there isn't."

He waved Lawrence away, grabbing her arm with one hand. His fingers sank through the thick material of her parka, biting her flesh. "Guess we'll have to look for it ourselves."

"No!" Gabrielle shouted. She could imagine what they would do to her cabin, her supplies, looking for it. "If I had the map, don't you think I'd have found the gold by now?" she reasoned. "Do you see any gold? Do you even see any mining equipment?"

Taylor released her arm, letting her stand on her own. "Maybe not. Your father told me you didn't take to the gold like some. But he said you'd come around, and when you did, you'd have the map."

Gabrielle sighed heavily, letting her eyes drift shut for a moment. *Alex,* her mind screamed. *Jack, anyone . . . please help me.* She knew she couldn't tell them where the map really was. They'd track Alex down and kill him in cold blood. She opened her eyes. "So go ahead and look for the map. I'm telling you, it's not here, but you're welcome to look."

Taylor grinned. "We intend to." With a nod of his head, Parsons and the other two men pulled long hunting knives from their belts and began ripping through the cabin. They emptied her crates of supplies on the floor, cutting open the cloth bags of salt, sugar and flour. They strewed her clothes across the room, emptying her crates of personal belongings. They found her father's last bottle of whiskey and drank it, laughing as they ripped through a lifetime of possessions.

It was all Gabrielle could do to keep from crying as she watched a year's worth of supplies being dumped on the floor. They would barely leave enough provisions for her to get through the winter, but she refused to let them see any weakness in her. She stood stock-still in the middle of the room as pandemonium reigned around her.

Finally, Parsons approached Taylor. "She's right, it's not here, boss."

Taylor grunted, giving a nod. "If it was my map, I don't guess I'd keep it here, either." He reached for his own parka that hung on the peg on the wall. "All right. Blindfold her and get her on the sled. We can't stay here. That Indian is liable to come by sticking his nose into things, and then we'd have to kill him, too."

Parsons nodded, seizing Gabrielle by the arm and giving her a shove. "Let's go, bitch."

This time she gave no trouble. She knew she couldn't overpower her captors, but if she was careful, she had a chance of outsmarting them. And when she did, they'd all pay. . . .

Alex sighed, tossing a twig into the blazing fire. He'd made good time today, nearly twenty miles, he guessed. He'd pushed the dogs hard, trying to tire himself, attempting to drive Gabrielle from his mind. He hadn't set up camp until well after dark; and now the dogs were fed and watered, and it was time to turn in.

Alex stretched his legs, holding out his hands to warm them. The trouble was, he wasn't sleepy. He was tired, bone tired; his legs ached from running, and his arms throbbed from hanging on to the back of the sled; but he knew he couldn't sleep. Gabrielle haunted his thoughts. He heard her lilting voice in the wind; he saw her form around every bend of the river. He knew he'd done the right thing in leaving her behind. Unconsciously he patted the worn map in his breast pocket. She'd given it to him free and clear, and it was his passage back to Richmond. He knew the map would lead to a mother lode of gold. He could feel it in his bones.

Then what's bothering me? he asked himself. *I told her I couldn't stay; I told her nothing could be permanent between us and she agreed. She said she wanted no ties. She said she was happy with her life and wanted no changes.* Still, all he could think of was her wide, sad brown eyes and the tremble of her sweet lips as she accused him of betrayal. Alex gazed off into the darkness, studying the trees that swayed gently casting long fingers of shadow over him and his sleeping dogs. Earlier the sky had been an inky black, but then the moon had slipped from behind the clouds to shine bright, reflecting off the snow.

Alex stretched out on his bed roll, resting his head on Leopold. The dog whined, licking his new master's face, then laid his head down again. "What am I going to do, Leo, old boy? Will I ever forgive myself for leaving the little minx behind, whether she wanted to come or not?"

The dog lifted his head, blinking sleepily, and Alex reached back to stroke his thick coat. "You listening to me, Leo? I should have asked her to marry me; that's what I should have done. Of course, what reason would she have had to say yes? I'm a penniless man with no future and a child to raise." He stared up at the three-quarters moon above. "We'd have to live in Richmond. She'd hate it there." He exhaled slowly. "So why am I so miserable? Tell me that?"

He pictured Gabrielle asleep, alone in her narrow bed and thought of the moments he'd shared with her there. *You can't let her go,* an inner voice warned. *You'll regret it for the rest of your life.*

Alex suddenly scrambled up off his bed roll. "Leo, come on boy, get up," he ordered. "We're going home."

Quickly, Alex packed the sled and harnessed his dogs, dousing the fire with armfuls of snow. Within half an hour he was on his way south again along the riverbank. The dogs, fed and rested, yiped with excitement as they bounded across the hard-packed snow, pulling the sled and Alex aboard behind them. If

198

his calculations were right, he figured he could be at Gabrielle's cabin by mid-morning if nothing went awry. He might even get there before she woke.

Visions of slipping into bed beside Gabrielle's naked body warmed Alex's heart as he called out to the dogs, urging them faster. He didn't know what he'd say to her when he got there. He didn't know how he would convince her they belonged together or how they would settle their differences. He didn't care. All he wanted right now was to have his Gabrielle in his arms again.

The trip back down the river was not as easy as Alex had anticipated. In his rush to get back to the cabin, the dogs got tangled more than once in their traces, and twice he lost the path and veered west, then had to retrace his steps. The sun was climbing high in the sky by the time he reached the cabin's clearing.

Gabrielle's dogs came rushing toward the sled, barking and howling at the sight of the familiar face. Alex laughed, trying to release his own dogs from their harnesses without getting knocked into the snow. Finally, when all five dogs had been set free, he started for the cabin door. He hoped Gabrielle would be inside, but because she hadn't come to the door, he guessed she'd gone fishing or to tend her traps. "Gabrielle," he called.

A sharp howl of a dog came from behind the cabin, and Alex stopped to listen. The mournful sound repeated itself, and Alex started around the back of the cabin. There he found Tristan tied to a metal stake. Gabrielle's lead dog barked and howled, pawing at the snow. Puzzled, Alex slipped a knife from his belt and cut the rope that held the dog tethered.

"What's the matter, boy?" He tried to catch Tristan's

collar, but the dog leaped past him, racing around the corner of the cabin. Alex followed him suspiciously. Why would Gabrielle have tied her favorite dog like that? And on such a short length of rope? It didn't make sense, and it worried him.

Coming back to the front of the cabin, Alex found Tristan scratching at the door. Cautiously, he turned the knob on the door, letting the dog in first. As light flooded the room, he swore beneath his breath. Tristan pranced in circles, sniffing and pawing at the hardwood floor.

The place was in a shambles, flour spilled onto the floor, pots and pans strewn recklessly; there were even ashes piled in the middle of the table. "My God," Alex breathed. "The map! That bastard came looking for the map!"

Calling the dog, Alex stepped outside, closing the door behind him. Rage seethed within him as he harnessed his dogs again. He had to find Jack. He would know what to do, in what direction to go looking for Gabrielle. Leaping into the back of the sled, Alex called to the other dogs, coaxing them to run behind the sled. He was afraid to leave them there for fear of them starving while he was gone or getting caught in the storm he saw brewing in the west. Mya would care for them in the village. He didn't know how long it would take, but he was going to track down that filthy rat Taylor, who had kidnapped Gabrielle, and then he was going to kill him.

Jack listened to Alex's tale, his face void of any emotion. "It was good to come here first." The Indian nodded, beginning to collect a knapsack of necessities.

Mya sat on a stool near the stove, their daughter on her lap. "How long ago do you think they took her?"

Alex brushed his auburn hair off his creased brow. "I don't know. I'm not much good at reading signs in the snow. I'm not even positive it was Taylor who took her."

Jack gave a snort. "It was him. No one on the Tanana would dare it." He got down on his knees and pulled two rifles from beneath a bed. Ammunition and two large hunting knives followed. "You know what to do with one of these?" He held up the long-bladed knife, its steel gleaming by the light of the lantern.

Alex reached for it, replacing the smaller knife on his belt. "I learned to handle one on the whaling ship. Did a little carving, a little throwing. Got pretty good."

Jack slipped a sweater over his head and reached for his seal-skin parka, directing his words to Mya. "I don't know how long we'll be gone. We're going to go by and pick up Magee, then back to Gabe's to check the signs. I expect they took her south. No tenderfoot would travel north with a storm like this coming up. They must have a cabin they're hiding her out in."

Mya got up, brushing her hand against her husband's sleeve. "You watch the storm. My mother feels a bad one coming. You will do no good for our Gabrielle frozen in a snowbank."

Jack gave her the briefest smile, caressing her round cheek. "I'll take care, wife."

"And bring home Gabe?"

"And bring home Gabe," he answered. Swinging Mary into his arms, he kissed the child and handed her to her mother. "Let's go, Alex."

Mya made a motion in the air as the two men left the warmth of her cabin. "May the spirits be with you," she whispered as they disappeared into a whirl of falling snow.

Alex and Jack drove their dogsleds hard across the frozen Tanana and westward into the storm. They reached Beans Magee's at nightfall, waited until he gathered his gear and hitched his sled and then they headed for Gabrielle's cabin.

Jack ran behind his sled as long as he could, and when his legs ached to the point that they grew wobbly, he leaped onto the runners to catch a ride. He talked to the dogs as they ran, constantly encouraging them, just as Gabrielle had instructed he must do. He yanked at the string of bones tied beneath the sled, urging them forward with the clatter-clatter they made. Most white men used bells on the Tanana, Gabrielle had told him, but she preferred the natives' strings of fish bones or antler pieces.

Through the darkness the three sled teams raced, each taking its turn in the lead, breaking fresh snow for the two behind. Alex cursed the darkness as they pressed on, the snowstorm closing in around them. It was difficult for him to believe that daylight lasted less than six hours in the winter in this frozen territory. It hadn't bothered him when he was with Gabrielle, safe and warm in her cabin most of the time, but now it seemed an insurmountable obstacle. How were they going to find her with a good fifteen hours of darkness ahead of them? How would they even know which way to begin their search?

Alex's feet grew numb, and he leaped off the runners of the sled, running again. The blowing snow surrounded them, the wind whistling and howling until he lost all sense of direction. Only the sound of Jack's dogs ahead and the clatter of the bone strings on his sled kept Alex on the trail. By the time they reached Gabrielle's cabin, a full-fledged storm was upon them. The air was so cold that it burned Alex's lungs as he fumbled with the harnesses to release his dogs.

"Should we bring them into the cabin?" Alex called to Jack through the driving wind.

The native shook his head. "They'll bury themselves in the snow. They'll be warmer than we will." His words were practically lost in the wind, but Alex caught enough to understand.

By the time the three men got inside Gabrielle's cabin, they were nearly frozen. Alex fumbled in the darkness to light a match, finally managing to work his stiff fingers enough to strike one. The smell of sulfur filled the small cabin as he found the lantern on the floor near the fireplace and lit it.

Jack stomped his feet for warmth, stooping to pick a piece of firewood from the center of the floor. "We'll not be starting out tonight," he stated flatly, carrying the wood to the fireplace. "Might as well light up your smokes, 'cause it looks like we're going to be sitting a spell."

"What do you mean?" Alex peeled off his frozen parka, letting it fall among the other belongings littering the floor. "We can't just sit here. We've got to find Gabrielle."

Beans shucked off his parka and kneeled to start a fire in the fireplace. "Not tonight we don't. We'll freeze before we make five miles."

Alex clenched his fists in desperation. "You're not

even going to try?"

Jack lifted a hand to squeeze Alex's arm. "It's like Mya told me. We'll be no good to Gabe dead. She's safe enough for now. They're not going to kill her without the map."

"How can you speak about this so calmly?" Alex flared. "This is Gabrielle we're talking about!"

Magee fed the feeble flames on the hearth. "No way to take it but calmly. Gabe's a strong woman. She'll know just to hold out until we reach her. She'll know we're coming for her." He uprighted a chair that had been pushed on its side.

Alex heaved a sigh of frustration. "You're right; I know you're right." He was silent for a moment, listening to the mournful wail of the wind as it whipped around the cabin. "But if something happens to her, I'll . . ." He let his voice trail off into silence.

Beans Magee stood up, pushing his long mane of blond hair off his shoulder. His eyes met Alex's. "I know, son," he consoled. "I know."

Chapter Fifteen

Gabrielle struggled to keep her head up, but as she slipped in and out of consciousness, it rolled and lulled to one side, making her entire body ache. Coming fully awake, she twisted her hands tied behind her, trying to bring back some of the feeling. How long had she been tied to this chair?

Days had passed, she was sure of that, but how many? Two . . . maybe three? There was no sense of day or night in the cabin with the lanterns burning constantly and no sunlight seeping through the tiny windows. Since the storm had begun, three of her four captors had kept themselves busy playing cards on the floor and drinking whiskey. Only Taylor abstained, keeping to himself on a bunk built on the far wall.

Gabrielle turned her head to look over at him. "Bastard," she murmured to herself.

He was just lying there, staring at the wooden rafters above him. He hadn't decided what to do with her yet. She knew he had expected her to just hand over the map, but when she refused to change her story, he had grown dark and brooding. Taylor knew she had the map and that she was lying; he just hadn't figured out how to get the information out of her. He hadn't allowed anyone to give her any food, and her sips of water had been minimal; she knew he was hoping she'd grow weak and crumble. Other than an occasional slap across the face, he hadn't hurt her, though he'd threatened far worse.

Raucous laughter filled the squatter's cabin, and Taylor shot a threatening glance in his men's direction. "Pipe down," he ordered, "or I'll burn the cards."

Gabrielle turned away to avoid eye contact with him. He was growing impatient with the storm outside as well as with her. She knew she walked a fine line between life and death now, and she was trying not to rile his anger any more than necessary. Until she could figure out a way to escape, she had to keep herself alive. She had toyed with the idea that Jack might come looking for her, but she knew the chance was remote. It might be days before he came by her cabin to see her, and then where would he start looking once he found she was gone? No, it was up to her to save herself. Maybe once they were out of this cabin and moving again, she'd have a chance. If she could get one of their dogsleds from them, she knew she could get away.

Her eyes drifted shut as she thought of her own dogs. Where would they find food? And poor Tristan. Her captors had apparently tied him up to keep him from mauling them. She wondered if the dog was still alive. If only she hadn't driven Alex away the way she did. If she had had the damned map, she'd have given it to Taylor and saved herself and Alex both.

Alex . . . tears welled in her eyes as she thought of

him . . . his startling blue eyes, his thick red hair, the smile on his handsome face. She swallowed against the rising lump in her throat, wondering how he'd made out in the storm. If he remembered everything she'd told him, he'd be all right. He had to be.

Gabrielle's eyes flew open at the sound of boots on the hard-wood floor. It was Lawrence, the pig-tailed man. "So little lady." He cupped her chin with his hand, forcing her face upward. "Come up with any ideas where that gold map might be?"

Gabrielle squeezed her eyes shut, struggling to wrench away.

When she didn't answer, he squeezed tighter, threatening to break her jaw with his massive hand. "I'm speaking to you!" he growled.

Her eyes flew open. The man reeked of whiskey and stale body odor. His breath was foul. "I told you, there's no map," she whispered.

"What did you say?"

"I said there's no map," she repeated through clenched teeth.

He grinned, releasing her. His pitch eyes were void of any humanity. "You'd best be tellin' us, little lady, because Mr. Lucas Taylor is getting annoyed with you. He's going to turn you over to me, and then I'll make you talk." He laughed wickedly, fingering a tendril of her chestnut hair.

"Lawrence," Taylor called from his bunk. "What did I tell you about leaving her alone?"

Gabrielle jerked back, and Lawrence walked away. She heaved a sigh of relief as he settled himself down beside Gaddy and motioned to be dealt into the game.

"He's right, you know." Taylor pushed himself up

off the bunk and came toward her. His gait was slow and lazy; his gaze riveting her eyes to his. He smoothed the expensive angora sweater he wore as he came closer, a silly smile on his face. "You can make it easy for yourself, or you can make it difficult."

Never let them know you're afraid . . . her father's words rang clear and true in her ears. "I'm telling you, Taylor. There never was a map." She kept her voice steady, refusing to drop her gaze. "You should have done a little investigating before you murdered my father."

"He was cheating. He pulled the gun on me."

"Liar! I was there . . . remember?"

Taylor's face reddened with checked anger. "And who believed you?" His firm mouth twitched into a smile. "Certainly not the authorities."

"Only because you paid them off you son-of-a—"

"Ah ah ah," he interrupted, pressing a finger to her lips. "What did I tell you about your language? A sweet virgin like you shouldn't even know such words." He slipped his finger from her lips across her bruised cheek, lowering his voice. "You *are* a virgin aren't you, Gabrielle?"

She flinched against her will. A chilling blade of terror ran down her spine.

Taylor took her silence as affirmation. "Good, because when I get that map, what I had in mind was—" He broke off, withdrawing his hand. "Let's just let it be a surprise, shall we?"

Gabrielle swallowed hard, shifting her gaze to the floor. *Alex,* her mind cried out, *Alex help me!*

*　　　*　　　*

Alex lowered his head against the driving wind, running in the fresh sled tracks. After two days of holding up in Gabrielle's cabin, he had convinced Jack and Beans that they had to start searching for her. Though the snow was still flying, the wind had shifted course this morning, raising the temperature to near zero degrees. At his insistence, they had left the cabin with the first blade of dim sunlight.

Gabrielle was out there, he knew it. And she was somewhere near by; she had to be.

From the state of Gabrielle's cabin, Jack guessed that Taylor had several men with him, experienced men. They would have had to be to have gotten up river in the middle of the winter like this. But he also guessed that they were not from nearby, otherwise they would have come for Gabrielle sooner. Taylor must have come after her shortly after she left Seattle. It had just taken him this long to track her down and hire men to help him.

Alex covered his mouth with his hand, breathing into the wool mitten to thaw the ice forming on his growing beard. Speeding up, he hopped on the back of his sled, glancing behind him to check on Beans Magee taking up the rear. Jack was just ahead of him, running in his own sled tracks. Alex shook his head. The short, plump Indian was amazing. He never rode on the sled, never slowed down. He was a machine that plodded through the snow, his head lowered, his hands swinging at his sides. Alex guessed he could run all day and into the night without any trouble.

Earlier in the day they had approached a cabin south of Gabrielle's. The trapper who lived there knew her, but nothing of her disappearance. He told Jack that he

209

had heard male voices and two sleds pass by just before the storm hit two days ago. His suggestion was to check a cabin some four or five miles south on the west bank. He said a month back he had passed it and seen smoke rising from the chimney. When he went to greet the newcomer, his welcome had been far from friendly. A man with long blond hair had run him off with a shotgun.

Alex knew it was a long shot, but what choice did they have but to mush in that direction and pray that luck was with them and the kidnappers hadn't been able to outrun the storm. If they weren't in that cabin, Jack said they could be anywhere; it might take until spring to find them, and then there would be no guarantee they still had Gabrielle. If Taylor had murdered Rouge out of greed, he would have no qualms about killing Gabrielle.

That thought made Alex sick in the pit of his stomach. Why had he left her behind? He should have made her come with him upriver, or not gone at all. He groaned inwardly, ducking to miss a low lying branch as his dogs pulled the sled into a small clearing and down another crude path. *If I find Gabrielle,* he promised himself, *I'll make it work. We'll go after the gold together, and we'll go home to Richmond. I'll prove my love to her and make her want to come with me.* Images of Gabrielle flashed through his mind as he dropped one leg to the ground and gave a push, aiding the dogs. He thought of her thick chestnut hair, her upturned mouth, the haughty sound of her voice. God, but he loved her. . . .

Jack's sled up ahead slowed and came to a stop, bringing Alex out of his daze. "The cabin can't be more

210

than half a mile from here," Jack told Alex. "We go on foot from here. You have snowshoes?"

Alex nodded, digging into the bags he carried on his sled. "But why not take the sled in? It'll be faster."

Jack shook his head, fitting his own snowshoes onto his boots. "They'll hear the dogs. This way we take them by surprise."

Alex sighed. It was already growing dark, and the snow had stopped more than an hour ago. What if they reached the cabin and Gabrielle was already gone? What if she'd never been there? He pushed the thoughts from his mind, strapping on his snowshoes. When he was finished, he followed Jack's and Bean's lead, unharnessing his dogs and tying them all to a tree with one piece of rope he looped through their collars. Feeding them each a handful of frozen fish chunks, he fell in behind Jack and Beans, moving south.

Gabrielle was startled awake by an iron grip on her arm. "Wake up," a voice urged.

Her eyes flew open. "What? What do you want?" She squinted against the bright light of the lantern held in front of her face. It was Lawrence's buddy, Gaddy.

"Time to wake up, missy. Snow's stopped, and Taylor says we're movin' out!"

She glared up at him, blinking the sleep from her eyes. "Storm's passed?"

"Yup." He set the lantern on the floor and began to work at the knot that bound her hands to the back of the wooden chair. He had no more loosened the rope and slipped it from the chair rail when he was binding her hands together again.

211

Gabrielle gasped as he lifted her to her feet. Against her will, she swayed, almost toppling into him. Gaddy laughed, catching her gently around the waist. "Fallen for me, have you, missy?"

She struggled to upright herself, embarrassed by her weak-kneed state. "How do you expect a person to walk with her ankles tied together?"

He released her, giving her a broken-toothed grin. "Boss's orders. I'm to carry ya."

"The hell you will!" She started forward, inching one boot in front of the other.

Gaddy watched her for a minute. "Come on, let me carry ya. I ain't gonna harm ya."

She glared at him. "You don't think kidnapping is harming someone?"

He looked up to be sure no one else had reentered the cabin. "Weren't my idea. They didn't tell me they was gonna take you. We was just supposed to get that gold map." He scuffed at the floor with his boot. "I ain't never hurt a lady before. Killed a few men, but never hurt a lady."

"Got a heart of gold, have you?" She pushed another foot forward, heading slowly for the door. "If you're such a gentleman, how about loosening these ropes? They're cutting into my wrists." She looked up at him.

He shook his head frantically. "Oh, no. Lawrence, he told me to untie you from the chair, rope you back up again and carry you out to the sled. They got them all hitched up waitin'. If I don't do what Lawrence says, he'll kill me!" The huge man bobbed his dark head up and down.

Gabrielle turned away. "Then you're just as bad as the rest of them, Gaddy."

212

He followed after her. "Look, if you'd just tell 'em where the map is, I'd make 'em let you go. I wouldn't let Mr. Taylor sell you to that whore house."

Her breath caught in her throat. "That's what he's going to do with me?"

"Lawrence wants ya for himself. The two argued over ya, but Mr. Taylor, he's the boss, so he does the decidin'."

Gabrielle could feel herself swaying where she stood. The lack of food and water and decent sleep had taken a toll on her. If she didn't escape soon, she wouldn't have the energy to do it. She spoke in a tired voice. "Gaddy, I'm awful thirsty. Could you get me a drink of water?"

The man stroked his beard in indecision. "I was told not to give you nothin'."

"Come on, I can't escape by drinking a cup of water."

With a quick nod, Gaddy crossed the room, bringing her a tin cup of water. He held the cup to her lips, letting her drink.

Gabrielle drained the cup. "Thank you," she murmured.

Hesitantly, he reached out to button up her parka. "It's cold out there. Where's your mittens?"

She motioned with her head. "Lawrence put them in my pocket." She watched him as he dug in the side pocket of her parka and extracted the thick wool mittens. He moved hesitantly, almost in awe of her. *He might be my way out of this,* she told herself. *He's not like the others. He's no angel, but he probably wouldn't hurt me.* "Hey, Gaddy," she whispered softly.

He looked up, startled by the soft, feminine voice. "Yea?"

Before she could speak again, Lawrence stuck his head in the cabin door. "What are you doin' in there, Gaddy? Get your ass out here and bring the girl!"

Gaddy gulped. "Yea, Lawrence. I'm comin'." He leaned to scoop Gabrielle into his arms. "Sorry. But I gotta do what he says."

"Why? Why do you have to do what he says, Gaddy?"

The bear of a man stood holding her in his arms. "I don't know, I just do. I always done what Lawrence told me."

"Help me, Gaddy," Gabrielle begged. "I'll pay you, more than Taylor's paying you. You name the price."

He moved toward the door. "I don't know, missy. I sure like ya, but—"

Suddenly there was a masculine shout from outside the door and the echo of a rifle shot. Gaddy immediately set her on her feet, grabbing a rifle near the door.

"What is it?" she demanded.

"I don't know." He flattened himself against the wall, peering out the door. "You stay put."

"No, Gaddy." She struggled to follow him. "You've got to let me loose." Another shot cracked in the air, followed by two more. Outside the cabin she could hear Taylor shouting to Parsons and Lawrence. She didn't know who was out there; she prayed it was Jack. But whoever it was, this was her chance to escape.

Gaddy shook his head. "I let you go, and you'll run off. Taylor'll shoot you before he lets you go."

"I'd rather be shot dead in the snow than sold to a whore house on the docks in Seattle." Her voice was desperate. "Please, Gaddy."

214

The straggly-bearded man hesitated for a moment, then slipped a knife from his belt. "He's gonna kill me, he's gonna kill me," he muttered beneath his breath as he sawed at the bindings at her feet. As soon as they were cut, he started on her hands.

"Thank you! Thank you!" Her hands trembled as he pulled on the last of the rope that bound her hands behind her. Rubbing her wrists to bring back the feeling, she peered out the tiny window of the cabin. "A gun, Gaddy. I've got to have a gun if I'm going to get out alive." Rifles fired on and off, bullets ricocheting in the trees.

"Oh, no. This is the only gun I got. You can't have it, missy." He pressed himself against the wall, starting for the door. "Now you give me a minute and then you get, you understand me?"

She nodded numbly. "Can you see who's shooting at them?"

He shook his head. "Naw, they're hidin' in the trees." With one last glance in her direction, Gaddy slipped out the door.

Gabrielle watched him through the window. He ducked out the door and threw himself into the snow behind a woodpile.

"Where's the girl?" Lawrence shouted from the cover of the trees.

"Inside," Gaddy answered. Just then, another shot rang out, splintering the wood above his head. Lawrence's reply was lost to Gabrielle as the men opened fire on their assailants hiding in the brush just beyond the cabin.

Hands shaking, Gabrielle pulled up the hood of her parka and laced it tightly. She was without a weapon, no food, no water, but she could make it home if she could just escape her captors. Taking a deep breath, she stepped outside the cabin door.

"Gabrielle!" came Alex's voice from the brush.

She froze for a moment in shock. "Alex!" she screamed. Bullets rang in the trees again, and she threw herself to the ground.

"Get out of the way," he shouted, reloading his rifle.

"You son-of-a-bitch, Gaddy! I'll skin you alive," Taylor barked from the corner of the cabin. "What's she doing untied?"

Gaddy stuttered. "I . . . I don't know, boss!"

"You get across there and get ahold of her before I shoot you myself!" Taylor ordered.

Throwing a pleading glance in Gaddy's direction, Gabrielle began to crawl toward Alex's voice. She dragged her body through the snow, trying to ignore the sound of bullets ringing over her head.

Alex reloaded again from behind a great evergreen, giving Jack a nudge. "I've got to go in after her, Jack. One of them's going to kill her."

Jack gave a nod. "You be careful. I'll cover you."

Slowly Alex moved through the trees, making his way toward the side of the cabin. A man in a parka leaped from behind the trees, racing toward Gabrielle, and then a shot sounded. The man crumbled to the ground, staining the snow crimson. In the semi-darkness, he spotted Beans Magee behind him, flashing a grin. Alex gave a nod, moving closer to the cabin.

Suddenly a pig-tailed blond came out of the trees, headed straight for Gabrielle. "Alex," she screamed as

216

she stood up to run.

In an instant Gaddy was on his feet, aiming for Lawrence. "Don't you touch her, Lawrence!" His voice rang through the trees as he pulled the trigger on his rifle.

Lawrence fell to the ground under the impact of his friend's bullet, clutching his arm. Taylor came around the side of the cabin, aiming his rifle at Gaddy's back.

"Gaddy! Look out," Gabrielle shouted. But it was too late. Taylor fired twice, and Gaddy fell into the snow, face first.

Before Alex could reach Gabrielle, the man who had been shot in the arm was upon her. He grabbed her around the waist, dragging her toward the cabin. Gabrielle screamed, kicking and swinging her fists as she tried to escape his iron grip.

Alex lifted his rifle to take aim but immediately saw that he would risk Gabrielle's life by trying to shoot her captor. Cursing beneath his breath, Alex reloaded his rifle to stalk him. "You get the other one," he shouted to Jack over his shoulder as he flattened his body against the hand-hewn outer wall of the cabin.

Easing himself along the wall, Alex listened intently. "Gabrielle, I'm coming," he shouted.

"No, no," she cried. "He'll kill you. Get back, Alex."

Inside, Lawrence was dragging her toward the rear of the cabin. He'd lost his rifle but held a pistol to her head. "You shut up and stop that screamin' before I shut you up." He shook her so hard that it jarred her teeth.

Just then Alex burst into the room, a rifle poised in his hands.

"Drop it," Lawrence ordered. "Or I kill the bitch."

Alex took a deep breath, slowly lowering his rifle.

"No! No!" Gabrielle called. "He'll kill you, Alex. He's crazy!"

Lawrence's laughter echoed in the cabin as Alex's rifle hit the floor with a dull thud. "She's right you know," he said. "I am gonna kill you."

Chapter Sixteen

Alex's eyes narrowed as he stared at the pig-tailed man that held Gabrielle captive. Slowly he lowered his hands to his sides. "Release her, now!" his voice thundered.

Lawrence tipped back his head, his laughter harsh and threatening. "For a man who's gonna die, you're pretty calm, mister." He tightened his hold around Gabrielle's neck, and she gasped for breath.

"Alex," she moaned, pulling at Lawrence's arm. Her mind was confused, her vision growing blurry. In another minute she knew she'd faint from lack of air. She looked to Alex standing there motionless, a hell-bent look on his face. *Dear God, doesn't he know he's about to die?*

"I'll tell you where the map is, if you let her go," Alex enticed. He tried to ignore Gabrielle, concentrating on the captor's movements and Jack's knife belted to his own leg.

Lawrence loosened his grip slightly with interest. "What do you know about the map? Who the hell are you?" He drew back the pistol but still held Gabrielle tight in his arm.

"She's my woman. I took the map from her for myself." His voice became gruff and agitated as he took on the persona of a man not to be crossed.

"Then hand it over," Lawrence ordered.

It was Alex's turn to laugh. "You think I'd be carryin' it around, as much as it's worth?" He moved his right hand slightly, inching toward the long-bladed knife.

"Then go get it."

"Oh, no," Alex told him with clear, hard precision. "You've got to let the girl go first. I told you she's mine; she has nothing to do with this. This deal is going to have to be between you and me."

Lawrence smiled wickedly. Tightening his hold on Gabrielle, he pressed the barrel of the gun against her head. "You get it, or she dies."

Gabrielle whimpered but held herself perfectly still, squeezing her eyes shut. She had seen Alex's hand on the hilt of his knife. *Now,* her mind cried out silently. *Do it now!*

Lawrence spotted the knife in Alex's hand a second too late. The pig-tailed giant of a man cried out as the knife whipped through the air. He meant to pull the trigger on his pistol, but his reflexes were too slow. The well-aimed knife cut through the fabric of his parka, sinking deep into his chest. Lawrence loosened his grip on Gabrielle, the gun slipping from his fingers. A look of surprise passed over his face as he fell to the floor, his head hitting the cabin wall with a sickening thud.

Gabrielle crumbled to the floor beside the dead man, gasping for breath. Alex was beside her in an instant, cradling her in his arms.

"Gabrielle," he breathed, brushing a lock of hair off her cheek. "Gabrielle, are you all right? Can you hear me, love?"

She lifted her lashes, her dark gaze meeting a stormy ocean of blue. "Alex," she whispered. "He was going to kill you." A sob escaped her throat. "I was so afraid he was going to kill you."

"Shhh," he hushed, holding her tight against his chest. "It's all right, Gabrielle. I'm alive. I'm here."

"You came back." She clung to him desperately, inhaling his familiar heady scent. "I thought you were gone. You left me; I thought you were never coming back."

"I couldn't leave you. I couldn't do it." He showered her dirty face with kisses. "I could never leave you. I love you; I love you too much."

"Alex, Gabrielle?" Jack's voice came from the door.

"Did you get Taylor?" Alex stood up, lifting Gabrielle easily in his arms. She looped her hands around his neck, too weary to protest.

"He got away. Beans was hit, just a flesh wound, but while I was tending him, that bastard Taylor got away on a sled." His wide frame filled the doorway. "She all right?"

Alex gave a nod. "Pretty weak, but I don't think they hurt her."

Gabrielle held tightly to Alex, only half hearing their words. All she cared about at this moment was being safe in Alex's arms. Her heart sang with happiness. He'd come back to her! He came back!

Jack gestured behind him. "The man Beans killed was the one that beat you up."

"Parsons?" Alex's eyes grew dark. "You sure?"

221

"You can check, but I think so. Looks to me like the same man who came with you that day to buy supplies."

Alex cursed beneath his breath. "Hope he goes straight to hell." He pushed at Lawrence's body with the toe of his boot. "This one's dead, too. You haul him out while I see to Gabrielle. Then we'll have a look at Beans." He took control of the situation with ease, and Jack didn't question him.

Laying Gabrielle down gently on the bunk against the wall, Alex unbuttoned her parka. Her face was ashen, her chestnut hair dirty and tangled. "You scared me to death," he whispered.

"Me? *You* were the dead man, Mr. Alexander." She lifted her heavy lashes to study his face. Slowly she reached out to stroke his red-bearded chin. "What's all of this fuzz?" She laughed tiredly, letting him take off her parka and tuck it around her.

His hand went to his growing beard. "I've been a little too busy to shave these last few days." He gave her a smile. "Now you go to sleep while we get rid of him"—he gestured to Lawrence's body—"and fix Beans up."

"Beans? He's here?" She sat up, but Alex pushed her back down.

"Didn't you hear Jack? Beans Magee is going to be fine. Just a flesh wound."

"Taylor got away did he?" She closed her eyes, succumbing to the overwhelming exhaustion that washed over her.

"Sorry. We meant to kill him, but maybe we scared him off."

Gabrielle exhaled slowly, entwining her fingers in

222

Alex's. "I hope so . . . dear God, I hope so."

Alex sat with her until she fell asleep and then went to look for Jack and Beans. He found them outside; Beans was leaning against the woodpile while Jack was dragging Lawrence's body through the snow.

"You all right?" Alex grasped Beans Magee's arm. The blond woodsman gave him a crooked grin. "That son-of-a-bitch Taylor caught me in the arm. Just grazed me, but I fell back and hit my head on a stump." He rubbed the back of his head gingerly. "It's a wonder I didn't kill myself."

Alex laughed. "Well, when we get inside I'll take a look just the same . . . at your arm and your head." Giving him a pat on the back, he walked through the knee-deep snowdrift toward Jack. "Need some help?"

Jack dropped Lawrence's hands, straightening up to catch his breath. "Big as moose, he is, and that one, too." He pointed to Gaddy, dead in the snow.

"What are we going to do with the bodies?"

"Not much we can do. If it was up to me, I'd leave 'em for the wolves." Jack grinned, extracting a cigar from inside his parka.

Alex eyed him in shocked disbelief. "You're not kidding are you?"

Jack turned his back to the wind and struck a match. "It's what they deserve."

"True." Alex peered into the snowy forest. "But it's not right. I know we can't bury them, but we can at least cover their bodies with brush to keep the animals off them."

"That Parsons fellow left you along the river to die. It wouldn't have been long before the wolves would have been nibblin' at *your* toes." Jack puffed on his

223

cigar, his arms crossed over his chest.

"Just the same, they'll get what decent burial we can give them." With finality, Alex grasped one of Lawrence's arms and began to drag the body to the edge of the woods.

It was near midnight by the time the men buried the three bodies in brush and fetched the dogs from upriver where they left them. Deciding to spend the night in the cabin and mush home in the morning, they lit a fire in the fireplace and settled in for the night. They had thought of going after Taylor, surmising he couldn't get far, but decided against it. Gabrielle was too weak to travel far and needed to get home. Besides, Alex had assured Jack that from now on he'd be there to protect her.

Waving good-bye to Jack and Beans Magee, Gabrielle pushed open the door to her cabin. "Oh, Alex," she sighed. "Look what they've done!"

He came up behind her, wrapping an arm around her waist. "It's not that bad, I'll help you clean it up. Between the fishing and hunting and the flour we can rescue, we'll have plenty to eat until spring." *Plenty to eat until we leave this place,* he thought to himself. He had decided on the trip back to Gabrielle's cabin that when he left for Richmond, with or without the gold, she was going with him. When the right time came, after she'd recovered from her ordeal, he would make her understand why she'd never be safe there again, why she would have to come with him and become his wife.

"It's not just the food for us; this is my livelihood!"

224

She stood dejected in the doorway, staring at the chaos her kidnappers had created. Although Beans, Alex and Jack had righted the furniture, returned her cooking pots to their crates and swept the ashes off her table, there were still flour, sugar, salt and other precious dry goods dumped on the floor. Crates had been knocked over and ripped apart, glasses had been broken against the walls and her clothes had been cut into shreds and strewn everywhere.

Alex stood in silence, not knowing what to say to comfort her. He lit a lantern on the mantel and one on the table and got to his knees to start a fire in the woodstove.

Gabrielle closed the cabin door and slipped off her parka, ignoring the teeth-chattering cold. Spotting her rag doll beneath the bed, she retrieved her, hugging her tightly. "You poor girl, Laura, been through hell haven't you? First Papa rips you open, sews a map inside you and sends you off to Jack's, then a dog eats you up and then you get knocked around by a bunch of do-gooders!"

Alex came up behind Gabrielle, wrapping his arms round her. "You've been through hell yourself, little lady."

She shrugged, leaning against him. "I was so afraid I'd lost you, Alex. I thought I'd be all right. I thought I could let you go, but I couldn't." She stared at the fire blazing in the stove.

Alex turned her around, pulling her to him and crushing the doll between them. "I thought I could do it, too, Gabrielle. But I couldn't." He stroked her bruised cheek, a mark left by Lawrence.

She lifted her chin and raised up on her toes to brush

225

her lips against his. "I don't know what we're going to do, Alex."

"Hush," he crooned. "Let's not worry about it tonight." He kissed her mouth, her bruised cheek, her feathered brows. They were soft, fleeting kisses that soothed and healed.

Letting the doll slip to the floor, Gabrielle raised her arms to snake them around his neck. She moaned softly as he caressed one breast, his thumb teasing through the material of her layers of shirts and sweaters. Parting her lips, she accepted his mouth hungrily, exploring the cool cavern of his mouth with her tongue. "Sure glad you let me bathe last night, even if it was in a basin," she murmured. "You'd not have dared get near me as bad as I smelled."

He nuzzled her neck. "It would take more than that to ward me off."

"Ah, Alex, I missed you so much. I couldn't think straight for wanting you. Sitting tied to that chair, I should have been trying to figure a way to escape. Instead, all I could think about was you."

He laughed, deep in his throat, showering her with kisses. "It wasn't my affection you wanted," he told her huskily, "you just didn't want theirs."

She laughed with him, nipping at his lower lip as she lowered her hand to caress the evidence of his rising ardor through the material of his woolen pants.

"Witch," he accused, "minx . . . woods nymph—"

"What happened to wharf rat?" She ran her hand over his buttocks, pressing her hips to his and moving seductively against him.

Sweeping her up in his arms, Alex carried her to the bed and laid her down gently. She reached out, beckoning him, then welcoming the strength of his body pressed full length against hers. She took his mouth hungrily, threading her fingers through his thick auburn hair. Relieving him of his sweater and shirt, her fingers teased at the waistband of his thick woolen pants. "Take them off," she ordered with a giggle.

Alex held her smoldering gaze as he sat up to shed his remaining layers of clothing. "And what of you?" he whispered.

A smile tugged at the corners of her mouth as she allowed him to remove her clothes. When both of them were free from the burdensome things, he laid down beside her, letting his gaze range her full length.

"You're so beautiful," he murmured, tracing the fullness of one breast with his finger. Sighing, he lowered his mouth to take a pert nipple, teasing it with the tip of his tongue until she cried out with pleasure.

Arching her back, Gabrielle writhed beneath the caress of Alex's practiced hands. He took her mouth with his, deepening the kiss as his fingers played the sensitive flesh of her inner thighs. Moaning softly, she moved her hips to the rhythm of his hand, loosing herself in the sheer pleasure of his caress. "Alex," she cried breathlessly.

"Gabrielle," he whispered in her ear.

Her eyelids flew open, and she smiled as his gaze met hers. "You don't play the game very fairly," she teased, stroking the broad expanse of his chest. Now that his hand was still, her thoughts came more clearly.

"No?" He pressed his mouth to hers, his tongue darting out to taste the honey of her lips.

"No." Lifting her head to rest it on his chest, she

began a slow, deliberate assault on Alex's senses. Reveling in the sighs and throaty moans that escaped his lips, she stroked his body, bringing to him the pleasures he evoked in her. Sliding her leg seductively between his, she moved against him, covering his chest with soft kisses. Taking a hard male nipple in her mouth, she licked and suckled, her own breath coming faster.

Tracing intricate patterns with her tongue, she moved downward, a smile crossing her lips when Alex groaned, threading his fingers through her hair. Pressing hot, wet kisses to his burgeoning flesh, she taunted him until he thought he would go mad with wanting.

"Gabrielle," he called huskily. "Come to me, love." Half-sitting up, he rested his hands on her hips, guiding her as she straddled his powerful legs.

Gabrielle's breath caught in her throat as his rigid manhood met her soft femininity, and she moaned softly. Gripping his shoulders, she leaned into him, picking up a rhythm as ancient as time itself. Alex held her against him, stroking her shapely back, burying his head in her chestnut hair as they climbed higher in insatiable ecstasy.

Higher and higher they moved as one, Gabrielle lifting her hips faster as Alex's breath became ragged in her ear. Their lips met, and they kissed deeply, savagely, as she felt her entire body tense with urgency. Crying out Alex's name, her entire being shuddered with pleasure, and she clung to him, tears of joy staining her cheeks.

When Gabrielle had relaxed, Alex eased her onto her back, showering her dewy face with feather-light kisses. He crooned unintelligible words of love as he took her with one hard stroke, pushing her past the brink of all reason. Gabrielle lifted her hips to meet his demanding thrust, and she was caught in the tide of love again. Clinging to him, she crested the mountain of all-consuming pleasure again and again until with a final thrust and groan of euphoric pleasure, Alex's body became still.

For a moment, Gabrielle didn't have the energy to lift her heavy lashes, but finally she opened her eyes to study the sea of blue above her. "I love you," she mouthed silently.

"I love you," he returned, his voice throaty with spent passion. Rolling onto his side, Alex kissed the tears from her cheeks, stroking her damp, quivering flesh. Gabrielle sighed contentedly, moving to rest her head on his chest as her eyes drifted shut.

Smiling in the darkness, he pulled a blanket up over them both, enveloping her in his arms. "Sleep tight," he murmured against her chestnut hair as he closed his own eyes.

Sometime in the night, a loud clatter and a crash of metal jolted Gabrielle and Alex out of pleasant dreams. Gabrielle's eyes flew open as she scrambled out of bed. "Fire! Fire!" she shouted, pulling on her pants that lay on the floor.

Alex jumped up, reaching for his own clothes. Red-hot sparks leaped in the corner of the room where the stove sat, igniting the paper in the dish crate. Flames had already begun crawling up the wall of the cabin by the time Gabrielle reached the fire to beat at it with the blanket she'd pulled off the bed.

"It's spreading too fast," Alex shouted above the roar of the flames and the howl of the wind. By the light of the orange flames, he gathered blankets, clothing, shoes—anything he could find—and began throwing them out the door into the snow. "Come on," he ordered. "Get back, you'll be burned."

Gabrielle beat at the flames with the blanket, smothering first one small fire, then another, but she seemed to make no headway as she tripped over pieces of stove pipe that littered the floor. Backing up, she raised her hands against the intense heat of the flames, tears running down her cheeks as she realized the fire was getting out of hand fast.

"Gabrielle," Alex shouted grasping her by the shoulders. He yanked the blanket from her hands and threw it over her shoulders, lifting her into his arms. "It's going to blow, the powder!"

"Put me down," she ordered, struggling. "The harnesses. The dog harnesses."

Driven by the heat at his back, Alex ran out of the cabin, dumping Gabrielle into the snow. Turning back, he entered the cabin through a wall of flames to retrieve the dog harnesses and gun that hung on pegs near the door. Just as he turned to go, by the light of the fire he spotted Gabrielle's rag doll lying on the floor, flames surrounding it as the floor became engulfed. Throwing the gun and harnesses out the door he made a running leap over the rising flames and snatched up the doll.

Gabrielle stood frozen in terror, knee-deep in snow, watching as her cabin crumbled before her. "Alex!" she screamed. "Alex!" She coughed and choked, craning her neck to see him.

Suddenly, Alex appeared through the wall of flames, falling out the door and into the snow. Scrambling to his feet he ran for Gabrielle, forcing her into the snow. "It's going to blow," he shouted as he covered her body with his.

An instant later a resounding boom filled the air as Gabrielle's cache of black powder exploded. The hand-hewn walls of the cabin splintered under the impact of the explosion, and flames rose to engulf the entire wooden structure.

Gabrielle lifted her face from the snow, struggling to get out from under Alex. "My cabin," she sobbed. "Do something, for God's sake. It's all I have."

Alex rolled off her into the snow, keeping a tight grip on her arm. "Gabrielle, it's too late. It's gone." He wiped a smudge of soot from her cheek. "I saved the guns, the harnesses, some blankets and other stuff." He lifted her doll from the snow. "And I saved this."

Gabrielle took the battered doll from him, crushing it in her arms as she got to her knees. She broke into sobs, rocking to and fro as the front wall of the cabin gave way, crumbling to the ground. The fire popped and sizzled, extinguishing as the flaming rafters fell deep in the snow. "It's all I have in the world," she moaned. "All I have."

He crawled through the snow to her, pushing aside one of the dogs that leaped and barked in circles around them. Gripping her shoulders, he forced her to look at his fire-blackened face. "It's not true. You have me, and you have your life."

231

Chapter Seventeen

The first rays of dawn streaked the sky, reflecting off the new-fallen snow. The trees glimmered like spun glass, hanging low beneath their burden, groaning as the wind shifted. Heavy heartedly Gabrielle dug through the pile of clothing and assorted necessities Alex had managed to save from the fire.

The entire cabin had burned to the ground in the hours just before dawn. In the place where her father had laid the foundation more than twenty-five years ago lay a pile of charred remains. Here and there a piece of wood glowed red, but for the most part the fire had died. It had been contained to the cabin, not spreading to the surrounding forest because of the deep snowdrifts that surrounded it.

Alex came up behind Gabrielle, resting a hand on her shoulder. "I rounded up all of the dogs that ran into the woods when the fire started. They're all safe."

She gave a nod, lifting her boot out of the snow. "Where's the other boot, Alex?" She dangled it on the end of her finger by the lace.

233

He glanced about. "I don't know; it's got to be here somewhere."

"It's not here. I've looked everywhere." Her voice was strained. "What am I supposed to wear, Alex?" She gestured at her feet wrapped in two layers of socks and strips of leather he'd cut for her earlier. "I can't walk around in bare feet."

"I don't know, keep looking." He picked up a blanket and folded it with stiff, jaunty movements.

"I said I've looked, damn it," she snapped, throwing the boot to the ground.

He watched it hit the snow, then glanced up at her, his lips tightly compressed. "I didn't set your cabin on fire, Gabrielle. It was an accident. The wind shifted the stove pipe, the pipe separated at its joints and the sparks from the stove set the house on fire."

Her gaze fell to the snow. "I'm sorry," she whispered. "It's just that I don't know what I'm going to do now." She picked up her boot out of the snow and added it to the pile she was making on a cured moosehide. "Everything I owned was in that cabin. My supplies are gone, my money . . . everything that was ever my father's . . . gone."

"You've got one thing left of his," Alex ventured.

She looked up. "What's that?"

"The map," he said with insinuation.

She shook her head. "Oh no, I told you I wasn't going after that gold. I don't want anything to do with it." She took a step backward, raising her hands to him.

"It's the only thing you can do." He approached her slowly. "Come with me and we'll find the gold together. If the strike is as big as Jack says your father thought it was, there'll be plenty for both of us."

234

For a moment Gabrielle stood frozen, staring at Alex. Her face was ashen with the cold reality of his words. "So you get what you want after all, don't you?"

"Don't be silly. You think I planned this?" He ran a hand through his tousled auburn hair. "That's absurd. I had nothing to do with the fire and you know it. It just happened."

"And now I'll have to use the map—"

"Gabrielle, I wanted it for you. Your father wanted it for you. Why are you being so unreasonable?" He reached to touch her, but she drew back.

Her jaw was set, her hands clenched at her sides. "All right. You win. I'll go with you, but I'm warning you, Jefferson Alexander the fourth—" she shook a finger at him—"we're through, you and I, you understand me?"

He looked at her, a blank stare on his face. "What do you mean? I don't understand. I can't believe you could blame me for this." He raised his arms in exasperation.

She turned her back to him, jerking a sweater out of the snow. "I'm not blaming you. I'm just telling you I . . . I . . ." she stuttered, not knowing what it was she wanted to say. "I'm just telling you we're through!" she blurted. "I've had enough. I never had any problems until you came along. My life was just dandy without you. You're the one who wrecked everything. You made it all a mess. I want you to get your gold and get out." She was talking more to herself than to him now. "If we strike gold, I want you to take your share and go. I don't ever want to see you on the Tanana again. You got that?"

Alex gave a sigh, shaking his head. He turned

without bothering to answer her. There was no use talking to her in this state, he was sure of that. The best thing to do right now was to load the other sled and make their way to Jack's to get the supplies they were lacking. Luckily his own sled was still packed from his first expedition, so he already had much of what they needed. Once Gabrielle had rested and the idea of seeking the gold had settled in her head, she would see how irrational she was behaving. Snatching an overturned lantern out of the snow, Alex walked away, praying he was right.

Gabrielle paced the floor of the tiny dwelling Jack lived in, her arms crossed over her chest. "I see no other choice, Jack. Where else am I going to get the money to rebuild my trading post?"

The native stroked his beard. "You are probably right. If you want to start another post, you will need much money, money you can only get from *paydirt.*"

She spun around to face him, her voice hostile. "So you think I should go, too?"

Jack poked an unlit cigar into his mouth, a twitch of a smile on his face. "You were the one who said you were going. You had already decided."

"Well, it really is my gold, isn't it?" she reasoned with herself aloud. "I mean it was Papa's whether he staked a claim or not."

Jack just nodded, accepting a bowl of stew Mya handed him.

"If we hit gold, I can take what I need, go to Seattle and buy provisions and build the following spring. I think I'll put my place on this side of the river, maybe farther north. The Yukon's getting busy. You see it, more and more men coming in every spring." She paced faster, words spilling rapidly from her mouth.

Jack tucked his cigar in his pocket and spooned the stew into his mouth. "It's going to break soon, Gabe, the rivers are going to run with gold."

She grimaced. "All I want is enough to rebuild; I'll not be greedy."

Mya sat beside her husband on the bench, a bowl of stew in her hand. "So go and maybe you can settle with that man of yours. There is stew in the pot for you and him as well."

Gabrielle went to the tiny cookstove to dish out her own supper. "I wouldn't be counting on us settling anything, Mya. I've had enough of that man. He's nothing but trouble."

Mya made a clicking sound between her teeth. "For a woman who usually has much sense . . ." She let her voice fade.

"I can't believe my friends are all against me. Who is he to you? A stranger, a tenderfoot, a gold seeker . . ." She blew on a spoonful of stew and sampled the savory mixture.

"He is the man you love." Mya's ebony eyes met Gabrielle's.

"Yea, well, love isn't everything is it? It doesn't mean you can live with someone. It doesn't mean they can make you happy. Look at Papa. Rouge LeBeau loved my mother till the day he died. Couldn't stand the woman, but he still loved her. Used to visit her when we were in Seattle, you know."

Jack raised a dark eyebrow. "I didn't know."

"Sure. He used to go right there where she worked,

237

like a paying customer." She shook her head in disbelief. "He said she was the only woman for him, whore or not. Can you believe it?"

Alex came through the door with a flurry of snow. "Believe what?"

Gabrielle turned her back to him to fill her bowl again. "Nothing. Dogs fed?"

He slipped out of his parka. "They are, and the sleds are packed. We can go in the morning," he answered tersely. His patience was wearing thin. He didn't know how long he could put up with her behaving like this.

"Stew in the pot, Alex." Jack nodded his head in the direction of the woodstove. "You sure you two don't want to spend the rest of the winter here?"

"No," Gabrielle said adamantly. "We'll have to build fires to thaw the site where we dig, and then we'll just pile the dirt. When the river thaws, we'll use a sluice box and go through the dirt we've dug up all winter."

Alex turned to her. "Since when do you know so much about mining? I thought you said you never mined."

"I didn't, but you can't help hearing about it when you grow up in this territory," she told him coldly. Turning to Jack, her voice lightened. "I'm not going to tell you exactly where we're going because I think we'll all be safer that way. But I can tell you that we'll be on this side of the river, north of here, off on a small tributary."

Jack got up. "Just so you don't take chances. All the gold in the world'll do you no good if you're dead somewhere rotting on the bank come spring." He rested a hand on Mya's shoulder. "Guess we'll be

238

turning in now. Thought we'd sleep at Mya's mother's."

"Oh, no." Gabrielle snatched her parka from a peg on the wall. "I'll go sleep there. You can put him on the floor for the night." She jerked a thumb in Alex's direction and slipped out the door before anyone had a chance to speak.

For a moment Alex just stood there, staring at the closed door. Then he placed his bowl of stew on a small table and picked up his parka. "Excuse me, will you?" he told Mya and Jack. Stuffing his fists in his sleeves he went out the door, closing it quietly behind him.

"Gabrielle," Alex shouted. He could see her form moving between the hutlike structures by the light of the moon reflected off the snow. "Gabrielle, wait a minute," he ordered through clenched teeth.

"Like hell!" she shouted over her shoulder, moving faster.

Alex ran through the snow, catching up to her. He grasped her by the shoulder, forcing her to turn around. "Don't do this to me," he threatened. "I don't know exactly what your problem is, but I can't live like this."

"You're my problem." She poked at his parka with a mitten-covered hand. "You've forced me into something I don't want to do, and I don't like it. No one tells Gabrielle LeBeau what to do."

"I didn't force you into anything." He released his grip on her shoulder but held her with his stormy gaze. "You decided to mine with me."

"Only after I had no other choice," she spat.

Alex reached out to pull up the hood of her parka,

but she batted at his hands. "You're not being logical. You know I had nothing to do with that fire." He jerked up his own hood to ward off the freezing temperatures.

"I know that! I'm not that stupid." She laced up her own hood with stiff angry movements.

"Then what is it? I can't figure you out. One minute you're telling me you love me, the next—"

She interrupted before he could finish. "Who said there had to be any logic in it?" She gazed off into the distance, unable to look him in the face. "You were right; we could never be together, not permanently, and I just think it will be easier for me when you go if . . ." her voice caught in her throat, "if we just act like partners."

"You mean you don't want to sleep with me?" He caught her hand. "You don't want to make love with me any more?"

Tears threatened to spill from her eyes. *Why does he have to look so injured,* she thought. *I'm the one who's going to hurt when you're gone. You've got your daughter, your mother and sisters. I've got no one.* "Why are you making this so difficult?" She twisted a boot in the snow, listening to the crunch it made. They were Mya's boots, given as a gift after the fire.

"I'm not trying to make it difficult; I'm just trying to understand you, Gabrielle. You can't do this to people, you know. You can't do it to me. You have to make up your mind what you want in life." Unable to resist, he touched a lock of hair that lay against her cheek.

"I have."

"And you don't want me?" His voice was husky with emotion.

"I don't want your way of life." She pulled her hand from his, unable to stand the warmth he radiated. "I don't want your Richmond, Virginia and fancy talk. I want my dogs, my trading post, my friends. I want things to be the way they were."

Images of his father, his brothers, all of the family members lost in the war flashed before Alex. The sound of cannons echoed in his head; he heard his mother crying. "But they never can be the same, can they?" he whispered.

"No," she returned softly.

For a moment Alex stood there in the snow, in the darkness, staring at the dark figure of the woman he loved, and then slowly he turned and headed back for the warmth of Jack's home.

With the coming of morning, Gabrielle and Alex hitched their dogs and were off, moving north. They traveled on the frozen river, few words passing between them as they took turns in the lead. It was difficult work making headway. The sleds moved easily over the hard-packed snow; but every time they hit a snowdrift the sleds became buried or overturned, and then the dogs grew tangled in their traces. Again and again, Gabrielle and Alex unharnessed the dogs, righted the sled and rehitched the dogs only to have to repeat the process a mile farther along.

The frigid northwesterly wind whipped and howled at Gabrielle's ears until all sound was drowned out but the sound of her own breathing and the whoosh of the sled as it slid over the ice and snow. To keep herself warm she ran behind the sled most of the time, only hopping on the back of the runners when she was too exhausted to take another step. Alex followed her lead but rode only when she did.

As the day passed and the afternoon lengthened into evening, the sleds moved slower over the icy terrain. Man and dog grew weary as they moved farther from home and closer to their destiny. Finally, just after dark, Gabrielle slowed her dogs, bringing the sled to a halt. "Whoa, Tristan. Whoa boy," she ordered. "Good dog, good Tristan." Leaping off the runners she walked back to Alex. "Let's stop here for the night."

He nodded, rubbing his hands together for warmth. He'd been ready to stop a good hour ago, but he'd have sooner run behind the sled to the ends of the earth than to have told her. "Sure you don't want to go any farther?" He breathed into his mittens, trying to thaw the ice that clung to his red beard near his mouth.

Gabrielle grimaced beneath the hood of her parka. "Let me guess, you could run another hour or so?" she asked dryly. By the faint light of the moon, she caught a hint of a smile on his face, and she turned away before he saw her return the smile. "Do what you want, but we've had enough," she called over her shoulder.

Alex chuckled, watching her wade through the snow. She moved wearily, her head bent low against the driving wind. His heart swelled with pride. He had never known a woman in his life so strong willed, so willing to beat the odds in life. As she walked around her sled to get her dogs, she tripped and floundered into a deep pocket of snow. For a moment Alex stood still in indecision and then suddenly he was behind her, pulling her up by her arm and wiping the snow from her face.

"Let go of me," Gabrielle ordered, flailing her arms. "I can get up on my own."

He ignored her protests, setting her on her feet on solid ground. "Partners, aren't we?" He brushed the snow from her parka. "You'd do the same for me or Jack, right?" He watched her through the tunnel of his parka hood, enjoying her discomfort.

"Right," she answered, stalking away. "Now come on. We'll camp on the west bank."

It was nearly two hours before a fire was built and the dogs were fed. Energy waning, Gabrielle and Alex put their sleds together to make an alcove around the fire and settled on hide mats to have their own sparse meal. They ate dried moose jerky and a handful of dried berries, drinking large quantities of weak tea. Slowly they thawed before the blazing fire, leaning back against the sleds to rest. Their dogs lay around them, sleeping contentedly.

"Good first day, huh?" Alex asked. He stroked his bright red beard, brushing the last of the melted ice from it.

"Fair," Gabrielle answered. "I've made better; I've made worse." She stretched out her feet, wiggling her toes in the handmade boots as the feeling came back into her near-frozen flesh.

Alex picked up a stick and poked at the campfire roaring before them. For a long time he was silent, choosing his words carefully. Then he spoke. "Gabrielle, we're going to have to call a truce here."

"What do you mean?" She stared at the fire, not wanting to meet his gaze.

"I mean if we're going to work together, if we're going to find that gold, we've got to have some sort of an agreement."

She lifted her tin cup to her lips and sipped at her tea. "What kind of agreement?"

"We've got to agree to act like two civilized people about this. If we're going to be partners in this effort, we've got to be friends."

"I'm being civil."

"Barely." He glanced over at her, taking notice of the way the firelight played off her chestnut hair making it shimmer with red highlights.

She looked at him and he looked away. "We are friends, aren't we?" she asked, trying to make light of the conversation.

"Gabrielle, I'm too tired to go around and around with you like this. I'm talking about the fact that we can be friends and partners, without being lovers." He laid back, resting his head against the sled behind him. He'd rehearsed this speech over and over in his mind, hoping to conceal his heart-wrenching pain by the repetition of the words. "I'm gentleman enough to accept the fact that you no longer wish to be the object of my affections. But—"

She turned to look at him, swallowing against the rising lump in his throat. "But what?"

"But I can't live with you hating me. We can't work together like this. I can't."

She rolled onto her side to face him. "I don't hate you, Alex. I just don't want to be hurt. Can't you understand that?"

His gaze rested on her delicate oval face. "I'd never hurt you." He took her hand, sliding the mitten off to caress her cold fingers.

Gabrielle's eyes drifted shut. She had never imagined there could be any intimacy in one hand touching another, but there was. As he stroked the back of her hand, a warm shiver ran up her arm, spreading to her limbs. "I know you wouldn't hurt me on purpose, Alex. But when you leave, it's going to hurt."

"You could go with me to Richmond."

"I couldn't." She knew she should withdraw her hand, but she couldn't. Not just yet. "I don't want to," she finished bravely.

"I know you don't," he whispered hoarsely. "But it's something to think about." He lowered his lips to her hand, kissing her palm. "I would do everything in my power to see you were happy. I'd make you my wife."

Gabrielle gave a sigh, easing her hand from his. *You don't really want to marry me*, she thought. *You get back home with your friends and I'll soon be gone from your mind.* "It would never work, Alex."

He leaned over her, his breath warm on her cheeks. "We could make it work."

"I'd hate it there. This is where I belong." She lifted a hand to stroke his bearded cheek. "Why is it so hard for you to understand that this was never meant to be?" Tears brimmed in her dark eyes as the words slipped from her lips.

"I can't accept that, Gabrielle." He leaned forward to kiss her, but she pulled back.

"Please." She touched his lips with the tips of her fingers. "Don't make it worse. You're asking too much of me. You're asking me to give up my life here for you."

"You could have a new life. My daughter needs a mother."

She was mesmerized by his deep blue-grey eyes. "I'd be an awful mother and a worse wife. Go home and

245

find a good woman. The LeBeaus were not meant to be family women."

"Is that what it is?" He toyed with a lock of hair that curled at her ear. "You think because your mother—"

She cut him off. "I don't know what I think, all right, Alex? I'm so confused, I don't know which way is up. I said I would never love a man . . . but I fell in love with you. I swore I'd never use that map, but I'm on my way to mine for gold. I need time to think." She chewed at her bottom lip. "So let's just call that truce and go on from here."

"You'll think about my offer?" He laid back crossing his arms over his chest.

"Only if you'll think about why I'm saying no."

"It's a deal then"—he stuck out his hand to take hers—"partner."

Chapter Eighteen

Following the brittle map that had been Rouge LeBeau's, Gabrielle and Alex made their way north, traveling the solid road of the frozen Tanana river. The days passed easily as the two fell into a routine. They mushed from dawn until just after nightfall, thankful for the gradual lengthening of daylight as January slipped by. Following a tiny tributary of the Tanana, they veered off to the right and into the mountains, making the final leg of the journey.

Near noon in early February, Gabrielle held the map in her hands, brushing the snow off the crumpled paper. Pulling off a mitten with her teeth, she traced a thin line her father had drawn with her finger. "Around this bend in the stream and we're there, Alex!" she said anxiously.

"You sure?" He leaned over her shoulder.

She held the map out for him. "See for yourself."

He looked from the map to the turn in the tributary that bent right and then to the map again. "I'll be damned," he murmured.

Folding the map carefully, Gabrielle tucked it beneath her parka and slipped her mitten back on. "Come on!" Running toward her sled, she gave one of her dogs a playful slap on the back. "Mush!" she ordered. "Mush!" The sled jerked forward, and the dogs were off, barking excitedly.

Alex followed behind, running alongside his own sled. Around the bend they went, slowing as they spotted a clearing on the bank to the left. It was a man-made clearing . . . something they hadn't seen in days.

"Whoa, whoa," Gabrielle called to her dogs, running past them. She pushed back her hood, clambering up the north bank. "This is it, Alex! This is it!" Struggling up the snowy bank, she rushed into the clearing nestled at the base of a mountain. Trees had been felled to build a crude cabin a hundred yards into the woods, and conical-shaped dirt mounds littered the clearing. *Someone* had been prospecting here. Gabrielle could only pray that it had been Rouge and that no one had been here since.

Alex came up the bank behind her. "You think this is it?"

"If his map was right, this is it," she whispered. An eery feeling swept over her as she walked through the old camp toward the cabin. It was built with whole logs, the cracks chinked with mud from the tributary; it couldn't have been more than ten feet by ten feet.

Taking a deep breath, Gabrielle cut the leather thong that held the door shut with her knife and pushed it open. Letting the sunlight flood the cabin, she stepped inside. It smelled of damp wood and dust, of animal droppings and smoke. It also smelled of Rouge LeBeau. "This is it, Alex," she whispered. "Papa was here."

"What do you mean? How do you know?" He pushed in the door behind her, surveying the barely adequate shelter.

"I know." Her voice was haunting. "I can feel him; I can smell him; I can hear his laughter." She ran her hand along the interior wall, years of dust clinging to her mitten. Rouge hadn't even stripped the trees of their bark before he'd begun construction. The cabin was obviously meant to be temporary; he had built it just to keep the rain and snow off his back while he mined.

Alex draped his arm over Gabrielle's shoulder, staring at the refuse that littered the floor: a tin pot with a hole in it, a pile of Scotch bottles, an old rotten shirt. The things meant nothing to him; they were junk. But to Gabrielle, he knew, they meant memories, some good and some bad.

Gabrielle choked back tears as she stared at the crude wooden table against the wall. "Oh, Papa," she sighed. "Why did you have to die?" Wiping her tears with the sleeve of her parka, she turned and went outside. Alex followed quietly behind her.

"He always told me he wasn't going to be here for me." She sniffed, blinking back tears. "He knew. Somehow he knew." She looked out over the frozen stream at the mountains in the horizon, at the trees stretching high into the blue sky, and she sighed. "So?" She turned to Alex, who stood silently behind her. "Where do we start, partner?"

The following morning, Gabrielle and Alex began

the formidable task of excavating. Choosing two spots, they built fires and began to thaw the permafrost. Their plan was to dig shafts and pile the dirt, just as Rouge had done, and then in May they would begin Spring Clean-up. Once the stream became accessible, they could use a sluicing process to wash the lighter dirt away, leaving the gold, if it existed, in the bottom of the sluice box.

Gabrielle and Alex quickly realized that the process of excavating was slow and arduous. While Alex cut wood to fuel the fires, Gabrielle tended them. Then, late in the afternoon, the two dug side by side, barely making eight inches of gravel a day. A week after they'd arrived, they both agreed to try a sample of the dirt, panning it for gold. The few shallow shafts left by Rouge led them to believe they were right on target, but still they couldn't help wondering if they were wasting their time.

Nervously, Gabrielle heated a pot of snow until it melted and dug her gold pan out of a bag in the cabin. Without a word passing between them, Alex dumped a handful of dirt into the pan and added water. With great ease, she rocked the pan to and fro, letting the water wash down the front of her parka as it lifted away the dirt. Squeezing her eyes shut, she whispered a silent prayer and poured the rest of the water onto the frozen ground.

For a moment, Gabrielle and Alex stood stricken in disbelief. There, in the bottom of the rusty pan, glimmered tiny slivers of gold.

"God, Alex, look at it," she whispered.

He stuck a finger into the pan and pulled out a minuscule lump, holding it up in the sunlight. Part of the rock was black, but a part of it shimmered in the light.

"This is it, Gabrielle," he told her, his voice hushed. "This is what it will take to get my daughter back, to restore my home—"

"To build my new trading post . . ." she added.

Alex looked at her, the smile fading from his face. "Yea." Pulling a small leather bag from inside his parka, he slipped the slivers of gold safely inside and turned away. "Better get back to work, looks like we've got a storm coming in."

Dejectedly Gabrielle watched his back until he disappeared into the forest and then picked up her shovel. They had found gold, not the mother lode they were looking for, but gold none the less. So why weren't they happy? Why weren't they dancing a jig? She sighed, slipping her mitten back on. They had said nothing to each other about a future together since that first night on the trail, but still it haunted their minds. Tightening her hood, Gabrielle jumped down into the nearest shaft and began digging wholeheartedly.

The bleary winter days slipped by like leaves falling from a tree. Gabrielle and Alex worked from sunup until sundown digging and thawing ground and digging some more. Instead of trying to reach bedrock, they decided simply to excavate and depend on sluicing in the spring to bring them the gold they needed. They made an agreement that on July first they would pack and go, no matter what. Whatever gold they had on that day would be what they would take. They would destroy the map and swear never to tell a soul of the location of Rouge's find, nor would they ever return.

Time seemed to lose all meaning to Gabrielle and

Alex as they worked by day, falling into an exhausted sleep at dusk. They slept side by side on the floor in the tiny cabin, each avoiding the other's touch. As time passed, they grew used to the new relationship, and though it was often painful, they grew to tolerate it. There were many days when Alex and Gabrielle could not leave the cabin except to tend the dogs because of the extreme low temperatures and driving blizzards. But on clear days, they were up and working as the first streaks of dawn colored the sky. Some days they worked in total silence, their moods dark and brooding, but other days, they laughed away the afternoon, content to work at one another's side.

Winter slipped by and spring descended upon them. With the first falling rain, the snow began to melt, and the bank of the Tanana tributary turned muddy and brown. One morning in mid-April they woke to a thundering rumble of sound.

"What's that?" Alex leaped to his feet, pulling on his pants, and reached for a wool sweater that hung on the wall.

Brushing the sleep from her eyes, Gabrielle yawned lazily, stretching as she came fully awake. "It's the break-up, silly."

"What?" He stood on one foot, hopping as he tugged on a boot.

"Spring break-up. The ice on the Tanana is breaking."

Stuffing his other foot in a boot, Alex went out of the cabin. Gabrielle watched him from the doorway as she dressed herself. "Beautiful sight, wouldn't you say?" she called after him.

Alex crossed the clearing to stand at the bank of the

stream. The water was finally moving, great chunks of blue-green ice floating downstream. He glanced back at Gabrielle. "But the sound? Where's the sound coming from?"

She laughed, racing down the bank toward him. "It's the Tanana."

"But the main river is miles from here."

"I know." She grinned, catching his hand. "Want to go see it?"

"And lose a day of work?" He squeezed her hand, reveling in the feel of her touch.

She shrugged. "An ounce of gold?" She turned and started back up the bank, shivering with cold without the protection of her parka. "I'm going. Work if you like, or come with me. Makes no difference to me."

Alex stood for a minute watching the ice floes disappear around the bend and then scrambled back up the bank. Pushing barking dogs aside, he hollered, "Wait! I'm coming."

Gabrielle's laughter filled the clearing, her voice echoing high in the trees. Another spring had come to the Tanana, and she was glad she was there to see it.

Leaving the mining site and the dogs behind for the day, Gabrielle and Alex made an overland trek, crossing a mountain ridge and a valley to hike part way up a mountain to look down on the breaking Tanana.

The mighty power of the breaking ice was overwhelming to Alex. For the longest time, he stood there on the side of the mountain just looking down at the great rushing river in awe. The sound of the cracking ice was nearly deafening, even so high above it. It was a thundering roar that would forever be embedded in his mind.

"A sight, isn't it?" Gabrielle tossed a stick into the small fire she'd built on the ledge they rested on. "Except for those years I spent in Seattle, I've seen this every year since I was old enough to remember, and still it astounds me . . . frightens me." Getting to her feet, she went to stand beside Alex and stare down at the countenance of the beauty.

"Yea," he answered, unable to resist wrapping an arm around her waist. "I could say the same about you."

The following morning, Alex and Gabrielle set up a sluice box and began the step in mining that actually produced results. Setting a screened box, which they'd built from scraps, down in the stream, they began the arduous task of shoveling dirt into it. The swift running water of the spring thaw left the heavy gold chunks in the riffles of the box and washed the lighter materials away. On the first day of sluicing, Gabrielle and Alex were beside themselves with wonder as they lifted the slivers of gold from the box, but as the week passed, they grew accepting of the bag that grew heavier with each day and worked diligently to complete their task. Slowly they made their way through the conical-shaped piles of dirt that towered over the campsite, taking turns shoveling while the other worked the sluice box.

Late one afternoon, Gabrielle heaved a sigh as she dumped another shovel of dirt into the sluice box. Leaning on her shovel, she wiped her brow. "That's it for me today, Alex. I can't lift another shovel of dirt."

He looked up at her smudged face, shading his eyes from the bright sunlight. She was as beautiful as she had ever been, standing there covered in mud, leaning on the shovel, her chestnut hair swaying softly in the breeze. "Given up, have you?"

She dropped the shovel with a bang. "Indeed I have, and I'd recommend you do the same." She looked out over the running stream wishfully, scratching her arm beneath her prickly wool sweater. "I need a bath."

He laughed, lifting the sluice box from its cradle to carry it up the bank. "Just wait until we get into Seattle. We'll find some fancy hotel with a tub big enough for both of us." He grinned, glancing sideways at her.

At Gabrielle's insistence, Alex had made no advances toward her since they'd left her cabin downstream. Though he ached for wanting her, he had promised himself that if they were ever to be lovers again, she would have to come to him. When they first arrived at Rouge's campsite, she had avoided his touch like the plague; but then as winter turned to spring, she had grown more lenient and now, suddenly he realized she was reaching out to him with warmth. At first it was just a brief touch as she passed a shovel or a coffee cup, but lately she had actually been seeking his attention, making physical contact with each chance she got. Could it be that she had changed her mind? Did she still want him as much as he wanted her? He was afraid to be too hopeful.

"Lewd comments is it, now?" Gabrielle arched a dark eyebrow playfully. "You want to see lewd?" Suddenly on impulse, she was stripping off her clothes, first her boots, then her muddy pants, her underdrawers, her sweater and shirt.

Alex's mouth went dry as he watched her dumbfounded. "What are you doing?" He choked on his words, wondering if she expected him to look away.

"Going swimming," she answered saucily. With a jaunty gait she went down the bank, her slim hips swaying as she walked. *What are you doing?* she asked herself. *You're not only offering a swim, you're offering yourself.*

Alex eased the sluice box to the ground and followed her, walking over her discarded clothes. "Going swimming, are you mad?"

She laughed, her voice clear and tinkling, like a bell in a church steeple. "What's the matter, you Virginians don't bathe?" Suddenly her decision was made. After all of these months, weeks, days of wanting Alex, it was time she gave in to her true feelings.

"Not in water that's still got ice floating in it. . . ."

Gabrielle's feet hit the water, and she groaned, wrapping her hands around her waist. "It's really not bad, once you get in," she called over her shoulder. "Come on." Shivering, she ran a few feet and then plunged into the icy depths. The water hit her like a wall of lead, numbing her mind as well as her body. It was so cold that it took her breath away, but at the same time it was astonishingly exhilarating. Surfacing, she threw back her head, paddling with her hands. "Join me?" Her doe-brown eyes shimmered with hidden promise.

Alex licked his dry lips. His desire to stay warm and dry was almost as great as his desire to be in the water so near to Gabrielle's naked body. "If I die, will you inform my family?"

The corners of her mouth twitched. "About the gold or your dying?"

Alex's eyes met hers, and he was encouraged by the steamy gaze she held him with. Slowly he walked toward the stream, shedding his clothes as he went. "You're funny—" he pointed a finger—"very funny."

Her head bobbed up and down in agreement. "I know. Get your clothes off." Her tongue darted out to moisten her lips as he slipped the dark wool sweater over his head. How long had it been since she'd allowed her gaze to linger over him like this? Had his shoulders always been so broad, his stomach so muscular? He tugged at the waist band of his pants, and she looked away, her cheeks coloring against her will. The familiar heat of desire spread through her loins as images of Alex's body pressed against hers flashed through her mind.

"You're suddenly awfully quiet, Gabrielle." He stood on the bank, wearing nothing but a broad smile.

She cursed him beneath her breath. The lout knew how much she wanted him! When she heard a resounding splash, she looked up to see Alex disappear beneath the surface of the water. For a moment she couldn't see where he was, then suddenly he rose in the water just in front of her.

"Damn, but that's cold water!" He rubbed his arms briskly, trying to bring back some of the feeling.

Gabrielle reached out hesitantly to wipe the water from his brow. "You're shivering," she offered quietly.

His hand cupped her chin. "So are you." He took a step closer, his bare leg brushing against hers beneath the water's surface.

She gasped softly. The warmth of his flesh against hers made her heart flutter, her pulse quicken. He leaned into her, resting his other hand on her shoulder.

"I promised myself I wouldn't touch you, Gabrielle, not ever again, not unless you wanted me to." His voice seemed to come from far in the distance, barely audible over the rush of the river.

Her lower lip trembled. "I want you to . . ."

Alex brought his mouth down hard against hers, crushing her body against him. "God, Gabrielle," he muttered thickly. "You're enough to make a man crazy." He deepened the kiss, and she responded wholeheartedly, her arms snaking around his waist. Her tongue darted out to meet his, and she shuddered beneath the power of his onslaught.

Alex's hand ran down her back and over her shapely buttocks, caressing the curves of her supple flesh. He kissed her eyelids, the tip of her nose, then the arch of her eyebrows as he reacquainted himself with the tender places that made her cry out with pleasure when he touched them.

Gabrielle's breath came faster as she moved her own fingers over his slick, wet flesh. "I'm c-cold," she murmured in his ear.

Brushing his lips against hers, he lifted her into his arms and started for the shore. Gabrielle looped her arms around his neck and nestled her head in the hollow of his shoulder as he whispered soft endearments in her ear.

Alex would have liked to have laid her right there on the bank of the tributary and taken her. His groin ached, and his fingers trembled with wanting; but he immediately saw there was no place dry to put her down.

Recognizing his dilemma, Gabrielle laughed, her voice husky. "In the cabin," she whispered, her tongue darting out to lick at his ear. "Otherwise the dogs won't let us be."

Nodding, Alex hurried across the muddy clearing and pushed open the cabin door with his foot. Giving it a shove closed, he got to his knees and lowered Gabrielle onto the mat he slept on. Putting her arms out to him, she took his mouth greedily, her hands moving over his wet flesh with driven passion.

Laying himself over her shivering body, Alex brushed the wet hair from her cheek. "I never thought I'd feel you beneath me again." His voice rang with heartfelt emotion. "I love you; I love you so much, Gabrielle."

She moved her hips rhythmically, stroking his broad back. "I love you, too," she answered in his ear as she parted her legs to accept the evidence of his love.

Though Alex had wanted this reunion to be unhurried, the pounding of his heart in his own ears made him move with hard demanding strokes. Gabrielle cried out against his cheek, arching her back to meet her own exigency. Driven by the separation of body and soul in the past months, they moved with unbridled urgency toward the peak of utter fulfillment.

Tensing every muscle in her body, Gabrielle squeezed her eyes shut, burying her face in the crook of Alex's neck. Running her fingers through his thick auburn hair, she lifted her hips once and then again, groaning as she strained to pass beyond the point of return. Recognizing the change in the rhythm of her movements, Alex drove faster, and hand in hand they rose above the brink of all-consuming ecstasy.

Panting, Alex pressed his lips to her damp cheek, his breath hot on her face. "Tell me you'll marry me, Gabrielle. Tell me you'll come away with me."

"Yes," she heard herself say. "I'll marry you. . . ."

Chapter Nineteen

Alex rolled onto his side, lifting himself up on one elbow. "You'll what?" he stammered.

Gabrielle opened her eyes, a glimpse of a smile on her lips. "I said I'll marry you, Alex," she whispered, reaching to stroke his cheek. "I'll marry and I'll go to your Richmond. I can't promise you I'll like it; but I'll go, and I'll try to be the wife you want me to be."

"Ah, Gabrielle," he murmured against her hair. "Are you sure?"

"You taking back your offer?" She relaxed in the crook of his arm, her breath finally slowing to a normal rate.

"No, of course not; it's just that yesterday we were through and today—"

"And today I'm yours forever?"

He kissed her love-bruised lips in disbelief. "Exactly. I don't understand."

"What's there to understand? I thought I could live without you. I thought I could put distance between us, and when you went, I could go on with my life the way it was."

He twisted her wet hair around and around his finger. "But we can't, can we?" he asked tenderly.

"No, we can't." She rolled over on her side to face him, her hand resting on his chest. "I love you so much, Alex, even more than I love this land, and that's what it comes down to, doesn't it?"

"I wish you didn't have to make a choice." He caught her hand with his and brought it to his lips.

"I wish I didn't, either, but it can't be helped, can it? You've got your home, your family, your daughter. It's like Papa always told me, things never turn out the way you think they're going to."

"And what of Taylor?" he challenged.

"I can't spend my entire life being afraid of my father's killer, can I? Besides, you're right. How could he ever find me in Virginia? I'll be safe there, safe with you."

"I can't believe you're saying this; I thought I'd lost you. You seemed so happy with the new arrangement. I thought you were just going to let me walk out of your life." He laughed, his voice a low rumble. "I thought you were of stronger constitution."

"Stronger constitution? What's with you and your big words?" She rolled over on top of him, pinning his hands down at his side. Bright light streamed through the tiny window of the cabin, highlighting his fiery hair. "Is that the way you're going to talk to me when we get to Richmond? Because if it is, I'm not going."

With one quick movement, Alex flipped her over onto her back, covering her naked body with his. "Oh, no. There'll be no changing your mind now, Miss LeBeau. You're mine!" He let out a theatrical cackle of delight and buried his face in her neck.

Gabrielle burst into giggles, straining beneath him to free her hands, which he held pinned to her sides. "Stop! You're tickling me." She laughed, trying to wiggle away. "I'll do anything you say, but stop it, Alex."

Laughing with her, he lifted his head to look into the depths of her dark brown eyes. Their laughter dying, their lips mingled, and Alex sighed with contentment. "I'm going to make you very happy," he promised. "With the gold we're holding now we can live like royalty." His fingers brushed the tip of her breast, and her nipple puckered immediately in anticipation.

"I don't care about that; all I want is you. I want us to be happy." She moaned softly, her eyes drifting shut as his thumb caressed the sensitive bud of her breast.

"We will. I promise we will." He slid his head down, and she threaded her fingers through his thick hair, guiding him to a rosy nipple.

Dear God, I pray so, she thought, groaning softly as all sensible reasoning slipped from her mind.

The days slipped by as Gabrielle and Alex continued the sluicing process, and suddenly a Tanana summer was upon them. Alex complained that it was still cool, even on the warmest days, but Gabrielle only laughed, stripping off her clothes to plunge into the icy tributary. Content with her decision to marry Alex, she worked steadily at his side, anxious to finish the task of gold mining and get on with the new life she had chosen.

One night in mid-June, Alex suggested a celebration.

"Celebrate what?" Gabrielle asked tiredly, dragging several tools up the riverbank to store them for the night.

Alex shrugged good-naturedly. "I don't know, finding the gold, our engagement, you choose." He slipped small nuggets of gold into a leather bag, watching how they glittered in the sunlight.

"That's silly, Alex. You have to have a reason to celebrate."

He tucked the bag of gold into his belt, coming up the bank after her. Taking the tools from her arms, he matched her gait. "How about a map-burning party?"

She stopped on the path, looking up at him. "A what?"

"A map-burning party. We said we were going to burn the map, right?"

She nodded in confusion. "Right . . ."

"So let's do it tonight. We don't need it. You said you know how to get us out of here and to that steamer on the Yukon."

Gabrielle's lower lip trembled. She had agreed to burn the map, and she knew it had to be done; but a part of her wanted to keep it. It was one of the few tangible objects she had left of her father's. "All right," she said softly. "Let's do it."

He heard the hesitation in her voice. "You sure?"

"Yup." Her hand went to the knot of hair on her head. "But if we're going to have a party, we have to do it right. I want a bath, and you'll have to go bring us back something for a proper meal. I think I've had all of the dried berries and moose I can stand for one winter." She patted her stomach.

Laughing, Alex started up the path again with the

tools. "So a party it is! You go get yourself prettied up while I find us a rabbit. I'll be cooking tonight." He gave her an all-knowing wink, and she punched him in the arm.

Gabrielle watched from the tiny window until Alex disappeared into the woods with his rifle on his shoulder, and then she began to strip off her grimy clothes. They were coming up on their last few days of sluicing before it would be time to pack to go, and she was glad of it. Mining was a dirty, tiresome business, something she never wished to do again, and thanks to Rouge, she never would. The goldfield her father had discovered surpassed Alex's wildest dreams. In the few short months they had been mining, they had discovered enough gold to allow them to live comfortably for the rest of their lives.

Dropping the last of her clothes to the floor, Gabrielle scooped up an old towel and a bar of Mya's soap and set out for the river. Her dogs ran beside her, barking and nipping at each other's heels as they vied for their master's attention. Sadly, she reached out to scratch Tristan's ear.

She hated to leave her dogs behind; Alex had even offered to ship them by steamer and then by train to Virginia, but she'd declined. They were long-haired dogs, bred to run long distances and haul sleds through the snow. Here on the Tanana was where they belonged, and here they would stay. Before she left Jack in his village, she had told him that in July she and Alex would pick up a steamer for Seattle at Crooked Neck Bend on the Yukon River. She would leave her dogs there with an old native, Ury, and Jack would pick them up later in the summer. She had asked him to sell the team Alex had been driving, but now she supposed she would have to leave a message for him to sell them all, or keep them if he liked. They would be Jack's now that she wouldn't be returning to the Tanana.

Giving Tristan a final pat, she pushed him aside, and her doubts with it. What was wrong with her to always see the downside in everything? *I've got Alex don't I?* she asked herself. Going down the bank to the stream, she dropped her towel and dove into the frigid water, Mya's soap clutched in her hand. Surfacing, she shivered, rubbing the sweet-smelling bar over her skin, watching the rivulets of dirt run down her body to be washed away by the swift current. Working a lather through her hair, she tossed the bar onto the bank, which had dried with the winds of the summer, and began to rinse the chestnut mane. She was amazed at how long her hair had grown over the winter. It had been over a year since the last time she cut it! Rubbing her arms briskly for warmth, she walked to the shore and began to dry herself with the stiff towel.

By the time Alex had returned with a rabbit flung over one shoulder, Gabrielle had dressed in a pair of soft flannel pants and a matching long-sleeved tunic of a rich blue. They had been gifts from Mya, sewn with her own hands. Gabrielle hadn't worn them since she'd received them after the fire because she'd thought them too delicate for the life she led. But tonight, she decided, was the perfect night to wear them.

Alex came in the door, a contented smile on his face.

266

"You see how beautiful the sky is tonight?" His eyes lit up at the sight of her in the soft flannel clothing, her damp hair curled enticingly about her face.

Self-consciously Gabrielle ran her hands over the blue fabric. "It was all I had clean. My other clothes are soaking."

"You're beautiful." He kissed her lightly on the lips. "Now, how about I clean this rabbit up and get a fire started? I thought we'd sit outside on a blanket near the fire while our dinner cooks."

"We could bake those last two potatoes Mya gave us, and there's still those berries I picked yesterday."

"A feast fit for a king!" He leaned his rifle against the wall of the cabin and went back outside, whistling a familiar tune.

Later, Gabrielle and Alex relaxed on a blanket stretched out beside the fire. Though it was nearly ten at night, the sky still shone with the sun's brilliance as it moved westward. A hint of grey and pink stretched across the clear blue of a cloudless evening.

"Best meal we've had in weeks," Alex commented, rolling onto his side.

"You can say that again." Gabrielle patted her stomach, stretching out beside him.

He sighed, watching the flames of their campfire lick at the charred logs he'd just tossed in. "You know something, Gabrielle?"

She smiled up at him, stroking his bearded chin. "What?"

"I'm going to miss this . . . the fire at night, the openness of this land. I never felt so free."

"I'm glad," she murmured, smiling sadly. "I'm going

to miss it, too."

"Oh, but wait until you see Alexis. I just know you're going to love her! And the house, with a little paint and some furniture, it's going to be perfect. You'll never be cold again. Servants will light the fires in the fireplaces and heat water for your baths. I'll never swim in ice water again." His blue eyes crinkled with laughter.

"I hope you're right, Jefferson Alexander the fourth." Her lower lip trembled slightly.

"I am. Not backing out on me are you?" He toyed with a lock of her thick hair, watching it curl around his finger.

"Nope. I said I'd marry you and marry you I will. Now hand over that blasted map and let's have this done with."

Alex got to his feet, putting out a hand to help her up. "Here you go." He pulled the crumbled map from his pocket and pressed it into her hand.

Gabrielle accepted the bit of yellowed paper, and with one final glance at her father's scrawled writing, she offered it to the flames, watching them flare up as they caught the corner of the map and sucked it from her grasp. "There, it's done," she whispered.

"Done," Alex added solemnly. Then, taking her in his solid arms, he pulled her to him, and she rested her head on his breast. "Now," he said, "let's get on with our lives."

Just as they had agreed, Gabrielle and Alex left Rouge's campsite on the designated day, as close to

July first as they could figure. Leaving the two sleds, the mining equipment and anything else they could do without, they made two dog travoises to haul out the gold. The trip north, back up the tributary and along the Tanana to where the river met the Yukon River, was frustratingly slow. The gold was heavy and the dogs unused to pulling such an awkward contraption through the undergrowth. Still, Gabrielle and Alex made the best of the trip, enjoying the beauty of the surrounding mountains and valleys and the pleasure of each other's company.

Nearly three weeks from the time they left the campsite, they entered the "town" of Crooked Neck Bend. The settlement consisted mostly of natives living in various forms of cabins and huts with a few white men sprinkled here and there. Here Gabrielle said was a man, Godly Towers, who owned a small steamer used to run up and down the Yukon. It was her intention to hire Towers to take them to the mouth of the river and up to St. Michaels where they could catch a steamer to Seattle.

As Alex and Gabrielle entered the cluster of weary buildings known as Crooked Neck Bend, people came spilling onto the dirt street that ran no more than three or four hundred feet. They were immediately caught in the throng of the town's twenty to thirty residents. Dogs barked and children shouted as the group descended with fervent greetings.

"God love a porcupine! If it ain't Gabe LeBeau herself!" A middle-aged man, his head shaved bald, threw out his hand.

Gabrielle took it, giving it a shake. "Well God love a

269

porcupine, if it ain't Lucky Lou!" She laughed, turning to Alex. "Alex, I want you to meet Lucky Lou. Doesn't have a last name as far as I know; he's the mayor of Crooked Neck Bend." She stepped back to let Lou offer his hand. "Lou, this is Alex, my husband to be." Her cheeks flushed against her will.

"Husband! Well I'll be damned and sent straight to hell! Never thought you'd marry!" He ran a hand over his shiny pate. "Glad to meet you, Alex, got a nice little lady here." He grasped Alex's hand, pumping it excitedly.

Alex gave a nod, not quite sure what to make of this peculiar character. "Good to meet you, sir."

"I saw Godly's baby down on the river. Is she runnin'?" Gabrielle asked Lou.

"Never know from day to day, do ya?" He gave a chuckle, leaning to one side to get a better look at the travoises hitched to her barking dogs. "Where you headed?"

"Seattle."

"Hmmm, that right?" He stroked his whiskered chin. "Got any furs you want to unload?"

"Nope." She gave a smile. She and Alex had decided to tell no one about the gold they carried wrapped in hides and stuffed in cloth bags. There were too many dishonest men hard up for money to tempt fate. Out in this wilderness, men disappeared all the time over less than a fortune in gold, never to be seen again.

Lucky Lou glanced at the sled again. "In a hurry, are you?"

She laughed. "Did I say that?"

Alex stepped forward, draping an arm over her

270

shoulder. "Yes, in fact we are in a hurry, because as soon as we reach Seattle, we're going to be married." He gave Gabrielle a squeeze. "You see, I'm a very anxious man."

Gabrielle's dark eyes twinkled with amusement. "What can I say?" She lifted her hands in absolution. "He's an anxious man." Giving Lou a wink, she caught hold of Tristan's harness and urged him forward. "C'mon Alex, we'll see if we can hunt up Godly. It's still early yet. If we're lucky, he might not be drunk yet."

Shaking his head, Alex followed behind her, leading the second team of dogs.

That night Alex and Gabrielle camped just outside Crooked Neck Bend, down near the river bank. Lucky Lou had offered to let them stay in his cabin, promising a meal cooked by his two wives, but Gabrielle declined, saying she just wanted to get some rest before they left in the morning.

Alex and Gabrielle had managed to locate a relatively sober Godly Towers and had hired him to take them upriver. They would leave for St. Michaels the following day, sharing the ride with two gold seekers bound for home empty handed. Once Gabrielle and Alex had secured their passage, Gabrielle had taken her dogs out to Ury's just outside town and said a tearful good-bye. Scribbling a note of thanks and warm wishes, she gave the paper to Ury to pass on to Jack, telling him that she had gone to Virginia to be Alex's wife.

After a meal of fresh fish and turnips, Alex and Gabrielle had turned in to spend their final night out under the Alaskan stars. Wearily Gabrielle had drifted

271

off to sleep in the crook of Alex's arms. It wasn't until well after midnight that she was startled awake by the firm pressure of a hand pressed against her mouth.

Panic rose in her throat as her hands flew up to wrench the hand that threatened to suffocate her.

"Shhh," a voice came. "It's me, Alex. It's all right, just hush."

Gabrielle's eyes flew open in relief as he slid his hand off her mouth, pressing it to his lips. Slowly he pointed in the direction of the outline of Crooked Neck Bend's houses.

Straining to see through the grey darkness of night, she spotted the shadow of a man moving along the ground. A flush of fear prickled her flesh. Who was it? And what did he want? Whoever it was, he was up to no good, she was certain of that.

Lying quietly side by side, Gabrielle and Alex watched the man as he crept closer to their belongings piled just outside the ring of dim light cast off by their dying fire. Minutes stretched into what seemed like years as Alex waited, his muscles tense with anticipation.

Just as the intruder lay his hand on the closest bundle, Alex leaped up off his mat, swinging his rifle. "Hold it right there," he barked.

The dark figure jumped, started, then lit off across the clearing, moving as fast as his legs could carry him.

Alex fired a shot over the man's head and then a second. Gabrielle was at his side in an instant. "Don't go after him," she said, laying a hand on his arm.

"You sure?"

"Yea. It'll be light in a few hours. We'll be safe enough."

They stood watching as the man disappeared between the shadow of two cabins. "Do you know who it was?" Alex asked, reloading the rifle.

"Couldn't help but notice. It was the mayor." She turned to go back to the campfire, chuckling. "Didn't you catch the moonlight shining off that bald head of his?"

Chapter Twenty

Gabrielle nodded to the well-dressed man across the table from her, her eyes narrowing as she studied the cards she held tucked in her hand. "Hit me again." She dropped a dog-eared card, facedown.

"And you?" The man Joey waited for Alex to respond.

Alex grimaced, concentrating on his own cards. He glanced up at Joey, questioningly.

"Don't look at me!" Joey bit back a chuckle. "I've *been* out; I can't beat her."

Alex gave a sigh. "Damn, Gabrielle, you've whipped me again!" He slapped his cards on the table, lifting a glass of whiskey to his lips.

Gabrielle grinned. "Sorry, fellas." Returning her five cards to the deck, she reached for the pile of crumpled bills in the center of the table.

"Now wait a minute, aren't you going to show us what you had?" Alex covered her hand with his, preventing her from picking up the cash.

She lifted a sooty eyebrow. "Not hardly, now

unhand me before I pop you in the eye." She laughed as he released her hand, and she leaned into him, kissing him on the lips.

Joey shook his head, extracting an expensive cigar from the inside pocket of his black coat. "Quite a card player you got there," he told Alex. "Get her at the gaming tables and she could win a fortune!"

"Yea." Alex refilled his glass from the bottle on the table. "If I keep playing her, I'll have to marry her to keep from going broke."

The two men laughed as Gabrielle gathered her bills and arranged them neatly before tucking them in the breast pocket of the man's shirt she wore. She and Alex had picked up the mail steamer at St. Michaels without a hitch and were now steaming full ahead, their destination Seattle. There were several other passengers on board: Joey, who worked for a fur trading company out of Seattle, the two gold miners they had met in Crooked Neck Bend and a handful of other assorted characters, along with the crew.

To keep busy she played cards with anyone who would dare, taking the few dollars Jack had given her and turning them into a growing stack she kept safe in the chamber pot in the small cabin she and Alex shared. Their gold had been placed in wooden crates and stored down below, disguised in the rolls of cured hides. So far, they had managed to let no one know they were carrying more than a few slivers of gold dust.

"Well, I thank you for the evening's pleasant company, Gabrielle, Alex." Joey nodded, getting up from his chair. "But I think I'll retire."

"Good night." Gabrielle smiled.

"Good night," Alex followed in suit. He watched the

businessman leave the dining room of the steamer through a heavy paneled door. Turning back to Gabrielle, he poured himself another glass of whiskey. "Shame on you taking all of that man's money." His eyes sparkled with pride.

"Shame on me?" She laughed. "Shame on him for thinking he could beat me!"

"I didn't know you could play so well."

She shrugged good-naturedly, retrieving her tattered deck of cards. "Not much to do in mid-January. Papa and I played by the hour."

Alex moved to the chair beside her. "There's something I don't understand."

"What's that?" She took a sip from his glass, the fiery liquid burning a path down her throat.

"If Rouge was as good as you are, why did he have to cheat?"

"I don't know. I asked him the same question, but he could never tell me straight. I think he liked the excitement of doing something dishonest. He liked worrying that he might get caught." She looked up at him. "Funny, huh?"

Alex took her hand. "Yea. Funny." He studied her dark eyes. "Listen, Gabrielle, I've been thinking. What do you say we wait and get married in Richmond?"

"In Richmond?" Her heart gave an involuntary leap. Was he backing out? Had he changed his mind? "I thought you said we were going to be married just as soon as we got to Seattle." Her voice wavered. "I thought you said you couldn't wait to marry me."

He smiled, hearing the uneasiness in her voice. "I do want you to be my wife. I just thought that instead of making it a hurried affair, we could wait until we got to

277

Virginia, and then we could have a big church wedding. My family could all be there."

Gabrielle twisted her fingers in his, staring at the worn wooden table bolted to the floor. "Yea, I guess we could wait . . . I mean we've been living in sin all this time haven't we?" *Tell him no,* an inner voice warned. *Tell him you want to make it legal as soon as you reach Seattle or you're not going with him.*

Alex caught her chin with his hand, lifting it to make her look him in the eye. "There can be no sin in loving you the way I do, Gabrielle. It's just that I want to make this special. Most women dream their entire lives of their wedding day."

"If that's what you want, it's all right." Her lower lip quivered slightly.

"You certain? We can go ahead and find a priest the minute we get off the steamer if that's what you want."

"No. No, you're right." She managed a smile. "A big wedding would be nice."

He brushed her hair off her chek, leaning to kiss her softly. "I just want to make you happy."

"I know." Pushing back in her chair, she got up. "I think I'll turn in now." She retrieved her cards.

"Want me to come?"

"Nah, it's still early. You stay." She nodded in the direction of three crew members and one of the miners playing poker in the corner of the small dining room. "Maybe you can get into the game."

He nodded his russet head, glancing over in interest. "I'm not really tired."

"Then stay."

Later, Gabrielle lay huddled in her single bunk in their cabin, unable to sleep. Was Alex having doubts about their marriage? Now that they were in contact with other people again, did he realize how unconventional she was? She groaned, pulling the wool coverlet over her head. The steamer had hit bad weather, and the vessel was rocking viciously, making her stomach uneasy. Had Alex just changed his mind and couldn't tell her?

Then her voice of reason took over. *Am I being irrational? Maybe I'm the one who's reconsidering, and I can't admit it to myself.* She had to admit that the thought of marriage, the institution her father had cursed, did frighten her. *Maybe I'm blaming Alex for my own doubts,* she thought dejectedly. *After all, he said he wanted a church wedding for me.* Her mind in turmoil, it was a long time before Gabrielle finally succumbed to uneasy sleep.

Gabrielle and Alex walked out of the gold-broker's office and onto the street hand in hand. "I can't believe it, Gabrielle! I still can't believe it! We're rich, sweetheart!" He caught her by the waist, swinging her around, ignoring the curious passersby.

Gabrielle giggled. "Put me down, you fool. We'll be arrested for vagrants disturbing the peace of this fine city."

He set her on her feet, unable to resist stealing a kiss before he released her. "Yea." He looked down at his worn clothing. "Guess the first thing we need to do is find some decent clothes, a new suit for me, a pretty frilly dress for you."

She wrinkled her nose. "No, the first thing we need to do is find a hotel. You do the shopping. I'm going to sink myself into a tub of water, and I'm not coming out until I'm as wrinkled as an old piece of moose jerky."

"You want me to get you a dress?"

"Sure, why not. Your taste is probably better than mine when it comes to that sort of thing. You know what a lady's supposed to look like. Just no bustle, please."

He caught her arm, steering her in the door of the first good hotel they came upon on King's Street. "The broker says it will be a few days until he can make the arrangements, find a buyer, but he gave me a nice cash advance." He patted his jacket. "You can have anything you want, Gabrielle. Just name it."

She stopped on the front step of the hotel. "In here?" A huge sign bearing the hotel's name loomed overhead. The St. Lucy was one of the most expensive hotels in Seattle.

"You bet." He put his hand on the doorknob, pushing the glass-windowed door open for her.

Gabrielle stepped in hesitantly, taking in the hand-painted wallpaper and crystal chandeliers in the front entryway.

A rotund woman with her hair piled high and her face caked with makeup scowled from behind the front desk. "Can I help you?" She eyed Gabrielle and Alex suspiciously.

"A room please."

The woman lifted a painted eyebrow. "Sorry, it's cash up front. I'll have to see the color of your money, sugar pie."

Alex stepped up, pushing a bill of large denomination across the polished wood counter. "That be enough?"

The woman's face brightened. "I believe so, yes sir!" She took the bill, sliding it beneath the counter. "You folks just come from up north?"

"Just in on the mail steamer this morning," Gabrielle answered.

"Must have been a good year for you." She reached for a large leather-bound register book. "Name please . . ."

"Gabrielle LeB—"

"Mr. and Mrs. Jefferson Alexander," Alex interrupted, draping an arm around Gabrielle's shoulder. "We'd like a large room, and a bath sent up for Mrs. Alexander immediately."

Gabrielle dug the heel of her soiled boot into the thick oriental carpet that covered the hard-wood floor. She felt distinctly out of place. She and Rouge had never stayed in a place this fancy; they always took a room down at the docks.

"Shall we go?" Alex took Gabrielle's arm, the key to their room in his hand. Going up the steps, they took the third door on the left. "Here we are . . ." He inserted the key and pushed open the door.

Gabrielle gave a gasp of surprise. "I've never seen anything so beautiful!" The sitting room was furnished in red velvet, with wallpaper done in red and ivory. The bedroom was off to the side. "Look at it, Alex!" She ran leaping onto the monstrous bed.

He chuckled, dropping the key on a marble-topped side table. "A little garish, don't you think?"

"Garish?" She popped her head up off one of the frilly pillows. "What's garish?"

He looked at her beaming face. "Nothing, never mind. You stay here and wait for your bath. Don't let

281

anyone else in but the maid while I'm gone. You hear me?"

She bounced off the bed, running to pull back the heavy crimson drapes that covered the windows. "I hear, I hear. Go on with you. I'll be fine."

"You sure you don't want to go with me?"

"Positive. I hate shopping." She looked down to the street below, watching people pass.

"All right. Back soon." He blew her a kiss. "Behave yourself."

A few minutes after Alex had gone, a knock came at the door. "Who is it?" Gabrielle called.

"Maid, ma'am, with your bath," a shrill voice called.

Gabrielle lifted the latch on the door and turned the knob. "Come in."

A maid in a flounced black and white dress and apron filed past her, a man following with a huge copper tub in his arms. Three men came in behind them, toting buckets of steamy water. Once the tub was filled, the men made a quick exit.

"Shall I stay and assist you?" the maid asked, holding herself erect, a pile of fluffy white towels in her arms.

"Help? Help with what? God's sakes, you don't think I can wash myself?"

With a snort, the maid dropped the towels on a chair and started out of the bedchamber and through the parlor. "Well, if there's anything else, Mrs. Alexander, you call." She pointed to a thick braid rope that hung from the ceiling in the corner of the room. "Just pull the bell, ma'am."

"Thank you." Gabrielle let her out and closed the door, locking it behind her.

An hour later when Alex's key rattled in the door, Gabrielle was still submerged in the glorious bathtub. "Gabrielle? Where are you, love?"

"Here I am," she called from the bedroom.

He stuck his head in the door. "How long have you been in there?"

She laughed. "I told you I needed a bath." She leaned forward to get a better look at him. "Come around here, I can't see you. Have you got yourself some new clothes, Mr. Alexander?" she teased. "And a haircut, too?"

His cheeks colored as he came through the door. He was dressed much like he'd been the day he'd rescued Gabrielle on the docks nearly a year ago. He wore a dark double-breasted suit and a starched white shirt with a stand collar. In his hand he carried a black bowler hat. "So what do you think?"

She smiled proudly. "I'd not have recognized you on the street. I'd forgotten what you looked like shaved and with short hair."

"Just wait until you see what I've brought you." He pointed at her with the hat. "You stay here while I have the shopkeepers bring the boxes into the parlor."

"Boxes?" She rose halfway out of the tub.

"Calm down, it's just a few things for you to wear until we get to Richmond."

Gabrielle rolled her eyes as he went out of the bedroom, closing the door behind him. A few minutes later when the sound of men's voices and footsteps died away, he came back into the bedroom carrying a silky azure robe over his arm. "Mademoiselle!" He offered an arm, helping her out of the tub.

"This for me?"

"Uh huh, like it?" He helped her slip her arms into the luxurious lounging robe.

"Well, yea, I guess so. It's just that I never owned such a thing. After my bath, I just put my clothes back on."

Alex laughed. "Well, now you have a robe to put on. Now come see what else I've bought you," he said, leading her into the parlor.

Gabrielle gave a gasp. There were paperboard boxes piled everywhere, large and small, wrapped and unwrapped. "You bought all of this? Have you lost your head, Alex?" She lifted a cardboard lid and extracted a pair of women's lacy underdrawers. There were eleven more pairs just like it in the same box.

"You don't like them?" He fingered the wide lace on the legs of the drawers. "I can take them back and get something different if you like."

"No. It's all right. Two pairs would have done, that's all." She proceeded to move from one box to the next, overwhelmed by his extravagance. There were day dresses and skirts, shirt waists and bonnets, not to mention the piles of ladies' accessories. "Did you leave anything in the shops?"

Alex laughed, watching her pull a gown of forest-green serge from a large box. "I know you didn't want anything too fancy. I thought you could wear that to supper this evening."

"Supper?" She looked up wide-eyed.

"Sure, I thought I'd take you out your first night in town." He folded a pair of silk hose and returned it to its box. "Don't you want to?"

She chewed at her lower lip in indecision. "I thought we could just stay here tonight and have something sent

284

up. I don't know that I'm ready for so many people."

"Nonsense." He slipped an arm around her waist, pulling her close. "I just want to take you out and show you off. I promise, we'll make an early night of it."

Not wanting to disappoint him, Gabrielle nodded her consent. "All right, but just a small place, somewhere not too busy. We don't want to end up running into Taylor."

"Is that what you're worried about?" He kissed her fragrant lips. "I think we've heard the last of him; besides, the map is gone, and the gold is safe with the broker. Our worries are over. Now go on and get dressed." He fondled her bottom playfully, and she smacked at his hand.

"Reservations for two for Jefferson Alexander," Alex told the maitre d'hotel of the restaurant in the finest hotel in Seattle.

The man in the dark suit nodded, checking off the name on a piece of paper with the great flourish of a plume pen. "This way, sir, madam . . ." The man led them to a small table in the corner of the dining room. Men and women at the other scattered tables looked up with interest.

"Thank you." Alex allowed Gabrielle to take a seat against the wall, and he sat down across from her.

The maitre d'hotel cleared his throat. "The special for the evening, sir, is baked patridge stuffed with salmon. Will that do?"

"Yes. That will be fine. And a bottle of wine while we wait." He smiled across the small table at Gabrielle as the man dismissed himself. He reached over the painted china plates to take her hand. "Don't look so frightened."

"I don't like it here." She batted at the chiffon veil of her hat.

"What do you mean you don't like it here?"

"People are staring at me." She withdrew her hand from his and slipped off the green gloves that matched her new dress.

Alex chuckled. "You're paranoid. No one is looking at you, but if they are, it's only because you're the most beautiful woman in Seattle."

Gabrielle twisted her hands beneath the linen table cloth. "You don't understand. I don't know how to act in a place like this."

"Act? There's no acting to it. You just have to sit here and talk with me and eat your supper when someone brings it." He sighed, lowering his voice. "There's nothing to be afraid of."

"Who says I'm afraid?" She started to say something else but immediately closed her mouth when someone returned with a bottle of wine and two crystal wineglasses.

Alex poured the wine and passed her a glass. "Drink," he urged. "You're just nervous."

She sipped the wine, peeking over the rim of the glass at the other customers in the room. The ladies and gentlemen speaking in low voices were all so well dressed; they seemed so refined. Gabrielle's hand trembled. She didn't belong here, but she knew that if she was going to marry Alex, she was going to have to get used to being out in public.

"Feeling better?" Alex took her hand again. "The hotel is very nice. We could move our things here if you wish. It's just been built."

She shook her head, rubbing her neck. The veiled hat she was wearing was so heavy that it was making her neck stiff. It was a huge billowing affair with thick ruffles of Spanish lace, and dyed green and black feathers. She thought it hideous when Alex had pulled it out of the hat box, but he was so pleased with his choice that she couldn't bear to tell him. "No. I like our room just fine. And like you said, we're only going to be here a few days."

He lifted his glass to his lips, sampling the familiar vintage. "We can take a train out of here at the end of the week. The gold broker suggested I hire a guard to ride with the money until I deposit it in a bank in Richmond." He smiled, watching the way the light from the gas lamp at the table cast golden shadows over her smooth skin. "You're beautiful," he whispered.

She smiled in return, beginning to feel a little better. The wine had calmed her nerves. She knew she had nothing to fear. "I may be, but the lace on these drawers is driving me mad!" She slipped a hand beneath the table to scratch viciously.

Alex grinned. "We'll have our meal, and then we'll go back to our room so I can take care of that little itch for you." His voice was husky with insinuation.

Gabrielle lifted her glass in laughter, then froze, the glass in midair.

Alex stared at her stricken face. "What's the matter? Are you all right?"

Her stomach gave a lurch as she managed to set her glass on the edge of the table. Suddenly she couldn't breathe. Her heart beat rapidly beneath her breast as she struggled against the sudden light-headedness she was feeling. She couldn't lift her gaze from the door of the restaurant.

Seeing that she was staring at something or someone behind him, Alex turned in his chair. He saw nothing but the other seated guests and a well-dressed man and woman just coming in the door. "What is it?" he murmured.

"Alex," she gasped, wiping her mouth with the linen napkin, "I have to get out of here."

"What do you mean? What is it? Taylor?" His handsome face was a mask of concern.

"It's Alice," she said in a weak voice, "my mother."

Chapter Twenty-One

"Your mother?" Alex turned back around, gazing at the customers that filled the room. He didn't see any whores. "Where, Gabrielle?"

She took a deep breath, averting her eyes to stare at the china plate in front of her. "There, Alex, don't you see her? At the door..." The pain that she'd suppressed so well flooded Gabrielle as she struggled to remain in control of her emotions. That woman, her mother, had abandoned her, had broken her father's heart. Alice LeBeau had never given a damn about anyone but herself.

Alex glanced back at the door in total confusion. The only woman he saw was standing in the entryway, speaking quietly to her escort. She was tastefully dressed in a deep blue, organza gown and a discreet veiled hat. The woman's hair, piled high in an elegant coiffure, was honey-colored and as shiny as spun taffy. He turned back to Gabrielle in disbelief. How could that well-spoken woman possibly be the whore, Alice LeBeau, Gabrielle spoke of so disdainfully? "Are you certain?" he asked.

"Am I certain?" Gabrielle managed a bitter chuckle. "What, you don't think I can recognize my own mother?" She lowered her head, blocking her face from view as Alice and her gentleman were seated.

"No, of course not. I mean . . ." He sighed, squeezing her hand in comfort. "It's just that she doesn't appear to be the woman you've spoken of."

"I have to admit she's moved up in the world since I last saw her. Maybe her friend's keeping her. But just because she's dressed well and can talk proper-like, that doesn't make her any less a whore!" She yanked her hand from Alex's grasp. "I have to get out of here."

He got immediately to his feet. "She didn't recognize you; we could stay and eat."

Gabrielle shook her head emphatically, already coming around the table. "No. I can't stay here. I can't breathe. I've got to get out of these suffocating clothes. You stay if you like." She started past him, but he caught her arm.

"It's all right, love," he said softly. "We'll go." Walking at her side, they made their way through the dining room.

Just when Gabrielle thought she'd made her escape, a familiarly grating voice came from behind.

"Gabrielle," Alice cried gaily. "Is that you, dear?"

Gabrielle stopped dead, her hand trembling in Alex's.

"We can go," he whispered in her ear. "Just ignore her."

"No," she breathed. "I can't spend my whole life running." Gathering her nerve, she turned slowly around. "Alice?" she managed.

"Gabrielle." The woman with the taffy-colored hair waved a gloved hand. "Come, come, how nice to see you again." She smiled graciously.

Gabrielle propelled herself forward toward the small table where Alice was seated. Alex followed at her heels.

"Geoffrey, this is Gabrielle, an old friend," Alice introduced.

The middle-aged gentleman got to his feet, giving a nod. "So nice to meet you."

Gabrielle nodded in return. "This is Alex, Jefferson Alexander the fourth," she corrected herself. Her mind went numb as the small talk passed between them. What kind of game was her mother playing that she hadn't introduced her as her daughter? Though she had never paid her a lick of attention, she'd never denied her before. "No, just arrived by steamer this morning," Gabrielle stumbled back into the conversation.

Alex felt her sway and caught her arm. "Well, we must be going. It's been a long day. Nice to have met you both."

"Good-bye," Gabrielle whispered, allowing Alex to steer her toward the door.

"Oh, Gabrielle," Alice called after her. "I'd like to call on you. Where are you staying?"

When Gabrielle didn't asnwer, Alex spoke for her. "At the St. Lucy. Mr. and Mrs. Alexander."

Alice's china doll mask fell for an instant, then suddenly she became the same lighthearted woman her clients sought her for. "The St. Lucy, then. Look for me tomorrow."

Gabrielle left the hotel's restaurant on Alex's arm, managing not to make a scene, but the moment they were out on the street, she turned on Alex viciously. "How could you? How could you do that to me?" She started down the wooden plank sidewalk, her feet moving rapidly beneath the heavy skirts of her new gown.

Alex was forced to run to catch up. "How could I what?" He pushed back his hat on his head.

"You told her where we're staying, Alex. Now we'll have to move."

"Don't be silly." He followed her down the street, turning onto King's Street. "Why would we move?"

"Because she won't leave us alone. When she finds out how much gold we brought back, we won't be able to get rid of her. The woman's a leech."

"Gabrielle, for Christ's sake will you slow down?" He caught the sleeve of her gown. "I just thought you might want to say good-bye. I just thought—" He stopped in mid-sentence as two women and a man passed them, staring curiously. He lowered his voice as they approached their hotel. "She's still your mother. You're never going to see her again."

"Oh, yes I am. I'm going to see her tomorrow, thanks to you!" She pushed open the glass-windowed door of the St. Lucy and hurried up to the front desk. "Key, please," she stated flatly.

The painted woman behind the desk looked up with interest. Obediently she slipped their room key from a hook beneath the counter and handed it to Gabrielle. "Have a nice supper?" she asked.

"No, I did not. Could you please have something sent up?"

"For you and Mr. Alexander?" It was obvious to her that the couple was having a disagreement.

292

Gabrielle glanced at Alex, who waited for her at the bottom of the staircase down the hall. "Yes, I suppose so."

"And what would you care for?" The woman smiled, her makeup creasing at the corners of her mouth.

"Anything. Anything will do." She spun around, heading for the stairs. The moment Alex let her in the door, she was tugging off the monstrous hat she wore perched on her head. Flinging it to the floor, she stomped into the bedroom.

Alex followed. "Are you quite through with your little temper tantrum?" he asked dryly.

She gave a sigh, moving to the windows to pull the heavy drapes. The room was silent for several moments before she spoke. "I'm sorry, Alex." She turned to face him. "I shouldn't blame you. That woman, she makes me crazy. All of those people looking at me . . . the fancy dishes, the clothes . . ." She tugged at a ruffle at her bodice. "I'm just no good at this."

He tossed his bowler hat onto a velvet-covered chair. "You were doing just fine."

"I was so nervous about being out with you with all of those people, and then she appeared." She put up her hands in surrender. "I didn't know what to do."

Alex gathered Gabrielle in his arms. "It's all right; you did fine. Now don't worry about it. Alice will come tomorrow, you'll say your good-byes and that will be the end of it." He stroked her back soothingly.

"I hope so." She sighed, resting her head on his broad chest.

"Now why don't you let me get you out of this." His fingers were already moving nimbly down the back of her new gown.

"Please." She wrapped her arms around his waist. "The lace itches so bad. I told you it would take me some time to get used to wearing these trappings."

Alex lowered his mouth to hers, and she leaned into him, a shiver of anticipation running down her spine. Their breath mingled, and she moaned softly, snaking her hands up around his neck. She ran her fingers through his thick hair, inhaling his familiarly masculine scent as she lifted her chin to let him kiss the length of her neck. Unbuttoning the last of the tiny green beads that ran down her back, Alex slipped the shoulder of her gown down, moving the strap of her corset cover with it. "Since when did you start wearing one of these things?"

She laughed deep in her throat, running her hands over his stiffly starched shirt. "The corset went out with the empty boxes. I just put on the cover. You'll not catch me trussed like a goose."

"I didn't think so, but the dressmaker insisted I take the thing." He slipped the gown down farther, nibbling at the silken flesh of her shoulder. Letting the gown fall to a heap at her feet, he swung her easily into his arms.

"What about the supper?" She stroked his clean shaven chin as he laid her gently on the large bed.

He pressed his lips to hers. "The door's locked," he said huskily, shrugging off his tailored coat. "Just have to wait, won't it?"

When the knock came at the door the following afternoon, Gabrielle's heart gave a lurch. Brushing her damp hands nervously over her jersey skirt, she got to her feet. "Do I look all right?" she asked Alex.

He smiled, picking his hat up off a small marble-topped table in the bedroom, and stepped into the parlor, closing the door behind him. "You're beautiful." He kissed the top of her chestnut head. She had pulled her hair back loosely into a chignon at the nape of her neck, letting a few wisps fall free to frame her oval face. "You sure you don't want me to stay?"

She laid her hand on the door knob. "I'm sure. Go see about hiring the guard. If we're going to leave on the Tuesday morning train, it's got to be done."

"I know, I just hate to throw you to the lions."

The knock came again, only this time more insistent and Gabrielle rolled her eyes. "Don't worry about me. I can handle her." She lifted her chin to let him kiss her gently, then she took a deep breath and opened the door.

Alice LeBeau entered the parlor of their hotel room with the rustle of taffeta and lace. "Afternoon." She nodded demurely to Alex. "Mr. Alexander, how pleasant to see you again." She fluttered her eyelashes, and Gabrielle groaned aloud. The woman never changed; she was always looking for a potential customer.

"Good-bye, Alex," Gabrielle murmured, resting her hand on the back of his coat.

He nodded in Alice's direction and put on his hat. "Good afternoon, ladies. I'll have refreshments sent up as I leave the hotel."

"You're not staying, Mr. Alexander?" Alice laid her hand gently on his arm.

"No. Sorry, I can't. I've business to attend to." He stepped back and she smiled, releasing him.

"Pity." She pulled off her dyed kidskin gloves and

laid them on the settee against the wall. "We could have gotten to know each other better."

Throwing Gabrielle one last glance, Alex went out the door.

"So, Mother," Gabrielle leaned against the paneled wooden door. "What do you want?"

"Want?" Alice sat on the velvet settee, taking notice of the pile of paperboard boxes beside her. She lifted the lid off of the box the dressmaker had just delivered that morning. "Do I have to want something to come calling on my daughter? It's just been a long time since I've seen you."

"So, I'm your daughter today, am I? Why wasn't I yesterday?" She ran her hands down over her slim-fitting bleached muslin shirt waist.

Alice fingered the rich fabric of the traveling coat in the box on the settee. "Is that what you're mad about? Oh, pooh. You don't think I could tell Geoffrey I was old enough to have a daughter your age, do you?"

Gabrielle gave an exasperated sigh. "Since when do your gentlemen friends take you out for supper?"

"Watch your mouth!" Alice stood up, pulling the coat out of the box. "You've no right to speak to me like that." She pushed her arms into the sleeves, trying on Gabrielle's new coat.

"And why not? What are you to me?" Her voice wavered as she stared in disbelief at her mother. The nerve of the woman, trying on her new clothes!

"I gave birth to you, girl."

"And that was the end of your responsibility wasn't it?" Gabrielle said accusingly, coming to stand before Alice.

"I can't believe you still blame me for that after all

these years. Nice coat, did it come from Barker's?" She went to the gilded mirror that hung over the rosewood sidetable and stood sideways to gaze at her silhouette. "Is it my fault I couldn't abide that wilderness, that crude little cabin, those Indians? Your father and I just didn't get along. I was never meant to be a wife and mother, just not cut from the right cloth."

"My father loved you," Gabrielle challenged.

"Your father was like any other man. He took what he wanted from me, but he gave nothing in return." Alice fingered the ebony braid that ran along the cuffs of the coat.

"That's not true. Papa wasn't like that; Alex isn't like that."

"If you think so, it's only because that husband of yours hasn't shown his true colors yet."

Gabrielle folded her arms across her chest. "Alex isn't my husband."

Alice spun around, lifting a shaped eyebrow. "Oh, no?" Her mouth twitched in a smile. "I thought he introduced you as the Mrs. Alexander . . ."

Gabrielle turned to present her back to her mother. "We're going to get married, just not until we get to Virginia. He's from Richmond."

Alice's laughter filled the small parlor as she shrugged off the coat and dug into a hat box. "If he hasn't married you by now, my dear naive daughter, then he's not going to marry you."

Gabrielle spun back around. "That's not true. We are going to be married. We just decided we'd wait until we reached Virginia." She tried to control her trembling hands. How was it that her mother always knew how to cut her to the quick?

Alice gave an all-knowing nod, returning to the mirror. "I understand you deposited a large sum of gold with a broker yesterday." She removed her hat pins and began to try on her daughter's new bonnet.

Gabrielle stared in disbelief. "How do you know? Who told you?" she demanded.

Alice glanced up at her daughter through the reflection in the mirror. "The man I was with last night, Geoffrey, does business with several gold brokers. When I saw you dressed the way you were yesterday, I knew you'd come into money; I just didn't know how." She turned her head this way and that, trying to decide if she liked the hat. "I just asked Geoffrey to do some checking. He'd do anything for me. So would most of my customers."

"Mother! Would you please stop trying on my clothes? Take them, take them all, just stop picking through everything."

Alice turned around. "Why, thank you," she said sweetly, returning the hat to its box. "The coat, too?"

"Take it," Gabrielle ordered through clenched teeth.

"I certainly will. I mean there'll be plenty more where this came from, won't there? At least as long as your man keeps you."

"Half of the gold is mine, Mother."

"Smart girl. At least you'll have something when he moves on. Something to take back to those filthy dogs of yours." She put her own hat back on. "Did you say we were having refreshments?"

"I think it's time you went."

"What do you mean? We were having such a nice visit."

Gabrielle stepped up to her mother. "Why didn't you

come to Papa's funeral?"

"It's not that I wasn't sorry he was dead—"

"Just too busy, were you? Too busy with your *customers,*" she demanded.

"That's not true and you know it. Rouge and I came to an understanding several years back." She faced her daughter squarely. "I was always glad to see him."

Gabrielle laughed bitterly. "Glad to take his money for your services."

Alice raised her hand to slap her daughter's face, but Gabrielle caught it in midair. "Get out," she ordered. "Get out of my life and don't you ever come back. All of these years I felt guilty. Papa told me it wasn't my fault you left, but I didn't believe him." She lowered her mother's arm slowly, refusing to release her. "But you know Papa was right. You didn't care about us; you only cared about yourself. Once a whore, always a whore."

Anger welled up in Alice LeBeau's face. "How dare you speak to me like that?" She jerked her arm free. "Look who's calling the kettle black. Living with a man, letting him buy you fancy things because you sleep with him." She yanked her gloves off the settee and thrust her hands into them. "What's the difference, tell me that? I take money; you accept a room in a hotel and a nice coat and hat."

"Get out," Gabrielle shouted. "Get out of here!"

Alice grabbed the hat box off the settee, heading for the door. "You'll regret this someday, Gabrielle. There'll come a time when you'll need someone. I know I haven't always been there for you, but I'm all you have."

"Get out!" Gabrielle ordered, swinging open the

paneled door to the hall.

Alice moved unhurriedly through the door, Gabrielle's hat box under her arm. "Good day, daughter."

Gabrielle slammed the door in response, then, spotting the traveling coat in the open box, she scooped it up off the settee. Yanking open the door again, she threw the box through the door. "You're forgetting something, Mother!" she shouted, then closed the door with a resounding bang.

The shadows were lengthening into afternoon when Alex slipped the key in the lock of their hotel room door and stepped inside. "Gabrielle? Where are you?" He slid his hat on the table and went into the bedroom, a small box clutched in his hand. He spotted her laying facedown on the bed. "Gabrielle?" he said softly.

"Yes?" Her voice was muffled by the pillow she rested on.

"Are you all right?" He sat down on the corner of the bed and rolled her over. Her face was tear stained, her eyes red and swollen. "What's the matter, love?"

She sniffed, reaching for the handkerchief that lay beside her on the bed. Her hair had fallen from the neat chignon, her shirt waist was wrinkled from lying on the bed and one stocking had come loose from its garter. Her head ached, and her throat was sore from crying. "Everything."

He stifled his desire to laugh. "Everything?" He reached to take her in his arms, but she resisted him. "The visit with your mother that bad?"

She sniffed again, squeezing her eyes shut. "I was thinking, Alex. Maybe this isn't such a good idea. Maybe . . ." She blew her nose. "Maybe you should just take your share of the gold and go back to

300

Richmond by yourself."

"Gabrielle, what's wrong? What did your mother say to you to make you change your mind?" He got up off the bed to retrieve a face cloth and dip it in the washbowl on a stand near the bed. Sitting back down beside her, he wiped her face gently. "Tell me, Gabrielle."

"She . . . she said—" Fresh tears streamed down her face. "Mother said I was naive. If . . . if you hadn't married me by now, you'd never marry me. She said I was no better than a whore myself. . . ."

Alex cursed beneath his breath, drawing her into his arms. "That's what she said, and you believed her?" He brushed back her damp hair, kissing her forehead.

She clung to him, swallowing against the rising lump in her throat. "I didn't want to, but maybe I am naive, I don't know. . . ."

"Shhh," he hushed. "It's all right, now stop crying. It's not true." He dabbed at her swollen eyes with the facecloth. "I love you, Gabrielle. I've always loved you. Now get up and fix your hair." He set her on the bed and got up.

"I don't want any supper."

"We're not going to supper. We're going to put an end to this once and for all." He tugged at her hand, bringing her to her feet.

She studied his clear blue eyes. "I don't understand."

He brushed his lips against hers. "What's there to understand? Tuck in your shirt and find your shoes. We're getting married."

Chapter Twenty-Two

Alex slipped the key in the hotel room door and turned the knob. Giving the door a push, he tucked the key in his pocket and turned to Gabrielle. He had never seen her so beautiful as she was tonight. Her dark eyes sparkled with happiness, her soft lips whispering silent promises of love. He bowed gracefully. "Mrs. Alexander?" His voice held a slight southern drawl.

"Mr. Alexander." She mimicked his voice, then gave a giggle, curtsying in return.

With one quick movement, Alex swept her into his arms, crushing his mouth against hers. Her arms slid up around his neck as she leaned into him accepting his greedy kiss. Their tongues met in a dance of love, with Gabrielle withdrawing only when she was breathless. Alex buried his face in the bodice of her gown, inhaling the sweet scent of her full breasts.

"Alex . . ." she murmured in his ear, "will you strip me here in the hall?"

"I could," he answered huskily, tugging at the tiny pearl buttons of her shirt waist with his teeth.

Gabrielle threaded her fingers through his thick, short-cropped hair, nipping at his ear. "Inside, please. Before we embarrass ourselves and everyone else in the hotel. And put me down, you fool."

Alex's laughter echoed in the hallway as he pushed through the door of their room and closed it with one polished shoe. "Come to think of it, you are getting a little heavy."

Playfully, she beat him with her fist as he lowered her to her feet. "That's not very nice to tell your wife." Her fingers moved lightly beneath his coat, surveying his broad chest.

His mouth came down on hers again. "And certainly not my rich wife," he murmured against her lips. Their breath mingled again, and Gabrielle molded herself against the length of his body, reveling in the feel of his hard, muscular frame pressed to her soft curves.

Running her fingers over his lips, she stared up into his familiar blue eyes. "I can't believe you did it. You married me."

His eyes drifted shut as her fingers moved over his cheekbones, the ridge of his nose, the arch of his eyebrows. Her movements were tantalizingly light, sending shivers of desire down his spine. "I told you I would marry you. I told you I loved you . . . love you."

"I know," she whispered. "I guess I thought it was too good to be true. I love you so much. I never expected to be this happy." Alex lifted a hand to brush against her breast, and she smiled, covering his hand with hers. "What of our wedding supper?"

He groaned, his nimble fingers starting down the line of buttons on her white shirt waist. "I forgot."

"Well, I didn't. I'm starved."

"You are?" He grinned boyishly. "For me or for supper?"

"Both, but if I don't get something to eat, I'll be too weak to roll in that big bed with you. I haven't had a bite all day." He slipped his hand between the folds of her shirt waist, and she sighed, moving one skirted leg provocatively against the hard bulge of his rising manhood. "You're so bad," she whispered. "Can't you wait?"

He lowered his mouth to her breast, his tongue darting out to dampen the filmy cloth of her chemise. "Do I have to?"

His tongue made contact with the tip of her breast, and she groaned softly. "Yes, you have to."

Just then a knock came at the door. "Yes, who is it?" Alex called, his face still buried in the fold of his wife's open shirt waist.

"Your supper, Mr. Alexander," the voice replied from the hallway.

"Couldn't you just leave it outside?" Alex asked.

Gabrielle giggled, trying to push his head away. "Alex!" she murmured.

"Sir?" The voice called.

"Just a minute!" Gabrielle said. "We're coming." Her hands flew to her buttons as Alex reluctantly lifted his head. Taking care that she was covered properly, she went to the door. "Sorry," she apologized, swinging it open. "Just newly wed, you know how it is."

"Ma'am?" the young gentleman said, his eyes widening.

"Nothing." She winked at Alex, who stood in the

305

parlor, his hands stuffed in his pockets, an amused smile on his face. "Just bring it in. The table will be fine." She pointed to a rosewood side table near the settee.

The boy hurried to set down the tray and then darted back out into the hall to retrieve the bottle of wine he'd left outside the door. "Anything else?"

"That will be all." Alex flipped the young man a coin, wrapping an arm around Gabrielle's waist.

The boy stared at the coin and then broke into a grin. "Thank you, sir."

"You're welcome. Close the door behind you." Alex smiled.

The boy stood frozen for a moment, then his face reddened and he backed out the door. "Good night," he called, pulling the door closed.

Gabrielle burst into laughter, spinning around to face Alex.

"What's so funny?" he asked, taking her hands.

"Nothing. I'm just happy."

"Well, let's quench your hunger, so I can quench mine." He tweaked the end of her nose playfully and then went to uncover the huge supper tray.

Gabrielle and Alex dined on roast beef, thick slices of sourdough bread spread with sweet butter and fresh ripe peaches. Sitting on the floor of the parlor, they ate their wedding picnic on the plush oriental carpet, laughing and talking as they took their fill. Finally, when their supper was finished, Alex stretched out, resting his head on Gabrielle's lap, nestled in her abundant skirts. He had stripped off his coat and neck scarf and now was content to bathe in his new wife's beauty, watching as she finished the last of the peaches.

"What are you looking at?" Gabrielle smiled, wiping her mouth with her sleeve.

"Just your lovely face." He grinned, handing her a linen napkin off the floor. "Use that."

She stuck her tongue out at him but did as he told her. "I told you I wasn't very civilized."

"Sometimes I think it's part of the act."

"The act?" She took a sip of wine from a hand-blown glass.

"You know what I mean, Gabrielle Alexander. You like to goad me. You know better than to wipe your mouth on your sleeve."

Her mouth twitched at the corners. "It was closer than the napkin."

Alex growled, sitting up to push her over. Laughing, she struggled to escape, but he pinned her down, pressing his damp mouth to the hollow of her neck. "Enough chatter. You've had your meal, and now I'm going to have mine."

Gabrielle relaxed beneath him, threading her fingers through the hair at the nape of his neck as she parted her lips to welcome his probing tongue. He brought his knee up between her legs, and she moved against him as his searing mouth sought the valley of her breasts. Pushing roughly at the material of her bodice, Alex fought to release her straining breasts. "Damned buttons," he muttered.

Gabrielle laughed at the sound of tearing material as she ran her hands over the broad expanse of his back, kneading the hard line of his muscular shoulders. She arched her back, groaning as his hot, wet mouth made contact with her bare breast. Moving beneath him, she slid her hands over his buttocks and down his thighs, her breath coming faster as his tongue lathed her budding nipple.

Rolling onto their sides, their mouths met fiercely as Gabrielle fumbled with the buttons on his trousers. Driven by the caress of his hand beneath her skirts, she released his throbbing loins, making him moan with pleasure as she fondled him. Slipping off her lacy drawers, Alex planted fierce, maddening kisses to the delicate folds of her womanhood. All conscious thought slipped from her mind as she guided him over her, parting her legs to accept him.

With a single thrust, Alex entered her, and she cried out with sudden fulfillment, laughing in his ear as he moved against her. Lifting her hips to join in his rhythmic dance of love, she moved faster, calling his name. With a quick and final thrust, he spilled into her, collapsing with a groan.

When Alex's breath came evenly again, he lifted his head to take in her dark eyes. "I hadn't meant for our first time as man and wife to go so quickly."

Gabrielle laughed, wiping his damp brow with her palm. "Guess we could have taken off the rest of our clothes." She rustled the skirts of her cordelette, with a giggle.

Alex rolled off her and onto his side, pushing back the plate the roast beef had been served on. "You make a man forget himself." He stared up at the ceiling with amusement. "At least I could have taken you to the bed."

"Well," she whispered seductively in his ear. "I'll give

you a few minutes, and then we'll try again. I'll make it slow this time, I promise."

On Tuesday morning Gabrielle and Alex boarded the Union Pacific train for the long cross-country trek to Richmond, Virginia. With their money safe in one of the boxcars, guarded by an armed man, they embarked on their journey with lighthearted exuberance. Gabrielle was so delighted to be married and know that Alex would be hers forever that she refused to allow herself to worry about what their life would be like once they arrived in Richmond. For the present, she wanted only to be at his side and to be happy.

The days that passed were a pleasant blur for both Gabrielle and Alex. Though the trip was long and the traveling dirty, they spent the hours reveling in each other's company. Twice they got off the train and took a stagecoach to the next train station, their money and the guard remaining with them. Seated side by side on the hard benches of the train and stagecoach, they ate picnic lunches and laughed away their afternoons, watching the countryside as they moved eastward.

It wasn't until the afternoon that they were to arrive in Richmond that Gabrielle suddenly became quiet and withdrawn.

"What's the matter, love?" Alex tugged on the sleeve of her brocade traveling suit. She'd dressed carefully that morning, changing outfits three times. She wanted to look right for his family; she wanted to make a good first impression.

Gabrielle swallowed against the rising lump in her

throat. "What if they don't like me, Alex?" She looked up at him with dark anxious eyes. "I'm not your wife Amber."

He smoothed the chestnut hair that peeked from beneath her fringed capote bonnet. "No one expects you to be Amber."

"But you said yourself everyone liked her." She gave a sigh. "She was such a lady and all."

Alex took her hand, pressing it to his lips. "I love you Gabrielle, and you love me. That's all that matters. They're going to like you, but even if they didn't, it wouldn't matter. You and I, that's what's important."

"And your daughter."

He squeezed her hand. "She's only a little girl. She'll love you as much as I do. You'll see."

Gabrielle looked away, staring at the passing wheat fields, doubt still clouding her mind. "I sure hope you're right, Jefferson Alexander the fourth, because if you're not"—she shook her head—"you and I, we're in trouble."

When the train pulled into the bustling station of the Richmond Potomac Fredericksburg Railroad, Alex hurried Gabrielle off. After speaking briefly with the man who had guarded their money coming east, Alex hailed a hired carriage and they were off.

Sitting beside Alex in the open carriage, Gabrielle tried to forcibly slow her pounding heart. She didn't know why she was so nervous. After all, if she could face Alice LeBeau, she could take on anyone, couldn't she?

"I've had the money transferred to our family banker." He patted her knee. "I still can't believe my luck. When I left here more than a year ago, I had nothing but my daughter, and she wasn't really even mine. I mean, I'd visited with her, but I was never able to care for her. And now look at me, a rich man able to care for his child and home, and a beautiful wife to boot."

Gabrielle smiled grimly. "I feel like I'm off to a hanging . . . my own."

He laughed, wrapping an arm around her waist. "Don't be silly. You're going to be fine. We're going to be fine." He looked out over a rolling field of corn. "I had your money put in a separate account. You can withdraw from it freely."

She looked over at him. "You didn't have to do that. We're married; as my husband the law says everything I own is yours." As the words slipped from her mouth, her chest tightened with pride. He understood how important it was for her to still be herself, to be Gabrielle and not just Mrs. Alexander. He understood that she still needed to feel like she was in control of her life, even in this strange new land.

"I did have to do it that way. You're not like the women who grew up here, or in New England. You've tackled more than most men do in a lifetime. The money you earned is yours. I'll not take it."

Gabrielle slipped her hand in Alex's. "Thank you," she whispered. "I love you."

"And I love you; now let me see a smile. We're almost home."

"This is it?" She studied the small fields on each side of the dirt road that they had turned onto. Some fields were planted in crops Gabrielle didn't recognize, while others were just overgrown in weeds.

The carriage moved up a long driveway which was lined with ancient elm trees. It was dark and cool beneath the heavy shade of the trees, and it smelled of green leaves and dark humus. "It's very pretty," Gabrielle murmured.

"Wait until you see the house. It needs some work, but you'll see, it's going to be beautiful."

A moment later she gasped as the manor house came into view. It was a giant, three-story antebellum-style structure with intricate woodwork framing the windows and skirting the roof line. It was also sadly in need of repair. Several shutters on the front windows were missing. The brickwork was cracked, the paint was peeling and weeds grew where flower beds had once flourished.

"He wasn't kidding," Gabrielle murmured beneath her breath. It looked to her like the whole place needed to be burned to the ground!

The carriage pulled into the rutted circular driveway, and the minute it lurched to a stop, Alex leaped out. Gabrielle got to her feet, handing him his bowler hat. "How do I look?" he asked, handing her down.

She laughed nervously. "I'm supposed to say that, not you." Just then the front door creaked open, and Gabrielle took a deep breath, turning to face her new family.

"Jefferson!" A large, dark-haired woman dressed in black came hurrying out the door. "Son! Son! You've finally come home."

Alex released Gabrielle, going to the woman. "Mother, could you just once call me Alex? You know I

312

hate Jefferson." He hugged her, kissing her on the cheek. Stepping back, he held out his arm to Gabrielle. "Mother, I want you to meet someone." He grinned. "This is my wife, Gabrielle."

His mother's face fell. "Your wife? Your message didn't say you had a wife."

Gabrielle had a sudden urge to turn and run, but instead, bravely she stepped up, offering her hand. "Mrs. Alexander, it's nice to meet you finally."

Margaret Alexander hesitated for a moment, then put out her arms. "You must excuse me; I apologize. Just surprised, that's all." She hugged Gabrielle. "We never expected Jeffer . . . Alex to remarry, not after he lost his Am—" She cut herself off, her cheeks reddening.

Alex gave her a pat on the back. "It's all right, Mama, Gabrielle knows all about Amber as well as Alexis." He offered an arm to each Mrs. Alexander and then started for the front door. "Now where is that daughter of mine?"

"Well, dear, we weren't certain what day you'd arrive, so of course she's at Clarice's home in town." Alex's mother turned to Gabrielle. "My daughter's house is far more suited to raising a child than this drafty place."

Gabrielle gave a nod, followed by an unladylike gulp. If possible, the interior of the house was in worse shape than the exterior. The wallpaper in the entryway was torn and water-stained, the plaster on the ceiling damp and crumbling. A three-legged table leaned pitifully against one wall, a candle sitting in its center, the wax having melted and congealed down one side.

313

The room was otherwise void of furniture. Just ahead and to the left loomed a winding staircase sporting missing banisters and uneven steps.

Alex pressed his hand to the middle of Gabrielle's back, clearing his throat. "Gabrielle, Mother asked if you'd like a mint iced tea."

Gabrielle's head snapped up, her cheeks coloring. She was so shocked by the state of Alex's "estate" that she hadn't heard what her mother-in-law had said. "Why, yes. I would, Mrs. Alexander."

"Now, now, we'll have none of that." She took Gabrielle's arm, leading her to the right. "I'm Margaret to you. All of my friends call me Margaret, and I do hope we'll be friends."

Gabrielle smiled genuinely. She laughed to herself as they made their way through a sparsely furnished room into another. What was wrong with her to be so nervous about meeting Alex's family? His mother was being far nicer to her than her own mother had ever been!

"Now I want you to tell me all about you and Alex, how you met, when you were married . . ." Margaret indicated a worn horsehair chair. "Sit. You must be exhausted from that nasty, dirty trip."

"No. Actually, I'm not. It was very nice. I'd never been on a train before." Gabrielle sat down, reaching up to take off her capote bonnet.

"Well, ladies, while you have your tea, I think I'll see to our baggage. It should be arriving any moment." He leaned to give Gabrielle a peck on the cheek. "I'll be back shortly."

She smiled up at him. "Take your time. I'll be fine."

Alex slid his hat next to Gabrielle's on the table

314

beside her chair. "If it suits you, Mother, I thought we'd go to Clarice's after our baggage has arrived. I'm anxious to see my Alexis."

"Fine, dear. Whatever you say." Margaret clutched her hands. "I'm just so happy you're safe and home, son."

Alex's blue eyes sparkled. "I'm glad to be home."

Chapter Twenty-Three

Gabrielle sat stiffly on the velveteen settee, a china tea cup and saucer balanced in her hand. Alex sat beside her, fidgeting nervously as he spoke with his sister Clarice and her husband Edward.

"We're so pleased you've returned, Jefferson. Mother's in desperate need of a man around the house." Clarice smoothed the dowdy grey-checked material of her walking skirt, pointedly ignoring Gabrielle. Other than a curt "good evening" she had not spoken a word to Alex's wife since she arrived.

"Yes, we're glad to be here, Gabrielle and I both." He leaned forward, trying to peer into the hall. Clarice's townhouse was not overly large, but it was new and furnished lavishly. "Alexis *is* coming down, isn't she?"

"Why, yes, yes of course. I just thought you might like to chat before I had her sent down. Children can be such a nuisance amidst adult conversation."

"How is she? Growing?"

"Like a weed in my rose garden. She must constantly have new frocks bought for her, and it's impossible to keep her in proper shoes. The expense is enormous." Clarice's voice lacked the distinctive southern drawl that Gabrielle found so evident in everyone else's speech here in Richmond.

Alex stiffened. "Yes, well, I'm sorry that I haven't been able to send more money, but now that I've returned, I'll take full responsibility for her. I'll repay you for whatever you've spent to care for her."

Clarice clicked her tongue. "Now, little brother, are you certain you should be tossing your money about like that?" Her curiosity getting the best of her, she leaned forward, lowering her voice. "Just how much gold did you bring out of that wilderness?"

Gabrielle sipped from her tea cup, listening irritably to the conversation between Alex and Clarice. Clarice's husband, Edward, sat across the room, reading a newspaper and puffing on a long, tapered cigar. He seemed pleasant enough, speaking to Gabrielle when they'd been introduced. But once she and Alex had been escorted to the parlor, he had immediately retreated to his corner, absorbing himself in his reading. He had not lifted his head or spoken a word since his earlier greeting.

Shifting uncomfortably, Gabrielle gave a sigh as the sister droned on. She wished desperately that Margaret had accompanied them, then at least she would have had someone to speak to. Gabrielle realized she wasn't the most mannerly person on earth, but she was certain it was rude to ignore a guest in your home. If there was one thing Rouge LeBeau had taught her, it was hospitality. When someone came into his cabin, it was the best chair, the finest whiskey and the last of the stew for that guest.

"Clarice, it's getting late," Alex said. "I'd like to see

my daughter now."

Gabrielle glanced up at Clarice as the middle-aged woman lifted herself out of her chair. "Very well, but I'm warning you. She can be rather difficult so near to her bedtime."

"Clarice, she's my daughter." Alex stood up, handing Gabrielle his hat. "I just want to see her."

The moment Clarice was out of the room, Gabrielle dropped her tea cup on the side table with a rattle and a bang. Glancing over at Edward, she forced a smile. "I really don't think we should stay long, Alex. I'm tired, and Clarice said it's Alexis's bedtime," she said, her voice obviously strained. "Maybe we could just come see her tomorrow. Take her somewhere, for a ride or something."

"I just want to see her." He stuffed his hands in his pockets, pacing the thick woven carpet.

"I know you do, it's just that—"

Clarice came through the door. "The nursemaid is bringing the child." She glanced over at Gabrielle as if just noticing her for the first time. "More tea?" She smiled artificially.

"No. No thank you, Clarice. I was just telling Alex I thought we should only visit a moment or two and then we should go."

"Trying to keep him from his daughter are you?"

"No, it's not that." Gabrielle was so startled by Clarice's accusation that she was at a loss as to what to say. She glanced over at Alex; his back was to her. Why was he offering her no help? Gabrielle looked back at Clarice. "I just thought—" At the sound of footsteps in the hallway, Gabrielle cut off her useless explanation. Clarice had already turned away.

A woman appeared, dressed in billowing white skirts, leading a small child in a nightgown by the hand. Gabrielle couldn't resist a smile. Alexis was a beautiful child, just as Alex had said, with large, round blue eyes and a head of honey-yellow hair.

Alex's eyes grew misty as he watched his daughter from across the room. Although he wanted nothing more than to cross the room and sweep her into his arms, he resisted the impulse. After all, his daughter hadn't seen him in over a year. She probably didn't even recognize him.

"Alexis," Clarice said starkly, "this is your father."

Gabrielle remained seated on the settee, watching Alex as he moved slowly toward his daughter. Getting down on one knee, he spoke in a low voice. "Good evening, Alexis."

The child twisted her hands in her white nightgown. "Evening, sir," a small voice replied.

"I'm very glad to see you. Your papa's missed you very much."

The little girl puckered her lips. "I haven't a papa. Aunt Clarice says he's run off chasin' gold rainbows. He'll not be back."

Alex heard nervous laughter coming from Clarice behind him, but he ignored her. "I did go looking for gold, love, and I found it. I've come home to be with you. Would you like to come with me and live in the big house with Grandma Margaret?"

Alexis slipped her small hand into her nursemaid's. "No thank you. I have a home, here with Nurse." She tugged on her nurse's hand, obviously dismissing her father. "I've been nice to 'im like you said. Might I have that hot chocolate now?"

"Take her, Louisa." Clarice gave a wave of her hand, and the child was bustled away.

Alex got stiffly to his feet. "She's beautiful," he said, trying to cover his disappointment. He realized his daughter would be shy with him, but he had hoped he could at least speak with her. "I'd like to come get her tomorrow. Gabrielle and I want to take her on a picnic."

"She has lessons, you realize. We run on a schedule here. It's the only way to raise a child." Clarice rested her hands on her ample hips.

Alex took Gabrielle's hand, raising her to her feet. "Surely she must get time to eat. I won't keep her that long."

Clarice showed them to the door. Edward remained in the parlor, reading his newspaper. "I suppose we can make the exception this one time." She brushed an imaginary speck of dust from her shirt waist.

Alex stuffed his bowler hat on his head. "Good, because we'll be by at eleven-thirty." He rested his hand on Gabrielle's shoulder. "Ready, Gabrielle?"

Gabrielle gave a nod, not daring to say a word, because if she spoke, she knew she wouldn't be able to contain herself. Fancy folk or not, she'd like to tell Clarice how rude she and her husband were and that she had no right to tell Alex's child that he'd abandoned her.

The moment Alex urged the carriage forward, Gabrielle swept off her bonnet. "God sakes, Alex. The woman's got nerve hasn't she, tellin' Alexis you had run off on her!"

"Well, maybe that's not what Clarice actually said." Alex spoke softly. He was hurt by his daughter's words,

321

but he still wanted to give Clarice the benefit of the doubt. He wanted to believe his sister had looked out for Alexis's best interest.

Gabrielle pushed back in the leather seat, crossing her arms over her chest. "Those words were too big to have ever come out of that child's mouth, and you know it." She paused, sighing when Alex said nothing. Linking her arm through his, she leaned against him. "I'm sorry; I just don't like to see your daughter turned away from you, that's all. I think the sooner we bring her home to live with us, the easier things will be. You're her papa; you've come home to her now, and you don't need those snooty folks' help anymore."

"I told Clarice we wouldn't move her right away. I thought I'd let her get used to the idea for a while. We could go get her, take her places, see her at Clarice's and let the idea sink in a little."

"Do what you want." Gabrielle ran her fingers through her hair, letting the wind loosen the pins that held it up. "She's your daughter, but if it was up to me, I'd have brought her home tonight. Damnation, can't you see, she thinks that nursemaid of hers is her mama!"

"I'm going to start on the house right away. I have workmen coming in the morning." He glanced over at Gabrielle. "I thought we'd bring her home when the place was in better shape. She's used to living very comfortably."

Gabrielle studied the passing scenery. "Seems to me, what she needs most is a little love."

The picnic outing the following day was an abysmal

322

failure. Clarice didn't have Alexis ready when Alex and Gabrielle arrived to pick her up, then once they reached the place Alex had chosen on the bank of the James River, the child refused to eat. Not only did she refuse to eat, but she wouldn't even get out of the carriage. She told Alex, with a rather sarcastic bite to her tongue, that young ladies did not sit on the grass and soil their frocks. Besides, she had explained, Aunt Clarice would make her go without her supper if she mussed her new outfit.

No matter how hard Alex tried to coax her out of the carriage, she refused him. Then when he climbed back into the carriage to try and talk with her, she pointedly ignored him. She said he wasn't her father, and she wasn't moving anywhere. She liked Nurse just fine.

Leaping out of the carriage, a discouraged look on his face, Alex came to sit in the grass on a blanket next to Gabrielle. She had pulled off her hat, stripped off her shoes and stockings and unbuttoned several buttons of her new ivory-colored shirt waist.

Gabrielle glanced over at Alex, noting his dejected grimace. "It's not gonna happen over night, you know. If Alexis thinks her father abandoned her, you just can't show up one day and say, 'Here I am, your papa, love me,' and expect her to come running into your arms." She looked away. "I just think it's going to take time."

Alex drew up his feet, resting his hands on his knees. "I can understand her being shy but she . . . she's—"

"She's a brat," Gabrielle interrupted.

Alex's brow furrowed angrily. "What did you say?"

"You heard me right. I said that little angel you were expecting to come home to is a brat."

"I can't believe you're saying this."

"I'm not saying it's her fault; I'm just saying the child's got no manners."

"I can't believe you'd say such a thing about my daughter," he repeated. "I love Alexis."

"I'm saying it because it's the truth. All right, so she didn't want the lemonade, did she have to throw it all over you? Did she have to bite your hand when you tried to help her into the carriage?" When Alex looked away, Gabrielle gave a nod, daring a slight smile. "Just 'cause she's a brat don't mean you can't love her. It doesn't mean *I* can't love her."

"So what do you propose I do about this brat of mine?" Alex demanded tersely.

"I told you." Gabrielle could feel the anger rising to color her cheeks. "Get her out of Clarice's house and into yours, leaky roof and all."

"I can't do that. I promised my sister I'd give Alexis some time and that the improvements on the house would be made first."

Gabrielle snatched up her bonnet and got to her feet. "Then I don't guess there's anything that can be done," she snapped, walking away.

Gabrielle followed the shoreline of the pond, muttering to herself as she stalked through the tall grass. It was so damned hot here in Virginia that she thought she'd cook, and it was September for God's sake! Nothing seemed to have gone right since they arrived. The house was a wreck, Clarice didn't like her, Alexis was obviously going to be a problem, and now she and Alex were squabbling.

Dropping into the grass, Gabrielle hung her head between her knees. "Oh, Papa," she murmured aloud.

"Why did I leave the Tanana? What am I going to do here? Who am I going to be?" She plucked at the material of her skirt dejectedly. Since they had arrived yesterday, she and Alex hadn't had time to exchange two words. She missed her dogs and her friends, she was uneasy in her new surroundings and she couldn't even get Alex's attention long enough to tell him. He was suddenly so preoccupied! Gabrielle's throat tightened. *Is it always going to be like this?* she wondered.

When Alex came for Gabrielle a few minutes later, she was still sitting there in the grass, her bare feet dangling in the water.

"There you are," Alex said.

"Here I am."

"You shouldn't have gone off; I didn't know where you were. It's not safe." He offered her his hand to help her to her feet.

"You telling me I can't go where I please?" She pushed aside his hand, getting up herself.

"No. It's just that women don't wander around unescorted."

"Who escorted me when I lived on the Tanana, answer me that." She studied his stormy blue eyes.

"That's different."

"Why? I took care of myself just fine before you came along. Sometimes my father was gone for weeks at a time. I caught my own meals; I cared for my dogs; I did my own trapping and cured the hides."

Alex exhaled slowly. "You're not on the Tanana any more, and there are certain rules . . . society's rules." He grasped her arm. "Gabrielle, you could be attacked."

325

She was silent for a minute, looking away, then she turned back to him. "I'm sorry," she whispered. "I said I would try, but this is all so new to me."

"I know," Alex answered, taking her into his arms. "It's all right. I didn't mean to get angry with you back there; it's just that I didn't expect Alexis to dislike me like this."

She brushed her lips against his. "It's not just you," she teased. "Alexis doesn't like anyone, except maybe Nurse."

He grinned. "Come on. Let's get the brat back to her aunt. I've got an appointment with the carpenters this afternoon." He took her hat from her hand and placed it on her head. "Now give me a kiss."

She leaned slowly into him, resting her hands on his chest. She kissed him slowly, deliberately, pressing her hips against his. Then she withdrew, spinning around. "Race you," she cried over her shoulder as she bounded through the grass.

Gabrielle glanced at the clock on the mantel in her bedchamber. It was nearly ten o'clock and Alex still hadn't come to bed. *Typical,* she thought. In the two weeks that had passed since their arrival in Richmond, she'd seen little of her husband. He was always busy with the carpenters or masons who were renovating the house, or he had an appointment with his banker. Gabrielle and Alex spoke in the hall and at the dinner table but saw little else of each other. At night, when he finally came to bed long after she had retired, he fell into an exhausted sleep.

Gabrielle gave a long sigh, getting up off the bed to

326

go to the window. Pushing open the window, she leaned out, letting the cool breeze blow into the room. It still seemed hot to her, though Alex's mother was already talking about crisp fall mornings. Gabrielle chuckled. It had never been this warm on the Tanana in the heat of summer!

Leaning against the window, she stared absent-mindedly at the grass far below. She studied the long fingers of light that fell on the lawn, cast from the lantern-lit window. Hearing laughter, she leaned to catch a glimpse of two young black servants dashing across the lawn arm in arm.

There were so many things that confused her here in Alex's Virginia, but the attitude toward servants was the most difficult thing for Gabrielle to accept. Soon after she'd arrived, she'd been chastised by Clarice and laughed at by Alex's mother for getting up to help clear the supper table after the family had finished eating. Here, the servants, all black men and women, cooked meals and did the cleaning. Not only was it improper for Gabrielle to pick up her own dirty dish, but in Clarice's eyes, it was criminal!

It just didn't seem right to Gabrielle, someone else scraping her dish or washing her underdrawers. It was such a belittling custom that she felt uncomfortable at every meal. She had attempted to express her reservations to Alex, but his only reply had been that that was the way it was in Richmond. All of the old families retained servants, and she would just have to get used to the idea. He'd adapted on the Tanana, and now she would have to adapt to Virginia.

Leaving the window, Gabrielle went to the wash bowl on a table and began to strip off her white shirt

327

waist. *No sense waiting up for Alex,* she told herself, dropping the shirt to the floor. She peered at herself in the cracked mirror that leaned against the wall on the table. She barely recognized herself with her hair so long. Picking up the glass pitcher, she poured a healthy portion of water into the wash bowl, then picked up a sponge from the table, dipping it into the water. Washing her face, she let the cool water run down her neck and dampen the bodice of her soft muslin chemise. At the sound of the lifting latch on the bedroom door, she turned with surprise. "Alex?"

Alex came through the door, closing it behind him. "You were expecting someone else?" He sat in a chair and pulled off his shined black-button shoes.

"No, just not expecting you." She went back to her washing.

He loosened his neck cloth and removed it, throwing it over the chair. "I'm sorry, Gabrielle. I know I haven't had much time to spend with you, but there are so many things to do." He ran his hand through his auburn hair. "So many responsibilities."

"I don't mind that you're busy, but I mind that I'm not. What am I supposed to do?" She stepped out of her skirt, letting it drift to the floor.

"Do?" Alex slipped off his coat.

"Yes, do."

"Well, you're not supposed to do anything. You're my wife, a wealthy woman. Mother never *did* anything."

"Alex." She turned to face him. "I'm bored stiff. I don't have anything to take up my time but take Alexis out for her walks or shopping or have tea with your sisters. And I can tell you now, Loretta and Sue Anne don't like me any better than Clarice does. If I have to drink another cup of tea or buy another hat, I'm going to lose my mind!"

Alex got up from his chair and came to her, stripping off his shirt. "Why didn't you say anything before?"

"I did. You just didn't hear me!"

"Ah, Gabrielle, I'm sorry." He took the sponge from her hand and began to stroke her chest, washing away the heat of the day. "It's just that I've been so busy."

"Too busy to listen to your wife?" She tried to retain the anger in her voice, but she couldn't resist a sigh as he slipped the strap of her chemise down. Cool water trickled between her breasts, and she laughed deep in her throat.

Alex kissed the soft flesh of her shoulder, dipping the sponge back in the wash bowl. His lips met hers for a brief moment, and then he lowered his head to the valley between her breasts, his tongue darting out to catch a trickle of water. "I've missed you," he murmured.

"Missed you, too. You ought to come to bed earlier." Gabrielle threaded her fingers through his thick auburn hair, inhaling his heavenly scent.

Alex eased her chemise down around her waist, then to the floor, touching one pert breast with the sponge. Her nipple puckered beneath the cool water, and he sighed, taking the pink bud in his mouth. Gabrielle moaned, swaying against him as she stroked his broad bare back. Rivers of sensation coursed through her veins as he suckled, still stroking the sponge over her bare flesh.

"I love you," he whispered, lifting his head to take in her dark eyes. "I do."

"I know you do. I just miss my home." She took the sponge from his hand and tossed it into the wash bowl. Together they walked toward the bed. Sliding in, Gabrielle rolled on her side, watching Alex as he stripped off his pants. Dropping them to the floor, he slid in beside her, wrapping an arm around her waist as he drew her closer. Their lips met just as the first cry of warning sounded. . . .

"Fire!" someone shouted from outside. "Fire!" came the voice again.

Alex leaped from the bed, rushing toward the window. Sticking his head out, he spotted a servant below. "Jesse, what is it?"

"Fire, Mista Alexander. Fire!" the boy shouted, pointing to the rear of the house.

Seeing the great billows of smoke rising through the air, Alex spun around. "Dress! Hurry, Gabrielle," he shouted. "The house is on fire!"

Chapter Twenty-Four

Gabrielle hitched up her skirts to wade through a pile of rubble. "God sakes," she breathed, staring at the charred skeleton of the rear of the house. "It's a wonder the whole place didn't go up."

Alex looked up at her sharply. "What are you doing here? A beam could fall and crush you."

Undaunted, she made her way to her husband. "Figure out what started it?"

Alex shook his head. His face was smudged with soot, his auburn hair singed on one side. There were dark circles beneath his eyes, evidence of his sleepless night. "I can't believe it; it looks like arson."

Gabrielle felt a twinge of fear. "Arson? You think someone started it?"

"It's what I said didn't I?" he snapped. "Now go on, Gabrielle, get out of here."

Her lower lip quivered in indecision. Where was the man she'd married, the man filled with laughter and tales of the wide open sea? This wasn't the Alex she knew. This was a man doubled over with the burden of his responsibilities, an unhappy man. "All right, I'll go. Maybe Alexis would like to come over and play."

"No."

"No? Why not? She told you yesterday that she wanted to come for tea. It's the first time she's said more than two civil words to you. Don't you think you ought to have her?"

"I just don't know if it's safe." He pulled a handkerchief from his pocket and wiped his damp brow. "Maybe we just ought to keep her away from here until we find out who started the fire."

Gabrielle rested her hands on her hips. "Do you . . . do you think this could have something to do with me?" She spoke haltingly. "I mean with Taylor?"

"Nah. He wouldn't follow this far. He probably never made it off the Tanana. Not alone." He didn't sound convinced.

Gabrielle hesitated. "Well, guess I'll go see Alexis. I'm going to go crazy if I don't get out of here. Maybe we'll go into town and try on some more dumb hats."

She was hoping Alex would laugh, but he didn't. He had already turned away and was moving a blackened chest of drawers. Two of the three rooms in the house that had burned had been empty, but the other had been used for storage. In the fire, Alex had lost portraits of his father and grandfather and furniture that had been moved to the rear of the house while the workmen started on the front rooms.

Gabrielle turned with a sigh. "Bye."

"Good-bye," Alex answered blackly. Then added, "Take a servant with you to drive the carriage."

She didn't bother to argue but just nodded her head. She'd be damned if she'd take anyone with her! She

332

needed no nursemaid.

Alex turned to watch Gabrielle disappear from view down the long passageway. He sighed, shaking his head dismally. "It's not what I expected," he murmured. Nothing here was the way he thought it would be, not his daughter, not his home, not even his mother and sisters. Instead of looking forward to rebuilding his family's fortunes here in Virginia, he found himself dreaming of falling snow and the roar of the breaking ice on the Tanana. He suddenly felt hemmed in, like he couldn't breathe. Had Virginia changed or had he? As much as he hated to admit it, his heart just wasn't in this land anymore; it was there in the vastness of the Alaska Territory, in the mountains, in the valleys, on the Tanana River.

Still, he had managed to keep his thoughts to himself. He saw no need to tell Gabrielle just how much he missed the wilderness, or her sled dogs or their way of life on the river. His life was here in Virginia now, and he would have to resign himself to that fact, just as his wife had.

Kicking at a pile of blackened rubble, Alex moved to the window to stare out over the fields. The worst thing was that he knew Gabrielle wasn't happy here, either. In the process of trying her damndest to fit in, she had lost that sparkle of vitality in her eyes that had attracted Alex to her in the first place. Not only was she putting up with his spoiled daughter, his snobbish sisters and his long hours of little attention, but now she might be risking her life to be at his side. If Taylor or one of his henchmen had set fire to their home, there was no reason for him to believe they wouldn't try something else. And what if they succeeded? Alex groaned, tightening his fists at his sides.

"Could Taylor possibly have followed me and Gabrielle here?" he wondered aloud. It just didn't seem logical, yet when gold was involved, men weren't always that sensible. He realized that now. Still, it seemed a bit farfetched. Perhaps the fire had been an accident. Perhaps a servant, snooping where he shouldn't have been, started the fire by accident and was now afraid to admit it. That seemed a better explanation. Turning back to his work at clearing the blackened room, Alex nodded to himself. Yes, that sounded more likely, but just to be sure, he'd keep a watch on Gabrielle just the same.

Stepping over a bucket of wet plaster in the front hall, Gabrielle went up the creaking front steps, muttering to herself beneath her breath. Who did Alex think she was to be ordering her about? Take someone with her indeed! Fetching her hat and a purse of money from her bedchamber, she came back down the steps two at a time. Ten minutes later, she was on her way in a small open buggy led by two chestnut mares.

Ignoring Clarice's protests, Gabrielle picked up Alexis and headed into town. In the past two or three days, the child had begun to open up to Gabrielle, trusting her hesitantly. Though Alexis still feared her father and was wary of him because of the tales Clarice had concocted, Alexis had found a friend in Gabrielle.

Laughing, Gabrielle urged the horses forward at an easy pace. She had learned to drive the small carriage in only an afternoon of tutoring by the old black man that ran Alex's stable. Just as she had a knack for controlling her dogs, so did she have that talent with horses. A whisper in the creatures' ears and a pat on the rump and even the jumpiest carriage horse was on its best behavior.

"Where are we going?" Alexis asked. She sat perfectly still beside Gabrielle in the carriage with her hands crossed neatly in her lap.

Gabrielle glanced at Alex's daughter. "Good Lord, girl, don't you ever fidget? We're going to buy us some fishing poles." She patted her knee.

Alexis smoothed the skirt of her lace frock where Gabrielle had mussed it. "Aunt Clarice uses the rod on little girls who fidget. What are we goin' to do with fishin' poles?"

"Fish! What else you silly goose?" Gabrielle's laughter was followed by a giggle from the little girl beside her.

"You know somethin', Gabrielle?" Alexis said hesitantly.

"What?"

"I like you. You're very nice to me, even when I'm not so nice to you."

Gabrielle passed the reins into her left hand and put her arm around Alexis's shoulder. "Well, everyone likes you, sweetheart."

"Nah." She shook her head of perfect curls. "Not really. Aunt Clarice buys me things and makes me pretty and smart, but she don't like me. She says I'm shiftless like my papa. She never takes me anywhere like you do."

"Well of course she must take you somewhere, girl. How else do you get all these fancy dresses you're always sportin'? She must take you somewhere to buy them."

Alexis shook her head again. "Nope. The seamstress

comes to the house. Nurse tells her what Aunt Clarice wants made. I like to go out. I like ridin' in the buggy." She beamed.

"Well, how would you like to come live with us? With your papa and I?" Gabrielle pulled the carriage up in front of an ancient general store in the corner of town.

"I . . . I don't know." She twisted her hands.

"Your papa's real nice; you just have to get to know him. He loves you very much."

"Aunt Clarice says—"

"I don't care what Aunt Clarice says. Your papa is the best man I've ever known, and I know you'd love him like I do if you'd just give him a chance." Gabrielle pulled the break on the carriage and tied the reins to the lever. "Now are you ready to get these poles or are you just going to sit there all day?"

Alexis broke into a grin, then jumped up off the padded leather seat. "I'm goin' if you are!"

"Good." Gabrielle leaped easily to the ground and reached up to help Alexis. Together, hand in hand, they entered the general store.

After selecting two cane poles, some hooks and fishing line, Gabrielle led Alexis to the front counter where an old man with a crippled leg waited on them.

"Afternoon, ladies. I see you're going fishing."

Alexis's head bobbed up and down. "We sure are. I've never been fishin' before."

The old man's eyes widened. "You haven't! A girl your age needs to know how to fish and certainly a girl as pretty as you!"

Gabrielle slid several coins over the worn wood counter. "Can you tell me where we can get some ice cream? Somewhere near here where there won't be too many people." She tugged playfully on one of Alexis's honey-colored curls. "My friend and I, we're not much for crowds."

The grey-haired gentleman winked. "Down High Street and around the corner. It's an old place, was there before the war just like this one. Martha's Bakery. I understand she makes the best ice cream in the whole city."

Gabrielle accepted her change and reached for her poles.

"No, no. I'll have a boy put them in your carriage; you go have your ice cream." He smiled, patting her hand. "Where you aim to go fishing?"

"On the James I guess. You know any good spots?"

The man's grey-green eyes sparkled mischievously. "Do I!" He motioned with a finger for Gabrielle to move closer.

Ten minutes later, Gabrielle and Alexis were seated at a small table in the bakery's window, feasting on large bowls of vanilla and chocolate ice cream. Gabrielle had been so lonely these last few days that she was enjoying the little girl's company immensely. And Alexis was thrilled to have someone really pay attention to her for the first time in her life.

Just as they were finishing their ice cream, the bell on the front door rang, and a man entered the small bakery. He was a big, ill-smelling man, dressed poorly with a dark stocking cap pulled over his head. He glanced at Gabrielle, then looked away when she looked at him. When the clerk came to wait on him, he bought one yeast roll and turned to go, his dark beady eyes on Gabrielle.

337

"Are you done, Alexis?" Gabrielle asked uneasily. She watched the man watching her go out the door and down the street. Suddenly something didn't seem right. The man was looking at her so oddly, as if he was trying to identify her. Of course she knew she had never seen him in her life.

"I'm done." The child wiped her mouth on the cloth napkin and got to her feet, picking her bonnet up off the table.

Leaving a coin on the table, Gabrielle urged Alexis out the door, checking the street before they stepped onto the walk. For just an instant she caught a glimpse of the man again, and this time there was another man with him, a big black man with powerful hands. "Let's hurry, Alexis," Gabrielle murmured, taking her hand.

"Hurry? Why? I thought you said we had all day."

"We do." Gabrielle glanced over her shoulder as they hurried down the street. "But the fishing is best this time a day, and we want to catch fish, don't we?"

Cutting the corner sharply, Gabrielle spotted Alex's carriage which she'd left in front of the general store. Her breath came faster at the sound of footsteps behind her. "Hurry, Alexis," she ordered, pulling the girl along. Reaching the carriage, she lifted the child into the seat and untied the horses. Leaping up on the seat, her skirt akimbo, she clicked to the horses, urging them forward. Hurrying down the street, she passed the two men on foot, and she glared at them. They turned and watched her disappear at the end of the street.

"Who are those men?" Alexis asked, as Gabrielle urged the horses into a trot.

"You saw them, too?" Gabrielle pushed her bonnet back off her head. "I don't know, sweety. I don't know." She looked to Alexis, wiping the concerned look off her face. "Now, how about some fishing?"

Keeping an eye on her back, Gabrielle led the horses down by the James River, picking a spot where she saw several other people enjoying the warm fall day. Tying the animals to a tree, she led Alexis down the path, singing a silly ditty with the child. Catching a shiny black cricket for each of them, she baited their hooks, laughing when Alexis turned her head away in horror. Coaxing Alexis to sit in the grass, she proceeded to instruct the little girl on the finer points of fishing. While she spoke, she continually glanced behind her, still uneasy.

Had those men been following her? *They were staring, weren't they?* she asked herself again and again. Jigging her line, she watched Alexis get to her feet to study a blooming fall flower. "Don't go far, Alexis," she ordered.

"I won't." Alexis giggled, picking one flower after another.

Gabrielle sighed, leaning back in the tall grass, a weed dangling from her mouth. Reassuring herself that she and Alexis were safe enough here in the open, she relaxed a little, letting her thoughts wander.

Nothing seemed to be going the way it was supposed to. She had married Alex and come east to be with him. She left the Alaska Territory because she was lonely, yet she was just as lonely here, maybe more so because everything was so unfamiliar. Alex didn't seem to have time for her . . . or need. When she had offered to help

339

with the building or fall harvest he had laughed. Suddenly he seemed so distant. When they were on the Tanana, he had never hesitated to tell her what he was thinking, what he was feeling, but now he was silent. He still said he loved her, and she believed him; but the spark was gone from his eyes. He just seemed so tired, so weary.

Though his mother Margaret was pleasant enough, she was constantly making demands on him: have this fixed, speak to this creditor, call on that ill family friend. And his sisters were just as bad. Everyone said they were glad to have him home, but no one gave him any joy. Not even his daughter gave him happiness because she was so suspicious of him.

A tug on the fishing line brought Gabrielle out of her daze. Where was Alexis? "Alexis," she called. "Where are you? Alexis!" she called louder. Getting to her feet, she peered over the tall grass. Alex's daughter was nowhere to be seen.

Gabrielle's heart pounded in her ears as she ran down the path, the fear tight in her throat. "Alexis," she screamed. "Answer me! Where are you?" Coming to a clearing, she spotted a man in a dark coat leaning over Alexis.

"Alexis!" she cried, running toward her. "Come here!"

Alexis turned to face Gabrielle. "Here I am. Didn't you hear me?"

Reaching her, Gabrielle grabbed her arm roughly. "I told you to stay with me." Her voice wavered with relief as she looked up at the man. He wasn't one of the two who she'd seen on the street.

"I'm sorry, ma'am. I meant no harm." The man with the moustache took a step back. "I just wanted to speak to your daughter; she is so pretty."

"It's all right." Gabrielle steered Alexis away. "Really, it's all right. She just scared me."

The man gave a nod, sweeping off his hat. "Good day," he called after the striking young woman, then gave a shake of his head and turned to go.

Gabrielle hustled Alexis down the path, wiping her own damp brow with her leg-o'-mutton sleeve. "You scared the wits out of me. You do that again, Alexis Alexander, and friend or not, I'll bust your little bottom."

Alexis's lower lip quivered. "I'm sorry. I was picking flowers. I heard you, you just couldn't see me."

Gabrielle gave her a squeeze. "Don't cry. It's all right. Just remember what I've told you." Reaching the spot where they'd been fishing, she tugged off her straw hat and sent it flying. "It must be a hundred degrees out here today," she murmured.

"It is kinda hot," Alexis echoed.

Gabrielle turned to her, a mischievous grin on her face. "When was the last time you went swimming, Alexis?"

"Swimming?" Her father's blue eyes widened. "N-never! Nobody ever took me swimming before."

"Five years old and you've never been swimming?" Gabrielle sat down in the grass to tug on the buttons of her new shoes. "Then I guess we'd better settle that right now."

"Swimming? You're going swimming?" Alexis's curls bounced jubilantly.

"You too, now get those clothes off." Tossing her shoes in a pile, Gabrielle started on her stockings. "Well, what are you waiting for?"

Alexis's little mouth formed a perfect "O." "I can't go swimming, I haven't a bathing costume."

"Who needs a silly old bathing suit?" Gabrielle started on the buttons of her stiff shirt waist. "What have you got under that ruffly mess?"

"Got my drawers and a chemise of course." Alexis stared in disbelief as Gabrielle shed her shirt waist and started on the buttons of her skirt. She'd never in her life seen an adult unclothed before.

"Well, strip 'em off!" Gabrielle laughed. "Come on, come on. If the fishing's bad, the swimming's got to be great!"

Alexis stood frozen, her arms drooped at her sides. "Aunt Clarice'll have my hide if I take my clothes off out here by the river."

"Pooh! Who's going to tell the old grouch?" Standing in her chemise, Gabrielle spun Alexis around and started on the buttons of her lacy lawn frock. "Besides, you're moving in with your papa and me, aren't you?"

"Yea. I guess I am." She covered her mouth with her palm, stifling a giggle. "I've never heard of anyone stripping their clothes off outside. What if someone sees us?" She wiggled her arms, letting Gabrielle slip the dress to the ground.

"Those other people are up around the bend, but what if they do? We're not naked are we? Where I come from, we swim without a stitch on." She dropped a kiss on the end of the little girl's nose. "Now come on, last one in is a sour scrap of moose meat!"

Diving into the water, Gabrielle surfaced and

reached out for Alexis. The child came to her without hesitation, and Gabrielle smiled. Alex would be so pleased. His daughter was going to be just fine. All she needed was a little attention, a little love. Gabrielle waded into deeper water with Alexis beneath her arm. "Just wait until your papa sees you tonight," she told Alexis. "Boy is he going to be happy with us!"

Chapter Twenty-Five

"Gabrielle, what the hell happened? I thought you took a driver." Alex looked from his dirty-faced wife to his mud-splattered daughter. "Where have you been? Clarice expected Alexis to be home hours ago!"

Gabrielle clutched Alexis's hand tight in her own. "We went fishing, then we went swimming, and then after we got dressed we had a mud fight." She smiled, then became indignant when he refused to do the same.

"I was afraid something had happened to you," he said through clenched teeth.

Gabrielle could feel the anger rising to color her cheeks. "I told you I could take care of myself didn't I?" She wiped at her muddy cheek.

"And my daughter, what of her?" He rested his hands on his narrow hips. "Just because you're fool enough to risk your own safety doesn't mean you have the right to risk hers! Didn't you understand me this morning when I told you I thought someone started that fire? Gabrielle, I think someone might be trying to kill you."

345

Gabrielle could feel Alexis's small hand trembling in her own. "That's enough, Alex," she said stiffly. "I'll put Alexis to bed, and then we can talk about it."

"To bed? She's got to be taken to Clarice's. My sister's worried sick."

"So, send one of those servants of yours over with a message. It's time Alexis started living here, here with her father," she told him tersely. Before Alex could say another word, Gabrielle pushed past him, leading his daughter up the front steps.

Climbing over a pile of lumber, she led Alexis into a small bedroom on the south side of the house, just across the hall from where she and Alex slept. "The hall's still a mess," Gabrielle said soothingly, as she began to help Alexis out of her mud-stained dress. "But I had your room finished first."

Alexis gave a gasp of wonderment. "It's beautiful, Gabrielle." She beamed, staring at the freshly papered walls. "Is that my bed?"

"Certainly is, picked it out myself." She went to the small nightstand and lit a lamp. "I found it in the attic. It was your papa's bed; I thought you'd like it."

Alexis bit down on her lip, the smile falling from her face. "He didn't want me to come, did he? Nobody ever wants me around," she said quietly.

"No. No, that's not true." Gabrielle got down on her knees, taking Alexis by the shoulders. "He's mad at me because he told me not to go out alone. But he wants you here. The only reason he left Alaska was to come back to you." She slipped off the little girl's damp chemise. "You have to believe me."

Alexis lifted her heavy eyelashes. "I wanna believe you, Gabrielle. Nobody's ever been nice to me like you,

346

not even Nurse."

Gabrielle's chest tightened. Alexis's eyes mirrored her father's; they were the same clear blue with the same streaks of soft grey. "I love you, Alexis," she murmured, hugging the child against her.

Hesitantly Alexis lifted her arms, wrapping them around Gabrielle's neck. "Can I stay? Are you sure I can stay?"

Gabrielle brushed Alexis's dirty hair off her face, smiling. The perfect sausage curls were damp and stringy, and her tiny pert nose was smudged with mud from the river bank; but her eyes held a sparkle in them that Gabrielle had never seen before. "I said you could, didn't I?"

"I wouldn't want Papa to be angry with you." She spoke the word "Papa" carefully, as if frightened by it.

"You let me worry about Papa, and you worry about Alexis. All right?"

Alex's daughter grinned. "Boy, is Aunt Clarice gonna be mad. She said I was livin' with you over her dead body. Said you weren't fit to raise puppies!"

"Let her be mad. Now you wait right here while I fetch a wash bowl. Then you clean up and get into bed, and I'll bring you something from the kitchen." She gave Alexis a wink. "Be right back. . . ."

An hour later Gabrielle had tucked Alexis in for the night and had bathed herself in an old tub she'd had one of the servants fetch from the cellar. Wrapped in a soft flannel dressing gown, she sat at the end of the bed she and Alex shared, a thread and needle in hand trying to sew the ruffle back on Alexis's new frock. Alex hadn't come upstairs yet, but she knew it would only be a matter of time

347

before he came storming in. When the door to their bedroom finally opened, she resisted the impulse to look up.

"I can't believe you did this. I was scared out of my wits, Gabrielle." He slammed the door shut, yanking at his neck cloth. "Well?"

She looked up, lifting an eyebrow. "Well what?"

"What have you got to say for yourself?"

"Nothing to say. I'm sorry I scared you, but I'm not sorry I went. You can't keep me locked up here forever."

"If someone is after you, you or Alexis could have been killed!" He pulled off his dark tailored coat and tossed it onto a chair.

Gabrielle dropped her attention to her sewing as she tried to suppress her anger. "I won't take her out anymore without a driver."

"That's not good enough!"

She shot him a dark, warning gaze. "It's going to have to be. I told you I can care for myself. I always have, and because I married you doesn't mean that's going to change." She got to her feet, moving to the window, the sewing scissors in her hand.

"You've got to start acting like a young woman! You're a wealthy married woman with a position as my wife. You can't traipse about like you were a man. The next thing I know you'll be wearing breeches again."

Moisture formed in the corners of Gabrielle's eyes as she lifted the scissors to her hair, combed out like a halo on her shoulders. "You have no right to say these things," she murmured as the scissors opened of their own accord.

Suddenly Alex's hand was on hers, his voice deep

and foreboding. "You cut one hair from your head and I'll—"

"You'll what?" Gabrielle flung, spinning around. The scissors clattered to the wooden floor. "You'll spank me? You'll lock me up?" Her stricken face was colorless. "You'll stop loving me?" She turned and ran for the door. "I knew I never should have come here," she shouted. Slamming the door behind her, she raced down the front steps in the darkness, ignoring Alex's pleas as he called her name.

Leaning his head against the closed door, Alex sighed heavily. *She is right; she should never have come,* he thought to himself. *But I shouldn't have, either.* "Why did I ever think this place would make me happy?" he said aloud to the empty room. "Why did I ever think I would make a difference to Alexis?" *Because she's your daughter,* his mind responded. *Because she's your responsibility.*

Turning, he took a deep breath, debating whether or not he should go after Gabrielle. Then, hearing a small voice, he opened his bedroom door. It was a soft sound, barely audible, but it was coming from the room across the hall. Hesitantly he opened the door. "Alexis?"

"Yes . . ." the tiny voice answered.

"What's the matter?" he called through the darkness.

"I'm . . . I'm afraid," she whispered.

Alex came and sat down on the corner of her bed, reaching to light the lantern. "Afraid? Afraid of what?"

"What's the matter with Gabrielle?" Alexis sniffed, trying to be brave.

"Nothing, we just had a fight." He pushed a lock of honey-colored hair off her cheek. Light from the lamp threw a circle of golden rays across the bed, illuminat-

349

ing his daughter's angelic face. "She'll be all right."

"You certain?"

"I am because I'm going to make it better. I love her you know, just like I love you." He smoothed the light blanket that covered her.

"You do?"

"Um hmm. You two girls are the most important people in my life. The only people I care for." His words brought a lump to his throat.

Alexis pulled her hand from beneath the covers and slipped it into her father's. "I'd like to stay with you and Gabrielle."

"You would?"

She nodded slowly, her blue eyes round in seriousness. "If you want me."

Alex groaned, leaning forward to take his daughter in his arms. "God, Alexis, that's all I want. I want you and Gabrielle to be happy." He squeezed her tight, then lowered her back onto the bed and tucked the covers around her. "Now, I'm going to leave this lit lamp on the mantel, all right?"

"You will? Aunt Clarice said it was wasteful to let the lamp burn at night. She always made me sleep in the dark."

"Even when you were afraid?" Alex moved to the door.

She nodded solemnly. "Even when I was afraid."

He smiled. "Well, no more. Your papa's got plenty of money to keep lamps lit, now go to sleep." He blew her a kiss off his palm and then went out the door, closing it quietly behind him.

Alex found Gabrielle beneath a huge oak tree near

the garden, playing with a pile of rabbit-hound puppies. She was sitting in the grass in her night robe, wrestling with one of the friskier pups. Even before Alex spotted her in the moonlight, he heard her soft lilting voice. "Gabrielle," he called softly.

"Here," she answered in the same hushed tone.

He came to the oak tree and stood over her, studying her delicate oval face. "I'm sorry."

She looked away. "So am I. It was a stupid thing to try and cut my hair."

He chuckled. "It was a stupid thing to do the first time. You told me how much it hurt you. I didn't want to see you hurt."

Gabrielle scratched the little brown puppy's ear, and it nipped at her fingers. "This isn't going to work, Alex."

"What isn't?"

"You and I."

"It is." He got down on his knees, taking her hands. "It has to. I love you so much."

She reached out to brush his cheek with her palm, her anger spent. "Just because we love each other doesn't mean we can live together," she said sadly.

"Don't talk like that. I need you; Alexis needs you." He pulled her against him, smoothing her gown with his hand.

"Alexis needs her father. I'll never be of any use to you here. I'll only be trouble." She lifted her hands to wrap them around his neck, lowering her head to his broad shoulder. "It was silly for me to ever say it would work. You were right; we should have waited until we got here to be married. We should have made sure it would work."

Alex's eyes grew moist. "Shhh. Don't say that. I've no regrets." His voice was hushed and softly masculine.

"Maybe not yet, but you will. I'll never fit in here. I miss the snow, the silence. There's too many people, Alex. They make me hurt inside, touching, staring, judging."

"I don't know what to say. I don't know how to help you."

"Let me go back," she dared.

"Go?" He pushed her back so that he could see her face. "Go where?"

"Home," she whispered.

"Home?" His clear blue eyes darkened with emotion. "Your home is here with me."

She shook her head, clinging to him. "My mother was right. I'm not fit to be anyone's wife, not yours. We LeBeaus, we weren't meant to be married. We weren't meant to be penned in." She sniffed, leaning against him again. She couldn't bear to see the pain on his face. "I'll only hurt you. I'll make you unhappy, you'll see."

"No. No, I won't let you. Just let me get things straight here at the house, and then things will be better. I'll have more time for you."

"And what of the fire?" She stroked the nape of his neck, reveling in the feel of his thick hair between her fingers. "Today I think two men followed me. They knew who I was."

Alex shook his head in disbelief. "The more I think about it, the more I realize how silly this is. It wasn't arson, just a foolish accident. A servant said he saw one of the stable boys in the house just before the fire broke

352

out," he lied. He hated to hide the truth from Gabrielle, but he was desperate. She couldn't leave him. He wouldn't let her. "How could anyone know you were here? It wasn't Taylor, was it?"

"No. I've never seen these men in my life. But they were watching me. I think they followed Alexis and me."

He brushed back the hair off her shoulder, kissing the crook of her neck. She smelled of wild flowers. "But you're not sure?"

"Not positive, but—"

"I think we're being paranoid, Gabrielle." He brushed his lips against hers, and she responded, looping her arms around his neck. Alex eased her onto her back in the grass, pushing aside a nosy hound pup.

Gabrielle clung to Alex, returning his kisses with feverish desire. Her world seemed to be crumbling around her. Nothing was right anymore. Nothing felt right, nothing but this, the two of them here beneath the stars.

Alex pushed her deeper into the grass, covering the length of her body with his. Gabrielle strained beneath him, moaning deep in her throat as he tugged at the tie of her wrapper, pushing back the soft flannel to reveal her satiny flesh shimmering in the moonlight. Cupping a breast in his hand, Alex kissed her swelling nipple, encircling the tiny bud with his tongue.

Gabrielle bit back a cry of delight, raking her fingers over his shoulders, arching her own back in encouragement. Hot flashes of exquisite pleasure surged through her limbs as the rhythm of her breathing changed with the motion of his callused hand on her

353

breast. His mouth met hers, and she strained against him, threading her fingers through his thick, sweet-smelling hair. "Alex," she cried. "Alex, I love you. . . ."

"I love you," he echoed, taking her mouth. His tongue darted out to trace the line of her lips, then delved deep to conquer the cool inner lining of her mouth. Running her fingers over his shirt, Gabrielle fumbled with the buttons. Their clothes fell to the grass as he gave her aid, whispering soft words of encouragement.

Free of their burdensome clothing, Alex rolled onto his back, pulling her on top of him. Laughing, Gabrielle kissed a path from his eyebrows to the crisp hair of his chest. Taking the tiny bud of his nipple in her mouth she suckled, bringing a moan to his lips. Moving downward, she kissed his quivering flesh, her tongue teasing him into a frenzy.

"God, Gabrielle," he said thickly, lifting her by her shoulders. When her face was above his again, he rolled her onto her back, easing his leg gently between hers. Gabrielle moved against the pressure of his knee, lifting her hips and parting her thighs to accept his first thrust. When he entered her, she cried out, then he was still for a moment, waiting for her to catch her breath. Finally he began to move, slowly first, then with greater speed.

Molten fire surged through Gabrielle's veins, lifting her toward the velvety softness of fulfillment. Higher and higher she climbed in Alex's arms, straining against him, moving with him, reaching for the glittering stars that dotted the sky above them. The pulsating need deep within the core of her being drove her faster as she lifted her hips to meet his virile thrusts.

Suddenly the world exploded around them; white light flashed through Gabrielle's head, shattering all possible thought. Then slowly she drifted back to earth and the reality of the world around her.

Alex gave a satisfied sigh, rolling off Gabrielle to lay beside her in the grass. He rested his arm comfortably around her waist, listening to her breath as it came more regularly. Lifting his hand, he tickled her flat stomach, and she giggled.

"Look at you lyin' naked in your own yard! Shame on you," Gabrielle teased, pushing aside his hand. She lifted herself up on one elbow.

He laughed, stretching his tall frame. "Feels good out here, doesn't it? I feel like I can breathe outside," he added thoughtfully. "Know what I mean?"

She ran a hand over his chest. "I do. The air's different here than in the house, isn't it? It's not just my imagination?"

"No. It's not your imagination." He caught her hand in his and raised it to his lips. "Everything is so busy here, there's no time to look at the stars or just breathe the clean fresh air."

"You sound like you miss the Tanana," she murmured softly.

Alex rolled on his side to face her. "I do. Want to know the truth?"

She nodded silently.

"I want to go back. I wish I could—"

"Only you can't . . ."

He smiled sadly. "Only I can't."

Gabrielle brushed her palm across the stubble of his unshaven cheek, her heart swelling with momentary

355

happiness. The thought that Alex missed the Alaska Territory made her feel good inside. It didn't matter that his responsibilities would prevent him from ever going back. What mattered was that he wanted to. "Guess it's time we went in," she murmured, sitting up to shrug on her dressing gown.

Alex sat up slowly. "Suppose you're right. With my luck Mother or Alexis will appear."

Gabrielle laughed, offering her hand to help him to his feet. Lifting up on her toes, she kissed him. "I hope you're not too angry about me bringing Alexis. I just thought she needed to be near you."

Alex wrapped his arms around her, holding her close. He rested his chin on her head, inhaling her fragrant hair. "I'm not. You're right. I just hadn't had the energy to go and argue with Clarice over her. I feel guilty taking Alexis from her and Edward. They have no children, you know."

Gabrielle gave a snort of disgust. "You can thank the Lord for that. She's a rotten mother. She doesn't give a damn about Alexis as long as she's dressed properly!"

"Gabrielle," Alex admonished. "It's not true."

"It is, but I'll keep my mouth shut." She laced her fingers through his hair, kissing him in apology.

"Enough said, now shall we go to bed, wife?" He slipped his hands around her slim body, letting the robe fall to her sides.

She leaned into him, savoring the feel of his hard, naked body pressed against hers. "I'd rather sleep out here." She lifted her chin to let him nuzzle her neck.

"I know. Me too, but in we must go." He leaned to sweep her into his arms, and Gabrielle laughed aloud, tipping back her head in merriment.

"To bed we go Mr. Jefferson Alexander the fourth," she declared. "But what about your drawers?"

Alex's eyebrows furrowed in confusion, then he followed the line of her finger as she pointed into the darkness. By the light of the moon, he spotted one of the hound pups dragging his new trousers across the lawn.

Chapter Twenty-Six

The following morning Gabrielle took Alexis out to the dog pens to see the new litter of hound puppies. The little girl squealed with delight as the pups surrounded her, licking and jumping.

Alexis put out her chubby hands to pet them, laughing when a dark speckled pup sucked at her finger. "Puppies!" she cried. "I never played with puppies before." She plopped herself on the ground without a thought to her lacy blue and white frock.

"Never played with puppies? Where have you been living, girl? The moon?" Gabrielle caught a pup by the scruff of the neck and lifted him, letting the sweet smelling ball of fur lick at her face.

"I've seen 'em, but I never petted one before."

"Wait. Let me guess." Gabrielle dropped the pup into Alexis's lap. "Aunt Clarice wouldn't let you because they would muss your frock," she said in disbelief.

Alexis gave a nod. "I used to watch them from the window when we came to visit Grandmother Margaret, but we don't come very often."

Gabrielle tucked a lock of hair behind her ear. "Well, from now on, you can play with them whenever you want. Because I like a little girl with a rumpled dress."

"Can I have one? Can I take one to bed with me?" Alexis rolled onto her back, letting the puppies climb over her and tumble to the ground in a wiggling heap.

Gabrielle frowned. "I'm afraid not. Your papa got very angry with me the other day when I brought that old mama hound into the parlor. He's given me strict orders. No dogs in his mother's house." She unbuttoned the two top buttons of her white shirt waist so she could breathe more freely. She didn't mind wearing the skirts so much—at least they weren't suffocating like the slim fitting shirt waists—but oh, what she wouldn't have given for a pair of men's Levis and a flannel shirt.

Alexis rolled onto her stomach, pushing her face into the fat belly of a rolling puppy. "Well, pooh on Papa, that's what I say!"

"Alexis Alexander!" came a sharp voice from behind. "Get to your feet immediately, child!"

Gabrielle spun around to see Clarice standing behind them. Alexis scrambled to her feet and ducked behind Gabrielle's skirts, slipping her hand into her new friend's.

"You could have said good morning, Clarice," Gabrielle said tartly, tightening her grip on Alexis's trembling hand.

"Good morning indeed! First you kidnap Alexis, and now you've got her rolling in the dirt like a pickaninny!"

"Kidnap her!" Gabrielle chuckled. "You handed her to me."

360

"I gave you permission to take her into town to purchase a new hat!" Clarice's face swelled with engorged blood. "I understand you had her swimming in the river," she said with disgust. "She could have been drowned!"

"Not with me hanging on to her she couldn't have!" Swinging around, Gabrielle took Alexis's hand, kneeling in front of her. "You run up to the house, sweet. Go into the kitchen and tell Cook to give you an apple cookie, all right?"

Alexis bobbed her head and turned to go, but Clarice's voice made her stop. "Alexis Alexander, you get in my carriage this minute!"

Tears of fright welled in Alexis's eyes as she looked to Gabrielle in confusion.

"Do as I say," Gabrielle said in a hushed voice, giving her bottom a pat. "Now."

With a squeak, Alexis bounded off, running across the rutted lawn as fast as her little legs could carry her. Seeing her safe, Gabrielle stood up, swinging around to face her incensed sister-in-law. "She's Alex's child and she's staying here, Clarice," Gabrielle said through clenched teeth.

"Who do you think you are?" Clarice's face was turnip-purple with rage.

"Your brother's wife and the step-mother of his child!" Gabrielle didn't care what Alex had to say about patience, she'd taken enough from this rude, meddlesome biddy!

Clarice shook her head in disgust. "You're nothing but trash, you little tramp. I've held my tongue for my dear brother's sake, but no longer."

"How dare you," Gabrielle murmured, taken aback.

"You don't belong here, so why don't you just go back from where you came? Jefferson will never be anything as long as he's got you hanging around his neck. You think Alexis will be able to get into a decent school with a step-mother with the kind of reputation you have? You think we don't know you spent the whole winter in bed with my brother? Jefferson told me you didn't get married until just before you left Seattle!"

"Since when is it any of your damned business?" Gabrielle was trying to block out the woman's words; she was trying to ignore her, but she couldn't. Clarice just kept going on and on, ranting and raving in that high, shrill voice.

". . . Jefferson doesn't need you. He doesn't want you; everyone knows it. He's just too much of a gentleman to say so. The only reason he married you was because he thought it was the honorable thing to do after you threw yourself at him."

Gabrielle took a step back, her mind reeling. "That's not true. Alex loves me."

"Loves you? The only thing he loved was your gold, and now he's got it, doesn't he? How can you be so stupid, girl? How can you be the only one that doesn't see it?"

"Stop it!" Gabrielle shouted. "Just stop it!" She covered her ears with her hands. "I don't want to hear anymore." Against her will, tears began to slip down her flushed cheeks.

Clarice pointed an accusing finger, following her. "Well, you're going to hear it. You're ruining Jefferson's life, and you're going to ruin Alexis's too if you stay here!"

A sob wracked Gabrielle's body as she turned away. She knew it wasn't true, none of it. She knew Alex loved her, but Clarice's wicked words combined with her own insecurities gnawed at her sense of reason.

"Now I suggest you pack a bag and be on the next train out of here. There's one leaving at eight in the morning, bound for the West Coast." Turning, Clarice left Gabrielle and stalked across the lawn.

Gabrielle sank to the ground, lifting a brown puppy into her lap. The little dog licked at her tear-stained cheek as she dashed at her eyes with the back of her hand. "I've got to get out of here." She sniffed. "Got to think . . ." Getting to her feet, she brushed the grass off her skirts and headed for the carriage house.

When Gabrielle set out in the two-seated carriage, she didn't know where she was headed. Her tears clouded her vision as she made her way down the dusty road, urging the matched chestnut mares faster. The wind tore at her face, whipping her straw bonnet from her head to blow down the road, but she gave it no mind. Taking the road along the river, she grew calmer, letting the mares fall into an easy trot.

What right did that woman have to say those things to her? Images of Alice LeBeau and her words of warning echoed in her head. Her mother had said the same, hadn't she? She'd called her own daughter a whore! *Am I that stupid that I don't see it?* Gabrielle wondered. *Am I so in love with Alex that I don't realize he really was only interested in the gold?* She moaned aloud, reining the horses to a halt near the river. Leaping out of the carriage, she tied the reins haphazardly to a hitching post and started down the path that ran along the river.

She was so confused! Nothing seemed right, and she didn't know what to do about it. Gabrielle lowered her head as a middle-aged couple, arm in arm, passed her.

"Good morning," they said, nodding pleasantly.

"Morning," Gabrielle muttered, passing them by. A little farther down the river, out of sight of the other people that sat fishing or just enjoying the fall morning, she sank into the grass.

"God sakes, Papa! What am I going to do?" she moaned aloud. Picking up a small stick, she tossed it into the water.

Three quarters of a mile down the river, Mickey Jordan and Goliath Baron eased their ancient rowboat into the water and jumped in. Mickey, a dirty blond, pushed aside the fishing poles and took the oars, beginning to row. Goliath, the black man, sat in the bow of the boat, his cap pulled low over his face.

"You sure you seen her?" Mickey asked, rowing steadily.

"Yes, I'm sure." Goliath smiled, tipping his hat in the direction of an old couple fishing on the bank. "I told you she'd be back. It's where she come yesterday and the day before, ain't it?"

"I don't know about this murderin' stuff, Goliath. I don't like it. Not one bit. 'Specially if we got to wait for the pay money to come from Seattle."

"I told you, Mickey, it's going to be well worth our while. This Mr. Taylor's offerin' a high price on her head."

"What'd she do? Pretty enough little thing. Hard to believe she could do somethin' to make a man so mad he'd have her kilt. 'Specially with him livin' out there and her here."

"It's not our business, Mickey, so just keep rowin'."

"I'm rowin', I'm rowin'!"

The rickety rowboat moved downstream slowly as Mickey continued to row steadily. "Here, Mickey, here's where we leave it." Goliath pointed into the reeds, pushing his cap back off his face. "You think you're gonna sneak up on her in this dinghy?" The bow hit the shore and Goliath jumped out. "You gonna come sneakin' up on her and say 'Hey, little girlie, hold still while I get out of this boat so's I can hit you over the head and kill ya!'"

Mickey shook his head. "I didn't say that, Goliath, and you know it! Don't be puttin' words in my mouth." He waded through the water, caught the bow of the wooden boat and tugged on it, pulling it onto the shore.

"You ready now?" Goliath tapped his booted foot impatiently.

Mickey wiped his runny nose on his sleeve. "Ready to go with ya, but I ain't ready to be hittin' the little lady over the noggin' with that there axe handle you got."

Goliath turned around. "What do you mean? You said you'd do it." He shook the long axe handle he'd retrieved from the bottom of the boat.

"I didn't say it; I never said it." He shook his head emphatically. "I didn't never say I was gonna do the whackin'. You said I was." Mickey pressed his dirty finger into Goliath's potbelly.

Goliath raised the axe handle threateningly. "You do as you're told Mickey, or you'll get it, too," the black man said. "Now take this and let's get going before she up and moves."

Mickey accepted the axe handle with shaking hands.

"I don't like it," he murmured beneath his breath as he followed Goliath through a patch of cattails. "Don't like it at all. What if I don't hit her hard enough the first time?"

"Hush now, before I hush you myself," Goliath ordered.

Gabrielle rested her chin in the palm of her hand, tossing another stick into the water. She'd been there nearly an hour, muttering to herself, and still she hadn't come to any conclusions. She wished desperately that she had someone to talk to: Jack or Mya or even one of her sled dogs. Anything would be better than sitting here alone in this strange place mulling over her dilemma. She loved Alex so much, and now his daughter had found a place in her heart. But was Clarice right? Was she really doing more harm than good staying here in Virginia?

The snap and crackle of moving brush behind her made Gabrielle turn just in time to see the shadow of a monstrous man swing a large stick over her head. She screamed, tensing her muscles to roll out of the way, but her voice was lost in the sound of the rushing water as swirling darkness overtook her.

The first sound Gabrielle heard as she slowly drifted toward consciousness again was the sound of water lapping beneath her. Her face was pressed against something hard and rough as she lay crumpled in a heap. Forcing herself to lay perfectly still, she waited to gather her wits. *A boat! That's where I am . . . someone has put me in a boat!* Recalling every survival rule she had learned on the Tanana, she fought back the paralyzing fear that crept up her spine. Where were they taking her? Was it the men who had followed her yesterday? Why? What did they want with her? Was she being kidnapped, or was that blow meant to kill?

"Come on, Mickey, let's get into the boat," she heard a deep male voice say.

"I'm a'comin'," answered another man, distress obvious in his voice. "I just wanted to get rid of the stick. It's got blood all over it, Goliath!"

Gabrielle took a deep breath, realizing it must be her own blood that covered the weapon the man had just disposed of. Then she felt it, the warm, damp sensation that oozed down over her ear and trickled to pool in the crook of her neck. She wondered faintly how injured she was, but she knew she couldn't be too bad off if her mind was functioning. Feeling the rock of the boat, she forced herself to remain relaxed to keep her abductors from realizing she was no longer unconscious.

The boat tipped again; and then there was the sound of wood scraping wood, and Gabrielle felt the boat begin to move backward through the water. *What am I going to do?* she thought frantically. *How am I going to get away?* It was difficult to suppress the desire to jump up and dive overboard, but she realized she wouldn't have a chance against these two men. If one of them followed her overboard, he could drown her as easily as a kitten.

"Golly, Goliath, look at all that blood," Gabrielle heard the man rowing say.

"People bleed when you kill 'em, Mickey, old boy."

Kill? They meant to kill me, Gabrielle thought. *Dear God, help me,* she prayed silently. *What am I going to do?* Panic rose in her throat until she thought she would choke, but then her father's words came to mind: "Panic is another word for corpse," Rouge LeBeau had told her time and time again. Swallowing against the lump in her throat, she tried to continue her shallow breathing.

"How're we ever gonna get our money, Goliath, that's what I wanna know?" the man rowing said. "How's that Mr. Taylor gonna know we done our job right?"

Taylor? Gabrielle shuddered inwardly. She couldn't believe that after all of this time, with this distance between them, he was still pursuing her. Only this time he wanted her dead. Why dead? And how did he find her? How could he possibly have known she was in Richmond?

"'Cause it'll be in the newspapers when they find the body. Haven't you got any sense, Mickey?"

Gabrielle heard the man, Mickey, cease rowing, and for a moment the boat just drifted. "How 'bout here, Goliath? This where we should dump her?"

"Yup. Looks good to me. You go ahead while I watch to be sure nobody's comin'."

"Me? I'm not doin' it. How come you're gettin' paid more than me, and I'm doin' all the dirty stuff, Goliath?" The big man stood up, rocking the boat, his feet so close to Gabrielle's face that she could smell the leather of his wet boots. "I just kilt this little girlie, and there you are sittin' pretty as can be with your arms folded across your lap!"

"Mickey, this ain't the time to be discussin' this. You'll get your money, all right? Now just throw the body overboard before somebody sees us."

368

The boat rocked again as Mickey took a step forward, the corner of his boot catching Gabrielle's hair. She grimaced at the pain but remained silent, wishing the man would just shut up and throw her overboard.

"Nope. I ain't gonna do it, Goliath."

"What do you mean you ain't gonna do it?" Goliath raised his voice then lowered it.

"I mean I ain't throwin' her over. You do it."

"Look at her! She's dead. I ain't touchin' her!" Goliath stood up in the bow of the boat, and it rocked again.

"Look here, Goliath. The way I sees it is if we get caught, I'm the one who knocked her, and I'm the one that threw her in the drink. What'd you do? You tole me to kill her, and you're gettin' most of the money." Mickey shifted his weight, and the boat rocked violently.

"Hey! Watch it, dumb ass, you're gonna tip the boat!"

"Tip it? What do I care if I tip it?" Mickey shifted his weight purposely, and the boat rocked so hard that it rolled Gabrielle on her side. It took all of her willpower to remain relaxed, like a ragdoll, like her Laura, and let her body flop over. "If'n it tips," Mickey went on angrily, "she'll roll out, and I won't have to dump her." He continued to rock his body and water splashed into the boat.

Goliath sat back in the bow, clutching the side of the boat. "But you'll dump us, too," he shouted above the sound of the pitching boat.

"I don't care," Mickey answered. "You're the one

that can't swim!" And with that, the man stomped his booted foot, and the boat tipped over.

As the cool water splashed Gabrielle's face and she took a deep breath, she heard Mickey throw himself into the water. Goliath cried out and fell with a bigger splash as Gabrielle felt herself roll from the boat to the water.

Gabrielle allowed her body to sink beneath the surface, letting the cold water of the James River revive her. Then, cautiously she moved her arms, then her legs, praying her limbs would obey her. Feeling light-headed by now, she knew she had to resurface. Turning away from the sound of splashing water, she raised her head above the surface just long enough to catch a breath of air and dove again.

She didn't know if one of the men had seen her; she prayed they hadn't, but she kept swimming. Her instincts told her to get as far away from the danger as possible. Gabrielle resurfaced three times before she felt the slope of the bank beneath her and decided to have a look behind her. Her heart pounding, she brought her head above the surface. Pushing her wet hair off her face, she found her would-be murderers nowhere to be seen. But as she pulled herself exhausted toward the reed-covered bank, she heard them just around the corner of the bend in the river.

Gabrielle could hear loud splashing and shouting, and she couldn't help wondering if the man Mickey was going to leave his partner to drown.

"Kick your feet," she heard Mickey calling. "Good a time as any to learn how to swim, Goliath."

"Help me!" the black man cried out, his voice garbled. "I'm drownin'!"

370

"You're not drownin', you're swimmin', now come on, just a little farther."

Panting, Gabrielle shook her head, pulling herself into the shallow water where reeds grew. *I'm safe enough from them now,* she thought as she pulled herself onto solid ground.

Chapter Twenty-Seven

For a long time Gabrielle lay on the bank of the river, her head cradled in her arms. The voices of her captors had faded until she was certain they were gone. Mickey had waded out and rescued Goliath after they had agreed that they'd split the payment for killing her fifty-fifty. Gabrielle couldn't help laughing at the irony of the situation. The two of them had been so busy arguing over the money that neither had checked to be certain her body had sunk in the river. If Taylor had hired two men with a little more sense, she knew she would be dead at this moment.

Sitting up, Gabrielle ran a hand through her hair. Warm, sticky blood oozed between her fingers, and she winced. Touching the wound lightly, she found a small cut beneath her hairline at her forehead. Lifting up her soaked skirts, she tore a piece of material from her chemise and dipped it in the river water, applying the compress to her head. *Awful lot of blood for such a small cut,* she mused, leaning back in the reeds that lined the shore. The funny thing was that all of that blood was probably what saved her life; it was apparently what had made her attackers think she was dead.

Now that Gabrielle realized she was safe, her mind was suddenly flooded with disjointed thoughts. "My God," she whispered. "If Alexis had been with me, they'd have killed her, too!" She shuddered at the thought, drawing in her knees to rest her chin on them.

I can't stay here in Virginia, she told herself. *If I do, I'll be risking Alex's and Alexis's lives, too. Sooner or later Taylor is going to realize I wasn't killed, and then he'll send someone else after me.* "Is that the only way we're going to escape him, Papa?" she asked aloud. "By bein' dead?" Tears ran down her cheeks. She didn't want to leave Alex or Alexis, but after all of the things Clarice had said and now this, she knew she had no other choice. Everything was suddenly too clear. She couldn't risk their lives for her own needs. She had to go back to Alaska, only this time it would have to be into the Yukon, or deeper into the interior, somewhere where Taylor would never find her. *Better yet,* she thought grimly, *maybe I should just let him find me and put an end to the cat and mouse game. After all, what will life be now without Alex?*

Gabrielle fought back the tears that blinded her vision as she clutched her knees tightly, rocking to and fro. "Oh, Alex," she groaned. "I love you; I don't want to leave you. I wish there was another way. Maybe if I loved you less. . . ."

Numb with disbelief, Gabrielle sat there on the bank until she grew numb with cold. "Guess I better be going, Papa," she said aloud, her teeth chattering. "I've got to be practical about this." If she was going to leave

374

Virginia, she knew it would have to be soon. "I'll be on that morning train," she whispered. "But I'll need money and traveling clothes." Lifting the wet compress to her head one last time, the white cotton came away clean, and she knew the wound had stopped bleeding.

Hugging her arms to her chest to ward off the chill, Gabrielle got to her feet and climbed up the bank. "I'll just leave . . . no farewells." She knew there would be no way to ever make Alex understand. If he did love her as he said, as she thought, he wouldn't let go. Then of course, if what Clarice said was true, he wouldn't stop her, and that would hurt more. *No, it's better this way,* she thought, *better never to know, better to always believe he truly loved me.*

Shivering, Gabrielle pushed her way through the reeds in search of the path that would lead back to her carriage. Once on the path, she ignored the occasional stare, hurrying to the horses and carriage she'd left at the hitching post. *Go ahead and stare now,* she thought bitterly. *Where were you when those men were trying to drown me?*

Reaching the carriage, Gabrielle untied the horses and was off, headed toward Alex's home, an old blanket wrapped around her for warmth. She had to change her clothes before she caught her death, but she was hoping she could sneak in and out before anyone really noticed her. Of course, who would notice? Alex would be busy as always, and Margaret gave her no mind except to be pleasant when they ran into each other in the downstairs hall.

In the carriage house, Gabrielle leaped to the ground as a newly-hired stable boy caught the harness. "Good lordy, what happen to you, Mrs. Alexander?" His eyes grew wide with a mixture of shock and concern.

Gabrielle managed a quick smile. "Fell in the river, Roy. Silly wasn't it?" She brushed self-consciously at her skirts like she'd seen the other women do. "But hold the carriage, I'm just going to run and change, and then I'll be going into town."

"Shopping, ma'am?"

She turned to go. "You could say that."

Slipping inside the front door, Gabrielle ignored the two men putting up wallpaper in the entryway. Going up the front steps, she hurried down the hallway. Relieved that no one had seen her, she rested her hand on the doorknob of her bedchamber.

Just then, Alexis's door swung open. "Gabrielle?"

Gabrielle jumped, pressing her hand to her thudding heart. She laughed nervously. "You scared me, Alexis."

"Sorry." Then the little girl gasped. "What happened to you? I thought Papa said no more swimmin' this year."

Gabrielle tugged on one of Alexis's curls. "I fell in the river; I didn't go swimming, silly goose." She opened her bedroom door and Alexis followed at her heels.

"You went down to the river without me?" She went to perch herself on the bed. "I thought you said I could go fishing again with you."

Gabrielle began to peel off her wet clothing. "I didn't go fishing."

"Then what were you doin' at the river? Aunt Clarice was lookin' for you. I hid behind the chair in the parlor 'til she went away."

Gabrielle reached for a gown of soft grey flannel and a dry chemise. "I was at the river because . . ." She

376

sighed not having the energy to come up with a decent lie. "Why don't you go see your papa? I'm sure he'd like your company."

Alexis fussed with the ribbon on the bodice of her frock. "I'd rather go with you."

Gabrielle's head snapped up. "Go? Go where?"

She shrugged. "Wherever you're goin'. I saw you from my window. The carriage is still hitched waitin' for you."

"You can't go with me, Alexis." Gabrielle shook her head. "You stay here with your papa. I want you to be with him."

Alexis stuck out her lower lip. "But I want to be with you."

"You can't be with me, Alexis," Gabrielle snapped. "Now go on!"

Alex's daughter got up quietly and crossed the room, her high-button shoes tapping on the hardwood floor.

Gabrielle watched her for a moment, and then put out her arms to her. "I'm sorry, Alexis. Come here." Gabrielle got down on one knee. "Just because you can't always have what you want, doesn't mean someone doesn't love you." Gabrielle fought back the tears that threatened to flow as Alexis came to her. Wrapping her arms around the child's slight form, she hugged her tight.

"I'm sorry," Alexis whispered. "I didn't mean to make you mad at me."

"I'm not mad at you, but I'm not your mother." A lump rose in Gabrielle's throat. "Alex is your papa, and the two of you have a lot to catch up on. A papa should be important to a little girl. I told you, he loves you very much."

"Do you have a papa?" Alexis regarded Gabrielle with Alex's blue eyes.

"He's dead now, but when I was your age, he was the most important person in the whole world to me." Gabrielle smiled sadly. "Now go on and be a good girl, and I'll see you this afternoon, all right?"

"All right." Alexis went to the door.

"And Alexis, could you please not tell your papa about me fallin' in the river?"

The little girl nodded her head and disappeared through the door.

With a heavy sigh, Gabrielle finished dressing and went to the mirror to brush out her wet, tangled hair. She stared at her reflection, barely recognizing herself. Who was this woman with the rich brown hair below her shoulder and a sullen mouth? Taking a bit of black ribbon, she tied back the wet mass and hurriedly left the room.

Her decision made to leave Richmond and Alex, Gabrielle moved mechanically, yet methodically. She went to the bank and withdrew sufficient money to get her back to Seattle and to buy supplies and build a new cabin, leaving the remainder. It was for Alex; he deserved it. Then she went to the old general store the crippled man owned and bought a pair of men's pants, a simple shirt and a wool coat. On impulse she bought a red flannel hat with a wide brim, much like the one that had burned in her cabin. Then she returned to Alex's home. She moved through the evening meal like a sleepwalker, smiling, speaking when spoken to, trying to behave as if nothing was wrong, as if this was not the last night she would ever spend with her husband.

After the meal, hand in hand, Alex and Gabrielle led

378

Alexis upstairs and tucked her into bed. Closing her door quietly, Alex wrapped an arm around Gabrielle's waist, nuzzling her neck. "I thought we could go to bed early," he murmured.

Gabrielle's eyes drifted shut as she inhaled his familiar masculine scent. Her fingers brushed the nape of his neck, and she tried to force to memory the feel of his lips against her skin. "That would be nice." Her voice was barely a whisper.

"You all right?" He lifted her chin, studying her dark eyes.

Gabrielle nodded dumbly, afraid to speak for fear she would burst into tears. "Just tired," she managed. Her voice caught in her throat, and she leaned to rest her head on his shoulder. Even in the shadows of the dark passageway, his blue-grey eyes seemed to bore into her very soul. Would his eyes haunt her forever, or would their memory be a comfort to her during the cold winters to come?

Alex stroked the back of her head, pressing a kiss to her forehead. "You go on. I have something to finish in the library and then I'll be up. I won't be long; I promise." Brushing his lips against hers, he released her and went down the hall.

Wearily, Gabrielle entered her bedchamber and began to undress. Pulling a long white flannel nightgown over her head, she splashed water from the wash bowl on her face and climbed into bed, turning down the lamp. Now that her mind was made up, she refused to let herself reconsider. She wouldn't allow herself to be so selfish as to risk Alex's and Alexis's lives for her own needs. She had lived without Alex before; she could do it again.

She had decided she would sleep a few hours, and then, before dawn she would get up and go. By the time Alex awoke and became concerned about her whereabouts the train would be ready to depart. She had considered leaving him a note of explanation, but she didn't know what to say. She didn't know how to make him understand that whether he loved her or not, their marriage was never meant to be. She knew the LeBeaus were loners, and she should have left it that way. She should never have permitted herself to believe she and Alex could ever be happy together. It was his own fault she was in this mess to begin with, and now it was up to her to right it.

When Alex came to bed a short time later, Gabrielle was still awake, waiting for him. Undressing quietly, he turned out the lamp and slipped in beside her, reaching out to take her in his arms. "What's this?" he whispered. "Since when have you taken to wearing nightgowns to bed? Take it off."

She rolled over to face him. "I don't feel like it, Alex."

He laughed, brushing her cheek with the back of his hand. "I just want to hold you. We don't have to make love; I just want to feel you against me." He stroked her arm through the soft material. "Come on," he coaxed.

"All right," she whispered. "I could use some holdin'."

Alex watched her sit up and pull the gown over her head. "You sure you're all right?" he asked. "You've been acting so odd tonight."

"I'm fine. I told you I'm just tired." She laid back down with her back to him, and he put his arm around her. "Maybe fighting off a cold in my chest or

380

something," she added.

"You're not . . . not pregnant are you?" he asked quietly.

She shook her head. *If only I was,* she thought. *Then I could take a part of him with me.* "No, Alex. I'm not pregnant."

"Would you like to be?" he asked hesitantly. They had never really discussed children. Alex had assumed it was a part of marriage. He was actually surprised that she wasn't with child yet.

"Alex . . . could we—" Her voice caught in her throat. "I'm really tired. Can we talk about it tomorrow?" Her chest ached with the pain of her breaking heart. If he didn't shut up, he was going to make her cry, and then what would she say? What explanation would she give?

"All right." He stretched out, pressing his lean body against hers. He knew something was wrong, but it was obvious she didn't want to talk about it tonight. *Maybe tomorrow,* he thought to himself. *Maybe I'll take the day off from work on the house, leave Alexis with Mother and the two of us will go somewhere for the day. She's just feeling neglected, that's all.* Snuggling closer, he closed his eyes. "Good-night, Gabrielle. I love you."

"Good-night," she answered in a voice that was barely audible. "I love you."

There nestled in Alex's arms, the sound of his breathing and the feel of his arm tight around her waist comforted her, and finally she fell asleep.

The case clock in the upstairs hallway chimed four as

381

Gabrielle slipped quietly out of her bedroom, a cloth satchel containing her money and her rag doll in her hand. There had been no tearful farewells to Alex. She had kissed his lips, smiling sadly over his sleeping face and then had dressed and gone. If she allowed herself to falter, she knew she'd never be able to accomplish what had to be done. Moving silently across the hall, she went into Alexis's room and kissed her good-bye and then made her way down the front steps.

Cloth satchel in hand, Gabrielle made her way out of the house and across the lawn. It would be a long walk to town, but she didn't want to take the carriage and then have to leave the horses tied at the train station until Alex finally found them. *Besides,* she told herself, going down the driveway, *the walk will do me good.*

Just then, one of the hound puppies came from behind a tree, racing after Gabrielle, yipping with pleasure at having found a human companion.

"Shhh," Gabrielle whispered, kneeling in the grass. "You'll wake 'em all up." She scratched the brown puppy behind his spotted ear and then deposited him on the grass. "Now you stay," she ordered, the minute she walked away, the puppy came bounding after her.

Gabrielle tried the technique again, this time offering the pup a piece of ham from the slices she carried in her bag. The puppy ate the meat and then came after her again, howling as it made its way down the tree-line drive.

Laughing at the little dog's antics, Gabrielle scooped him into her arms, cuddling him inside her wool coat. "What am I going to do with you?" she murmured. For a moment she stood in indecision; then dropping her bag on the lawn, she made her way back up to the house and in the front door.

Going quietly up the steps, Gabrielle carried the little brown pup into Alexis's room and lifted the covers, depositing him beside the sleeping child. The puppy turned three times and then laid down, warm beneath the quilts. With one last glance at Alex's daughter, she left the house, refusing to look back. "Good-bye, Alex," she whispered as she went down the lane. "I love you."

Alex pounded his fist against the wooden door of Clarice's townhouse. "Clarice, answer this door!" he ordered through clenched teeth.

The door swung open. "Jefferson, how nice of you to call." Clarice smiled sweetly.

He pushed his way in the door. "Where is she?"

"What are you talking about?"

He knotted his fists at his sides, his face red with anger. "Gabrielle, where is she?"

"How should I know?" Clarice replied indignantly. She crossed her arms over her bosom.

Alex took a step forward, raising his fist to point a finger. "Don't play stupid with me, dear sister. I haven't the time. Now tell me where she's gone."

Clarice took a step back, intimidated by the threat in her brother's voice. "Jefferson, I assure you I—"

"My name is Alex. It's been Alex since I was a child so don't you ever call me Jefferson again." His stormy grey eyes narrowed. "Now you tell me where my wife's gone or so help me God, Clarice, I'll strike you!"

"I . . . I don't know." Her voice shook with sudden fear. She'd never seen her brother so volatile.

"Alexis told me you had words with Gabrielle yesterday," he accused. It was nearly noon and he was frantic. No one had seen Gabrielle since she went to bed last night, and he feared something terrible had happened. None of her clothes were missing; the horses were all in their stables. She had just disappeared. He was terrified that Taylor or one of his men had gotten to her.

"What does a child know?" Clarice asked, trying to gain her composure. She couldn't believe it! The little tart had actually taken her advice.

"I knew there was something wrong with Gabrielle yesterday; I just didn't know what. Now tell me what happened."

"She's gone," Clarice blurted out.

"Gone? Gone where?" Alex swallowed against the rising fear in his throat.

"Back where she belongs, I would guess. Some dockside *Ladies' House* maybe?"

Alex raised his hand to strike his middle-aged sister, but caught himself in midair. "Are you so selfish that you won't allow me just a little happiness?" he asked bitterly.

Clarice cringed, backing up in the small entryway until her back was against the papered wall. "Don't be foolish. She'll ruin your life. She's nothing but a—"

"She's my wife!" he shouted. "Tell me what you know, now!" His angry, masculine voice echoed in the high-ceilinged hall.

Clarice shrugged. "I sent her packing. I told her you didn't love her, that you only wanted her gold . . ."

Alex's face fell.

"I told her we knew the sordid truth of her past. I told

her she'd ruin your life and Alexis's if she stayed." She straightened her posture. "I told her the truth."

Alex spun around, his back to his sister. He could feel the rage bubbling up inside him, threatening to spill over. His chest ached for the pain Gabrielle must have experienced from his sister's words. "I can't believe you did it, Clarice. I can't believe it," he whispered.

"It was only for your own good. For Alexis's."

Alex turned slowly around, scrutinizing her pale face. "You know, I actually believe you." He shook his head sadly. "And I'm sorry for you. But why? I told you I loved her. I told you she made me happy."

"She was nothing like Amber—"

"I didn't want another wife like Amber!"

Clarice trembled. "All I ever wanted was what was best for you, for my loved ones."

Alex looked away, his eyes clouding with moisture. "I told you that I loved her, but there's no way I can make you understand that is there? You don't know what love is."

"I love my Edward; I love you. Why do you think I did it?"

"No. You don't love your husband. To love someone you have to be willing to sacrifice. Gabrielle gave up her entire life to come to Virginia and be with me. You wouldn't sacrifice your cherry tart at supper time for Edward," he sneered.

"How dare you!"

"No!" he shouted. "How dare you!" Spinning around, he made three long strides to the door.

"Where are you going?" Clarice ran after him.

"To the train station."

"The train's gone, left this morning."

Alex ran a hand through his thick hair. "Then I've got to get a schedule; I've got to see when the next west-bound train is leaving."

"You can't go after her," she argued, following him as he took the front marble steps two at a time.

"Oh, you're wrong. I can. And I'm taking Alexis with me. . . ."

"No!" Clarice protested. "You can't!"

Alex leaped onto the horse he'd left tied to the hitching post. "Oh, I can," he said with a nod. "And I'm going to." Sinking his heels into the bay's side he rode off in a fury of dust, ignoring his sister's pleas.

Chapter Twenty-Eight

Gabrielle stepped off the stagecoach at the Union Pacific Railway Station in Seattle, clutching her wool coat and lowering her head against the driving rain. She had taken the stagecoach from Portland because she had been told it would be faster but had ended up losing two days while a wheel was being repaired. Cursing beneath her breath, she started down the street, her satchel held tightly in her hand. Turning onto King's Street, she lifted her head in search of the St. Lucy, the hotel she and Alex had stayed in. Spotting its wooden sign blowing in the wind another block up, she hurried, shivering with cold.

Pushing open the front door, she stepped into the entryway and went up to the front desk.

"Can I help you?" The same rotund woman with the painted face who had been there before glared suspiciously.

Gabrielle slipped her red felt hat off her head, letting her damp hair fall to her shoulders. "Yes. I'd like a room." She ignored the water that ran off her boots and puddled on the thick piled carpet.

The woman's round face lit up, her thick makeup cracking at the crinkles near her eyes. "Mrs. Alexander! How nice to see you. We have the same room you stayed in before available. Mr. Alexander will be joining you, won't he?"

"No," Gabrielle responded tiredly. "Different room, a small one. He won't be joining me."

The woman lifted a painted eyebrow but said nothing, turning to reach for a key. "How long'll you be staying with us?"

"Not long. Can you find out when the next steamer is headed north? I'll take a sloop if I have to. I'll pay you." Her voice was dull and lifeless.

"Sure, sugar pie, I can take care of it for you. Won't be hard. I hear they're settin' up another line, gonna run all winter. Things been busy here since we got word of the strike on the Forty Mile River."

Gabrielle glanced up in interest. "At Forty Mile, you say? How big a strike?"

"I don't know, but big from what I hear. I'm sure someone down closer to the docks can tell you. We been busy as bees since the word came down. Men settin' out and it's near winter. Do anything for a bit of glittering rock, won't they?" The woman slid a key across the desk and opened the large register book. "Let's see here." She licked the point of her pencil. "That'll be Mrs. Alexander in room twelve."

"No." Gabrielle shook her head. "Just Gabrielle LeBeau."

She looked up but said nothing, then leaned to scribble in the book. "All set." She smiled at Gabrielle.

Gabrielle scooped the key off the desk and turned to

go. "Send up a bath, will you?"

"I will indeed," the woman called after Gabrielle as she went up the steps.

Letting herself into the hotel room, Gabrielle dropped her satchel on a chair and flopped down on the bed. The room was much smaller than the one she and Alex had used. This one had only one room with no parlor, and the bed was only big enough for one person. Still, it was elaborately decorated with rosewood furniture and deep-brown velvet drapes.

Sighing, Gabrielle let her eyes drift shut. In the weeks that had passed since she had left Alex in Virginia, she had moved like someone caught in a dreamworld. She ate, she slept, she watched the passing scenery as the train moved west, but she felt nothing. At the end of the line in San Franciso, she had taken a stagecoach into Rosenburg, Oregon, then a train into Portland. By that point, she was beyond thought or feeling; she was numb. But she refused to allow herself to dwell over the past. Her life had been adequate before Alex had come along; she had been happy, and she was determined to make herself happy again. She felt no bitterness. She was thankful for the year she had had with him, and she would keep those memories locked safe in her heart forever.

But now it was time to get on with her life. She needed to get supplies and building materials and be on her way before Taylor found her. She figured she would buy some dogs and take them north with her. She'd move her supplies as far upriver as she could, and then she'd leave them until spring and mush on up to Jack's to spend the winter. In the spring she'd hire a steamer and ship the supplies upstream. She didn't know where she would build a new trading post; she'd worry about that when the time came.

A knock came at the hotel room door, and Gabrielle sat up. "Come on in," she called.

A maid came in with towels, followed by a boy carrying a copper tub. Gabrielle stood and waited while the tub was filled with steaming water, and then she dismissed them both. Stripping off her damp clothes she threw them over a chair to dry and sank into the velvety softness of the water. With a sigh, she leaned back, closing her eyes.

As she rested her weary body in the hot tub, she couldn't help wondering what Alex was doing right now. She was caught between hoping he missed her dearly and hoping he didn't miss her at all. She knew it would be easier for him if he was relieved she was gone, if what Clarice had said about him being too much of a gentleman to tell her was true. But in her own selfishness, a part of her hoped he still loved her. Whatever was the case, she was certain that in time he would meet someone else, someone who would make him a proper wife and a decent mother to Alexis.

In the days that followed Gabrielle's arrival in Seattle, she kept herself busy bargaining for supplies and looking for some sled dogs to purchase. In the evenings she went down to the Full Moon Saloon where her father had been killed and talked with his old cronies. From them she learned that there had indeed been a large strike at Forty Mile. It was made by a man named Howard Franklin off one of the tributaries of the river and was expected to be bigger than the Stewart River sandbars of '75–'76. The news of the strike excited Gabrielle. With the rush of gold seekers that would follow, if she could build a trading post in a strategic place, she'd be able to make a good living.

Four days after Gabrielle had arrived in Seattle, a knock came at the door of her hotel. Surprised because she had called for neither food nor a bath, she went cautiously to the locked door. "Yes, who is it?" Her eyes went to the new Colt pistol she'd purchased, which she kept on the stand next to her bed.

"It's your mother, Gabrielle. Let me in, love. I'm near soaked from the rain." She rapped on the door again.

"Alice?"

"I said it was me, now open the door!"

Against her better judgment, Gabrielle opened the door a crack. "What do you want?"

Alice sighed, running a hand over her elegant coiffure dampened by the downpour outside. "Must we go through this again?" She pushed her way through the door and past Gabrielle. "I heard you were back in town; I came to comfort you."

Gabrielle's eyebrows furrowed. "How did you know?"

Alice smiled sweetly, removing her cloak. "I told you before, dear, nothing happens in this town these days that your mother doesn't know about." She sat down on the only chair in the room, removing her long leather gloves. "I have to tell you I told you so, but your man didn't keep you very long, did he?" Her eyes went to Gabrielle's hand. "No wedding ring, either."

Gabrielle crossed her arms over her chest. "We *were* married; it just didn't work out." Her own voice sounded strange in her ears. She wondered how she could discuss this so calmly with her mother.

"I'm sure you were, dear," she said patronizingly. "Now tell your mother, what are you going to do with yourself?" She lifted a finely sculpted eyebrow taking in her daughter's shabby appearance. "Now that you have no money—"

Gabrielle gave a snort, turning away. "I have money."

Her mother straightened in the chair with interest. "But what happened to your fine clothes, the gowns, the hats?"

Gabrielle stuffed her hands in the pockets of her men's woolen pants, scuffing at the rug with her booted foot. "I dress this way because I want to."

"You mean he didn't take your share of the gold?"

"No, I brought—" She cut herself off, turning to scrutinize her mother. She had realized a long time ago that Alice LeBeau was not a woman to be trusted. "Why do you ask?"

"Just concerned for your welfare." Alice shrugged delicately as she got to her feet.

"Why do I find that hard to believe?" Gabrielle asked sarcastically.

Her mother pulled on her cape. "You're so suspicious, child. As bad as your father was. Now, I have a surprise for you." She worked at the buttons of the expensive overcoat. "I want you to come to my home; I've someone I want you to meet."

"Your home?"

Alice smiled, lifting her chin. "I'm a kept woman these days, and I want you to meet him."

"I . . . I don't think so." She shook her head. "I'll be leaving any day now. I've got a lot to do."

"Nonsense. If you're abandoning your poor old

mother again to go off into that wilderness, the least you can do is come and see how well taken care of I am."

Gabrielle followed her mother to the door. "I really don't want to."

"Please." Her mother turned to her, a hint of sincerity in her voice. "I'm a respectable lady now."

"He's going to marry you?"

"Why would I want to marry anyone? I made that mistake once; I'll not do it again." She pushed a folded piece of paper into her daughter's hand. "Here's the address. Tonight, six o'clock? I have two maids and a cook."

All sensible reason told Gabrielle she shouldn't go. Her mother had given her nothing but pain her entire life. So why did she care if she was happy, if she had a man keeping her off the street? Because she was still her mother. . . . "All right. Tonight. But I can't stay long. I've found a man who has some sled dogs to sell. I'll be going out to see them in the morning."

Alice lifted her hood. "Tonight, then."

Gabrielle closed the door, leaning against it. Looking at the piece of paper in her hand, she crumpled it with a sigh.

Dressed in a new sweater and flannel pants, Gabrielle arrived at the address her mother had given her, with a bottle of good Scotch whiskey tucked beneath her arm. It was just after six-thirty, and the rain had finally ceased. Taking a deep breath, she lifted the knocker on the paneled door and let it fall. "Stay with me on this one, Papa," she whispered. "I'm going

393

to need you."

The elegant door swung open. "Gabrielle! I was so afraid you weren't coming. You're late." Alice was dressed in a deep-blue serge gown with large sapphires dangling from each ear. Her face was painted subtly, her honey-colored hair pulled back in a nestle of curls at her neck.

"I couldn't make up my mind whether or not I was coming." She looked up at her mother standing in the light that streamed from the door. "Are you going to let me in?"

Alice laughed, stepping back. "Come in . . . come in. Excuse my poor manners."

Gabrielle moved past her mother and into the entryway of the newly built house. "Quite the little homemaker, aren't we?" She glanced up at the crystal chandelier hanging overhead.

Alice leaned to brush her lips past her daughter's cheek. "I thought you'd be happy for me."

"Oh, I am. I just can't help wondering what it is you want from me."

Alice shook her head. "Always the cynic, weren't you, daughter. Your coat?" She motioned to a maid standing discreetly in the doorway of the parlor to the right of the entryway. "Carla, take it will you?"

Gabrielle shrugged off her heavy men's coat, handing it to the maid. She held out the whiskey to her mother. "For you. I know how much you always liked good liquor."

Alice let out a sigh, accepting the bottle. "And I thought you were going to come and be nice." Her gaze went to the label, noting the year the whiskey was bottled.

She tucked a wisp of hair behind her ear. "You're right," she conceded. "I was. I'm sorry."

"There, there, no harm done. It's no news to me that you've never been particularly fond of your mother." She lowered her voice to be certain it didn't carry to the maid's ears. "But I'd like to put the past behind us."

"I'm leaving, Alice, in a few days. I doubt I'll be coming back." Gabrielle heard her mother's peace-making words, but she didn't believe them, not for a minute. Alice LeBeau never offered anything, not even her friendship, without expecting something in return.

"Are you sure you want to go?" Alice folded her hands demurely. "The territory will surely be an unsafe place for a woman with all of those men heading north now. You heard of the strike at Forty Mile—"

"I heard."

"But you still intend to go?" Alice led Gabrielle into the parlor.

"I'm still going. It's my home; it's where I belong. Now where's this gentleman of yours? He must be a good man to offer you so much." She gestured with a hand at the room, tastefully furnished.

"Oh, Malcolm is. Please, sit." Alice indicated a red-colored velvet settee. "He's been too good to me."

"Funny. I don't remember you mentioning a Malcolm in August." Gabrielle stroked the velvet with her palm, remembering the settee she and Alex had sat side by side on in his own parlor only a few weeks ago. Her throat tightened at the thought of him, and she looked away, hoping her mother wouldn't notice the tears that pooled in the corners of her eyes.

"Actually, I haven't known him long. I only saw him a few times, just after you left, in fact, and then he asked me to move into his new house here with him." She settled herself on a chair across from Gabrielle. "You see, he's had an injury. He lost a leg to frostbite up north last winter, somewhere on the Tanana, I think."

Gabrielle shook her head. "My, I wouldn't wish that on anyone. Frostbite's a painful thing. Alex—" She cut herself off, looking away. Why couldn't she get him out of her mind. Would he haunt her forever? "How did it happen?" she asked quietly.

"Actually, I don't know. It was such a painful experience that Malcolm prefers not to speak of it, and I haven't pressed him. He's been so good to me that I saw no need." She got to her feet. "Well, shall we go in to supper. Malcolm said he would be down in a moment."

Gabrielle got up and followed her mother down several steps into an exquisitely furnished dining room. A fire burned in an ornate stove in the corner of the room, adding to the atmosphere of warm opulence. "Pretty," she murmured, turning to study a portrait on the wall.

"I'm glad you like it" came a deep male voice from behind.

A shiver of primal fear ran down Gabrielle's spine, and for a moment she was too paralyzed to move. She knew that voice! There was no mistaking it. Slowly she turned to face Lucas Taylor.

"Gabrielle, I want you to meet Malcolm Rosenwood." Alice swept up the two steps that led out of the sunken dining room, catching Lucas's arm.

Gabrielle forced back her rising terror as her eyes met his. What game was he playing? Speechless, all she could manage to do was nod her head in his direction.

Taylor was dressed impeccably in a black, single-breasted sack suit, a pristine white collar peaking from beneath the coat.

"Gabrielle, how good to meet you at last. Your mother has told me so much about you." He came toward her slowly, with the aid of a cane, his gait hampered by the wooden leg that tapped on the hardwood floor.

Gabrielle stifled the urge to confront him here and now. *No,* she thought. *Better to hold my cards and see what he's holding first.* "Good to meet you, too," she heard herself say.

Taylor's dark eyes glistened. "Your mother was afraid you wouldn't come." He put out his hand to take hers and pressed it to his lips.

Gabrielle's eyes met his, and he smiled, showing even white teeth. She couldn't believe how dashingly handsome he was in his fine coat and gilt cane. How could her mother not know this was the same man that had killed Rouge LeBeau only the year before? "I . . . I've been very busy," Gabrielle stuttered. "I'm headed north as soon as my supplies come in."

"Are you now?" He released her hand and started for the upholstered chair at the head of the long dining table. "Not many women in that territory. It's a dangerous place; I've been there, you know."

Gabrielle's eyes narrowed. "Have you, now?" Gaining control of her emotions, she slid into the chair just to his left. Alice was seated to his right. "Where?"

He smiled charmingly. "On the Tanana. Do you know it?"

Alice eyed Malcolm, then her daughter. She wasn't quite sure what was going on between the two of them, but she didn't care for it. She didn't like the sparkle of interest in her lover's eyes. She had worked too hard for this position as his mistress to lose it to this little chit, daughter or not. "Now Malcolm, you know very well Gabrielle knows the Tanana. I told you it was the unfortunate place where she was born." Alice nodded to the maid that stood in the doorway, and the woman dropped a curtsy, disappearing into the kitchen.

Gabrielle reached for her glass of wine, sipping it. She couldn't believe she was sitting here speaking so civilly to the man who had murdered her father, to the man who had attempted to murder her! She leaned back as the maid served the first course of the meal, a steaming bowl of creamed soup.

Gabrielle listened quietly as Alice and Lucas chatted pleasantly. Gabrielle nodded occasionlly, speaking when necessary, but concentrating on watching Lucas and trying to figure out what he was up to. Tonight, Lucas Taylor appeared to be the perfect gentleman. Who would know that a few months ago he had kidnapped her and threatened to sell her to a brothel? He spoke quietly, was attentive to Alice and was a charming conversationalist. But Gabrielle saw through his façade; she saw him watching her from the corner of his eyes.

It was not until after supper, just before dessert, that Gabrielle finally got the chance to speak to him alone. Alice got up from the table, excusing herself to check and see what was holding up the baked pie. The moment she was gone from the room, Gabrielle turned to Taylor.

"What the hell are you doing?" she asked quietly, her voice thick with venom.

"Doing?" He leaned back in his chair, extracting a cigar from a gilt case on the table. "Having dinner with my mistress."

"What are you doing with my mother? Who the hell is Malcolm?" She leaned in toward him, her anger stronger than her fear.

"I met your mother just after you left town. I would have returned to Seattle sooner, but I was ill." He poked the cigar between his teeth. The man was perfectly relaxed, feeling entirely in control of the situation.

"You should have died on that river instead of just losing your leg. . . ." Gabrielle whispered.

Lucas's hand darted out to catch hers, squeezing it viciously. "You little bitch! It's because of you that I lost my leg!"

"Me?" Gabrielle tried not to let her voice shake. She was scared. "Who came after me? It was greed that took your leg, your own greed."

He tightened his grip on her hand, making her rise up in her chair. "Just wait. You're going to pay. It may take time, but you'll pay."

"Why not kill me now?" she dared. "Do it yourself instead of sending idiots to bungle it."

He smiled, the cigar still clenched between his teeth. "Too messy. To easy to get caught. Besides, I want your money. Your mother says you brought back your half of the gold strike."

She struggled to wrench her hand free. "I'm going to tell her who you are, what you're trying to do! What you tried to do to me."

He released her hand, and she fell back against the chair. "Tell her and I'll kill her while she sleeps. Besides, she wouldn't believe you and you know it. She fancies herself in love with me." He lit the thick cigar with a candle that burned near his plate.

He's right, Gabrielle thought frantically. *She won't believe me.* "But my father. You killed my father. There's records to prove you were charged with my father's death. It wouldn't be that hard for me to prove you're the Lucas Taylor that killed Rouge LeBeau," she treaded carefully.

He shrugged. "There are records that prove I was found not guilty. It was self-defense. And as for my name, it's no crime to change one's name. I can assure you that there is more than one man who has changed his name in this town. I only did it because there were too many . . . shall we say bad rumors connected with Taylor." He exhaled slowly, watching the cigar smoke rise above his head.

Gabrielle's hands shook as she lowered them to her lap. She had to get out of there! She had to book her passage before he caught up with her. She couldn't live like that, watching her back. She rose up out of her chair, her napkin falling to the floor. "I . . . I have to—"

"Gabrielle." Alice came floating into the dining room. "Where are you going? You haven't had dessert."

"I . . . I . . ." Gabrielle stuttered, too shaken to reply.

"Gabrielle has a headache, dear." Taylor smiled handsomely, falling back easily into the role of the gallant protector. "I suggested she go back to the hotel and rest." He got to his feet, reaching for his cane. "I thought she could come another evening, when she's feeling better."

Gabrielle hurried past her mother and through the

parlor into the front entryway. Alice followed her. "Are you all right, dear? Would you like me to have the carriage brought around?"

"No." Gabrielle shook her head, swallowing against the nausea that rose in her throat. She felt trapped, like an animal in deep snow. No matter which way she turned, or how hard she fought, she didn't seem to be able to break free of Taylor. "Just my coat, Mother." She could hear Taylor coming through the parlor, his peg leg tapping on the polished floor.

A maid came in and handed Gabrielle her coat. "Thank you," Gabrielle murmured, stuffing her fists in it as she opened the door. "Thanks for the meal, Mother, it . . . it was good."

"Are you certain nothing's wrong?" Alice looked at her with a hint of genuine concern.

Taylor entered the entryway, slipping his hand around Alice's waist. "I'm quite sure she'll be fine, won't you, Gabrielle?"

She nodded her head. "Yes, yes, fine. Good-night." Without looking back at them, she ducked out the door, closing it behind her. Turning down the street, she ran as fast as she could over the icy walk. "Alex . . . Papa . . . anyone, help me."

Chapter Twenty-Nine

Alex wrung out the cotton cloth over the washbowl and kneeled to wipe Alexis's flushed face. The little girl moaned softly, twisting away to roll over on her side beneath the bedcovers. Persisting, Alex brushed the cool cloth over her brow, mopping up the tiny beads of sweat that clung to her pale skin. Heaving a sigh of relief, he pushed back a lock of golden hair off her cheek and tucked the covers tight beneath her chin.

At least the fever had broken, and that was what the old woman had said was important. Getting to his feet, Alex dropped the cloth in the washbowl on the night table near the bed and went to stare out of a small window. Rain trickled down the glass clouding his vision so that he could barely see the San Francisco street below. He damned his luck silently as he watched a horse and carriage hurry through the rain down the paved street.

How could Alexis have gotten sick so fast? And why in San Francisco? If only they could have made it to Seattle. Alex was caught between concern for his sick daughter and concern for Gabrielle. He had to get to Seattle! With every passing day, he had felt her moving farther and farther from him, until he could barely hear her voice in his mind or feel the touch of her hand beneath his. And what if she hadn't made it to Seattle? Carrying all of that money she had withdrawn from the bank, anyone could have knocked her over the head for one tenth of the amount!

Or what if she reached Seattle and caught a steamer and was already headed north into the Alaska Territory? Alex leaned forward, pressing his forehead against the cold window pane and squeezing his eyes shut. It would take months, even years, to find her once she disembarked at St. Michaels, especially since she didn't want to be found. And now that he had Alexis with him, how could he drag her over the miles and miles of snow and ice searching for Gabrielle?

Alex tightened his fists in frustration, turning away from the window. He was going to make himself crazy thinking like this! He had to be optimistic. He had to believe he would find her. His chest tightened with heartfelt pain. How could she just have left him like that, no note, not a word? Though he had realized she wasn't happy in Richmond, he didn't know she was so miserable that she would just walk out on him. He was her husband for God sakes!

Alexis stirred, and Alex moved to the bed, sitting on the edge. "Papa," she murmured. Her eyes fluttered open. "Papa, where are you?"

"Here I am, Alexis." He took her hand. "Here's your papa."

She squirmed beneath the heavy quilts, tightening her hold on his hand. "Papa, where's Gabrielle?" Her tongue darted out to moisten her dry lips. "You said we was goin' to Gabrielle."

Alex reached for a tin cup of water on the table beside the bed and lifted her with a hand, pressing the cup to her lips. "Drink. We are going to Gabrielle, in Seattle, just as soon as you're better."

Alexis drank thirstily, then laid back on the pillow. "I'm hot, Papa. I don't like this place. Where are we?"

"At a hotel in a place called San Francisco. We got off the train because you were sick." He smiled at her, returning the cup to the night table. "But you're much better now. The lady, Mrs. Forester, who helped me look after you said you're going to be fine. Just another day or two of bed rest and then we'll be on our way." He stroked the little girl's damp forehead, thankful the hotel proprietor had been able to get his mother to come in and look in on Alexis after the doctor had gone. If it hadn't been for the kind old woman, he wouldn't have known what to do for his daughter.

"I want to go now, Papa. I want Gabrielle. I miss her." Her lower lip jutted out. "And where's my puppy?"

Alex grinned. He knew she was feeling better; this was the first time she'd asked for Mister Ballentine in three days. Reaching below the bed, Alex pulled the sleeping puppy from the box and dropped it in his daughter's lap. "Here he is."

"Mister Ballentine." Alexis laughed, stroking the wiggling pup. It was the same brown puppy with the spotted ear that Gabrielle had left in Alexis's bed nearly three weeks ago.

Alex shook his head, unable to resist giving the dog a pat on its back. How Alexis had convinced him to bring the puppy, he didn't know. Imagine, his mother had said, a man with a child and a puppy crossing the country by train. Impossible, she had told him. Well, it wasn't, and he had almost proved it. "All right now, little lady," Alex said to Alexis. "Give him a kiss and then back in the bed he goes. You're as bad as your Moth—" he cut himself off. "As bad as Gabrielle with her dogs. Now it's time you went back to sleep, time we both went to sleep."

Alexis did as she was told, telling the pup goodnight, and then handed him to her father. Alex returned the whining Mister Ballentine to his box beneath the bed and leaned to tuck his daughter in. "Now you go to sleep, and I'll see you in the morning."

Alexis nodded compliantly, her eyes already drifting shut. "Yes, Papa."

"Good night, darling. Say your prayers, and add an extra special one for Gabrielle, all right?" he whispered.

"Okay," Alexis answered sleepily. "Good-night." Her eyes flew open. "And Papa . . ."

"Yes?" Alex ran a hand through his auburn hair.

"Thank you for comin' back to Richmond to get me."

He laughed, moisture gathering in the corners of his eyes. "You're welcome."

The morning after Gabrielle had dinner with her mother and Lucas, she went down to the docks early to secure passage on the next vessel that left port headed for Alaska.

"I don't care if it's a steamer, a sloop, or a rowboat," she told the old man at the rickety desk in a shipping line office. "I've got to get out of here, today if it's possible."

The grey-haired man clicked between his teeth, shaking his head as he went over a smudged list of departures. "Best I can do is a steamer tomorrow morning, missy. We're busy as I ever saw it, and I been in here nigh on ten years. The *Mary Bella* is bound for St. Michaels." He looked up, taking in her masculine appearance as well as the bulge of her revolver beneath her coat. "In a hurry are you?"

She nodded, glancing out the window. "You could say that."

"You could catch something over to Vancouver Island and pick something up out of there in the next day or two."

"No. I've got dogs to transport. Can I take 'em on that steamer?" She shifted nervously, looking out the window again. She hadn't slept at all last night for fear of Taylor, and this morning she had almost been too frightened to go out on the street.

"Yup. That can be arranged. Name please."

"Ummm . . ." Gabrielle hesitated. "Alexander, Alexis Alexander."

The man scribbled her name. "Don't make no difference to me, hon." He looked up at her. "Done. They'll be loadin' live stuff at daybreak. The ship's leavin' on the outgoing tide, around eleven."

Gabrielle nodded, pushing a hand deep into her pocket. "Good. Now how much you want?"

He stated his price, half now, half when she left port tomorrow, and she complied, slipping the bills over the wooden counter. Though passage had gone up considerably since last year, she said nothing. All she

407

wanted to do right now was get out of Seattle alive.

"You come in here in the mornin' after you're loaded and pay up the rest," the old man instructed.

Thanking him, Gabrielle slipped out the door and moved inconspicuously up the street. Returning to the St. Lucy Hotel, she asked the desk clerk, Gerta, to have the supplies she'd ordered delivered to the docks in the morning. Then she met the Frenchman she had hired to take her out of the city to pick up her dogs. The rail-thin man was a brother-in-law to Gerta, and she had promised he would be both discreet and trusting.

Locating the gentleman who was selling the sled dogs just outside the city, Gabrielle chose four strong husky mixes and loaded them into the Frenchman's wagon. She also purchased a wooden crate to transport each dog on the steamer. Ordinarily she wouldn't have paid the extraordinary price the dog seller quoted for the boxes; she would rather have built her own. Unfortunately she didn't have the time, so she handed him a wad of bills and was off in the wagon headed back to Seattle with new dogs.

Reaching the St. Lucy after dark, the Frenchman, Francis, helped her unload the crates and dogs and tie them in a barn behind the hotel. Thanking him and paying him generously, she said good-bye and then settled on a blanket beside her new dogs to spend the night with them. Well before dawn she was up and gathering her things from her hotel room. Francis returned with his wagon and took her and her dogs to the docks. They arrived just as the sun was rising in the eastern sky.

Nervously, Gabrielle approached the crewman on the *Mary Bella* who was directing the loading of the vessel. "Excuse me. My name is Gabr— Alexis Alexander. I've got dogs to ship. My other supplies should already be here." She glanced uneasily behind her.

There were men everywhere with horses and wagons, moving crates and shouting orders. The gulls overhead wailed mournfully, and the water lapped rhythmically at the sides of the moored steamers. It would have been an exciting morning filled with sights and sounds and anticipation of a journey, but instead, Gabrielle was apprehensive. Her nerves were raw from the sleepless nights and her fear of Lucas Taylor. And worse yet, her imagination was getting the best of her. She kept thinking she heard Taylor's voice, or saw his shadow behind her.

The crewman leaned to study his list of passengers and their supplies. "Nope. Don't see no Alexis Alexander and no freight for her, either. Don't see no women." He pushed back his knit cap and called an order to another crewman on deck. "Sorry, ma'am."

"But . . . but I paid half of my passage." She looked at him in disbelief.

"Look lady, if you paid, your name would be on this list."

"But it must be there. You just didn't see it." She grabbed the lapel of his wool coat. "I've got to get on this steamer. I've got to get to St. Michaels," she told him desperately.

The burly crewman looked down at her hand on his lapel, and she released it. "All I can tell you is there ain't no ladies travelin' on this vessel. Check the office. It must be a different day, different boat."

"No. No I'm certain it was today, the *Mary Bella*."

409

He shrugged, backing up to make way for a large wooden crate being swung on a crane. "Check the office." He pointed to the building she'd been in the day before and turned away.

Gabrielle hurried to the office and swung open the door. To her surprise, the old man wasn't there. Instead, a seedy-looking character with a long scraggly beard and mustache was seated in the old man's chair.

Swallowing hard, Gabrielle stepped up to the counter. "Excuse me."

The man didn't look up so she repeated herself a little louder. "Excuse me but there seems to have been a mix-up."

The man got slowly to his feet and came to lean on the counter. "Yea?"

His breath nearly knocked her over. "There's a mix-up," she insisted. "I was in this office yesterday and paid half of my passage for the *Mary Bella.* For this morning. I've got my supplies stacked up outside on the dock."

He looked at her, only one blue eye focusing on her face, while the other rolled lazily. "You didn't pay me nothin'. Pretty little female thing like you, I'd've remembered."

"No." She shook her head, taking half a step back. "I didn't pay you. It was an old man. Here yesterday morning."

He spat on the floor. "Don't nobody work here but me. You see anybody else?"

"No. No, I'm sure it was here . . ." Gabrielle let her voice trail off into silence. *My God,* she thought. *Has Taylor been here?*

"Look here, female. You ain't on this list, and you

410

ain't gettin' on it. You understand?" He pulled a long knife from his belt and began to carve at his dirty fingernails.

"What . . . what do you mean? I paid good money. Who said I'm not?"

"That was the message I was to give you. You're supposed to know who it's from."

Gabrielle's heart skipped a beat. "The old man who was in here . . . where is he? What did you do with him?"

"You just better get out of here and quit asking questions," he threatened, pointing at her with the knife. "Because sometimes people who ask questions get hurt. If you know what I mean."

Gabrielle took a step back, then turned and ran out of the office, leaving the door swung wide open. Racing to the open wagon where Francis had her dogs, she leaped in beside him. "Back to the hotel."

"But, mademoiselle—"

"Please, now!" she insisted.

The Frenchman slapped the reins, and the horses lunged forward. As they hurried down the street, Gabrielle looked over her shoulder just in time to see the shadow of a man with a cane limp into the shipping office she'd just come from. Covering her hand with her mouth, she gasped.

"Mademoiselle, what is it?" Francis reined in the horses and headed down the warehouse-lined Water Street.

"I can't tell you," she murmured.

"You can't tell me? What does this mean? I see you are in trouble."

She shook her head emphatically. "No. Anyone I tell

might be in danger, too. Just take me to the hotel . . . please. And unload my dogs. I've got to go somewhere, to see someone." She had to get to Alice to warn her—without Taylor knowing.

Francis studied the young woman whose face was ashen with fear. "Perhaps I could help you. . . ."

She laid her hand on his arm. "Yes. You could."

"Tell me."

"After you leave me at the hotel, could you go back to the dock and find a warehouse to store my supplies until I can find passage on another steamer? That stuff can't sit out in the rain, it'll be ruined."

He nodded, pulling into the alley that led to the barn behind the St. Lucy hotel. "Anything else, mademoiselle?"

She leaped out of the wagon the moment it came to a stop. "Yes, could you get a schedule of the next vessels leaving here for St. Michaels?" She stuffed her hands in her pockets. "I don't want to buy passage yet; I just want to know when they're going."

Francis jumped out of the wagon and went around to unload the first dog crate. "Yes. For you I will do it."

"Thank you," she whispered. "Here, take this." She offered him a bill of large denomination but he shook his head.

"You have paid me more than enough already."

She stuffed it into the front of his vest and turned to go. "Take it, Francis. The money, it doesn't matter to me."

He smiled, calling after her. "It will be a good Christmas this year for my little ones."

She waved good-bye over her head, disappearing around the building.

First, Gabrielle went into the hotel. "Gerta, I'll be stayin' a little longer," she told the woman who took care of the front desk.

"Problem, honey? Didn't that Francis take you to the dock like he was supposed to? Because if he didn't—" She hit her palm with her fist.

Gabrielle laughed nervously. "No. Francis has been wonderful. There's just been a mix-up down at the docks." She tried to sound casual. "I'll be leaving in a couple of days."

Gerta looked as if she didn't quite believe Gabrielle, but she nodded her assent. "All right, you got your room for as long as you need it." She leaned forward until her large breasts rested on the counter. "You in some kind of trouble? Runnin' from the law maybe?"

Gabrielle heaved an exasperated sigh. "No. Not the law, but if anyone asks for me, say I've gone. Say I'm headed for—" she threw up her hands—"for the Kenai."

Gerta nodded. "Don't you worry, honey. Nobody'll know you're here by these lips." She pressed her fingers to her mouth, painted a deep ruby.

"Thank you," Gabrielle whispered.

Taking a deep breath, Gabrielle rapped on the door of the townhouse where her mother and Lucas lived. She knew she was taking a chance, but she had to warn her mother. When no one answered, Gabrielle tapped lightly again.

When the door swung open, a maid in starched white nodded her head. "Yes?"

"Is my mother . . . is Alice in?"

413

"May I ask who is calling?" She indicated with her hand that Gabrielle was to come, but Gabrielle balked.

She suddenly felt as if she could trust no one. What if it was some sort of trap? What if Alice wasn't home? What if only Taylor was here?

"No." Gabrielle took a step back. "If she's here, could you ask her to come outside?"

The maid studied her masculine attire critically but bobbed her head. "Very well." She closed the door quietly.

Gabrielle slipped her hands into her pockets, shivering. Snow was just beginning to fall over the city, blanketing its imperfections with a veil of pristine white. Smiling to herself, she lifted her chin to catch a single flake on the end of her tongue. It was good to see the snow again. When the door swung open, she jumped.

"Gabrielle!" Alice tightened her fingers on the knitted shawl draped over her shoulders. "Why on earth didn't you come in?"

"Is he here?"

"Is who here? Come in this minute. I'll not have you standing on the stoop."

"Taylor, Rosenwood, whatever the hell his name is!"

Alice stiffened. "Malcolm?"

"Yes. Is he here?"

"No, but he'll be right back. What is this all about?"

Gabrielle took a deep breath. "Mother," she blurted, "I have something to tell you about him, something you're not going to like."

"What? That he killed Rouge?" Her voice had turned frosty.

"You . . . you know?"

"He told me everything the night you were here, after you'd gone."

"Well, don't you . . . aren't you—"

Alice cut her off. "He told me how you had made it out to be murder. Rouge was the one who pulled the gun, and you know it. The drunken ass, he was always doing stupid things. It was a wonder he lived as long as he did!"

"No. You don't understand." Gabrielle shifted her weight from one foot to the next, frantic to make her mother understand. "It's lies—all lies!"

Alice's hand slipped from the shawl to crack sharply against Gabrielle's cheek. "How dare you come to my home, proposition a man that belongs to me and then carry tales when he turns you down! A whore's whore, hmm?"

Gabrielle's hand flew to her cheek. "Proposition him! Mother, he tried to kill me; he kidnapped me. He's trying to kill me now!"

Alice laughed, tipping back her head with grim amusement. "He thinks you're a little mad, and you know, I wonder if he's right." Her eyes narrowed. "Actually, I think you're jealous."

"Jealous?" Gabrielle wrapped her arms tightly around her waist, shivering with cold.

"Jealous because you lost the only man you'll ever have, and I've had my choice." She smiled wickedly.

"Mother, Alex is my husband. I left him because of the man you call Malcolm Rosenwood." Her voice dropped to a whisper. "I was afraid for our lives!"

"That's absurd!" Alice's eyes grew large with rage. "What could Malcolm possibly gain from your death?"

"That son-of-a-bitch wanted Rouge's map, and now

he wants to kill me for revenge. He lost that leg on the river when he was chasin' after me!"

"You hold your tongue!" Alice stepped out onto the stoop, shaking a finger at her daughter. "I'll have you know that that man is my husband, and I'll not hear it from you!"

"Your . . . your husband?" Gabrielle stammered in disbelief. "No . . . it can't be!" She stumbled backward off the step, nearly losing her balance. "I came here to warn you. He told me he would kill you."

"Kill me?" She laughed. "Malcolm loves me. Now go, before he comes home and sees you. I won't have him disturbed."

Gabrielle took another step back, staring at her mother's cold, uncaring face, and then she turned and ran down the street, the sound of her boots muffled by the new fallen snow.

Chapter Thirty

Gabrielle stretched out on the narrow bed in her hotel room, still fully clothed. She had meant to spend the night in the barn with the dogs, but it had grown too cold outside. She'd been forced by the driving wind and snow to come in out of the elements and spend another sleepless night worrying where Taylor would show up next.

Reaching out to be certain her revolver was still on the night table, Gabrielle turned up the oil lamp until it cast bright light over her bed and against the wall of her room where the door was. Twice she had gotten up to be sure it was locked, but still she watched the knob. In her state of exhaustion, she kept thinking she saw the knob turn, but whenever she got up to investigate, the hall was empty.

Groaning aloud, Gabrielle rolled onto her stomach. She was making herself crazy, and if she didn't get out of Seattle soon, she would be. She had gone over and over the events of the past year in her mind, trying to figure out what she had done wrong, what she could have done to prevent this. But nothing came to mind, except the fact that she supposed she should have kept Alex out of it all together. She should never have become involved with him; she should never have fallen in love with him.

But how was she to have known then what she knew now? Was she supposed to have left him there in the snow to die? A smile played on her lips. "Oh, Alex," she murmured, remembering his smile. "You made me so happy." She remembered the feel of his hair twisted in her fingers, the taste of his mouth against hers. Her breasts tingled at the thought. How could life be so bitterly unfair? How could Lucas Taylor keep her from the only man she had ever loved . . . would ever love.

Gabrielle had toyed with the idea of gunning Taylor down, just like she'd been told men did in the West. But no matter how much she hated the man, no matter how much she thought he deserved to die, she knew it could never be at her hands—not at least until it came to the two of them, until it was his life or hers. She'd never be able to live with herself if she killed him when his back was turned.

Sighing, Gabrielle propped herself up on one elbow. She was so tired; she would have liked to have taken a brief nap, just ten minutes or so, but she was afraid. Taylor had said he was coming for her; he said he would find her. She supposed she should have moved to another hotel, but what good would that do? Lucas Taylor seemed to know everyone in the town, or at least to have paid them off. She wondered absent-mindedly what had happened to the old man she had spoken to in the shipping office the day before. Had he quit? Been fired? Would his body wash up on the shore somewhere? She prayed the man was all right.

Resting her head on the pillow, Gabrielle stroked it with her palm. Images of her mother flashed through her mind. "Can you believe her, Papa?" she said aloud, trying to keep herself awake. "I tried to warn Alice. I tried to make her understand she was in danger, but she didn't believe me. She said terrible things." Gabrielle squeezed the pillow in frustration. "What did I ever do to deserve this? What made her hate me so? You loved me, Papa. I think Alex loved me . . . I know Alexis did, but why not my own mother?" She stared at the pulled drapes, dry-eyed. There were no tears left.

She rubbed her cheek against the pillow, her eyes drifting shut for an instant before she forced them open. *Think of Alex,* she told herself. *That will keep you awake.* Mentally she began to count the times they had made love, the times they had cut wood together or checked trap lines in the snow. The memories were so good, better memories than anyone deserved. In the back of her mind she could see Alex laughing, wrestling with the dogs outside the cabin. She could see him sinking into her old copper bath tub, grinning. She could see the firelight playing off his rich, auburn hair and smell his freshly bathed body pressed close to hers. Slowly, against her will, without her realizing it, Gabrielle's eyes drifted shut.

The next thing Gabrielle knew, she was startled awake by something. Her eyes flew open, and she suppressed the urge to leap out of the bed. She was lying facedown, her head resting on the pillow. She could dimly make out the outline of the drapes on the window. Suddenly every nerve in her body was on edge; something wasn't right. The lamp had blown out

419

on the night table, and the air in the dark room had somehow changed. She breathed shallowly, listening. . . .

Was that someone else's breath she heard, or was it her own? Sweat beaded on her forehead as a board creaked near the other side of the bed. The gun! She needed the gun! With one swift motion she rolled over, slamming her hand on the night table. A shock of cold, stifling terror washed over her. The gun was gone. . . . She heard the match strike, and light filled the room.

Taylor sat on the chair near the bed, leaning forward to light the lamp. Slowly, methodically, he lit the cigar that protruded from his mouth. "Good evening." He smiled wolfishly.

"Where is my mother? What have you done with her?" Gabrielle swung her feet over to leap from the bed, but Taylor raised her own Colt 45 pistol, aiming it at her head.

"You mean my wife? Home, sleeping where good wives should be."

"Why did you marry her?" Gabrielle demanded.

He smiled, tapping his temple with a well-manicured fingernail. "Can't you figure it out? She is your only heir."

"Alice? She can't be. If something happened to me, my husband Alex would inherit whatever I had."

Taylor chuckled deep in his throat. "Come, come, little girl. We all know this husband is a figment of your imagination. Your mother said so herself."

"My mother—"

"Hold your tongue," he threatened, lowering his hand until his wrist rested on the arm of the chair. He kept the pistol aimed at her. "Now, as I was saying, your mother is your only heir. So when you kill yourself with your own weapon," he lifted it menacingly, "your dear bereaved mother will inherit your fortune."

"But she can't! What do I have to do to make you believe I was married to Alex. The records . . ." She put out a hand in desperation.

Taylor shrugged, removing his own pistol from beneath his coat to lay it on the table, gleaming in front of her. "Even if you were married, which is highly unlikely, who would know? Who would believe it?" He puffed on his cigar. "Records can be destroyed as easily as they can be made. Besides, it's not just the money." He beared even white teeth, his eyes narrowing. "I owe you. I lost my leg in that God damned wilderness because of you."

Gabrielle flung herself from the bed in blind anger, screaming as she swung a fist at Taylor, catching him in the jaw before he tripped her and shoved her to the floor. Lifting his peg leg, he pressed the carved wooden stub into her stomach until she squirmed with pain. Then, he stepped on her hand with his good foot, forcing her fingers open. "Take the gun!"

"No," she moaned, shaking her head. Tears blinded her vision. "If you're going to kill me, do it!" she demanded. "But be a man about it!"

Shoving Gabrielle's gun into her hand, Taylor laughed, and Gabrielle screamed as loud as she could. Suddenly the sound of splintering wood followed by an enraged masculine voice filled the room. Someone lifted Taylor up over her and threw him against the wall. As Gabrielle tried to force her limbs to move, she heard the thud of fists meeting flesh and the clatter of steel hitting the floor.

"You God damned son-of-a-bitch," Alex shouted, slamming his fist into Taylor's face. "I'm going to kill you, you hear me, you greedy bastard!"

Gabrielle lifted her head from the floor. *Alex! Alex!* her mind screamed. Willing her limbs to obey, she pushed off the floor, spinning around to face the battling men.

"Oh, my God," she murmured, her hand flying to her mouth.

Enraged, her husband sank his fist into the soft flesh of Taylor's stomach, and the man groaned, doubling over. Caught off balance, the two fell to the floor, and the back of Alex's head hit the corner of the night table, sending Taylor's pistol skittering across the floor.

"No!" Gabrielle screamed as Taylor rose up from Alex's motionless body. Grabbing the china water pitcher off the table, Gabrielle swung it as hard as she could, shattering it over Taylor's head. Cold water sprayed, and white and blue pieces of china flew in every direction as she hurled herself into Taylor kicking him beneath the chin with her booted foot.

Taylor fell back against the hardwood floor, stunned for a moment, then began to crawl toward the door. Alex groaned, and Gabrielle fell to her knees. "Alex? Alex?" she cried out, grasping his shoulders. "Are you all right?"

His eyes flickered open then closed, and she shook him vigorously. "Alex wake up! You've got to stay awake," she begged. She wiped the blood from his cheek with her palm, groaning aloud. "Oh, God! Alex, don't leave me now." Then she spotted Taylor's pistol on the floor beneath the bed, and she lunged for it, vivid with rage. Scrambling to her feet, she swung around to face Taylor retreating through the door.

"Turn around!" she shouted. "Turn around so I can see your face when I shoot you, you sorry son-of-a-bitch!" She rested her finger on the trigger, dashing at her eyes with the back of her hand.

Taylor continued to walk, leaning heavily on his cane.

"I said stop and turn around!" she ordered.

Taylor tipped back his head, filling the hall with laughter. The sound of footsteps coming up the stairs reached Gabrielle, and she dashed after Taylor. Going through the doorway of the room into the hallway, she leveled the heavy pistol, poised to shoot. To her horror, she spotted Alexis and Gerta coming up the steps.

Gabrielle froze. "Get back!" she shouted, waving the pistol. "Get out of his way, Gerta!"

Gerta screamed, shrinking against the wall, Alexis clutched against her as Taylor passed them, taking the steps two at a time. Gabrielle ran down the steps, firing the pistol at him from the bottom of the landing, but it was too late. She caught a glimpse of Taylor's head as he slipped out the front door.

For a moment, Gabrielle just stood there, the smoking pistol hanging from her fingers. "I would have killed you, Lucas Taylor," she swore. "I would of done it!"

"You all right, honey?" Gerta came down the steps, her dressing gown flying open, as she dragged Alexis after her.

"Gabrielle!" Alexis shouted, throwing herself against her.

Gabrielle let the gun slip from her fingers and fall to

423

the floor with a loud clatter. "Alexis." She threw her arms around the child, lifting her. "You came. Your papa came for me."

Alexis clung to Gabrielle, resting her head on her shoulder. "Where's my papa?" She smiled. "Me and him, we're good friends. He let me bring my puppy you gave me, Mister Ballentine."

Gabrielle gave the child another squeeze and then set her feet on the floor. "Your papa's upstairs, but he's got a little bonk on the head; so I want you to stay here with Miss Gerta while I tend to him. Okay?"

Alexis looked apprehensively at Gerta, then back at Gabrielle. "But I want to see my papa."

Gerta took the little girl's hand. "Come on, sweety. You come on around the back with me, and we'll see if we can't find some cookies and a bit of hot chocolate for you."

Alexis brightened. "You got chocolate? I like hot chocolate."

Gabrielle gave Alex's daughter a small push. "Go ahead and I'll be down to get you after a while." Then she turned and ran up the steps, practically colliding with Alex as she came around the corner to her room. "Alex!" She threw her arms around him, nearly knocking him over.

"Gabrielle," he whispered in her ear. "I thought you were gone. I thought I'd lost you," he told her, his voice thick with emotion.

"You came for me; you came back. Why did you come?" She buried her face in the crook of his neck, inhaling his familiar masculine scent. She brushed at the nape of his neck with her fingers, trying to make herself believe he was truly there.

"Of course I came for you. But you should never

have left. I'm your husband; I love you. I thought you loved me."

She sighed, looking up at him. "I left because I loved you, because I loved Alexis. There were these men . . . Taylor sent them . . . they tried to drown me . . ." A jumble of words tumbled from her mouth as she clung to Alex, afraid to let go. "I was so scared, but I was more scared for you—"

"Shhhh," he hushed, forcing her head against his chest. "You can tell me about it all later. Just tell me if you're all right. Did Taylor hurt you?"

She shook her head.

"You could have shot him with one of the guns that were on the floor."

"I tried. Didn't you hear the shot? But Alexis and Gerta were in the way; I was afraid I would hurt them."

Alex stroked her tangled chestnut hair, reveling in the sound of her voice. "Is Alexis all right?"

"She's fine. She went to the kitchen for cookies with Gerta. I was afraid you were hurt." She hesitated. "Should we call the law on Taylor?"

Alex shook his head. "Never argue with a dog in his own yard. You should know that, Gabrielle. It would be his word against ours. He won't dare come back here tonight." He rubbed at his head and laughed. "Got knocked out cold, didn't I? Some hero." Alex tipped back her chin with his hand, brushing his lips against hers. "What are you going to do with me? I'll never be of any use to you on the Tanana."

Her eyes widened. "On the Tanana?"

"Well, that's where we're going, aren't we? I want to show Alexis what real snow looks like."

She stared at him too startled to speak. "You mean you're . . . we're . . ."

He kissed her again, pressing his mouth hard against hers. "I mean we've left Richmond for good and my money as well. I gave it all to Mother for the house and the property. I only brought what you left behind. I'm a penniless man"—he grinned—"looking for a wealthy woman."

"Oh, Alex!" She rested her head against his hard chest, listening to the rhythmic beat of his heart. "I love you, I love you, I love you!" She covered his travel-worn coat with a shower of kisses.

"It's late. Don't you think we ought to be getting to bed?"

She looked up at him, her eyes narrowing. "Bed? A few minutes ago you were unconscious, and you're thinking about bed? You should rest."

"Well—" he lifted an eyebrow—"I was thinking of bed—but not sleep."

She shook her head, clicking between her teeth. "Bad, bad, bad," she teased. "And what about your daughter?"

He shrugged. "Gerta had better have our old room open for us. Alexis can sleep in the parlor—otherwise we'll be going elsewhere."

"In the middle of the night?"

He leaned to nip at her neck, his breath warm and raspy in her ear. "In the middle of the night. I've waited too long already."

A shiver of desire tickled at Gabrielle's spine, and she backed up, holding him at arm's length. "All right, all right. I'll find Gerta. You see if you can straighten up that room. I think we broke a few things."

*　　*　　*

An hour later Gabrielle and Alex had tucked Alexis in on the settee in the parlor of their hotel room and had retreated to the bedroom. It was the same room they had occupied before. Alex closed the door quietly, leaning against it, a broad smile playing on his lips. "I can't tell you how relieved I am to leave Richmond behind. I thought I belonged there, but I don't. All I could think of the entire time I was there was the river and the sound of the ice breaking." He shrugged. "Silly?"

Gabrielle drew the crimson drapes on the windows. "No," she murmured, turning to him. "Not at all. I see the snow." She squeezed her eyes shut, breathing deeply. "I smell the cold air; I hear the ptarmigan's call." She lifted her dark lashes. "I hear your voice calling me in the forest."

Alex came to her, wrapping her in his arms. He kissed the top of her head, stroking her back. "All I want is for you to be happy. No more gold mining; I know how you feel about that. We'll build a trading post again if you want."

Her fingers worked nimbly at the buttons of his shirt. "I bought some dogs, some supplies, too. I was going to build a new cabin, close to Forty Mile, maybe." She pushed aside the shirt, running a palm over the hard muscles of his chest.

"Forty Mile sounds good to me." He brought his mouth down hard on hers, and she leaned into him, parting her lips to taste of him.

She withdrew hesitantly. "Tell me something," she whispered as he pressed his lips to the leaping pulse at the base of her neck.

"Yes," he answered. "Anything."

"What . . . what took you so long? If you were coming, you should have been here days ago." She held her breath, waiting for his answer.

With a single motion Alex swept her into his arms and carried her to the bed. "Alexis was sick, in San Francisco."

"Sick?" She lifted her head off the pillow, laying her hand on his chest.

He smiled, pulling her sweater over her head and then stretching out beside her. "Just a fever, an ague the doctor called it." He reached out to fondle a rounded breast possessively.

"But she's all right now?" There was a warmth beginning to spread from Alex's hand to her breast, to every limb on her body.

"She's all right now," he answered, lowering his mouth to the bud of her breast.

Gabrielle's eyes drifted shut, and she moaned softly. "It's been too long. I've missed you so much," she breathed. "I've missed this."

Alex teased her nipple with the tip of his tongue, coaxing it into a hard nub, then moved to the other breast. He could feel Gabrielle's hands on his back, caressing his tired muscles, washing away the pain of separation and uncertainty.

Sitting up to take in her dark eyes, he shrugged off his shirt and pants, then got on his knees to tug at her pants. She smiled up at him, reaching with a hand to stroke his cheek. When he had removed the last of her clothing, she put her arms out to him, inviting him to stretch out over her. She needed to feel every inch of his body against hers; she needed to know this was real.

"You're so beautiful," Alex whispered, kissing the

bridge of her nose. He laced his fingers through her thick rich hair, moving his hips provocatively against her.

The force of his hard, bulging loins against her bare leg made her light-headed. She lifted her hips with his, matching his rhythm as she accepted his mouth greedily. Completely aroused, she moaned softly in his ear, stroking his firm buttocks. Showering her face with kisses, Alex made his way down her body, his tongue teasing her flesh until she quivered with desire. But still he taunted her, reveling in the sound of her rapid breathing and the soft whispers of encouragement that escaped her throat.

"Alex, please." She shuddered, reaching to take his shoulders and guide him over her. Parting her legs, she cried out with relief when he took her with one long, hard stroke. He buried his face in her hair, taking in the scent that clung to her damp skin.

"I love you, Gabrielle LeBeau," he whispered, moving slowly. "I will love you for this time and the next."

Gabrielle opened her eyes, heavy-lidded with wanton desire. "You really do, don't you?"

He brushed his lips against hers in a feather-light kiss. "I really do," he answered. "More than you'll ever know."

Her eyes drifted shut. "Then show me," she murmured. "Show me, Alex."

Chapter Thirty-One

The following morning, after a picnic breakfast on the bed, Alex left Gabrielle and Alexis in the hotel and went down to the docks to secure passage for them on the next steamer headed for St. Michaels. He'd decided he should report Lucas Taylor to the authorities, but out of fear for her mother's life, Gabrielle had insisted he not go.

"Let's just leave," she had begged. "He won't follow us into the territory again, not with that bum leg of his. He'd never make it, and he's smart enough not to try."

"What if he sends someone after you again? If he can reach as far as Richmond, don't you think he could send another of his henchmen after you in Alaska?"

Gabrielle shook her head emphatically, taking Alex's hands. "Please. Let's just go. If someone comes after us, we'll deal with it when the time comes. I'm afraid for Alice, okay?"

He tenderly brushed a lock of hair off her shoulder. "Okay. But you two stay right here until I get back." Pressing a kiss to the top of Alexis's blond head, he had left them.

Returning at noon, Alex banged on the hotel room door. "It's me, Alex, let me in Gabrielle."

She unlocked the door and swung it open. "I was worried about you; where've you been?"

He stepped in the door, his arms burdened with boxes.

She rolled her eyes. "Not more clothes?"

He dropped the parcels on the settee. "Well, look at you." He motioned to her men's flannel pants and bulky sweater. "This is no way for a lady of your means to be traveling."

Gabrielle's eyes narrowed dangerously. "You telling me you don't like the way I dress, Mr. Alexander?"

He laughed, taking her in his arms. "I love you just the way you are, but for sentimental reasons, I couldn't resist the gown in the box." He turned to Alexis who stood in the door in a wrinkled blue smock with Mister Ballentine in her arms. "And there's something for you, too, sweet."

Alexis dropped the puppy on the floor and clapped her hands, bouncing up and down. "For me! What is it? What is it, Papa?"

Alex led his women by the hand to the pile of boxes on the settee and pulled off the lid of the largest of the bunch.

Gabrielle laughed, digging into the box to remove the woman's forest-green brocade gown. "I can't believe it; it looks almost like the one I was wearing when I met you."

"Almost, but not quite. No more black for you. There's a bonnet and gloves here, too." He brushed his

432

lips against hers and then reached for another box. "And this is for you, Miss Alexis, and it was harder to find than Gabrielle's present."

Alexis pried the lid off the box and dug into it, wrinkling her nose as she pulled out a small pair of grey flannel pants and a thick wool sweater. "It's not a frock. . . ."

"Nope. It's not, because where we're going young ladies won't be much in need of frocks." He tweaked the end of her nose, and she laughed.

"I'm going to look just like Gabrielle then, huh?"

Her father nodded. "Just like her."

Gabrielle rested her hand on his. "Thank you. It was a nice surprise."

"And that's not the best surprise." He crossed his arms over his chest. "I found a steamer leaving this afternoon."

"This afternoon?" Gabrielle's dark eyes widened with disbelief. "How?"

"Well, don't get too excited. I booked us passage on a steamer to Vancouver, then we'll be taking a sloop to St. Michaels." He shrugged. "Not great traveling, but I thought you wanted to get out of here."

"I do."

"Do you . . ." he paused. "Do you want to say good-bye to Alice?"

She turned away. "No. Our last words were enough for me. Besides, I think she'd be safer if I stayed away."

"All right, then." He turned to face Alexis. "Well, ladies, let's get packed. We've got to get down to the docks."

"My dogs."

"They've already been taken care of, and I had Gerta, down at the front desk, find her brother-in-law to have your supplies moved from the warehouse."

"I can't believe it. How did you accomplish in one morning what I couldn't manage in two weeks?"

"Simple negotiation." He grinned. "I threatened to break heads down at the shipping office if they didn't find us a steamer today."

Gabrielle's dark eyes sparkled. "Just the kind of man I need."

He gave her a wink. "Now come on, let's get moving. Francis will be back with his wagon to pick us up shortly."

It was mid-afternoon when Alex, Gabrielle and Alexis reached the docks and located the steamer they were to sail on. Standing on the dock, Alex draped his arm over Gabrielle's shoulder, watching the waves of blue-green water break in the harbor. Snow was falling lightly to add to the several inches that already covered the ground.

Alex brushed a few flakes off the end of Gabrielle's nose, and she laughed. "Feels good, doesn't it?" She put out a gloved hand to catch the flakes.

"It does," he answered contentedly. "We're ready to go. Got the money?" His blue-grey eyes twinkled with amusement.

She lifted the cloth satchel she held on her arm and opened it for his inspection. "Sure do." Then she glanced up at him with concern. "Laura. Where's Laura?"

"What?"

"My rag doll. Where's Laura? I thought she was in the bag."

Alex took the bag, searching through it. "You're right, she's not here."

Gabrielle chewed at her bottom lip, trying to recall the last time she'd seen her rag doll. "Alexis." She turned to the little girl throwing crumbs of bread to the sea gulls on the dock.

"Yes." Alexis came running, bundled in a warm parka her father had purchased.

"Alexis, were you playing with my doll at the hotel?"

Alexis hung her head. "I'm sorry. I didn't know I wasn't allowed."

"No. It's okay." Gabrielle stooped to be eye level with the child. "You can play with her; you can even have her. It's just that my papa gave her to me, and she's all I have left of him. She's a special doll-baby. Do you know where she is?"

Alexis grimaced, obviously trying to think. Then her face lit up. "She's under the settee. I was playin' it was a bear cave. Are there bears where we're going?"

Gabrielle laughed, flooded with relief. "Yes, there are bears. Now go back to feeding your gulls." She went to Alex who was speaking to a man overseeing the loading of the supplies.

Alex glanced up. "Did Alexis know where Laura was?"

"Yes. At the hotel. I'm going to get her."

Alex caught her hand. "Alone? I'll go with you."

"And what? Drag Alexis all the way there and then back again? You stay here and make sure they load everything that's mine. I don't want to get up there and find we've got no flour or salt."

"I said no, Gabrielle; it's not safe. Taylor could show up anytime. Wait until I'm done here, and I'll take you." He returned to his conversation with the crewman.

Gabrielle sighed, walking away. *Is this the way it's going to be now,* she wondered. *Am I never to be free to go anywhere alone again?* She glanced back at Alex, who was still engrossed in his conversation. It seemed so silly to stand there and wait on him. Taylor wouldn't dare try anything now that he knew Alex was here. She watched the movement on the steamer; passengers were already boarding. Laura was just a silly old rag doll, but she wasn't going to leave her behind.

On impulse, Gabrielle went to Alexis, who was on her hands and knees on the dock, coaxing a sea gull to eat bread scraps from her fingers. "Alexis?"

The little girl looked up, beaming. "Look at 'em all, Gabrielle. Can we take one with us? A friend for Mister Ballentine?" She turned back to the gulls.

Gabrielle laughed. "No, you cannot take a sea gull with you on the steamer. Now, I want you to do something for me."

"Yes?"

"Hold on to the satchel and give it to your father when he's done over there. Tell him I went after Laura and I'll be back in a few minutes. Go ahead and board, and I'll be back directly."

Alexis's chubby fingers closed around the handle of the satchel. "Sure." She offered another piece of crust to a sea gull, laughing when the bird snatched it from

436

her hand.

There was so much commotion on the dock between the arriving passengers and the crane loading supplies onto the deck of the vessel that Gabrielle was able to slip away without Alex noticing. *It's just silly,* she told herself. *The St. Lucy is only a few blocks away. I'll be there and back before Alex notices I'm gone.*

More than halfway to the hotel, Gabrielle stopped on the wooden walk, realizing she didn't have her pistol. She tugged at her bottom lip with her teeth in indecision. She'd left the weapon in the satchel back at the dock. Should she return to get it? *No,* she decided. *I'll just hurry. If I go back, Alex will insist he come, and we might miss the steamer.*

Reaching the St. Lucy only minutes later, Gabrielle retrieved the key from Gerta and went up to the room she and Alex had occupied. Pulling up her stiff brocade skirts, she got down on her hands and knees to search for her doll. Sure enough, there beneath the settee was Laura with her yarn hair and missing eye.

"There you are! Almost left behind, weren't you?" Gabrielle hugged the tattered poppet. Stroking the doll's hair, she smiled to herself. This morning, after counting on her fingers, Gabrielle had realized she was probably pregnant. She hadn't told Alex because she knew he wouldn't want her to make the trip north. But as soon as they reached Alaska, she would tell him. Wouldn't he be surprised? Singing a silly ditty of Rouge's to herself, she locked the hotel room door, returned the key and headed for the docks.

Drawing in a deep breath of the crisp, salt air, Gabrielle went down King's Street and onto Water

437

Street. The snow muffled the sound of her feet as she hurried, anxious to be safe in Alex's arms again. Turning the corner of the winding street, she looked up at the warehouses looming above, casting shadows on the rutted street. Feeling uncomfortable, Gabrielle walked faster, clutching her rag doll to her bodice. Was that the sound of footsteps behind her?

She spun around but saw no one. Turning back, she paused to think. Was she being paranoid because this was the street that Taylor had tracked her on more than a year ago? She glanced behind her again, wishing desperately that she had returned to get that pistol. She saw nothing.

Lifting her skirts, she hurried along the wooden walk built next to a warehouse. She heard nothing but the sound of her own feet and the sound of her own rapid breathing. A board creaked behind her, startling her, and she spun around.

Lucas Taylor stepped through the door of the warehouse. He held a gleaming pistol in one hand, his gilded cane in the other. He was dressed handsomely in a dark overcoat and a charcoal-grey bowler hat.

"So," Gabrielle breathed. "I'm not to escape you."

He grinned, bearing even white teeth. "I said I would find you. You have a debt left unpaid."

"I owe you nothing," she said through clenched teeth. Oddly enough, she was not frightened. The anticipation, the fear of when he would appear had been worse.

"Don't owe me?" He laughed grimly. "The exchange is simple. Your life for my leg."

Gabrielle lifted her arms in surrender. "So shoot

me." She forced a genteel smile.

Taylor's brow creased. This was not quite the way he had expected this to go. All of the months he lay in that stinking cabin waiting for the stump of his leg to heal, he had imagined what it would be like to murder this woman. He had expected pleading words, tears, wild promises, but never this cold, hard acceptance.

"Well? Are you going to do it? Because if not, I have a steamer to catch, you know." Gabrielle could hardly believe the words that were slipping from her mouth. She was braver than she had thought.

Taylor pulled back the hammer with a resounding click. At that instant a voice came from down the street.

"Gabrielle," the voice called. "Gabrielle, are you there?"

Gabrielle could hear Alex's footsteps as he ran toward them. "Here," she called out daringly. "I'm here, Alex."

Alex came around the building with the satchel in his hand and stopped dead not more than twenty feet from Taylor and Gabrielle. "No!" he shouted.

Taylor raised his cane in salute. "So we meet again, Mr. Alexander. She is your wife isn't she?"

"What do you want?" Alex demanded, staring at the pistol Taylor held poised on Gabrielle.

"You know what I want. I want her dead."

"She never did anything against you. A helpless woman? You're going to kill a woman?"

Taylor laughed. "Helpless? Her? Not hardly."

Alex looked down at the satchel he held in his hand. "Our money, her money. Here, take it." He offered the bag. "It's all we have left of the gold."

"How much?"

Gabrielle crossed her arms over her chest, her skirts rustling. "Plenty. You want it? It's yours."

"Yea, I want it. Throw it over here." He waved the gun. "But don't do anything stupid, Mr. Alexander, because I'll shoot her."

"You intend to shoot her anyway," Alex treaded carefully.

"That's right, I do. But if you try to come after me, I won't kill her on the first shot, maybe not the second."

Gabrielle's hands trembled. "Give him the money, Alex. Then go. No need for both of us to die."

Alex's stormy blue-grey eyes met hers. "Don't say that," he told her softly.

"Throw the bag!" Taylor ordered.

Alex did as he was told, and Taylor scooped it off the ground, opening it to glance inside. "Nice, very nice. And now, Mr. Alexander, you are excused."

"I'm not leaving without my wife." He stood stock-still, his fists knotted at his sides.

"Please," Gabrielle begged. She tossed her rag doll through the air, and Alex caught it. "It's for Alexis," she murmured. Against her will, tears began to slip down her cheeks. "Now go on, do as he says."

Gabrielle heard a sound behind Taylor and looked up. There, standing in the middle of the road was Alice dressed in a sapphire-blue lady's overcoat and a veiled hat. In her hand she held a shiny new pistol, aimed at Taylor. "You lied to me, Malcolm," she accused bitterly.

Taylor stiffened, his eyes widening with surprise.

"What are you doing here?" he shouted.

"You lied," she repeated. "You lied to me about everything, didn't you? What Gabrielle said was true, wasn't it?"

"Put down the gun, Alice, and go. This is none of your concern."

"The hell it isn't; she's my daughter."

Taylor laughed, still holding the gun on Gabrielle. "Some mother you are." His voice rose to echo between the warehouses.

"It doesn't matter. Good or bad, I'm still her mother. I won't stand here and watch you murder her."

"And what are you going to do about it, Alice? You couldn't hit the side of the warehouse with that gun."

"Mother," Gabrielle called. "I—"

"Just hush, Gabrielle. You and I both know what I am, what I'll always be, but that doesn't mean I haven't got principles."

"Alice," Taylor threatened, glancing sideways at her. "If you don't put that gun down and go, you're out of my house."

"Out of your house? It's mine, too, wouldn't you say! You married me, you stupid bastard, remember? You married me to get my daughter's inheritance when you killed her. Only, I guess she really is married." Alice looked at Alex. "So, you wouldn't have gotten a cent anyway."

"Alice! I'm warning you one last time. If you want to live, you'll go home now!"

"Threatening me? Is that it, Malcolm, or is it Lucas now?" Alice took a step closer, pulling back the hammer of the pistol.

Gabrielle screamed as Taylor whirled around to face Alice, pulling the trigger on the gun. At the same instant, Alice fired, and Gabrielle felt herself shoved to the ground by Alex's strong hands.

The sound of the shots echoed in the empty street, and the smell of powder filled Gabrielle's nostrils as she struggled to get up out of the snow. Lifting her head, she spotted her mother standing in the street, the pistol still frozen in her hands.

Alex rolled off Gabrielle and helped her up. Lying only a few feet away was Taylor's motionless body. Gabrielle looked from Taylor to her mother and then back at Taylor again. "You killed him," she breathed.

Alice nodded her head, coming slowly toward her daughter. The huge sapphires that hung in her ears glittered in the sunlight. "I did, didn't I?" She pushed at the dead man's hand with the toe of her high-buttoned shoe. His hand flopped back in the snow, lifeless.

Gabrielle held Alex's hand tight in hers for a moment and then ran to fling herself into her mother's arms. Alice dropped the pistol into the snow, accepting her daughter's embrace awkwardly. "You'll go to jail," Gabrielle cried. "They'll hang you."

"No." Alice shook her head, stepping back. "It was self-defense. I have a feeling the town was ready to be rid of this man. They won't press charges. Everyone hated him anyway."

"I don't know what to say, Mother." Gabrielle studied Alice's face.

Alex squeezed Gabrielle's arm lightly. "You'd better say good-bye," he said quietly. "Alexis is on the steamer; we can't miss it." He stepped back to let mother and daughter say their final farewells in private.

Gabrielle looked up at her mother. "You certain you don't want me to stay? Just until things are cleared up?"

Alice shook her head. "No. You've got a life with that man so go on and have that life." She smiled genuinely. "He loves you very much."

"I love him, too," Gabrielle whispered. It seemed so strange to be speaking to her mother like this. Had they ever talked without hostility in their voices? "Why don't you come with us?"

Alice laughed, clasping her gloved hands. "No. I made that mistake once, but never again. Besides, you and I would be at each other's throats before we hit St. Michaels." She reached out to touch a lock of her daughter's thick hair. "My life is here, and I am what I am." She smiled sadly.

Gabrielle spotted her cloth satchel in the snow and leaned to pick it up. "At least take some of the money." She offered the bag.

Alice laughed. "Keep your money, build your trading post and raise your filthy dogs," she said without malice. "Malcolm has left me a good deal of money and a nice home. Maybe I'll build myself a first-class bordello and gambling house."

"Alice, you're incorrigible."

Her mother shrugged delicately. "Being a lady was too damned boring anyway."

"Gabrielle," Alex called. "We've got to hurry."

Alice gave her daughter a nudge with her gloved hand. "Go on. And good luck to you." She glanced at Taylor's motionless body in the snow. "He'll not trouble you again."

For a moment Gabrielle's dark eyes met Alice's, and then she smiled. "Good-bye and good luck to you, too . . . Mother." With one final look at Alice's youthful face, Gabrielle took the arm Alex offered her.

"Come on," he told her as the steamship on the dock gave a loud moan signaling its departure, "we'll have to run for it!"

Gabrielle laughed, hitching up her brocade skirts to her knees. "Race you!" she dared, already bolting ahead of him.

As the steamship puffed its way through Puget Sound, Gabrielle leaned over the rail, her arm linked through Alex's. Seated only a few feet away on a wooden crate was Alexis, grinning broadly, her puppy held tightly in her hands.

Taking a deep breath, Gabrielle exhaled slowly. Snow was just beginning to fall from the sky to blanket the ship's deck. "Doesn't it smell good?" she murmured, shaking her head to let the wind ripple through her long, chestnut hair.

Alex chuckled as he swept off his bowler hat to keep it from blowing away. "Doesn't what smell good?"

"The snow, the ocean . . . the freedom. Oh, Alex, we're going home."

His blue-grey eyes met hers, and he leaned to press a kiss to her rosy lips. "Home," he echoed. "To a place we never should have left."

"Don't say that," Gabrielle murmured, glancing back at Alexis. "If we hadn't gone back to the states, we wouldn't have her with us. But will she like it, do you think? What if she's lonely without other children to play with—without roads and schools and towns?"

"Then we'll build them, darling," Alex promised, pulling her tightly against him, "together."

"We could—couldn't we?" Gabrielle answered softly. "Because we've got a whole lifetime ahead of us."

Now you can get more of HEARTFIRE right at home and $ave.

**Preview
Four Brand New
ZEBRA
Heartfire
Romance Novels...**

FREE for 10 days.

No Obligation and No Strings Attached!

♥

Enjoy all of the passion and fiery romance as you soar back through history, right in the comfort of your own home.

Now that you have read a Zebra **HEARTFIRE** Romance novel, we're sure you'll agree that **HEARTFIRE** sets new standards of excellence for historical romantic fiction. Each Zebra **HEARTFIRE** novel is the ultimate blend of intimate romance and grand adventure and each takes place in the kinds of historical settings you want most...the American Revolution, the Old West, Civil War and more.

<u>FREE</u> Preview Each Month and $ave

Zebra has made arrangements for you to preview 4 brand new HEARTFIRE novels each month...FREE for 10 days. You'll get them as soon as they are published. If you are not delighted with any of them, just return them with no questions asked. But if you decide these are everything we said they are, you'll pay just $3.25 each— a total of $13.00 (a $15.00 value). **That's a $2.00 saving each month off the regular price.** Plus there is NO shipping or handling charge. These are delivered right to your door absolutely free! There is no obligation and there is no minimum number of books to buy.

TO GET YOUR FIRST MONTH'S PREVIEW...
Mail the Coupon Below!

Mail to:

HEARTFIRE Home Subscription Service, Inc.
120 Brighton Road
P.O. Box 5214
Clifton, NJ 07015-5214

YES! I want to subscribe to Zebra's HEARTFIRE Home Subscription Service. Please send me my first month's books to preview free for ten days. I understand that if I am not pleased I may return them and owe nothing, but if I keep them I will pay just $3.25 each; a total of $13.00. That is a savings of $2.00 each month off the cover price. There are no shipping, handling or other hidden charges and there is no minimum number of books I must buy. I can cancel this subscription at any time with no questions asked.

NAME

ADDRESS   APT. NO.

CITY   STATE   ZIP

SIGNATURE   (if under 18, parent or guardian must sign)   2420
Terms and prices are subject to change.